Eternal Desire

CLARISSA ROSS

CRIMSON ROMANCE

F+W Media, Inc.

This edition published by
Crimson Romance
an imprint of F+W Media, Inc.
10151 Carver Road, Suite 200
Blue Ash, Ohio 45242
www.crimsonromance.com

Copyright © 1979 by W. E. Dan Ross

ISBN 10: 1-4405-7289-5
ISBN 13: 978-1-4405-7289-0
eISBN 10: 1-4405-7290-9
eISBN 13: 978-1-4405-7290-6

Cover art © 12RF

Chapter One

A wave of cold air brushed Della Standish's lovely face like the breath of some phantom come to block her way. The twenty-two-year-old English beauty came to a halt in the dank, dark passage. The wavering flame of the candle she held reflected on her pale oval face and long, auburn tresses. Fear distorted her features as she peered into the shadows with her exquisite green eyes.

"Raphael!" she called out. Her frantic cry echoed in the dark depths of the catacombs. But there was no reply.

A moment ago the handsome Prince Raphael had been at her side. Now he had mysteriously vanished. She was completely alone.

She swung around and plaintively called out again, "Raphael! Please answer me!"

There was only the grim echoing of her anguished plea for help followed by the silence of the tomb. The shadows of the narrow stone-carved passage mocked her.

The charming Prince Raphael had brought her here to view the famed catacombs of Rome. They had descended from gardens filled with blood-red gladioli to the blackness of the underground passages. The Prince had warned her to keep close by him because of the danger of being lost underground. Unfortunate visitors to this eerie place had been known to slowly go mad while trying to find their way out of the maze of the dead.

Tens of thousands of bodies were buried in the narrow passageways and recesses. It was a place of eternal chill.

Though it was an August afternoon in the hot summer of 1890, no hint of the sun's warmth touched this black cave.

It was always night in the subterranean place. It was the dark world of the dead. Used by Christians for centuries as a burial vault, the maze of passages stretched almost endlessly; to be lost here without a guide was to be doomed.

She was trembling and her eyes widened with the terror of her plight. She ran a few feet back and the candle almost went out. This brought her to a frightened halt.

"Please!" she prayed. "Please let this end!"

As if in a miraculous answer to her tautly whispered prayer, she heard, from a distance, Raphael's slightly accented voice cry out, "Della! Where are you?"

"Here!" she cried out at once. "Here! Do come to me!" And she waited in the weird darkness with her heart pounding with fear.

She thought she heard footsteps approaching and then all at once there was the welcome sight of a candle's glow: Prince Raphael was walking toward her with a lighted taper in his hand.

Delia ran to greet him breathlessly. "Raphael, what happened? I almost died of terror!"

He placed an arm around her and consoled her. "You managed to get too far ahead of me. I lost my way at the turn. Don't worry! We'll get out of here somehow!"

. . .

Della felt this bizarre adventure had begun on a bleak afternoon in late May of 1890. Sir Roger Drexel, the family solicitor, had contacted her at the great mansion in Doane Square to tell her he would make a late-afternoon call on a matter of urgency. She had thought little of it at the time, supposing that it had to do with some business document that required her signature.

She was the heir to the Standish fortune and legally the head of the family firm's many enterprises, though in fact she had nothing to do with the day-to-day workings of them. Sir Roger looked after legal matters and a group of competent managers took care of the various businesses. Still, from time to time, her approval was required.

"What a bore!" she had grumbled to her prim Aunt Isobel Moore, a sister of her late mother who had been with her since the death of her parents.

Aunt Isobel, tall and thin with a dried-up face which belied her kindly nature, replied, "You have no right to neglect your small duties. The estate brings you a fine income every year."

"I suppose you're right," Della had smiled at her aunt. "But I'd counted on going to the dressmaker's today. All my new summer clothes are waiting for fittings."

Aunt Isobel, as drab in dress as of feature, said, "You'll have other days for that. You must be here when Sir Roger Drexel arrives."

"I will be," she promised.

Standing by the velvet drapes at a window overlooking the square, she gazed out at passing horse-driven carriages and sighed.

Aunt Isobel sat primly in a high-backed chair by the fireplace of the high-ceilinged, elegantly furnished living room. The old woman said, "If your sister Irma had lived it would all have been different for you."

Della, who was wearing a chic green linen suit, glanced at her aunt over her shoulder and said, "Much would surely be different if that were true."

And so it would have. Twenty years earlier the dark shadow of tragedy had come to hang over the family. A wicked governess had vanished in the night, taking with her Della's twin sister, Irma. When the loss was discovered in the morning every step was taken to find the vindictive woman and recover the child. But to no avail.

Police and private investigators alike gave up attempting to find out where the woman had gone and what had happened to the missing two-year-old. All the wealth of Delia's parents had been useless in the face of this tragedy. It was as if the woman and her child captive had vanished from the earth.

In the end that was the opinion of most. It was felt that perhaps the woman had accidentally drowned and the young Irma had perished beneath the waters of the Thames with her. The woman was known to have an admirer of dubious character who worked on a river scow. But he could not be found either.

Delia's mother had been a frail person and the loss of a beloved child had not helped her health. When a bout of pneumonia swept the city in 1876, she was one of the plague's victims. It was said that she had died pleading with her husband not to give up the search for the missing Irma which, at that time, had already been in progress for years.

Della had been only eight at the time and her Aunt Isobel, who had been called in during her mother's illness, had remained with her and tried to console her. But Della would always remember her tall, mustached father coming out of her mother's bedchamber with a look of shocked sorrow on his aristocratic face.

Seeing her, he impulsively fell to his knees sobbing and took her in his arms. She began to cry as well, for she knew that her mother must have died.

And so she had. Aunt Isobel remained in the fine house which now was somber and silent. The servants moved about on tiptoe for weeks after the death of a beloved mistress. Delia's father began to be absent from the house more and more, and all too frequently when he returned he was in a drunken state.

There were periods when he seemed to repent his fall into drunkenness and then he would remain at home and be most attentive to Della. These were times of unbelievable happiness for her, all the more so because she knew they wouldn't last.

Nor did they. Invariably he returned to his drunken ways and brought sorrow to them all. Somehow he managed to look after the family business so they did not suffer financially. And he kept his word to his dead wife by continuing to employ private agents to locate the little kidnapped girl, whom everyone else believed to be dead. He would not give up if only because he must fulfill his late wife's dying request.

Aunt Isobel had protested petulantly, "It is wrong! A foolish quest! And it keeps the tragedy continually with him! No wonder he drinks."

"But Mother pleaded that he not give up the search," Della reminded her aunt.

"She was delirious and dying when she made the request," Aunt Isobel said tartly. "He should have ignored it!"

"Father wouldn't," she said quietly. She had great love and respect for her sole surviving parent.

"I warn you it will lead to no good," the prim older woman predicted.

And unhappily her prediction proved all too true. One evening about a year later word was brought to the mansion in Doane Square that her father had suffered an accident. He had toppled down the winding stairway of his club and been taken unconscious to a hospital.

Della and Aunt Isobel at once rushed to the hospital. By the time they reached her father's side he was dead. She learned the tragic fact that his fall had taken place because he was drunk. So she was now alone except for Aunt Isobel and some distant cousins.

Della had been numbed by this second bereavement. But Aunt Isobel had stood by her and instilled courage in her. This had always been a characteristic of the stout-hearted maiden lady and she was not going to allow Della to grow up without infusing her with some of it.

As a result Della became a lively, adventurous young woman with many admirers rather than a meek, sorrowful and shy girl. Life took on an even, pleasant tone in the old mansion and the search for her missing twin was dropped. It was agreed by Aunt Isobel, Sir Roger Drexel and even by Della that it was a sad, futile business and there was no point continuing it.

At twenty-two, Della still had not found a young man whom she wished to marry. Aunt Isobel had accused her of being too much of a flirt and too difficult to please.

"Watch out or you'll end up an old maid like me," Aunt Isobel had threatened.

"Perhaps I might enjoy that!" she'd said with a smile.

"You might now," the older woman said. "It's all fun when you're young and able to turn every male head. But when you're older and less attractive, it's a different matter. You'll wish you had a husband."

Della had raised her chin in a show of confidence and said, "I know many wives, some young ones, who don't appear all that happy!"

"And a good many more that are! A husband and babies! What else should a woman ask for?"

"Romance, for one thing!" Della declared. "And a little fun as well!"

"You're spoiled!"

Della laughed. "If I am, dear Aunt Isobel, then you are wholly to blame since you have been both mother and father to me all these years!"

Aunt Isobel's dried-up face showed the hint of a smile, but she said, "I haven't put such ideas in your head. It's those wicked, romantic novels you've been reading!"

"They've taught me a good deal about life and men!"

"I'll warrant that! But all the wrong things!"

"I wouldn't say so!"

"I will," Aunt Isobel insisted. "You went with that young lawyer apprenticed to Sir Roger's firm for most of a year. I thought it would be a match. And then you dropped him!"

Della's cheeks crimsoned. "I don't wish to discuss that!"

"Just the same, Henry Clarkson was a good-looking, pleasant young man."

"He had no vision or true humor and a head full of dull law!" Della exclaimed.

"There are no perfect men!"

"There must be some better than Henry Clarkson," Della said, turning away so her aunt could not study her expression. The fact was she had liked Henry Clarkson a great deal, but there had been an unfortunate circumstance that had ended their budding romance.

While driving with a girl friend in a carriage in the park one day, she had happened to look across the road and seen Henry Clarkson at the reins of a carriage drawn by a frisky black horse and with an equally frisky, black-haired young woman at his side.

Later, when she had challenged him about this, he had behaved most guiltily and insisted that the girl was a school friend of his sister. He had agreed to show her some of London. But the more she probed the more she learned about his attentions to this girl. It had not been a matter of a single afternoon, friends of hers had seen him with the dark girl at other times and places.

So, in spite of his protests that it had all been most innocent, she had broken off with him abruptly. He'd made several requests to see her since, but she'd always refused him. When they met at parties she did her best to avoid him. But it had been difficult for her and she'd needed all her courage to put on a brave front and turn to other swains who interested her not at all.

This was her situation at the moment. She rarely went out with a young man twice. And since she knew hosts of the most eligible young fellows in London and because she was lovely enough to capture their fancies, she had no lack of male companions. The price she was paying was to be considered a heartless flirt!

And this was too bad. Since she was anything but that. Often she sat alone mourning the unhappy twist of fate that had parted her from the one man she'd truly cared for. But she let no one else guess.

So now she found herself in the great living room with her aunt, awaiting the arrival of Sir Roger Drexel. She respected the tall old man with his craggy face, heavy white hair and sideburns and booming voice. In a way he had become a kind of father figure to her.

Sir Roger arrived exactly at four as he had promised. He had the military bearing of the former cavalry officer he was and made a magnificent figure in his gray trousers, fawn vest and brown frock coat. His cravat was also of dark brown. He approached Aunt Isobel with a smile on his face and bowed and kissed the back of her hand.

"You look in good health, Miss Moore," he boomed in his loud voice.

Aunt Isobel's dried face showed pleasure. "I'm as well as I can expect for one of my years!"

"Years! Ha!" the grand old man said, dismissing her age with the gesture of a huge hand. "You are in the prime of life, ma'am."

"I'd hardly say that!" Aunt Isobel replied.

"I say you are," the big man said, his eyebrows almost meeting as he frowned. "For I'm a good many years your senior and I'm not about to pop into my grave!"

Della laughed and went to kiss him dutifully on the cheek as he leaned down to her. "I can't ever imagine you doing that, Sir Roger!"

"Well, the Sudanese tried to do me in when I was in the army but without any luck," the big man laughed. "I enjoy life."

"I know you do," Della said, taking one of his huge hands in hers. "Now do come and sit by the fireplace with Aunt Isobel."

He drew back. "No," he said. "I'd rather you sat down. I'd like to stand for a little."

"Truly?"

"Yes. I've been seated in my office all day until now," Sir Roger Drexel said. "By the way there's some talk about town that the Queen has a cold."

"I hope it's not serious," Aunt Isobel said with some alarm.

The white-maned Sir Roger shrugged. "Well, at her age any illness is to be considered. But the direct word from the palace which came my way suggested she's resting as comfortably as can be expected."

"Then she is likely in no danger," Della said. "She is such a sturdy old woman. We've come to think she'll live forever."

"And she'd better and stop that rogue of a son from taking the throne," Aunt Isobel said with some anger.

"Edward?" Sir Roger inquired mildly. "What have you against the poor man?"

"He has too many women for one thing!" Aunt Isobel said.

Sir Roger sighed. "Well, temptation is often thrown in his way. He's waited a long time for his chance to be King. I like the man and I sympathize with him."

A knowing look wrinkled Aunt Isobel's face. "For all I admire you, Roger, you are a male. So I'd expect you to favor him."

Sir Roger chuckled. "Well, there you have it. But let me get down to the serious business of my being here."

"Why did you come?" Della asked.

The big man's face became grave. "I don't think either you or Miss Moore can possibly guess."

"Out with it, man," Aunt Isobel insisted.

Sir Roger took some papers from an inner pocket, lifted the pince-nez that hung from a velvet cord about his neck, and adjusted them on the bridge of his nose. He said, "I only received these papers hours ago, and so I have not had too much time to study them." Turning to Della, he added, "I ask you to prepare yourself for a shock, my dear."

"What sort of shock? Have we suffered some grievous business loss?" she asked.

"No, I wish it were as simple as that," the old lawyer said. "The fact is I received this message only early this morning that your long-missing sister, Irma, is alive and well."

Nothing he might have said could have come as more of a shock. Both Della and her aunt rose to their feet. Della was the first to recover her voice. "You can't mean it!" She gasped.

"I'm completely serious," the old man said.

"Explain!" Aunt Isobel begged him.

"After twenty years! And all that searching!" Della said tautly. "Where is she?"

"In Italy," Sir Roger said.

"Italy!" Aunt Isobel echoed.

"In Rome, to be precise," the old lawyer said. "It appears she has been there all these years. No doubt some of the investigators must have come close to discovering her and just managed to miss doing it."

Della stared at the lawyer. "She's twenty-two! My own age! My twin! And most surely a stranger to me!"

"That is so," Sir Roger said. "As I follow it, the woman who stole your sister went to Rome. There, she found employment in the house of one Prince Sanzio."

"A prince!" Della said in amazement.

"There are a good many of them over there," Sir Roger said. "Much more common than in England."

"Did my sister grow up a servant in this man's house?"

"No. Because she was attractive and he a childless widower, he adopted her. The woman who did the kidnapping pretended the child was her own and offered her to the Prince."

"How dare she do such a thing," Aunt Isobel said in annoyance.

Sir Roger said, "She felt this was the best way of concealing the child. And she kept her secret until after her death."

"How did Prince Sanzio find out?" Aunt Isobel asked.

"The woman died recently and left a written confession," the old man said. "This was not immediately found, but as soon as it was I received this communication from Prince Sanzio."

"What does he say?" Della asked.

"He claims to be old and in poor health," Sir Roger Drexel said. "He has brought the girl up as Princess Irma Sanzio."

Della smiled in awe. "So I have a sister who is a princess!"

"An Italian princess," Sir Roger said. "However, Prince Sanzio fears he will die soon and he does not want the girl to be left alone. It is his wish that she be reunited with her family."

"Of course!" Della agreed.

Aunt Isobel spoke up: "Let us not be too quick in this matter."

"What do you mean?" Della asked her.

The old woman said, "Suppose it is a hoax?"

This left Della shocked. She asked Sir Roger, "You must think this all bona fide or you wouldn't have brought it to us."

The old lawyer's white eyebrows met again in a frown as he said, "I've gone into it all in as much detail as time allowed. I only received the message this morning."

"And?" Della said.

"I know there is a Prince Sanzio and that the crest on the letterhead on which he's written me is his actual crest."

"That does not prove much," Aunt Isobel said, still stubbornly refusing to believe the story. "Someone could have somehow stolen his notepaper and manufactured the message. It could be another scheme to drain us of money. There have been such attempts in the past."

"I know all that," Sir Roger agreed. "But there is no mention of money in this letter. It only states the facts and asks that Della come to Rome at once and be reunited with her sister."

Aunt Isobel looked more upset. "This man expects my niece to journey to Rome on the basis of his wild story?"

"I think it may be the truth," Sir Roger said solemnly. "I cannot think of anything he has to gain by it otherwise."

"Sir Roger is right, Aunt Isobel," Della said. "I think you are wrong to refuse to believe. It is wonderful! A dream come true! I only wish that my mother and father were alive to know about it."

"And I," Sir Roger agreed. "I think the tragedy of Irma's vanishing helped bring on the death of your parents."

"I'm sure of it," Della said. "And I want to meet this girl. If it turns out she isn't my sister no harm will be done."

"You sound so sure," her aunt said drily. "It could be a plan to get you to Rome and hold you for ransom. Have you thought of that?"

Della stared at her aunt incredulously and then at Sir Roger. "Do you think that, Sir Roger?"

The big man hesitated. "I suppose it is possible. You are one of the wealthiest young women in England."

"You see!" Aunt Isobel said triumphantly.

"Yet I doubt it is likely," Sir Roger said, rubbing his long chin. "I believe this letter to be genuine."

"Why does he ask that Della go to Rome?" the older woman demanded. "Why not send the other girl here?"

Della turned to her aunt and said, "She may be afraid to come here alone. Not sure what sort of reception she will get."

Sir Roger nodded. "I think Prince Sanzio wishes to see Della and know her. It is understandable."

"But it could be a wicked trap!" Aunt Isobel insisted.

Sir Roger said, "I would not under any circumstances allow Della to journey to Rome alone."

Della stared at him. "You think me incapable of making the trip on my own?"

"Not at all," he said. "But you must be protected. I would insist on sending along a qualified lawyer. And certainly your Aunt Isobel should journey with you as a companion!"

Aunt Isobel said, "I'm not sure I'm up to such a trip."

"Of course you are," Della said, turning to her. "If my sister is in Rome and alive I want to meet her and know her!"

Sir Roger said, "I shall try to get any additional information I can. In the meanwhile I would suggest that you two ladies prepare to travel shortly."

"I'm so excited!" Della said. "It's like someone coming back from the dead!"

"Just so long as we get the right Lazarus," her aunt said grimly.

"What do you mean?" Della asked.

"You heard Sir Roger say you are heiress to one of England's great fortunes. If this is truly Irma living in Rome, she will be bound to share the fortune with you."

"I don't care! There's enough for both of us!"

"I'm sure there is," Aunt Isobel said with irony. "But would you wish to share the family money with an impostor?"

"An impostor!" she gasped.

"Come," her aunt said, "surely you are not so naïve as to have overlooked that possibility."

"No!" she said indignantly. "The idea didn't cross my mind! I'm too happy to hear that my sister may be alive and safe. That I may have someone of my own flesh and blood to cherish!"

Aunt Isobel drew herself up primly. "I must say that puts me properly in my place!"

At once Della knelt by her aunt's chair and pleaded with her, "Don't make things more difficult. I do appreciate all you've done for me over the years. No one will ever mean more to me than you! But if my sister is alive I do want to go to her!"

"Your aunt made a sensible comment," Sir Roger warned her. "There is surely a danger that someone may have located a look-alike for you and now be hoping to pawn her off as your long-lost sister. The search for her is widely known and is the sort of thing to attract the unscrupulous."

She gave him a troubled look. "Don't tell me that when you've raised up my hopes!"

Sir Roger's stern expression softened. "I'm sorry, my girl. I did not mean to upset you. I had no choice but to bring this to your attention. And the chances are that we may have found your sister."

She rose to face him. "But you are no more convinced of it than Aunt Isobel?"

"Frankly, no," the old man said with a hint of embarrassment. "Yet I think the lead is worth you're making the journey to Rome. Just so long as you're protected against possible kidnapping or being tricked by an impostor, or in some other fashion."

"I see," she said quietly. "So I should not let my hopes raise too high?"

"That would be my advice," Sir Roger said. "Now I must be on my way, ladies. I'd like you to call at my office on Monday, Della. We can then work out more of the details."

"I was going to the country," she said. "But I will stay in the city and see you."

"Very good," the old lawyer bowed in his formal fashion. "I hope you will regard my news as good until it is proven otherwise."

Della saw him out and after she had watched his carriage drive away, she returned to the living room and the company of her aunt.

"I don't like it at all," Aunt Isobel said.

"You're being too pessimistic," Della complained.

"Rome is far away and in a foreign country," Aunt Isobel said. "We could all wind up in our beds with our throats slit open!"

"Nonsense!" Della exclaimed. "This is 1890. People travel everywhere with few problems, if any!"

The prim woman sighed. "I know you've been taken in by it. So has Sir Roger to an extent. But I feel it is simply a trap set up by some confidence man to get money from you!"

"The man who wrote the letter and adopted my sister is an Italian prince," she said with impatience. "He could be more wealthy than I am!"

"He likely lives in a cold, old castle with no money at all," Aunt Isobel warned her.

"I must find out if it really is Irma," Della said. "So I shall go to Rome no matter what you say."

"I realize that," her aunt answered with resignation. "And I shall accompany you. But I fear for the worst!"

After a while Della left her aunt to retreat to her room and think about this startling new development in her life. She had been too young when Irma was kidnapped to have any real memories of her. Or of the woman who had committed the vile crime. She only knew its effects had poisoned the lives of her parents and had a real bearing on her own happiness.

Now there was a chance the mystery might be resolved. That Irma might happily be restored to her rightful place in London society. That she might get to know this lost sister!

In a closet of her room there was a small velvet-covered trunk that had come into her hands on her father's death. Prior to that he had kept it in his room. Now she went to the closet and moved out the small trunk from the shadows to study it. She knew well its contents, ancient and yellowed garments of the child who had been stolen that night twenty years ago.

The trunk was not locked so she slipped back the catches and held it open. She could smell the ancient rot of the infant clothes, mildew mixed with a faint aroma of perfume. She lifted a tiny yellow baby dress and stared at it.

She knew that before her death her unhappy mother had spent long hours brooding over this trunk and its contents. Then her father had taken it into his room, a continual reminder of the tragedy. Now she had it.

The link with those distant days gave her an eerie feeling. Was Irma truly alive and grown up in Rome? Or was it part of some diabolical scheme to defraud her and round out the tragedy? She didn't know and she couldn't take the chance of not trying to find out.

Something deep within her made her decision unwavering. She owed it to her parents not to fail at this critical moment. She must go to Rome and find out the truth. And if Irma were truly alive, bring her back to London. In the meantime she would live in a state of tension. Difficult days lay ahead for her!

On Monday afternoon Della made the journey to Sir Roger Drexel's Fleet Street law offices. It was a pleasant day and she sat back in the open carriage enjoying the drive while the coachman sat on a seat high behind her guiding the reins of the brown mare.

Della loved London! There was the theater—she enjoyed every play whether it was an old-fashioned melodrama in one of the lesser theaters or a fine production of Shakespeare at the Lyceum. She liked equally the vulgarity of the music hall and the new plays about social problems. And she often went to the open-air entertainment at Earl's Court or the Crystal Palace.

She was a part of social Mayfair. Mayfair led a very carefully regulated life as a community. At various times of the year the houses of the aristocracy and of the very rich were filled for the season! At certain times carriages paraded in the park. Children went out with nurses or governesses, all the little girls of one family dressed alike. There were parties, receptions, balls, "drums" and dinners. The shops of Oxford Street, Regent Street and Bond Street showed their newest collections. The opera audience, in full dress, was brilliant and sometimes bored, but Della knew it was thought to be the most fashionable entertainment. When the season ended the dresses and uniforms, the liveried footmen and the starched nursemaids, the window boxes and stiff little park chairs would vanish, leaving the squares of Belgravia and St. James and the streets of Mayfair almost deserted.

Such were the dimensions of her world. And yet she knew there was another London. The world of the poor Londoner. Those who worked hard and lived in slum houses in mean streets. Whose diversions were limited to the public house, an occasional visit to a music hall and rarely a trip as far as Hampstead Heath on Bank Holiday. Drinking, fighting and swearing were common among these men and women. Few visitors came to their areas from outside, except for church missions and fashionable young ladies like herself doing social work.

Along with some of her friends, she had invaded these dark corners of the city on special enterprises. Certain parts of East London were quickly becoming inhabited by foreign immigrants, a large proportion of whom were refugees from the Russian pogroms. By industry, thrift and driving ambition many forged ahead to middle-class respectability. But many of the newcomers retained their own clothes, customs and the language of their birthplace.

The Chinese already had their own quarter in Limehouse, with the Japanese to be found in Bloomsbury, studying English and English business methods. It was an exciting age, Della believed; the first news photograph had just been printed in a London Daily and there were dozens of other amazing inventions said to be on the way.

Her carriage moved slowly along Fleet Street. Men in bowler hats and top hats and lads in caps flowed about in the busy thoroughfare. Because the weather was warming, there were occasional women in wide-brimmed straw hats. And one or two of the men sported straw boaters.

The carriage passed a two-decker, horse-drawn omnibus with a full complement of passengers and ads printed on its sides for

"Carter's Liver Pills," "Nestles Milk" and "Sanitas" disinfectant. Her driver brought the carriage to the curb by the great stone building in which Lawyer Drexel had his chambers and jumped down to help her to the sidewalk. She told him to return for her in a half-hour and went inside.

A young, bright-faced clerk was there to greet her. "And what is your business, miss?" he asked with a smile.

She was impressed by his manner. She smiled in return as she said, "I'm here to see Sir Roger Drexel."

"Yes, miss," the lad replied. "You would be Miss Della Standish."

"That is correct."

"Follow me, miss," the boy said. "Sir Roger is waiting for you."

She followed him down a short corridor to an oaken door marked *Private*. The boy knocked on it and from the other side came a reply in Sir Roger's booming tones.

The boy smiled and opened the door and said, "You can go right on in, Miss Standish."

She entered the big office and the tall Sir Roger stood up to come and meet her. She kissed him in her usual fashion and he saw her safely seated in a chair across the desk from his. He said, "Are you still keen about going to Rome?"

"More than ever," she said. "Have you learned anything else about Prince Sanzio?"

The craggy face of the old man showed a smile. "I have not been idle."

"So?"

"Prince Sanzio has a palace in Rome. He is not a poor man but neither is he wealthy. He is respected for his family name and it is known that he has an adopted English daughter."

"Which must be Irma!"

"Could be your sister," the old man corrected her. "We must not jump to conclusions. Prince Sanzio would benefit greatly if his adopted daughter came into half the Standish fortune."

She sat back wearily in her chair. "Why must money always be coming into it? I want to find my sister!"

"And so you shall—if she is your sister," Sir Roger Drexel said. "Yet your Aunt Isobel is right in fearing you might be stepping into a trap or that an impostor might be palmed off on you!"

"I don't think that is likely."

Sir Roger gave her a stern look. "Consider this: If the girl in Rome should be given acceptance as your sister and anything subsequently happened to you, she would then be the sole heiress."

"Why do you point out such an obvious fact?" she asked impatiently.

"To make you understand the possible dangers in all this," the lawyer said slowly so that it would sink into her mind. "You might be lured into a trap and then murdered if your sister is in the hands of unscrupulous people."

Chapter Two

Della listened to the old lawyer's grim warning but determination remained on her lovely face. She did not flinch at the risks as she replied, "But Sir Roger, do I have any choice?"

He raised his white eyebrows. "Meaning exactly?"

"All my life I have been haunted by the disappearance of my twin sister," Della told him. "I saw my parents die, if not from broken hearts, most surely as the consequence of the anguish they suffered. Their dearest wish was to find Irma."

"True."

"I therefore feel it my duty to follow this up," she said. "And I pray that I shall be reunited with my dear sister in Rome."

Sir Roger's weathered face showed approval. "Spoken with courage and wisdom," he said. "Your parents would be proud of you if they were alive."

She smiled thinly. "Thank you. I know Aunt Isobel will accompany me, though she may make protests to the contrary. She is as much interested in this as I am."

"That is good," he said with a sigh. "Still you can scarcely embark on a venture of this sort alone. I insist that a member of this firm accompany you to offer you the best protection possible every foot of the way."

"You think that required?"

"I consider it imperative."

"Very well," she said. "I suppose it would be best. I shall bow to your wisdom in this."

"Thank you, Della," Sir Roger said. "If you will excuse me for a moment I will bring the person I think ideal for the task in here." And with that he left the room.

She sat alone in the book-lined office wondering who the old lawyer might settle on. Perhaps some older member of the firm who had made the tour to Rome many times. Such a man would have a considerable advantage and perhaps also a knowledge of the Italian tongue.

Her back was to the door and so she heard Sir Roger and the man he had chosen entering the room before she was able to see them. As the two men came into view she gave a start! For the young man Sir Roger had in tow was no other than Henry Clarkson!

Sir Roger Drexel, clearly innocent of the breach between them, beamed at her and said, "I know you and Mr. Clarkson are acquainted!"

Sitting up in her chair, she said stiffly, "Yes, we have met."

Henry Clarkson's face was crimson and he bowed to her with some embarrassment. He said, "It is good to see you again, Miss Standish!"

She thought it to his credit that he at least did not take the liberty of calling her Della, as he had so often when they went about as a couple. The situation was, she felt sure, as difficult for him as for her.

Sir Roger showed an expansive smile. "It came to me in a second that Clarkson might be the ideal person to accompany you. Not that we can afford to lose him here in London."

She said hurriedly, "Pray do not work any hardship on the firm. Some older man might do just as well for this unimportant task."

"I do not consider the expedition unimportant," the old lawyer told her. "It could be that your journey might be fraught with danger."

"Surely not," she protested.

An unhappy Henry Clarkson turned to his superior and said, "I think it most important that Miss Standish be satisfied about who accompanies her. And, as you know, I'm fully occupied here with the settlement of Lord Mavor's estate."

Sir Roger brushed this aside. "I can put another man on that!"

The young lawyer's pleasant face showed his acute chagrin as he turned to her and said, "Please understand I do not wish to force myself upon you!"

"That is to your credit," she said primly.

Sir Roger Drexel eyed them with some perplexity and boomed out, "May I ask what all this means? I have been told that you two were on the point of being engaged. I would expect the chance of a journey together to Rome would suit your ardent state most agreeably. Yet you both protest and make excuses!"

Now it was Della's turn to feel her own cheeks burn as she explained, "We have not been seeing each other of late! And we surely are not on the point of becoming engaged!"

"That is the truth, sir," Henry told his superior.

Sir Roger studied them both for a moment and a smile slowly spread over his craggy face. He pounded his right fist in the palm of his left hand and exclaimed, "I understand now! You've had a lovers' quarrel! Damme, why didn't you say so?"

She sat in confusion, staring down at her hands. "It wasn't quite that," she said awkwardly. "We simply made up our minds not to see each other again."

"Miss Standish is telling the facts exactly," Henry Clarkson said loyally, although in truth this was not at all the case. She had refused to see him again despite his efforts to win her forgiveness.

Sir Roger boomed, "Call it what you will, I say it is a lovers' quarrel!" He was so emphatic on this that neither of them dared contradict him. Henry stood in unhappy silence and she kept staring down at her hands without trying any reply.

Then Sir Roger spoke again: "In any event I do not think your differences are of any consequence."

She looked up at him with incredulity in her large green eyes. "Not of any consequence?"

"No!" he said. "In fact it might be better this way. If you and Clarkson were mooning and lost in puppy love you might well be exposed to danger without realizing it!"

"What are you saying?" she asked the old lawyer.

Sir Roger eyed her smugly. "That I'm just as pleased you've had this difference. It means the arrangement would have much less personal feeling in it. Mr Clarkson would have his mind strictly on business and so would you."

"Do you think it wise, sir?" Henry said desperately. "We have had differences. More could arise if we were forced to make a long journey together."

Sir Roger asked, "Would your difficulties with Miss Standish make you any the less diligent in your protecting her as an agent of this firm?"

"Certainly not," Henry Clarkson said.

"Then that is all that matters," his superior replied.

It was Della's turn to protest. She said, "Am I not to be considered? I wish to feel comfortable with whomever is assigned to accompany my aunt and myself."

Sir Roger gave her a stern eye. "Do you not think that Mr. Clarkson would properly do his duty and properly keep his place? Why should you be uncomfortable?"

Despairingly, she said, "A stranger might be better."

"I cannot agree," the old lawyer said. "Clarkson speaks a smattering of Italian. He has visited Rome and he is young and agile should you need protection from physical violence. No one else in the firm meets those requirements. So I say he is the one who must join you and your aunt on this journey."

She sank back in her chair. "Perhaps we can discuss it later."

Sir Roger looked stubborn. "We can discuss it as much as you like. But I warn you I'm not about to change my mind. I shall go ahead with making the arrangements for your trip with Mr. Clarkson as the firm's representative to accompany you."

Henry Clarkson gave her a miserably apologetic glance and told the old man, "I have a client in my office, sir. May I go back to him now?"

"Go," Sir Roger said. "But consider this settled. We will have a meeting about it tomorrow."

"Yes, sir," the young lawyer said unhappily. And to Della, he bowed and said, "Good day, Miss Standish."

She nodded a silent farewell to him and he went on out. When she was alone with Sir Roger she told him, "You surely are aware that you're making both myself and Mr. Clarkson miserable."

Sir Roger shrugged. "Don't expect me to be a party to all your lovers' quarrels or much interested in them. I'm merely trying to do my duty as your legal advisor. And I maintain that Henry Clarkson is the man best fitted to see you through this business."

She took a deep breath. "What if I refuse?"

"Then I shall delay your departure until we reach some agreement!"

Della rose and complained, "That is a threat to stay me altogether; I think it most unfair."

"If I have to resort to unfairness to insure your safety I'm perfectly capable of it," was the old lawyer's reply in a tone which indicated he meant it.

"Am I to have no say in this at all?" Della exclaimed with frustration.

"Certainly, my dear," Sir Roger said, joining her to escort her from the office. "You may choose your wardrobe at will and decide how soon you wish to leave. The rest must be left in my hands."

She returned to the street in a state of confused anger. Events had taken a turn for which she was in no way prepared. She'd never dreamed that Sir Roger might decide on Henry as the one to accompany her on the adventure. She could understand the old man's confidence in him, but after their quarrel she could not imagine spending months in his company.

The carriage had not yet returned for her and she waited impatiently. The street was crowded but she was in such a quandary she hardly noticed anyone. As she stood there mulling the situation, she was suddenly bumped into by a tall, swarthy man in a dark suit, cloak and wide-brimmed black hat. Surely a foreigner in this London street.

The man halted and, removing his hat, bowed and said, "My regrets, *signorina*, I was lost in thought! I beg you to forgive me!"

She stared up at the lean, brown face and saw the man's intense, burning eyes. London had its share of foreign fanatics and anarchists and she had no doubt this was one of them.

She said, "It was nothing."

He kept staring at her. "You are too kind, *signorina*!"

Fortunately, at that moment her carriage appeared and she quickly got into it and was driven away. She looked back and saw the swarthy man still standing on the curb with his hat in his hand, watching her. It gave her a strange feeling.

Judging by his accent and appearance, he was probably an Italian. It was odd that she should have this meeting with one just after her conference in the lawyer's office. But then she realized she was being silly and placing too much stress on the event. London had many foreigners and it was not all that surprising this tense, self-absorbed one should have accidentally brushed against her.

She dismissed the matter from her mind and went on to her dressmaker's establishment, where she spent a trying hour having fittings. She advised the owner of the shop that she might be leaving London shortly and would need the dresses earlier than expected.

The middle-aged woman had not shown pleasure at this, but told her, "Most of my ladies are of the same mind, Miss Standish. They all want their work finished at once."

"You will do your best?" Della said.

"You may rely on that," the woman replied without giving her any definite promise.

So Della returned to her carriage again in not too happy a state of mind. It seemed that it was to be one of those days when everything combined to frustrate her. A brief call at her milliner's made her feel better, but when she went out to her carriage she was startled to see a familiar figure standing across the street watching her.

It was the swarthy foreigner in the wide-brimmed hat!

She was certain of it. With a feeling of panic she hurried to the carriage. As the coachmen helped her inside she told him to take her straight home. She tried to appear calm and not stare in the direction of the watching man. But as the carriage began to move she cast a glance at him.

He was still standing there and he was following her with his eyes. Perhaps it was another foreign man in a broad-brimmed hat, there were surely more than one of them in London, but she had a strong feeling this was the same man. And if so, what did it mean? He could not be there by sheer coincidence? He must have been following her.

It was a worrisome thought and one which she could not explain. Why should this unknown man be interested in her? Did it possibly have anything to do with her missing sister in Rome? Were her adventures to start in London rather than in the ancient Italian city? It could not be so. She was fantasizing wildly even to entertain such thoughts!

Rebuking herself, she decided it had all been quite ordinary. She had seen two foreigners who dressed and looked enough alike to catch her attention. One of them had happened to bump into her and he surely would not have done that had he been following her and not wanting her to know it. She was allowing her sense of the dramatic to take over. She must put the whole business out of her mind.

And this was exactly what she did. On entering the mansion in Doane Square she sought out her Aunt Isobel and talked only of her trouble at the dressmaker's and her difficulty in finding hats suitable for Italy's warmer climate.

Aunt Isobel, seated in her usual chair near the fireplace, said, "Why do you not pattern yourself after me? I intend to delay any new purchases until I reach Rome. I'm sure I can get better prices there and find materials favored in that city."

"It does make sense," Della agreed, seated on the arm of a divan near her aunt. "But I need something to start the journey with."

"You have dozens of dresses that would do."

"I suppose so," she said, sighing. "But that is not really why I'm so upset. That is not the worst of it!"

Her aunt's eyes widened. "May I ask what the worst is? Or do you think me too old to be included in your problems?"

She stood up and sighed and then began to pace. "You know I always confide in you, Aunt Isobel."

"When it suits you," her aunt said acidly.

Still pacing, she said, "It's Sir Roger! I saw him at his office this afternoon. I think he likes to enrage me!"

"Does he?"

"It would seem so."

"What has he done now?"

"You would not believe it," Della said, halting in her pacing and facing Aunt Isobel. "Whom do you think he wants to send to Rome with us?"

"How should I know?" the older woman demanded.

"Henry Clarkson!"

Aunt Isobel took a moment to react and then she began to laugh. Still chortling with laughter, she said, "Henry Clarkson!"

"I don't think it all that funny!" Della told her indignantly.

Her aunt's mirthful face resumed its usual prim look and she said, "There, dear, I didn't mean to make you angry. But you must admit, it is funny. After the quarrel you two had!"

"There's nothing funny about it," Della said. "I had my quarrel with Henry because he behaved in a despicable manner. A manner which I found it impossible to forgive."

"He came to you asking pardon."

"Too late!"

Aunt Isobel stared at her worriedly. "I have always felt you were too hasty in condemning him. I think the young man truly cared for you."

"How could you know that?"

"I have eyes and intelligence even if I am an aged spinster," Aunt Isobel retorted sharply. "Henry told you he saw that young woman a few times as a favor to his sister, and I think he was telling the truth."

"And I choose to think the opposite!"

"So you've made yourself and Henry miserable," her aunt said. "Don't think I've not been wise to what you've been doing. Dating all those other young men."

Della felt herself blushing. "What do you mean?"

"I mean you've been trying to make Henry Clarkson jealous!"

"Never!"

"Deny it if you like," the old woman said. "But that is how I see it. You may have even convinced yourself it's not true, but I believe it."

"Then you're wrong!"

"Do you care for any of the other young men you've been dating? I mean, really care, as you did for Henry?"

Della gave a deep sigh. "What has that to do with it?"

"Everything!"

"You're talking nonsense," Della said, turning away to hide her own troubled feelings. Her aunt's probings were coming dangerously close to the truth. Truth she didn't wish to accept.

"So Sir Roger wants Henry to accompany us," her aunt said. "I think he's made a wise choice."

She turned to her aunt again. "I'll never agree."

"Henry is young and a good lawyer," Aunt Isobel said. "He can protect you well. And because he cares for you he will be especially cautious."

Della was shocked. "You talk as if it were all settled? I've told you I won't have any part of Henry on the trip."

Aunt Isobel smiled. "I know Sir Roger Drexel. And I think he will have the final say."

"Don't be too sure!" she replied, though she knew it was all too likely her aunt was right.

Della temporarily forgot these problems because this was the evening she was attending a grand party at the home of Earl and Lady Grey. The Grey mansion in Mayfair was often the scene of fabulous parties and she was sure this one would be no exception. Her escort for the evening was to be the Honorable Davy Miller, a well-known young man-about-town.

She began preparing early, taking a long warm bath, and then carefully selecting what she would wear. All the while her personal maid, Jeffries, bustled about assisting. Della had chosen a rose gown and decided to wear pearls given to her by her late mother. Jeffries fussed over her hair, parting it in the middle and fixing in it ornate coils at the nape of her neck.

At last the elderly maid said, "I declare, miss, you look perfect!"

She smiled at herself in the mirror and was satisfied. "At least I look as well as I can," she said.

"And that is better than most girls your age," Jeffries defended her loyally.

Della gave her a teasing glance, saying, "I want to be at my best tonight. The Honorable Davy Miller is my escort!"

"Him!" Jeffries said, impressed. "According to the newspapers, he can have the choice of any girl he likes!"

She laughed. "Well, tonight I'm his choice."

Jeffries was all agog. "Let me give your hair a final touch, miss," she worried. "I do want you to be a beauty!"

Davy, handsome in white tie and tails, arrived for her sharply at seven-thirty. He was a large young man with a tanned face and golden hair. He had made his name as a cricket star and was constantly moving about the country playing the game.

"Dashed lovely!" was his comment as she came down the stairs and linked a white-gloved hand through his arm.

As Davy's carriage arrived at the Grey's, the street was filled with smart conveyances with elegantly dressed couples descending from them and entering the brightly lit entrance of the big house. On the opposite side of the street, and held in check by two sturdy bobbies, were a motley lot of common folk come to admire and be awed by this display of grandeur and wealth.

"Bloody disgrace!" someone shouted from the crowd as Davy and Della stepped from their carriage to join the party. "Waste of money!"

"Feed the poor!" a woman shrilled and started a clamor.

Then an indignant male voice cried, "Shut your ugly face! That's Davy Miller, the cricket star, and he's entitled to a night out with a lady toff!" This brought laughter and good humor back to the crowd.

Inside, the orchestra was playing and once through the reception line Della and Davy mingled with the other of their set. Davy fetched them some champagne from the bar and then they danced a polka.

The great ballroom was brilliantly lighted with several hanging glass chandeliers. The shining oak floor was nearly always crowded with dancers. Della knew almost everyone at the grand affair. The orchestra played waltzes, lancers and the quadrille. She danced with Davy most of the time.

During the waltz he said, "Your mind seems far away tonight."

"I'm sorry," she apologized with a smile. "I had a busy day. I'm soon leaving for Rome."

He showed surprise. "This is the first I've heard of it."

"The plan came about suddenly," she said as they moved gracefully about the floor.

"If it weren't the middle of the cricket season I'd follow you," the big man said.

"You mustn't neglect your game!"

"Can't," he said. "Just the same, don't let any of those Italian counts talk you into anything."

"That's not likely!"

He swung her around. "Everyone is watching us. We're the best-looking couple on the floor."

"You only think that!" she protested.

"It's true," he said. "I wish you'd change your mind about Italy."

"Can't," she said. "Family business." But she made no attempt to explain it to him. Sir Roger had advised her not to make mention of her long-lost sister until she was sure all was well.

A break came in the dancing and Davy left her to get some wine from the bar. She stood alone by one of the open windows that looked out on the gardens. The ballroom had become almost unbearably warm and she was thirsty. She had an idea Davy would be some time getting her a drink as there was a long line at the bar before he started for it.

"Della!" Her name was spoken urgently.

She turned to see Henry Clarkson standing beside her. She said, "What do you want?"

"To tell you I had nothing to do with Sir Roger's plan this afternoon."

"You made that perfectly clear."

He sighed. "I'm sorry you were embarrassed. I really did feel badly for you."

"That's very kind," she said with a hint of coldness.

He stood there ill at ease and finally said, "He still thinks I'm the one to go with you."

"I'm going to have to change his mind," Della said.

"I hope you can if that's what you want," Henry responded with a sincere look on his handsome face. "For myself, I'd be ready to go with you if that was your wish."

"You'd willingly make the sacrifice?" she asked with mild sarcasm.

"It would be no sacrifice on my part," he said. "Despite what you think, I still care for you, Della. I still love you."

She raised a hand to silence him. "This is neither the time nor place. And anyway, it's all a little late."

"Not too late unless you make it so," he told her.

"Please," she said. "Do leave me alone. Davy will be back in a moment."

"I saw you with him on the floor," Henry said. "You made a perfect team."

"Thank you," she said impatiently.

"It's my absence you wish, not my compliments," he said with a bitter smile. "I'm sorry, Della. I can't change the way I feel about you." And he turned and vanished into the crowd.

She watched him go with a sense of loss and dismay. Why did she always react as she had? Why not at least be pleasant to him? Perhaps it was because she'd cared so much and had been so deeply hurt. And why would he not be discouraged and turn away from her for good? Was it possible that he still loved her as deeply as he pretended?

These questions tortured her until Davy returned with their glasses of wine and even afterward. In fact, on the drive home from the party the big blond man complained that she had not been her usual vivacious self that evening.

"You lost your zest as the evening went on," he said as they sat in the dark seat of the carriage, his arm around her.

She smiled up at him. "I'm sorry. I told you I was tired and worried."

"You showed it," he said. "I think you should forget all about that trip to Italy."

"I wish I could."

He brought her close to him and kissed her for a long, ardent moment. Then he said, "Follow me around the cricket circuit. See England first and we'll have a party every night!"

"And ruin your form?" she laughed.

He joined in her laughter. "Better mine than yours," he said. And they sat close and content as the carriage rolled over the rough cobblestoned street.

Davy saw her inside and kissed her goodnight again. She left him in a pleasant, relaxed state and made her way up the stairway. The wine and the enjoyable evening had left her in a mood of easy languor.

Everyone in the mansion seemed to be asleep except herself. She had told Jeffries not to wait up for her because she felt the old woman was not up to it. But her bed had been turned down and everything laid out for her. Cold water had been run in her bath and there were jugs of hot water waiting for her to pour into the partly filled tub.

She undressed slowly and hung her gown up with care. When she had removed the last of her clothing she stood before the great oval mirror on one of the closet doors and admired her lithe body. She constantly checked to see that she was not putting on weight. As she studied herself she quickly took the pins from her auburn hair and let it tumble about her shoulders.

She was small-breasted with a naturally narrow waist, according to the fashion of the day. Her legs were long and slender with plenty of shape. She knew that some of her girl friends considered her figure too slim and boyish, but she preferred this to being on the stout side and having to battle with tight-fitting stays.

Moving on to the bathroom, she poured enough hot water into the tub to make a satisfactory mixture. Then she let herself sink into the water, temporarily fixing her hair up in a twist on the top of her head. The warm water caressed her shapely body and she continued to feel relaxed.

After a time she emerged from the tub and began drying herself with the large towel Jeffries had left for her. When she was thoroughly dried she put the towel down and, her nude body tingling from the brisk rubbing, she crossed the room to get her nightgown from the bed.

She never reached it. Halfway there she suddenly had the terrified feeling that she was not alone in the room. Then she saw a movement behind one of the long velvet window drapes at the floor-to-ceiling windows. In the next instant the drape was pushed aside to reveal the swarthy man in black cape and wide-brimmed black hat. He came quickly to her with a look of mad desire on his thin face.

Della cried out and turned to rush to the door and scream for help. But she was caught from behind and a rag doused in sickly-sweet-smelling ether was held tightly against her nose and mouth. At the same time the dark man held her naked body in check with his other arm. He seemed incredibly strong and she could not struggle free of his unwelcome grasp.

Then the ether began its insidious work and she slumped as she sank into unconsciousness. From that moment until she opened her eyes to darkness and the feeling of cold, she knew nothing. As she gradually revived she knew that her ankles had been tied and her hands bound behind her back.

She was still naked except that a blanket had been thrown around her. It had partly fallen away so that the chill of the night penetrated her. Now she began to take note of where she was. She could hear the panting and clanking of machinery and a steady kind of vibration. All this, along with the damp cold, convinced her she was stretched out in the bottom of a steam-driven craft making its way along the Thames.

Panic returned to her along with her wakening senses. Why? Why had she been captured in this fashion? And who was the sinister man in the hat and cape? Surely the same one who had followed her during the day. How had he managed to get into the house and hide in her room?

The tremor and noise subsided and she heard the wash of waves as the boat apparently made ready to dock somewhere. A moment later the man in black loomed over her.

"So, *signorina,* you have come to?" he said.

"Why have you done this?" she gasped.

"You do not know?" he asked with light sarcasm.

"No! You must be mad! Let me go! I'm willing to pay a reward!" she said frantically.

"Do not hurry things, *signorina,*" the man said in his menacingly accented fashion.

"What are you going to do?"

"Just now take you ashore," he said. "We have reached our destination."

And with that he leaned down and, gathering the blanket about her, lifted her up in his arms. Then he carried her up a few steps onto the deck and a moment later nimbly stepped over onto the docks.

A yellow fog lay heavy over the entire scene and she could not tell where they were. Somewhere along the Thames, probably still well within the city. He walked along with her weight apparently giving him no trouble.

She said, "I'm going to scream my lungs out for help!"

He gave her a vicious look. "One sound from you and I'll break that pretty mouth so that it will no longer be your pride!"

"Bully!"

"No matter," he said. "If you behave properly and make no outcry this need not go badly for you."

She did not believe him and yet she felt that for the moment she would be best advised to submit. Later she would somehow try to escape.

They reached a cluster of buildings and he went to one and rapped roughly on the door. It was opened after a moment and he carried her inside.

By the light of a candle in a holder on a barrel head, it looked like a stable. He took her over to a stall with a half-partition separating it from the rest of the room and put her down on the straw-covered floor.

"Not the sort of bed you are used to, *signorina*," he said with a grim smile.

"Please let me go!" she begged. "I will make no charges against you!"

He laughed unpleasantly. "I promise you that you will not do that!"

A door from the other end of the stable opened and she heard someone utter a long preamble in a tongue which was known to her! Chinese! Someone else joined the first man and there was an excited conversation between the two in their native tongue.

She stared up at her captor in dismay. "Limehouse! You've brought me to Limehouse."

"As good a hiding place for you as any."

She knew it as an area set apart from the rest of the city. A place in which the population consisted entirely of Chinese, Lascars, Maltese and a few Japanese. A place foreign to all that was Western, where opium dens and fan-tan saloons were as frequent as in any underworld of the East. A place where, despite the vigilance of the police, it was not wise for strangers to intrude.

"Don't keep me here!" she pleaded.

The swarthy man bent down and said in a low voice, "The price of your release is not too much. Just tell me what you have done with the jeweled Madonna!"

She frowned. "The jeweled Madonna?"

"Don't pretend ignorance! It has been sent to you!"

"I have no idea what you're talking about!" she protested.

He nodded. "So. You need more time to think about it. I can give you all the time you need. I'm going to cut the binding at your ankles. But your hands will continue to be bound behind you. And if you make any move to escape because you're able to walk, you'll find it to no prupose. There are armed guards outside every door." He removed the blanket from her nude body and then took out a knife and cut the thongs which had bound her ankles.

She said, "Let me have the blanket! It is not decent to expose me naked in this fashion!"

He shook his head. "On the contrary, I find you most attractive as you are!"

"Monster!" she said in a tremulous voice as she moved away from him. Leaning against the wall of the stall, she raised herself up to a standing position. She was weak and her head still light from the drugging.

"You have only to tell me where the Madonna is," he said, staring at her with hungry eyes.

"I don't know anything about a Madonna!"

"No?" he said, taunting her. "Soon you may be praying to her for help!"

Plaintively, she told him, "You are behaving like a madman and asking me about something of which I have no knowledge."

"Lies will not help," the man said. "It was sent from Italy to London. We know that. And it was sent to you!"

"Why? Who would send me a jeweled Madonna from Italy?" she demanded.

His smile was sinister. "I do not have to tell you. You know! You are playing a game and I am sick of games!"

"Go!" she said tearfully. "Let me be!"

"I will," he said softly. "But not for a little." And he methodically threw off his cloak, took off his hat and began removing his other clothes. She gasped at his audacity and huddled in a corner of the stall, forlorn in her nakedness.

"No!" she begged him. "No!"

He was stripped now, his hairy chest heaving as he came at her. There was a leering smile on his ugly face as his cruel hands reached out and dragged her from the corner to the middle of the stall.

There he pinned her down on the straw and despite her struggles, cries for help and moans, he cruelly took her. When he was sated he got up and stared down at her with contempt.

"You disappoint me, *signorina,*" he said. "I have had more pleasure in the brothels of Rome!"

She lay there sobbing as he dressed himself. She felt debased, beyond hope. She would never forget these nightmarish moments in which the act of love had been perpetrated in cruel parody.

The swarthy man in hat and cape stood over her again. He warned, "I'll give you a half-hour to remember where the Madonna is. If your memory fails you I'm going to turn you over to my Chinese friends. They shall have your favors one by one. They are not as choosy as I and will look on you as a rare experience!"

Chapter Three

Della fainted again. When she came to and opened her eyes she found herself looking up into the wrinkled faces of two old Chinese in black caps and native coats and trousers. The two chuckled over her and jabbered to each other, their conversation mixed with bursts of shrill laughter. As one of the old men reached out a skinny claw to caress her breast, she cried out and moved away in disgust.

This set them on another round of hysterical laughter, after which they padded out and vanished somewhere beyond the stable door. Her horrified thought was that they were going for others to return and gang-rape her. She had heard of white girls treated in such a manner in these Chinese dens and losing their minds as a result!

The swarthy man, whoever he was, had carefully sought out this spot to keep her hidden. The kidnapping had been managed smoothly and there was no question that he was grimly desperate to find the jeweled Madonna of which he had spoken. The only trouble was that she knew nothing about it or why anyone should send it to her from Rome.

Could it have anything to do with her sister? The sister who had recently been found and whom she was going to visit? There was no one else in Rome who could have sent a precious gift to her. She was convinced this could not be and the criminal who had abducted her had somehow come to a wrong conclusion—had in fact mixed her up in a business of which she knew nothing.

Perhaps someone close to her sister, someone who knew her, had been mixed up in the theft of a valuable Madonna. And when it was suspected the Madonna had been shipped out of the country, the thieves believed it sent to her. If only she could convince this madman that he was wrong!

Terror struck her again when the rear door of the stable opened and a half-dozen Chinese of various ages and sizes came in, jabbering as they leered at her with almond eyes. She shuddered and turned her back to them, trying to shut their weird talk and chuckles from her mind.

Her head pressed against the wooden planks of the stable's wall, she found herself truly praying for release. So desperate was her state that at first she did not hear the shouting from outside. The Chinese gathered in the stable were evidently aware of its meaning earlier than she, for they began to jabber louder and all scramble toward the rear door and then vanished through it. Heartened, she turned to hear more shouts and then the door sprang open.

Two of the river patrolmen led the way and following them was a man in plain clothes and Henry Clarkson still in the evening dress in which she'd last seen him at the party. The police ran on out after the fleeing Chinese while the man in plain clothes advanced to her, followed by Henry.

The detective draped the blanket over her and cut the heavy cords which had cut into her wrists. Seeing that the blanket served for modesty, he said, "We'll get you to a hospital. Those wrists are in bad shape!"

Henry offered a sincere, "Thank God, you're alive!"

She stared at the detective and then at him, and in a small voice asked, "How did you know?" Meaning how did they know where to look for her. But she did not hear the explanation if any came, because at that moment she became unconscious once again and remained so until she was in a hospital bed.

The broad, purple face of Dr. Walters, the family physician, loomed over her as she opened her eyes. He said, "Well, it is about time, Miss Standish."

Weakly, she said, "Doctor."

He took her hand and held it in his. "You must not worry. I knew you have been through a grim ordeal. But I'm convinced no permanent harm has been done!"

She noted that her ankles and wrists both pained, and saw that her wrists were bandaged. Her head ached wickedly and she had fits of trembling as she recalled her ordeal.

"Did they get him?" she asked.

"Who?" Dr. Walters wanted to know.

"The swarthy man! The one who kidnapped me!"

"No. He escaped," the doctor said. "Inspector Hogan will tell you about it."

"He attacked me," she moaned. "Treated me worse than an animal!"

"I agree," the bluff old doctor said. "But you are young and healthy. You will recover more quickly than you imagine. And I much doubt there will be any serious aftereffects."

She closed her eyes. It was easy enough for this doctor, who saw little, if any, of the sort of violence she had just experienced, to be bland about it all. But she would never forget it. And she could only pray that her rape would not result in her giving birth to a child of the swarthy monster who'd attacked her.

When she opened her eyes again the doctor had vanished and a nervous, middle-aged man was standing by her bedside. She recognized him as the plainclothesman who had come to her rescue with Henry Clarkson.

"I'm Inspector Hogan, miss," he identified himself.

"Thank you for saving me!"

He shrugged. "No more than my duty, miss. Though I was glad to do it. You can save some special thanks for the young man who was with me. That Mr. Clarkson."

"How did he come into it?"

"He was the one who broke the case," the inspector said. "Your aunt called Sir Roger Drexel and he sent Henry Clarkson to help."

"I see," she said, though she was still bewildered about it.

"Mr. Clarkson was questioning all the help when I arrived," the inspector went on. "And it was a smart move, miss. For one of the scullery maids up and confessed to seeing the man who abducted you. He had been leading her on with promises to marry her and the rest. And he got her to let him in the house, hide in your room until he captured you, and see him safely out at the end."

She said, "I knew there had to be someone on the inside to help him."

"And you were right, miss," the inspector said. "But when the girl realized she was caught and in trouble she told all she knew. She said the fellow was an Italian lately come to London. And a couple of times he'd taken her down to a boat at the Farrowgate Docks for lovemaking!"

"There was a small craft," she said. "That is what he took me to Limehouse in!"

"Yes, miss," the inspector said. "The girl also knew this Italian had friends in Limehouse. When we knew that, it was only a matter of going there and making a check of the buildings close by where the boat was docked. The girl had given us its description and name."

"He got away?"

"The Italian?"

"Yes," the inspector said with a sigh. "And we can't seem to find him. The Chinese are no help and he doesn't seem to have dealt with anyone else."

"He must have had confederates," she said.

"We can find none except the Chinese," the inspector said. "The fellow had to be mad. What was the point of it all?"

"I can tell you that, Inspector," she said bitterly. "He was looking for some kind of a jeweled Madonna which he claimed had been sent to me from Rome."

"From Rome?" the inspector said, mystified.

"It's a long story," she said wearily. "I'm sure some error was made. Nothing was sent me. Though I have had an urgent message from Rome concerning a twin sister who was abducted years ago."

Inspector Hogan's thin face showed interest. "Would you be so good as to tell me all about this."

She told him as much as she knew and all the while he made notes. She finished with, "It is possible Sir Roger Drexel can give you more information concerning this. He has the original letters sent us."

"Thank you," the inspector said, putting his notebook away. With a wry smile he suggested, "This is the sort of eerie case which I'm sure would be just right for Sherlock Holmes. But we have no Baker Street wizards at the Yard."

"That man is dangerous," she said earnestly. "I shall not feel safe until you find him."

"We shall do our best," the inspector said. "This story of a jeweled Madonna is puzzling. Apparently he was of the opinion you had this valuable item in your possession."

"He seemed sure of it. I don't know why."

"Could it have anything to do with this Prince Sanzio who sent you the word about your sister?"

"I don't know," she said. "It is most perplexing. I think some mistake was made. Wrong information given to the man who abducted me."

"That often happens in the underworld."

"But this man would not believe I knew nothing of such a Madonna. In addition he was sadistic and lustful." She turned her head on her pillow and sighed.

"You must try to put what happened out of your mind," the inspector urged her.

She gave him a grim look. "That is what my doctor told me. It will not be easy."

"I'm fully aware of that," the inspector said with a frown. "And depend on it we are following every lead in an attempt to locate the scoundrel."

"Perhaps the maid—the girl he seduced—knows more than she told you."

"We've questioned her thoroughly and have not been able to come up with anything new," the inspector worried. "But I expect we can try again. She became hysterical and it was useless to prod her further."

"I see."

"In any event we have an idea that the fellow only let her know so much. He was cunning enough. It may be that she really doesn't know anything beyond what she's told us."

Della realized this was all too likely to be true. "You may be right," she said.

The inspector left her and she rested. When she awoke the nurse brought her some broth and she felt a good deal better though her wrists and ankles were still hurting.

Then Sir Roger arrived with her Aunt Isobel. The old woman came to her and embraced her, tears streaming down her withered cheeks.

"I thought I had lost you!" her aunt lamented.

"It was a close thing," she said with a rueful smile.

Sir Roger glanced about the tiny, white-walled room and inquired, "Are they giving you good care?"

"I cannot complain at all," she told him.

Aunt Isobel now became indignant. "None of this would have happened if that wretched girl hadn't lost her head and let that villain get control of her. I hope she serves a jail term for what she did."

"I can see no benefit in that," Della said. "Discharge her without references but do not prosecute."

"Not prosecute?" Her aunt sounded surprised.

Sir Roger nodded. "I'm inclined to agree with Della. It could be a mistake to make charges against the girl and send her to prison. Better to give her a chance to rehabilitate herself."

"But think how Della has suffered because of her?" Aunt Isobel said.

"Sir Roger is right," Della said. "There will be no prosecution of the girl and let that be the end of it."

"And that dreadful Italian man is still at large. You might have gone to Italy if this hadn't happened. Perhaps it is a blessing in disguise!" her aunt went on.

"Extremely well disguised," she said wanly. "But it will make no difference. I intend to go to Rome just as I planned."

"You can't!" Aunt Isobel protested.

Sir Roger looked down at her earnestly. "After all this do you think it wise?"

"Do I have any choice?" she asked. "I must find out about my sister."

Aunt Isobel was upset. "Surely you cannot deny this Italian must have something to do with the other business of your sister being found!"

"It may be nothing but a coincidence," Della said.

"Or it could be much more," Sir Roger Drexel shook his head. "I tell you, I do not like it. Perhaps old Prince Sanzio has been mixed up in some sort of theft. And these others believe the loot was sent to you in London."

Della said, "There may have been a theft but I'm sure Prince Sanzio had nothing to do with it. Though he may be able to explain the mystery when I meet him."

"We shall be killed if we go," Aunt Isobel said dismally.

"You don't have to accompany me," Della said.

The old woman gave her an angry glance. "You know I won't let you go alone!"

"There is plenty of time to discuss that," Sir Roger said placatingly. "The main thing now is that Della recover. And our remaining here arguing with her is not likely to help."

Aunt Isobel calmed a little but said, "I'm only trying to take care of her."

"I'm sure you are," Sir Roger said. "And it will all work out. Just now we should leave and allow her to get more rest."

Della kissed them both and they went on their way. She was grateful for the quiet which followed. She had gone through a great deal and was not yet fully recovered. As she lay there she thought about it all and it seemed to her that whoever had stolen the jeweled Madonna in Rome must have learned about her from old Prince Sanzio. They might well have sent the Madonna to her in London, expecting to pick it up on some pretense.

But somewhere along the line the plot had gone wrong. Whoever had been sent with stolen treasure had either vanished with it to keep it for themselves, or the whole thing had been a hoax on someone's part: the Madonna had not been shipped out of Italy at all! She was sure she would get to the bottom of it when she reached Rome.

Her sleep that night was tormented by frightening dreams in which she was pursued by the man in the cape. His lean, cruel face was etched on her memory. She would not feel safe in London as long as he remained at large. And it worried her that he might still pursue her to Italy.

In this frame of mind her dreams were not surprising. Several times in the night she woke screaming. Her cries always brought a nurse running and each time she was given more sedative. All it did for her was make her sleep soundly for a short time and then the nightmares returned and she found herself trying to escape from the cruel attacker.

In the morning she felt better. Her doctor came by and pronounced himself satisfied with her condition. And later in the morning the nervous Inspector Hogan returned. He had little additional news, only more questions to ask her.

He stood by her bedside apologetically. "I have an idea that rogue has left London. He may even have skipped out of the country."

"You've not been able to trace him?"

"No," the inspector said. "We found the company who rented him the boat, but it was a cash deal and they could only offer the same description of him that you had already given us."

"So you gained nothing?"

"Nothing beyond the fact he appeared to be well supplied with money."

"I had dreadful nightmares of his chasing me last night," she told him.

"I'm sorry, miss. I only hope this was all some sort of strange mix-up and you'll not be bothered by this criminal or any of his cohorts again," the inspector said.

"I hope not," Della replied. But she knew it was all too likely that more would follow. Without knowing anything about it, she had somehow become involved in the theft of a treasure. "Have you heard anything about a jeweled Madonna?" she asked.

"No."

"No reports of a piece like it being stolen from some museum?"

"Not as yet, miss," the inspector said. "Though we no doubt will get notice if there has been such a robbery."

"The museum might not even be aware of their loss," she surmised.

"True, miss," he agreed. "In some cases these fellows have been clever enough to substitute fake pieces for the ones stolen. In which case a long while elapses before such a loss is known."

"He kept asking about a jeweled Madonna. Demanding that I tell him where it was hidden. Perhaps you might make some inquiries as to whether there are any well-known art items of that sort and where they might be located. Then you could pursue it further to see if one was missing."

Inspector Hogan seemed impressed. "A very good idea, Miss Standish. I shall at once launch an investigation along those lines."

"Possibly it may lead you to the theft and the criminals involved."

"I sincerely hope so, miss," the inspector said.

After he left she thought about it some more and was convinced she was on the right track. The jeweled Madonna had quite likely been filched from some museum, probably in Italy, though not necessarily. Whoever was involved had heard about her, likely through Prince Sanzio, and had decided to use her. An agent had been dispatched to bring a package to her for safekeeping. But the agent had never arrived! What had happened to him? And who had sent him?

She was still debating this when something she'd been wishing for happened. During his noonday break Henry Clarkson came to visit her. The serious young lawyer was the picture of sympathy as he came into the room.

Advancing to her bedside, he said, "Della, I trust you will forgive this visit."

"I do," she said.

"I'm glad to know you're recovering and I want to offer my sympathy for all you've gone through."

"That is good of you," she said, her eyes fixed on him.

"It was a terrible ordeal," he said.

She nodded. "But at least I learned something from it."

"You did?"

"Yes," she said, reaching out a hand to him. "I learned what a good friend you are and how unimportant the quarrel between us was."

The handsome young man's face brightened. "You really mean that, Della?"

"I'm offering you my hand as a token of our renewed friendship," she said sincerely.

He took her hand in his. "Della!" he said with some emotion. And he bent and kissed her.

She returned his kiss and then studied him with a sad smile. "It is too bad I had to go through such suffering to find out how wrong I'd been!"

"It doesn't matter now!" he said, happy with the situation as it was.

"I was wrong not to believe you!"

"My story did seem thin, but I promise you I told you the truth. She was merely my sister's friend. I had not been cheating on you!"

"I believe that now."

"I thought I had lost you to Davy Miller!"

"Not likely," she said. "Davy and all the others were just substitutes for you. I felt I had lost you and I was unhappy from that moment."

Henry squeezed her hand. "No need to concern yourself about that."

"Had it not been for your quick thinking last night that maid would never have confessed," she said. "I heard about it from the inspector."

The young lawyer looked embarrassed. "That was merely good luck. I felt someone on the inside had to be involved. I kept hammering at them and finally this young maid broke into tears and began to talk."

"The police might not have managed it as well."

"I have had training in court questioning."

"And you used it to advantage," she said. "My aunt and Sir Roger have been by to see me. And as you might expect, they both seem to think I should abandon going to Italy."

He frowned. "They're likely right. If your sister has been found why not have her come here? It seems likely that this attack on you stems from the business. Within a short while of getting the news you are abducted and nearly murdered by an Italian!"

Della sat up in bed and said in a confidential tone, "I do think there is some link between the two circumstances, but I don't wish to admit it to my aunt or Sir Roger."

"They are intelligent people," Henry protested. "They probably have come to the same conclusion on their own."

"They have and they are going to be difficult," she agreed. "But I must go to Rome as I planned. The fact that some Italian criminals tried to make use of me does not mean that Prince Sanzio or my sister is involved. Someone might have heard about me through them and used the information wrongly without their being aware of it."

"That is possible," the young man admitted.

"I think it is true," she said. "And that is why I must not give up going to meet my sister. Happily, I will have you to escort me."

Henry looked wryly amused. "I never thought you'd come around to it."

"You see what strange twists fate takes!"

"I'll be glad to accompany you if Sir Roger does not make it impossible," he said.

She stared at him. "How could he do that?"

"By refusing to let any of us go to Rome," the young lawyer said. "I'm a junior member of the firm. He could say he couldn't spare me."

"Then leave the firm and come with me anyway. I'll pay you!"

"He is your legal guardian," Henry reminded her. "He might stop you from using any funds for the venture."

Della gasped. It was a possibility she hadn't thought about. "You don't think he would threaten that?"

"It's possible if he felt it were for your good."

"But I must find out the truth about my sister. It is what my parents would wish!"

"Find out some other way."

"I think this Prince Sanzio is too old and frail to be willing to bring her to London," she said. "There is no other way."

"You're determined to go through with it?"

"Yes."

"In spite of what has happened?"

She nodded. "I must!"

He sighed. "Very well. When I talk with Sir Roger I will argue your case as well as I can. But do not count on his agreeing."

"We must find a way," she said.

His face shadowed. "They haven't caught that man yet. He may be mad. And he may have confederates. You can't tell how risky your situation is."

"The police think he may have already left the country."

"Let us hope they are right," Henry said. "You must exercise extreme caution when you leave the hospital. Not go anywhere on your own."

She wrinkled her nose. "You make my future sound so dismal."

"Because I want you to have a future," he said.

"Henry, dear," she said. "You always were such a worrier."

He smiled. "At least I have no need to worry about you and me any longer."

"No," she agreed. "At least that's settled."

"Rest yourself," he told her. "In a few days you will be home and this will all seem like a kind of nightmare."

She gave him a knowing look. "Nightmares seem to have a way of recurring."

Later she wondered why she had said it. Later she was to think that it had been a kind of second-sight. It was as if she'd looked into the future and saw what was ahead of her.

The next day Sir Roger Drexel came to see her again and remained with her longer. Seated at her bedside, the craggy-faced old man showed great concern.

"I'm worried about your insisting on going to Rome," he said.

"I will not change my mind."

"Even if it places you in great danger."

"I doubt that it will. I'll have Henry Clarkson to protect me."

Sir Roger raised his white eyebrows. "So you have made your peace with him?"

"Yes. I was wrong and ready to admit it."

"You weren't a few days ago," he reminded her.

She blushed. "Things have changed since then."

"My dear, you can be stubborn when you like. Don't deny it as it happens to be true!"

"I'll grant you that," she said.

"Too stubborn for your own good, often enough," he went on. "So?"

"Will you one day be ready to admit this visit to Rome ill-advised. Perhaps when it is too late."

"I'm committed to find my sister."

The old man sighed. "I might be able to prevent you going if I take a strong stand against it."

She reached out and touched his gnarled hand. "I'm sure you won't do that. It would be betraying your trust to my mother and father. Their dearest wish was that Irma be found and restored to the family."

He sat staring silently at her for a moment. Then he said, "Very well. I've been trying to find out more about this Prince Sanzio. I've contacted several people in my circle of friends who have lived in Rome."

"And what did you find out?"

"That all his life he has been a reckless gambler. So that now he lives in his palace with a horde of creditors daily at his door, having to live out his old age in genteel poverty."

"Perhaps I can help him. He ought to have something for adopting Irma and bringing her up to be a princess."

"You can decide that later," the old lawyer said. "I have tried to find out if he was ever mixed up in any criminal activity and have found nothing against his record."

"I'm sure he had nothing to do with the attack on me," Della said.

"Maybe not," Sir Roger responded. "But he has some friends who are not above suspicion."

"Oh?"

"There is a Count Barsini, a younger man than the Prince, and of evil reputation. His morals leave a good deal to be desired from all I have learned, and he has considerable wealth. From time to time he has played the role of moneylender at destructive interest rates to hard-up noblemen like the Prince."

She was at once interested. "Perhaps he is our man."

"It could be."

"The police should be told."

Sir Roger spread his hands. "Told what? That a man living in Italy is of evil character and a moneylender. I doubt if the London police would have any interest."

"They might if you explained that we had lately heard from Prince Sanzio about my missing sister. And shortly after, this attack was made on me by an Italian in search of stolen loot. Count Barsini could easily have heard about me from the old Prince and decided to use me as a decoy for some crooked game."

"Entirely possible," Sir Roger agreed. "But difficult to prove."

"If I were in Rome I'm sure the puzzle would all fit into place!"

"And you might find yourself in more danger," the old man worried.

"I think I have served my prupose," she said.

"I'm not at all sure," Sir Roger warned her. "All this talk about a jeweled Madonna may be sheer nonsense to throw us off. The real object may be to murder you so that your sister will be the sole heir to the Standish fortune."

"That would mean my sister or Prince Sanzio was part of such a plot. I cannot believe it of either of them. I'm sorry."

Sir Roger smiled bleakly. "Very well, then. I shall not argue with you further. As soon as you feel able I shall begin the arrangements for your transportation to Rome. I'll book for three, to include your aunt and Henry Clarkson."

"You can begin at once," she said. "I expect to leave the hospital tomorrow."

"I see," he said. "Well, the first step in your journey will be the boat train to Dover, then across the Channel on the ferry, and by train to Paris. After a brief stay in Paris you can board the express from Paris to Rome. You should arrive there within a week or ten days of leaving London. Depending on your stops along the way."

"I prefer not to stop anywhere," she told him. "Let me get to Rome as quickly as possible."

"I'll make the bookings with that in mind," he promised her. He rose and added, "I'll contact the hospital to find out when you're leaving and be here to see you safely into your carriage."

That night she slept better, waking only once. And the next morning her doctor informed her that she would be able to leave in the early afternoon. Her wrists were healing and her ankles much better. With the help of a nurse she dressed in the morning. Aunt Isobel had sent her a suitcase of clothing.

Henry Clarkson made another noon call and this time he shyly proffered her a bunch of roses. She was touched by his thoughtfulness.

"You need not have done this," she said. "I'm going home this afternoon."

"You can take them with you."

"No," she said. "If you don't mind I'll have the nurse give them to someone who is really ill."

He smiled. "They are yours to do with as you wish. And congratulations on winning your battle with Sir Roger."

"I know," she said. "It was touch-and-go. But he finally agreed to let me travel."

Henry said, "He has already started to see what bookings are available on the Paris-Rome Express. It is often sold out weeks in advance."

"I hope I don't have to wait too long. I have an odd feeling I should get to Rome as soon as possible. Otherwise something might happen to my sister and I may never meet her."

"Why do you think that?"

She looked at him ruefully. "No logical reason. Call it intuition."

Henry said, "You know that Sir Roger has developed a theory about what happened. He thinks it is a scheme to kill you and leave your sister as heir."

She nodded. "He broached that to me. I don't believe it."

"Prince Sanzio is in bad financial shape. And he is known to deal with some evil men."

"I still don't believe it," she said.

"It would be better if your belief is justified," he said. "But I'm worried that Sir Roger may be on the right track."

"We soon should know," she said. "Once we're in Rome."

"Do you want me to come and see you home this afternoon?"

"No," she said. "Aunt Isobel will likely come in the carriage to get me. And Sir Roger has promised to be here to see me safely into the carriage."

Henry laughed. "Then I mustn't interfere with him. Let him be the gallant!"

"Especially as we want him in good humor," she said with a smile.

"May I call on you tonight?" he ventured.

"Yes," she said. "I meant what I said. We are back where we were before the quarrel. Unless you want it different."

"You know I don't," he said quickly.

"Then I'll see you after dinner."

Henry kissed her good-bye and left in high, good humor. She felt much better and was impatient to leave the hospital. As she waited for the carriage she had a message from her Aunt Isobel telling her she was suffering from an infected tooth and would not make the journey to the hospital. But the old woman stressed that the carriage would be there for her at two o'clock.

Sir Roger arrived shortly before two and chatted with Della as she prepared to leave. He told her, "I think you can start your journey on Monday if that is all right with you."

Wearing a smart two-piece green woolen dress and a pert green hat, she was feeling much more assured. She smiled and said, "Monday would be excellent. I'll start preparing as soon as I get home."

"Do not push yourself," he advised. "You still look pale. And you have a long journey ahead."

They were still chatting when her nurse came in with a smile and said, "Your carriage is at the side entrance waiting for you, Miss Standish."

She thanked the nurse and Sir Roger carried her suitcase for her and escorted her out to the waiting vehicle. The coachman was seated above at the back of the closed two-seater, so Sir Roger opened the door for her and saw her inside. Then he placed the suitcase in beside her.

His craggy face thrust in the doorway, he told her, "I shall call at the house tomorrow."

"Thank you for your kindness. I know how busy you are."

The old man looked pleased. "Never too busy to look out for the daughter of old friends."

He closed the door and the coachman set the carriage in motion. She sat back and closed her eyes and listened to the clopping of the horse's hooves on the cobblestones and the creaking of the carriage wheels. She was on her way home; at last the nightmare was at an end.

After a little she opened her eyes and saw that they had moved into a different street. She gazed out at the wheeled traffic and the many pedestrians on the sidewalks and by the crossings. And all at once she frowned, for she recognized this as a strange part of London!

She could not be mistaken! She was certain of it! For a moment she debated that the driver might be taking a shortcut. His name was Miles and he was getting very old for his post. That was why she'd not expected him to help her in the cab when Sir Roger was there to assist. She could not believe that such an experienced driver had lost his way. And now the carriage was moving at a good pace.

Thoroughly upset, she turned and opened the small window which allowed her to communicate with the driver. "Miles," she called out, "why are we taking this route? I do not know it!"

There was no reply at all. And now panic began to take hold of her. She twisted her body so she might look out the small square and get a glimpse at the driver. It was then that a wave of trembling seized her. For the man at the reins was not Miles but the thin, swarthy-faced man who had abducted her. He was wearing a coachman's coat and hat but there was no mistaking him!

At the same time she made this shocking discovery the carriage picked up speed. She screamed in terror and tried to balance herself on the seat as the carriage careened wildly in its swift passage of the busy street. Once again she was a captive.

Chapter Four

The carriage rolled on at a mad speed. She saw the faces of startled bystanders on the street and heard angry cries. The vehicle veered sharply to the right, narrowly to miss collision with a heavy wagon drawn by two horses. The driver of the wagon was on his feet cursing as she lost sight of him. A moment later the carriage shot over to the left as a horse-drawn two-decker bus went by!

She was sobbing with terror and trying desperately to save herself from being hurled about. First she was at one side of the dark interior of the carriage and then the other. Ahead she heard a whistle being blown shrilly and as they came to the spot she saw a policeman waving for them to stop!

In that split second she made a desperate decision. Groping for the door handle, she pulled it open and made a leap to clear herself from the careening vehicle. She had the sensation of floating in the air for a moment and then she fell sprawling on the cobblestones.

The policeman came rushing up to her. "Are you hurt, miss?" he wanted to know.

Her hands were skinned and so were her knees. Her skirt had a tear in it and her hat was gone. With the policeman's help she struggled to her feet still in a daze.

"The carriage!" she mumbled.

"It's out of sight!" the policeman exclaimed in anger. "What's wrong with that driver? Did he go mad?"

"Tried to abduct me," she said, aware that a crowd had surrounded them.

"So that was his game," the policeman said. "I knew something was wrong when he didn't stop for me!"

She leaned against him. "I feel ill. Can you get me another carriage to take me home?"

"That I will, miss," he said. And waving his hand, he told the circle of onlookers, "Get moving, will you! The show is over! Make way for me and this young lady!"

The crowd obeyed him, at the same time mumbling about the wonder of it all. He led Della a few steps away and blew his whistle, this time to hail a passing carriage.

He saw Della into the carriage and found out her address to give the driver. Then he told her, "This fellow will see you home safely."

"Thank you," she said. "What about my own carriage?"

The policeman looked grim. "It's either smashed up somewhere or been stopped and the driver arrested. I'll make a report on it!"

Della thanked the policeman again and this time was driven properly back home. She knew this second attempt on her life was bound to arouse Sir Roger's ire and she hoped it wouldn't make him change his mind about her proposed trip to Europe. She saw no reason why it should. This second incident had merely proven that the swarthy-faced criminal was still in London and had not given up in his efforts to abduct her.

When she reached Doane Square she found Aunt Isobel already in a state. The old woman lamented, "We are all marked for death! I know it!"

"Why do you say that?" she asked, standing in the reception hall with the old woman.

"Why? I'll tell you why! Poor old Miles came stumbling back here half an hour ago with his head all battered. Two thugs stopped him and asked for information and before he knew it they'd dragged him from the carriage and taken him into an alley. They stole his hat and coat and left him for dead!"

"So that is how he got the coach!" Della said.

Aunt Isobel looked at her querulously. "What are you talking about?" And then it hit her. "How did you get back with the carriage stolen?" she exclaimed.

"I came in a public cab and do give me the money to pay for it, the driver is waiting," she told her aunt.

But Aunt Isobel was now regarding her with horror. "Your skirt is torn and your hands are cut! And you have a cut on your cheek and your hair is awry! What happened to your hat?"

"It's somewhere in the street, I suppose! Do give me some change!"

"In the street," Aunt Isobel repeated blankly. "I declare the whole city is lost in madness." And she went to get her change purse.

It took Della a while to explain everything to the older woman. Then Aunt Isobel insisted on calling Sir Roger and asking him to come to Doane Square at once. Meanwhile Della washed and changed into clean clothes and miraculously felt no serious aches or pains from her incredible experience.

Old Miles was not so fortunate. Della was so worried about him that she at once sent for a doctor. And before the doctor arrived Sir Roger was at the front door.

Sir Roger stamped in and glared at Della. "So it has started over again!"

She tried to appear calm. "Just a continuance!"

"Continuance be blazes!" the old lawyer said angrily as he marched ahead of her into the living room.

She followed him, saying, "I begged Aunt Isobel not to bother you!"

He turned to face her in a rage. "Would you have kept this from me?"

"I meant to tell you in time!"

"All London talking about the wild runaway carriage and the girl who leapt from it, and you would say nothing to me?"

"You're making it worse than it was!" she protested.

"You think so?" he said with sarcasm. "Miles half dead. Your carriage smashed and abandoned!"

"They found it then?"

"Yes. In the street following the one where you jumped out. The villain crashed it into a lamp post and then fled!"

"What about the horse?"

"Standing free in the carriage shafts which it drug away. The horse is all right."

"I'm thankful for that," she said.

"How can you be thankful for anything with all this starting again?" Sir Roger wanted to know. "Where is your aunt?"

"Aunt Isobel is down in the servants' quarters with Miles. The old man was badly beaten about the head."

"So it goes on!"

"No," she said. "I think this is the end of it."

"I wish I could agree, young lady," Sir Roger said sternly. "It seems to me you're ready to encourage this menace until everyone is murdered, including yourself."

"That is not true," she said. "You put me in the carriage. Why didn't you notice it wasn't Miles in the driver's seat?"

Sir Roger frowned and looked uneasy. He waved a huge hand. "I assumed it was Miles. I never even looked up."

"Nor did I until I realized I was being taken in the wrong direction."

"Jumping from that carriage wasn't smart. You might have been killed!"

"I wasn't," she said. "And anything would be better than being a captive of that man again."

Sir Roger paced and fumed. "I don't know what has happened to our London police. Used to be the best in the world. Now they let girls be abducted out of their homes and madly speeding carriages to go through the streets without being halted!"

"They made a brilliant try to halt the carriage," she said in defense of the police. "I know! I was there!"

The old lawyer glared at her. "And lucky to be alive! And don't tell me this state of affairs doesn't all stem from that Rome business!"

"I know we won't agree on that," she said mildly. "So lest us postpone the arguments until later. Just now I'd like to go see how Miles is making out. The doctor may have arrived."

This calmed the old man down a little. They made their way to the servants' quarters where the doctor was treating the elderly coachman. Aunt Isobel stood nervously in the corridor.

"How is Miles?" Della asked her.

"The doctor says he will recover," her aunt said. "But he is still very confused."

"Little wonder," Sir Roger boomed angrily. "Those criminals tried to kill him!"

Aunt Isobel gave him a pathetic look. "What are we to do, Sir Roger? How is this all going to end?"

Della broke in, "Sir Roger doesn't know any more than we do. London is not the safe, sane place it used to be. We can only hope this last failure will discourage those men."

Sir Roger shook his head in dispute. "You are wrong if you think that. They would not have gone this far unless they were ready to go further."

"So you think there is more to come?" Della said.

"I'm certain of it," he said.

•••

But in the end she won her own way. On the following Monday they started their journey, accompanied by many dire warnings from Sir Roger. Despite his pessimism, the first stages of the trip were completely uneventful. Their schedule called for them to stay overnight in Paris before embarking on the train for Rome.

They stayed at the Plaza-Athénée and had their dinner in the great dining room. All were delighted with the food and Aunt Isobel complained of being sleepy and went up to her room after dinner. She was in a bad frame of mind because she was still against the journey.

With the spinster gone upstairs Della and Henry were left to themselves. He hesitated with her by the hotel elevator and said, "It is still early. Would you like to take a look at Paris by night?"

"The can-can girls," she said eagerly. "I'd love to see them!"

"See them you shall!" the young lawyer said, pleased.

They left the hotel and hired a cab which took them from the broad tree-lined avenue where they were staying to the cheaper, more crowded Montmartre district. The driver let them out in a dark street before a one-story building from which sounds of music and merriment came.

"This is one of the famous can-can places," he told her. "You may even see the famed artist Henri Toulouse-Lautrec here. I was told it is one of his favorite spots!"

"Wonderful!" she said, thrilled.

Inside there was the clamor of lively music and the shrill singing of the can-can girls, along with their bold dancing on a brightly lighted little stage with a backdrop of a park scene. The air was filled with smoke, the odor of good food and a hint of body sweat. A fat maître d'hôtel led them through the crowded place to a small table near the front.

"A top table for the English demoiselle," he said, beaming at her.

Henry, in evening dress from their dinner at the hotel, stood out among the crowd. He smiled at the fat, mustached man and gave him a generous tip. The maître d'hôtel was properly grateful and sent a waiter rushing to take their orders.

They both ordered wine and gave their attention to the lively show. True to what she expected, the girls wore black stockings and colorful costumes which they held up most brazenly at certain points in the dance so that their garters, bare legs and white underthings were exposed. The crowd, a mixed one, greeted this part of the performance with loud applause and shouts of encouragement.

The entertainment ended for a little, leaving a lone violinist and piano to offer musical background for the drinking and dining which was going on.

Henry smiled at her and said, "I don't think you'll find Rome as exciting as Paris!"

Della eyed him archly over her wineglass. "I think these pretty dance-hall girls have a special attraction for you."

"It was you who urged me to come here," her handsome escort reminded her.

"True! It is such fun! One can forget everything here. I wish we didn't have to go to Rome, but there is no choice."

He said, "What if the girl turns out to be an impostor?"

"I will have at least tried."

"It is a long way to go on a mere chance."

"Prince Sanzio's letters seemed authentic enough. Irma was kidnapped and it is quite possible she turned up in Rome."

Henry nodded. "I'd be more willing to think it possible if there had not been those attacks on you in London."

"I don't think they had anything to do with my search for my sister, even though Sir Roger doesn't agree," she said. "And let us forget all that for the evening."

"Sorry," he said.

"It is fun being here with you," she told him.

Henry said, "I've often thought that Paris is the perfect spot for a honeymoon. Perhaps we can return again."

"Perhaps," she said, gentle amusement in her eyes. "We can talk about that after Rome."

"After Rome!" the young man complained. "I'll be glad when the business is settled!"

"And so shall I," Della said.

There was a stir at the other side of the big, dark room and Henry touched her arm and said, "See who is joining us!"

She stared in the direction Henry indicated and saw the headwaiter proudly leading in a dwarflike man wearing thick glasses, followed by a spectacular, tall blond girl with a boa thrown about her neck. She had seen many photo studies of the famed painter so she exclaimed at once, "It is Toulouse-Lautrec!"

"I told you he came here," Henry said as the waiter went about seating the little man and the tall, lovely girl.

"I can't believe I'm in the same room with him," Della said with delight.

"So Paris has not been such a waste of time?"

"I would never say that," she protested. "It is just that I'm in a hurry to get to Rome."

The famous artist received many people at his table. It seemed that a third of the patrons knew him and wished to pay homage to him. He accepted it all grandly and drank absinthe with his lady friend. Then the can-can girls returned to put on another bright show and this time direct their kicking and thigh exposure to the little man. He showed his pleasure by rising and applauding. Even on his feet he was barely taller than the table!

They left the busy place before the artist. Della knew they had an early train departure and didn't want to be too weary for the journey. Outside they picked a carriage from the waiting line and were driven through the murky streets to the Plaza Athénée.

Della was completely reconciled with Henry and she rested in his arms all the while they were driven to the hotel in the carriage, which smelled slightly of the stables. She smiled to herself as she recalled his earlier comment that Paris would be a perfect place for a honeymoon. She was of the same mind and hoped that it would be soon and with the handsome man at her side.

He had changed since their quarrel and now appeared to be a great deal more considerate. There was little of the stodgy young British lawyer, whom she used to resent, about him now. She decided their separation and reconciliation had been a good thing. Each of them now valued the other more.

The lobby of the hotel was quiet and almost empty of people. Henry saw her across to the elevator and they waited for it a moment. As they did so her eyes happened to settle on a man in an easy chair near the main doorway. He was reading a newspaper.

Just as the elevator arrived and they were ready to step inside the man lowered his newspaper slightly to stare at them. And for just a moment she had a stab of fear, for the face behind the newspaper resembled the swarthy countenance of her abductor!

"Come along," Henry said, guiding her into the elevator. And she did not have the chance of a second look at the man. Nor did she mention him to Henry, though the incident had worried her.

Henry saw her safely into the suite she shared with Aunt Isobel. The young lawyer lingered only long enough to kiss her goodnight and left for his own nearby room. She looked into her aunt's room and saw that she was asleep. Then she went to her own room and prepared for bed.

She undressed and put on a dressing gown and was studying herself in a hand mirror before the dresser. She moved the mirror in such a way that it reflected the window area. She was just in time to see a hand emerging from between the drapes!

She did not hesitate but screamed and with the mirror still in her hand rushed to her aunt's room and closed the door and locked it. Her Aunt Isobel awoke at once in a state of confusion.

"What is it, girl?" Aunt Isobel demanded with sleepy indignation.

"An intruder!"

"Where?"

"In my room! I saw only a hand through the drapes and I ran in here!"

"Is that door locked?" Aunt Isobel was now on her feet and slipping into a dressing gown.

"Yes! It may be the same man who came after me in London. I thought I saw him in the lobby as we came in just now!"

"Did you tell Henry?"

"No!"

"How could you be such a stupid creature?" her aunt demanded angrily.

"I thought I must be imagining things," she wailed. "I didn't want to upset him without reason!"

"Considerate!" Aunt Isobel said with sarcasm and crossed to the door and leaned her ear against it. "What now?"

"I don't know," she said. Then she decided, "I'll buzz for service. That will bring the night watchman!"

"Then do it!" her aunt waved to her. And her ear to the door again, she said, "I can't hear anyone moving about in the living room."

"I expect whoever it was has gone," she said. "They hoped to get to me before I could raise an alarm. When I came in to you they probably fled!"

Her aunt stared at her grimly. "Are you sure you saw the hand?"

She sighed. "And you wondered why I didn't mention seeing that familiar face to Henry? I'd have had the same doubting treatment."

"Did you buzz several times?" her aunt asked.

"Yes. I made sure someone would hear me," she said.

"Then we'll wait until he arrives at the suite door and then let him in," Aunt Isobel decided.

"That should be safe enough," Della agreed, still upset by the experience.

Several minutes more went by before they heard the light knocking on the door to the suite. Aunt Isobel gave her a warning look, unlocked the bedroom door, and went hurriedly across the living room and opened the door. A plump, elderly man in the hotel footmen's uniform stood respectfully outside.

In fluent French Aunt Isobel told him, "A man tried to get into my niece's room. From the balcony!"

The man looked amazed. "Is it possible?" he asked.

"Cone with me," Aunt Isobel said and led him to Della's room with Della accompanying them.

Aunt Isobel pointed to the yellow drapes at the big window. "She saw a hand appearing between the drapes!"

"A hand!" The man seemed surprised at every statement.

"There!" Della told him in her less-than-adequate French. "I saw it!"

The man nodded vaguely and with some caution pushed aside the drapes. He at once discovered that the French doors behind them were opened out onto the balcony. He turned to them with an expression on his round face which indicated he considered this unusual.

Then he stepped out onto the balcony and after a long moment came back in again. He looked apologetic. "I fear Mademoiselle was right. There is a rope hanging outside. It was used by someone from the floor above to reach this balcony."

"I knew it!" Della exclaimed. "Then you need only to find who has the suite above to know who the intruder was!"

"Yes. You must check on that at once," Aunt Isobel said. "The rope must be removed and the French doors locked from the inside. This is a disgraceful thing to happen!"

"I'm most unhappy!" the man said. "I shall inform the night manager!"

"And let us know what you find out," Aunt Isobel told him. "We'll be awake and waiting."

"Yes, madame," the plump man said, bowing and hurrying out.

"French hotels!" Aunt Isobel complained. "This would never happen at the Savoy!"

"I'm sure equally unpleasant things happen in London hotels," Della said. "And in any case it is our fault. That man is after me!"

"The hotel should offer you proper protection. Did you leave those French doors unlocked?"

"I don't remember," she said unhappily.

"What about informing Henry?"

Della said, "I see no reason to wake him. The intruder has gone."

"Suppose he comes back?"

"He won't!"

Aunt Isobel's withered face showed resignation. "It is a mystery to me how you can know so many things!"

"He won't take a chance in coming back here again," she said. "He'll try something else."

"Henry should be told!"

"We can tell him in the morning."

Aunt Isobel sat down disconsolately. "I don't like it!"

It was a while later that they heard the babble of excited French male voices coming along the corridor. Then the footman and a bald man in frock coat, clearly the night manager, appeared in the open doorway. The manager bowed and led the way as the two entered.

"*Madame et mademoiselle*," he said humbly. "I regret that you have been bothered by a cat burglar!"

Della rose to face him. "Who had the suite above?"

The manager spread his hands, "Alas, mademoiselle, it is empty! Not rented! The burglar picked the room's lock and let himself in and so down to your balcony."

"I think it all lax on the hotel's part," Aunt Isobel spoke sternly from her chair.

The manager showed perspiration on his bald pate. "I beg you to make no fuss, ladies. Nothing has come of it and to notify the police would be bad for the hotel."

"Bad for the hotel!" Aunt Isobel snifed. "And what, pray, about us?"

"The doors are locked," the apologetic manager said. "It cannot happen again." And he bowed and backed out dragging the surprised plump man by the arm.

Aunt Isobel told Della, "You will sleep with me in my room and see if we can survive this dreadful night!"

There was no more trouble. They had breakfast with Henry in the morning and Della brought him up to date with what had taken place.

Henry looked at her in dismay from across the breakfast table. "I cannot believe that you refused to wake me!"

"She did!" Aunt Isobel gloated.

"It seemed so useless!" Della despaired. "It was all over!"

"You could not be certain," he said, touching a napkin to his lips. "What would Sir Roger have to say if anything did happen and I was not on hand?"

"I'm sorry," she said.

"You place me in an impossible position, Della," he said earnestly. "I'm doing my best to protect you and you refuse to give my any cooperation!"

"I'll do better in future," she vowed.

"I hope so," Henry said in a hurt tone.

"Do not depend on it," Aunt Isobel warned him. "She has a way of doing only what she likes."

In a desperate attempt to get them off the subject, Della warned, "If we do not be quick with breakfast we may miss our train!"

That served her purpose. Little more was said. They finished their packing and had the expected delay in getting a carriage.

After that the driver misunderstood where they wished to go and took them to the wrong railway station. But in spite of all this they finally reached the Paris-Rome Express in time to board it.

The porter stumbled under the load of their hand baggage as he led them to their compartment. Henry had already taken care of the heavy pieces in the baggage car ahead.

The compartment was empty and she and Aunt Isobel at once collapsed in seats by the window as Henry was busy tipping the porter.

Aunt Isobel asked, "Do we have the compartment to ourselves?"

"I do not think so," he said. "It is for six and we are three."

Aunt Isobel said, "You should have bought the extra seats."

"It is not encouraged," he told her. "Space is hard to find on the train. It is heavily booked every day in the year."

Della gave him a smile of encouragement. "I think you've managed things very well."

"I have the tickets for the sleeping divan," he said. "I'll give yours to you later. And also the table number in the dining car."

"Surely we'll at least have a private dining table!" Aunt Isobel said in her demanding way.

"I believe sittings are arranged with the dining-car headwaiter," Henry replied politely. "I'm sure we'll have a good table and adequate privacy."

"Since we must journey to this outlandish place let us at least be comfortable," Aunt Isobel declared with true British spirit.

"Rome is the oldest and most cultured of cities," Della reproved her.

"And I wish I had never heard of it!" Aunt Isobel said grimly as she gazed out the window at the dark and bustling station yard.

There was a racket in the corridor. A woman's deep voice crying out angrily in French was answered by breathless protests from a male. Then the poor porter showed up again, accompanied by a most remarkable duo. The woman making the noise was large and heavy-boned and wore a monstrously ugly suit of some sort of plaid cloth. Pearls decorated her wrinkled throat and above her sallow, long-nosed face there loomed a broad-brimmed hat decorated with white and yellow wild flowers. The woman's wrinkled countenance showed immediate distaste at the sight of them.

Halting in the doorway she cried, "I do not like to be crowded! Is there another compartment available?"

"No, madame," the porter said abjectly. "This is your compartment!"

The woman came in glaring and then shocked them all by saying in English, "This is not as bad as I expected! You are all English, aren't you?"

Henry was on his feet. "Yes, madame."

"So am I," she said, to their surprise. "I have lived on the Continent for years so I'm fluent in most languages. My name is Madame Guioni, I am a widow. My late husband was important in the wine trade. Guioni Brothers. A famous name, if I may say so! Both brothers dead. I am now Guioni wines!"

"Happy to know you," Henry said politely and introduced Della and Aunt Isobel. Della was amused and Aunt Isobel looked outraged.

Madame Guioni briefly acknowledged the introductions and then proceeded to go on bullying the porter about where to place her bags on the overhead rack. Visible now in the corridor was a stout, sullen woman in black with a black bonnet on her head. She stood there saying nothing while all this commotion was taking place.

Madame Guioni sank onto the bench alongside Della with a sigh of resignation and made no attempt to tip the porter who lingered for a moment, then shrugged and vanished with a grimace on his thin face. Then the woman arrogantly waved the stout woman in black dress and bonnet into the compartment to sit beside her. The fat woman obeyed without saying a word but looked extremely frightened and uneasy.

"My personal maid, Rosa," Madame Guioni informed them after glaring at the unhappy woman. "She speaks nothing but Italian and rarely says anything of value in that! But she is a good worker and she understands me!"

"Those are the main things," Della said, amused.

Poor Rosa sat meekly with her hands in her lap and her eyes cast down. She looked neither to right nor left. It was clear that she had long ago given up any kind of communication with her employer which was not absolutely necessary.

"Stupid!" Madame Guioni went on. "But that is to be mingle only with the best people, the nobles and the mer-expected. Most Italians of her class are. Thank goodness I chant kings, and they are as intelligent as we British!"

Aunt Isobel glared at the horse-faced woman. "It is clear that your long years in Italy have not changed your insular viewpoint."

Madame Guioni returned her glare. "I do not know whether you have offered that as a compliment or an insult, madam. In any case I'm impervious to either."

Henry spoke up with obvious embarrassment to ask, "Shall we find it hot in Rome at this time of year?"

The woman sniffed. "This is not the season, if you understand me. But I'm not like some people, I do not mind the heat. I rather enjoy it! You must expect to wear light summer clothing!"

Della breathed a sigh of relief. "Then we have packed wisely"

Madame Guioni eyed her with cool interest. "May I ask which hotel you propose to stay in during your Rome visit. Some of them are incredibly bad!"

Della said, "We are to be the guests of Prince Sanzio at his palace."

"Prince Sanzio!" the woman repeated.

"Yes, do you know him?" Della wondered.

"A very old man, white-haired and feeble!"

"Yes, I believe that would be him," Della said.

Madame Guioni's eyebrows lifted. "I thought he had died long ago. The last time I saw him shuffling about at the Countess Friasco's he looked as if he already had one foot in the tomb."

Della was determined to be friendly with the difficult woman. She said, "He is very much alive and he has invited us to stay with him. Have you perhaps met his adopted daughter, the Princess Irma?"

"No," the woman said coldly. "Frankly the Prince does not travel in my set. So I do not know him well. I do not wish to alarm you but he is quite impoverished."

"Really?" Della said, pretending it to be news.

"Gambling was his ruin, or so gossip has it," the woman in the outlandish clothes confided. "Not that we discuss such things in the best circles, but word gets about."

"I suppose it does," Della said meekly.

"You must not expect the palace to be well kept. The Prince could not afford to keep it up properly. I hope your visit will be pleasant."

"I hope so," Della said.

"I'm sure we'll manage," Aunt Isobel spoke up spitefully. "After all he is a Prince."

Madame Guioni gave her an angry glance. "Titles do not mean anything to me! Especially Italian titles! My dear Carlos could have been made a count if it had pleased him. But he refused! A modest man who gave much of his fortune to the children of the poor!"

"I'm sure you've changed all that," Aunt Isobel snapped. And she turned to stare out the window and ignore them all.

Madame Guioni gasped. And after a moment said to Della in a low but audible voice, "Your grandmother is extremely senile! I noticed it in her when I first came into the carriage."

Della gave Aunt Isobel's back an anxious look and then confided to the arrogant Madame Guioni, "She is my aunt and not my grandmother, and she is very bright. It's just that she is weary that she's not in a good mood."

"She has every sign of senility," the woman sniffed haughtily. "I am a widow. It is true I did have to cut down on many of my husband's charities. But who would blame me? Who looks after a widow if she doesn't watch out for herself?"

"No one, I'm sure," Della said, sure that being agreeable was the only solution to their dilemma in getting along with the strange woman.

Madame Guioni eyed her with an almost friendly look. "You are a rather nice child, though lacking in spirit. You should keep that aunt of yours in her place. But I like you and this young man seems charming."

Della said, "My lawyer and my fiancé, Henry Clarkson."

Madame Guioni smiled revealing large, uneven teeth which added to the horselike cast of her face. Only her long nose refused to fit the equine pattern. "So you are engaged! Delightful! I only wish romance would come my way again! But it will never be! Dear Carlos often said the same thing. He vowed that if he were widowed he would never wed again. His sadness touched my heart."

"I'm sure he meant it as a tribute to you, madame," Henry said gallantly.

"True," she said with spirit. "You understand! I like young men! I have always said, if I should marry again, it will be to a young, handsome man!"

Della was having a hard time stifling her laughter as Henry's face turned a bright crimson. She smiled at the woman and said, "I'm sure your late husband must have been a handsome man."

"No," the woman shook her head. "He was not. He was tiny and had a squint. That used to bother me but I grew used to it.

But I could never have married his brother, he was impossible. A hump on his back and his thin face covered with black warts! He died from one of them in the end. His life was a disaster!"

"Sad!" Della sympathized.

"Both brothers dead and now I alone am Guioni Brothers," the big-framed woman said. "I promise you I would not marry in a foreign land again. But I make the best of it. I give magnificent parties! You must come to one of my parties!"

"You are very kind," Della said.

"I am generous by nature," Madame Guioni agreed. "I cannot help it. Dear Carlos often said he had never dreamt the sort of person I was before he married me! Everyone wants to attend my parties! The cream of Rome can be found at my little affairs!"

There was the sound of a whistle and the train gave a jerk and began to move slowly. Henry said, "I think we are on our way. And it seems the sixth seat is not to be occupied."

Madame Guioni frowned. "I tried to get Rosa a cheaper seat and couldn't. Look at her! Asleep like a contented sow!" And it was true.

The train began to pick up speed as it left the station behind. Then the door of the compartment opened and it became apparent that Henry had been wrong, there was to be a sixth traveler with them. A jolly looking, fat priest in black hat and black robe pushed through the door with a shabby valise in his hand.

Breathlessly he wheezed, "I am Father Anthony!"

Chapter Five

The train was gaining speed now and fortunately the noise level had grown to the point where it was possible to speak in a low voice without being overheard. Madame Guioni scowled at the newcomer who had struggled for a moment to place his valise in the rack above and then seated himself next to Henry.

Father Anthony had a fat, oval face and the pale blue shadow of his beard was obvious against his somewhat olive-skinned face. He had bright eyes and when he removed his hat his head proved bald except for a light fringe of gray hair. He sat back in his shabby robe and smiled amiably at everyone, including the sleeping Rosa.

Madame Guioni spoke to Della in a tone low enough for the good Father not to overhear. She said, "Rome is creeping with priests! They overrun the place like a plague of black bugs!"

"He seems a jolly nice sort," Della suggested.

"Lazy, I'll bet!" Madame Guioni said, determined to not like the newcomer. "He's grossly fat and far too contented. Of course they're all contented, they claim it's because they're looking forward to the next world, but I say it is because they do so well in this one."

"Still it is a life of sacrifice," Della said.

Madame Guioni eyed her sharply. "You are Protestant? Anglican, no doubt!"

"Yes," Della said.

"I have little time for Anglicans either," Madame Guioni said severely. "I cannot have confidence in a church brought into being by a king who beheaded most of his wives!"

Della smiled. "Ancient history, madame. The forming of the church was surely one of his good deeds."

"Then it was likely purely unintentional," Madame Guioni said sharply.

Father Anthony was smiling happily all the while, seemingly unaware that he was a subject of their conversation. He now brought a cigar from an inner pocket and looked at all the others with polite inquiry.

Speaking loudly, he asked, "May I be permitted to smoke? It is a good cigar and I promise its aroma will not be offensive."

Aunt Isobel glared at him in silence. Henry said, "I do not mind if the ladies have no objection."

Della smiled at the fat priest and said, "For my part, Father, I like the aroma of fine cigars."

"Thank you, my child," he said. And he glanced at Madame Guioni. "What about you, dear lady?"

Madame Guioni shrugged. "It is my opinion you will smoke your cigar whatever my opinion!"

"So I shall," he said. And he bit off the end and smelled it with an appreciative smile on his oval face. Then he told them good cigars and good wine are the comforts of the celibate.

Madame Guioni watched him with disapproval as he lit the cigar and puffed on it happily. Then she said loudly, "You like good wine?"

Father Anthony nodded. "I think I may be said to be a connoisseur of fine wines."

"I am Guioni Brothers," she said with some pride.

The fat clergyman leaned forward and cupped his hand to his ear. "I suffer from a slight deafness. I did not hear you clearly!"

Madame Guioni glared. "I said I am the owner, the sole owner, of Guioni Brothers wines. Have you heard of them?"

Father Anthony sat back with a look of distaste on his fat face. "I have heard of them," he said, puffing on his cigar. "I have even tasted them."

"And may I ask whether you enjoyed them?" Madame Guioni spoke above the noise of the train.

The fat priest studied the glowing end of his cigar. He said, "As a priest I am expected to be entirely truthful, as a man I attempt to be agreeable. You place me in a most difficult position."

"I do not understand," Madame Guioni shrilled.

"You wish my honest opinion?" he asked.

"I do," she said in her imperious fashion.

He puffed on his cigar. "Slop, madame! Slop for the unwary! The dregs of the grape!"

Madame Guioni sat up, seeming to swell in size. "How dare you say such a thing? Guioni Brothers wines sell fabulously well."

"I do not deny that, madame," Father Anthony said. "I wish you success. But you asked my opinion and I gave it!"

Della decided to turn the conversation away from this embarrassing channel. She said, "You speak English so well, Father."

He smiled modestly. "Thank you. As soon as I entered the compartment and heard you conversing I knew you were all English with the exception of that poor woman." He nodded toward the sleeping Rosa.

Henry said, "It seemed so natural I didn't think of it as being a tongue foreign to you."

Father Anthony looked pleased. "It is true I have no detectable accent, though my native tongue is Italian. I was in England for many years, attached to our bishop in London."

"No wonder you handle the language so well," Della said. "We are on our first visit to Rome."

"Ah!" Father Anthony looked ecstatic. "You will never forget it! I promise you! Rome is the most beautiful city in the world! I say this, not because it is the seat of the Mother Church but because I was born a Roman and I am never happy away from its boundaries."

"We are looking forward to it," Henry agreed.

Father Anthony puffed on his cigar and in tones of rapture said, "Wait until you see it all! The Capitoline Hill with the wonderful Piazza del Campidoglio, designed by Michelangelo, near the ruins of the Forum. The Arch of Titus, the three columns of the Temple of Castor and Pollux, the Arch of Septimus Servus, the Basilica of Constantine, and, dwarfing everything the Colosseum!"

"There is so much to see and learn about," Della said.

Father Anthony nodded. "The great city by the Tiber has it all. And do not let us forget the largest church in Christendom, the Basilica of St. Peter built on the very spot where the saint's holy bones rest. A masterpiece! And the buildings of the Vatican. I once worked in one of the museums open to the public."

This caught Della's attention. "There are many museums in Rome, I'm sure!"

"And the Vatican has the finest libraries and museums of all," the priest assured her. "A place of fabulous riches, for the most part collected by popes of the sixteenth and seventeenth centuries. They spent great sums to add to the splendor of the Church and of Rome!"

Della gave Henry a knowing glance and then asked the priest, "Have you ever heard of a jeweled Madonna?"

The fat man smiled indulgently. "My dear child, there are many jeweled Madonnas. The Madonna figure is prevalent in all Church collections."

Madame Guioni, who had been grimly quiet up to now, snapped, "A scandal spending the money of the poor on precious stones and idolatrous figures!"

Father Anthony looked mildly surprised. "You speak like a pagan madame. Are you not of the faith?"

"I am not," she snapped. "I pride myself on being a free-thinker."

"I trust you possess the needed equipment," Father Anthony said. And then to Della, "Do not miss the art treasures of my native city."

"I have heard so much about the glory of Roman art," she said.

The fat Father Anthony nodded. "We have the best. The Picture Gallery alone contains the works of great masters such as Giotto, Fra Angelico, Bellini, Leonardo, Titian, Veronese and Murillo. And the ten wonderful Raphael Tapestries are displayed there!"

Della said, "But you were a member of the staff at the Vatican Museum."

"I was," the prelate said proudly. "And with all modesty I must say our museums house the greatest collection of ancient treasures in the world. Treasures of every sort, mosaics, bronzes and statuary, including some examples of the jeweled Madonna of which you spoke."

"I must go there," Della said.

Father Anthony made a resigned gesture. "Only a fool would miss touring the Vatican. Our library has a half-million volumes and more than sixty thousand beautifully illuminated manuscripts. And there is the Sistine Chapel, unrivaled in conception and design. The work of the mighty Michelangelo! He painted the ceiling frescoes under agonizing conditions, lying on his back for nearly four years. His studies of the Old Testament figures are overwhelming. And you can compare his work of two decades later in the Last Judgment painted on the altar wall."

Madame Guioni declared, "I have never been near Vatican City and I never intend to go there!"

The fat priest smiled mildly. "I'm sure you've been missed, madame. But then the Church has always had its setbacks."

Henry, who had been saying nothing, now looked at Della and said, "I have to go forward to the dining car to see about our dining arrangements. Would you like to come with me and get a little exercise?"

She jumped at the opportunity to be out of the tense atmosphere of the compartment. "Yes, I should like that," she said.

Henry stood up, "Then let us leave at once."

Della leaned over to Aunt Isobel who continued to stare out the window and ignore the others in the compartment. She said loudly enough for the older woman to hear, "We're moving on to the dining room to make arrangements. We'll be back shortly."

Aunt Isobel nodded bleakly and went back to her window. The train was moving fast and swaying a good deal, so Henry and Della had to brace themselves by placing hands against the walls of the train passage.

When they were alone a little distance from the compartment, Henry turned to her with a smile. "I had to get out for a little!"

Braced against the inner wall, she laughed, "I know how you feel. Isn't that Madame Guioni awful?"

"Worst I've ever encountered. Makes me wince to think she is an Englishwoman. No manners at all."

"And the priest seems to bring out the worst in her!"

"She's a natural bigot! Has no respect for her servant or the country she lives in," Henry agreed bitterly. "And I doubt if her husband meant much to her beyond being a source of money."

"Aunt Isobel is in a rage and the madame is mostly to blame," Della worried. "I'm afraid it is going to be a difficult journey."

"Every passing minute gets us closer to the end of it," Henry said, trying to comfort her.

"And we'll be dining and in the sleeping area part of the time!"

"Which may save our sanity," he said.

"We must try and get Father Anthony's address in Rome," she said. "He could be very helpful to us as a guide!"

"And don't accept any invitations to Madame Guioni's," the young man warned her. "I don't want ever to see her again after we get off the train."

Della laughed, "Don't count on it! She knows we will be at the palace of Prince Sanzio!"

Henry groaned. "I'd forgotten that."

"But we can always be busy."

"We must," he said. "I can't endure the woman!"

They went on to the dining car and found the headwaiter. A suitably large tip from Henry assured all three of them an excellent table with a good window view. And after finding out the hours of seatings they made their way to the sleeping car and checked where their bunks would be. Della's was directly above her aunt's at the end of the car and Henry's was across from her. This made her feel more secure. He would be no more than an aisle away in case of an emergency.

On their way back along the rocking, noisy corridor they halted to embrace. Henry held her in his arms for a longer while than usual and she found the security of being pressed to him most satisfying. She no longer doubted that she loved this rather precise young lawyer. And she only wished that this business of seeking out her long-lost sister would soon be at an end and they could return to England and be married.

Henry must have been thinking the same sort of thoughts, for after his lips stopped caressing her, he said worriedly, "I wish we were going home instead of going to Rome!"

She smiled ruefully. "This has to be attended to first."

His arms around her, he said, "I keep worrying about you. After all that has happened I don't like you to be out of my sight for a moment."

"I'm sure nothing will happen."

"You keep saying that and yet things continue to come along and threaten you," he said. "I heard you mention the jeweled Madonna to Father Anthony."

"Without much reaction from him."

Henry frowned. "According to him there are a lot of them. I've always thought the talk about a stolen Madonna was a cover-up for the real business of killing you so this supposed sister in Rome can inherit your fortune."

"You're taking that line from Sir Roger."

"It's the logical motive," he told her. "And you must never forget that."

"I've been duly warned," she said with a smile. "We'd better get back to the compartment or Aunt Isobel will have a fit."

When they reached the compartment they found that Madame Guioni and her maid had also gone off somewhere and the fat priest was sitting with his head bowed in sleep. Aunt Isobel greeted them with a look of reproach.

"You were gone long enough," she told them.

"It took a while to find the waiter and get things properly arranged," Henry explained.

"We'd better have a good table," Aunt Isobel said.

"We will," Della assured her.

And they did. When their seating time came they were shown to the table Henry had picked out. Aunt Isobel was favorably impressed by the elegant dining car with its white-clothed tables and excellent waiter service. She smiled for the first time during the journey.

"I think I shall enjoy having my meals," she said.

"This is the best table in the car," Della told her. "And you can thank Henry for getting it."

Aunt Isobel said, "That is why Henry is with us. To protect us and to see we get the best. Isn't that right, young man?"

He smiled agreeably. "Those were my instructions from Sir Roger."

Her aunt sighed across the table. "I must say I feel you could have managed the compartment better."

"The train is heavily booked and for a long way ahead," Henry said.

"But surely we could have found more agreeable people to share it with?" Aunt Isobel complained.

"We have no choice in the matter," Della told her.

"That is evident," the older woman said grimly. "That Madame Guioni is the most dreadful creature! Her ugly face and overbearing manner, and that deep voice so used to ordering people about!"

Della said, "I'm sure her maid hates her."

"And remains asleep in self-defense," Henry laughed.

"She was miserable to that poor priest," Aunt Isobel went on. "Though I must admit he had the wit to parry with her and win most of the time!"

An excellent six-course dinner with wine put them all in a relaxed, pleasant mood. Aunt Isobel forgot her complaints and even began to speak hopefully of Italy. It was amazing what a good meal could do, Della decided.

They returned to the compartment for a short time before going to bed in the sleeping car. Madame Guioni and Father Anthony had also returned following dinner, but the maid, Rosa, was nowhere in sight.

Madame Guioni explained her absence: "I spoke with the railway conductor and was able to get her an empty seat in second class. He is refunding the difference in fare to me."

Della said, "I should think the convenience of having her with you would have been worth some extra money."

The coarse face of Madame Guioni showed a petulant look. She said, "The woman is a peasant! Useful enough in my home but a difficult traveling companion!"

Since none of them could imagine a more difficult traveling companion than Madame Guioni herself, this led to a long silence.

Then Father Anthony smiled at Della and asked her, "Is the purpose of your journey merely to see the beauty of Rome?"

"No," she said. "I have personal business with the Prince Sanzio."

"Ah," the fat man said approvingly. "Then all the wonders of the city will be a bonus! How fortunate you will be!"

"I hope we may see you when we reach the city," she said. "I'm sure there are many wonders you could point out to us that we might otherwise miss."

Father Anthony took out another cigar and went about lighting it. He said, "I shall have to report to the Papal officer whom I serve. But when my business with him is completed I shall have a few days. I'd be glad to spend part of them showing you around."

She said, "Thank you! You can always reach us at Prince Sanzio's palace."

"I shall write that down," the priest said and did so. Then he sat back puffing contentedly on his cigar.

Madame Guioni sat glaring at him for a few minutes. Then she jumped up and exclaimed, "I'm going to bed. Better to be there sleepless than to sit here and be asphyxiated by cigar smoke!" And she marched out.

Father Anthony removed the cigar from his mouth. "Am I annoying any of the rest of you?"

Aunt Isobel quite surprisingly said, "It is a fine cigar and I rather like its smoke. Continue, Father."

Della smiled and added, "I think that is true for all of us."

The fat priest said, "Then I shall continue to enjoy myself."

Della had an idea her aunt had only been so agreeable because it gave her a chance to disagree with the dreadful Madame Guioni. The two had at once become antagonists without any campaign being declared.

After a while Della saw both Aunt Isobel and Father Anthony nodding in light sleep. Then the plump priest rose and excused himself and announced he was also ready to retire. Goodnights were said and he went to the sleeping car.

Henry told her, "I'm going out to the end of the car. I want to stand on the platform and get some fresh air before going to bed."

"Go ahead," she said. "I shall be quite safe here with Aunt Isobel."

He stood up uncertainly and said, "You promise me you won't leave the compartment."

"No. I shall be right here," she said.

"I won't be long," he told her. He opened the door and made his way along the corridor until he was out of sight.

When the black curtain of night had fallen Aunt Isobel pulled down the blind at her window. She now rested her head back on the high seat and stared across at Della.

The old woman said, "I shall count the hours until we are back in London."

"You'll count a good many," Della warned her. "We've only started on our journey."

"It's a mistake!" Aunt Isobel sighed, returning to a familiar complaint.

"I think you should go to bed, you look worn out," Della said. "I'll accompany you in to your sleeping section."

"You promised Henry you wouldn't leave here!"

"So I did!"

Aunt Isobel struggled to her feet. "I can manage very well on my own. I have my ticket to give to the porter."

"Make sure," Della said.

"See!" Her aunt took it triumphantly out of her pocketbook. "I'm not all as senile as you seem to think!"

She smiled. "I don't think any such thing." And she rose to kiss her aunt and see her on her way.

At the compartment door, Aunt Isobel told her, "You go back and sit down. I don't want you to move until Henry returns."

"I won't," Della promised, sitting down again.

Now she was alone in the compartment. There was just a slight smell of stale tobacco smoke still in the air to remind her of Father Anthony. She felt she might learn more about the jeweled Madonna if she had a chance to question him further. He had held a responsible post in one of the Vatican museums and so probably knew any of the really valuable Madonnas by description.

She closed her eyes for a moment and tried to relax, but for some unknown reason she could not. Tension rose in her and she became restless. Being alone in the compartment late at night was not all that pleasant an experience. She began to wish that Henry would soon put in an appearance.

A uniformed trainman came by and poked his head in the door to inquire in French, "Does Mademoiselle not have a sleeping berth?"

"I have," she explained. "I'm waiting for a friend to return to say goodnight."

The trainman smiled knowingly. "Very well, mademoiselle, it is your choice. I merely wished to be of help if I might."

"Thank you," she said. And the trainman went on.

She sat back, nervously thinking that Henry had been gone far too long. Then she began truly to worry. Could something have happened to him? Was it possible that he'd had some sort of accident? The thought of this made her tremble! And she became angry at herself for not going with him.

There were open platforms at the juncture of some of the cars and he had sought out one of these. But such places could be dangerous with the swaying of the train. They were not lighted and were fairly narrow with steps descending on either side of them. A natural setting for an accident of some sort.

She became so alarmed she stood up, bracing herself against the swaying of the speeding train by placing a hand on the top of the seat. Just as she did so she was relieved to see the figure of Henry come into view in the corridor. He came to the door of the compartment and entered. The moment she saw his ashen face she knew something had happened.

"What's wrong?" she asked, going to him.

He took her by the arms and said in a taut voice, "I'm lucky to be alive! To be here with you now!"

"What do you mean?" she cried. "Tell me?"

"I went out to the open platform," Henry said. "I enjoyed the cool wind and was astonished at the train's speed! We're really moving along! I decided to take a step down and support myself by holding onto the railing on either side of the steps."

"And?"

"I'd barely stepped down when I was given an almighty shove by someone! I lost hold of the railing with my left hand and someone cracked my knuckles as I clung on with my right!"

"Oh no!" she said in alarm, aware that they were not finished with the menace yet.

"I turned to see who my unknown assailant was and before I could manage it, I was struck on the back of the head by someone's iron fist. I nearly lost hold altogether. My right hand slid down the rail and I ended crouching on the last step just a few feet from falling off the speeding train!"

"Then what?"

"I heard someone call out from the platform," Henry said. "A moment later hands helped me back up and I found myself facing an irate trainman and receiving a safety lecture!"

"Did you tell him what happened? That someone had tried to force you off the train?"

"I made an attempt, but it didn't impress him. His view was that another idiot Englishman had stumbled from the platform and almost lost his life!"

Her eyes were wide with fear. "But someone did try to take your life!"

"Nothing is more sure than that!"

"You must report it to the conductor!"

"It's already been done," he said grimly. "The trainman took me to him. I could tell by the way they reacted that they considered it all my own fault. And they insisted I had no right to be out there by myself."

"It was unwise," she said.

"Not under normal circumstances."

"These are not normal circumstances," was her bitter reply. "You should know that."

"I've been reminded of it."

Della gave him a worried look. "I was beginning to have a funny feeling. A sense of danger without knowing exactly what it might be."

"All the other attacks have been directly against you," he said. "I wasn't expecting this."

"From now on be prepared," she warned him.

"I will be."

"You are protecting me. So you stand between them and me. After they settle with you they'll go for me next!"

"Pleasant thought!"

"It seemed we'd at least be safe on the train."

"Forget that," he said.

"I know," Della said. "So we have an enemy on board. I wonder who?"

"We're not liable to find that out unless we're terribly lucky," the young lawyer said.

Della shuddered. "I don't think I can go in there and sleep!"

"You must," he said. "You have to have your rest and you should be safer in there than here. There is a porter on duty all night."

"And you'll be directly across the aisle from me," she said.

"Yes."

She looked up into his eyes. "I don't know what I would have done if they'd killed you!"

"They didn't," he said with a wan smile and kissed her. "Now come along before there are more problems."

Della was in no mood to stand there continuing the discussion. She let him escort her to her upper bunk and they bade each other goodnight. She knew she needed sleep badly but worried that it mightn't come.

After what seemed an interminable time she finally drifted off. But her sleep was broken by a series of terrifying dreams. She suffered the ordeal of her rape again, down to the last dreadful, cruel detail. And she saw the wild eyes of her attacker and felt his iron grip as he handled her like a cloth doll.

She swallowed in her sleep and opened her eyes as she came partly awake to feel a growing pressure on her throat. Panic swept through her as she gradually came to understand that a hairy hand had pushed through the drawn curtains of her sleeping berth and was now firmly holding her throat!

She could see nothing! The berth was in utter darkness! But in her ear there came a hissed whisper, "The Madonna! What did you do with it? Is it in your luggage or back in England?"

"Please!" she strained to breathe as the hand tightened on her neck.

"Where is it?"

"Don't know!" she croaked in a low whisper.

The hand cruelly increased its pressure. "You are lying! Little fool!"

Her attacker overplayed his role, for she could stand no more. At that moment she blacked out into a faint. And when she came to her forehead was drenched in perspiration and her throat hurt. But the menacing hand was no longer there throttling her.

After a moment she raised herself up and explored her aching throat with her fingers. Then she hastily slipped on her robe and slippers and, opening the curtains to the dimly lighted, swaying car, let herself down to the corridor by stepping on the edge of Aunt Isobel's bunk below.

She took a quick glance in at her sleeping aunt to make sure she was all right. Then she let the black curtain drop back and stood in the rocking corridor staring at the dozens of black-curtained sections reminiscent of shelves in a crypt. She knew which one was Henry's and went to it.

She touched his arm and spoke his name.

The young lawyer opened his eyes at once. He gave her a worried look. "What is it?"

"More trouble," she told him.

He was already on his way out of the berth. Reaching for his robe and putting it on over his pajamas, he asked in a low voice, "What now?"

"Someone came after me!"

"How?"

She told him, ending with, "I fainted or I don't know what would have happened next."

Henry looked angry. "I thought this car was properly guarded!"

"Whoever it was got in and threatened me for several minutes," she said.

"Let us see if we can find the porter," Henry said with annoyance.

She followed him down to the end of the car. And in the small section where the porter had his seat they found him fast asleep.

Henry stared grimly at the snoring porter and said, "There is your answer!"

"I see," she said.

He shook the porter and when the fellow woke up confused and wild-eyed, demanded to know, "How long have you been asleep?"

The porter was now recovered and apologetic. "Only a minute or two, monsieur. I have had to do double duty. I've been without sleep for almost thirty-six hours!"

Henry scowled at him. "That doesn't matter. You have neglected your duty and while you were asleep someone attacked this young woman."

The porter looked at her in disbelief. "It is hard to imagine with all asleep." He waved to the car. "We never have any incidents."

"Well, you've had one now," Henry told him. "I shall be forced to report you to the conductor."

The man shrugged. "As you wish, sir!"

The conductor was thin, crabbed and too old for his trying job. He greeted them with a look of annoyance on his wrinkled face and said to Henry, "So you are back with another complaint?"

"Not for myself," Henry said.

"That is a wonder!" the conductor said with sarcasm as they all sat in one of the deserted compartments.

"This may seem like nonsense to you but it is not to us," Henry told the man.

The uniformed old man eyed him bleakly. "That is quite clear."

"You do not understand," Henry went on. "I'm a lawyer accompanying this woman and her aunt to protect them."

The conductor said, "Then why expect me to do your work?"

"Because we are on your train!" Henry said with some anger. "These attacks began in London!"

"If the London police were not able to deal with them what can you expect of me?" the old man wanted to know.

"We have paid a good price for safe transportation," Henry said. "That includes proper security on this train. You have not provided it!"

The porter, silent up until now, protested, "I was on duty every moment. Just for a few seconds I fell asleep and Monsieur happened to come on me then."

Henry shot him an irate glance. "You do not know how long you were asleep!"

The conductor said, "I shall make a report and turn it in."

"Can't you make a search of the train for some hidden criminal?"

The conductor eyed him with ugly anger. "No one is on board this train who shouldn't be!"

Henry said, "Then one of your regular passengers must be the criminal!"

The conductor's thin, wrinkled face showed scorn. "I say, nonsense, monsieur!"

"You are being unfair," Della told him. "And you are taking a grave risk that we might be killed on your train. Then what will you do?"

The conductor glared at her in silence. Then he asked, "Would you ask that I rouse up every passenger and question them?"

"If that is the only way, yes," Henry said.

"No, monsieur," the conductor said with a wave of a scrawny hand. "It cannot be done. I shall place two porters on duty in your car and you may safely return to your sleep."

Henry sighed. "That is your last word?"

"It is, monsieur. I can send a wire ahead for the police in Rome to board the train when we arrive. In which case all will be held. You and the young lady will also be questioned."

"It isn't worth it," Della appealed to Henry. "You may as well let it drop."

"Very well," Henry said slowly. And he told the irate conductor, "I will expect to see the new porters on duty before we return to our bunks."

"I will arrange it at once," the conductor promised. It was evident that this was all they could hope for, so they settled for it.

Della slept little for the rest of the night. The morning was sunny and pleasant and word was that the train would soon be passing the Italian border. This proved correct as there was a boarding of the train by Italian officers and a brief questioning of them all before they had breakfast.

At the table Henry said, "We at least are in Italy and should reach Rome by early evening."

"Did you sleep well?" Aunt Isobel asked her.

Della gave Henry a warning look, as she did not intend to tell her aunt of the night's two frightening incidents. She told the old woman, "I slept as well as I could under the circumstances."

"I had nightmares," Aunt Isobel said glumly. "I had the sensation of excited voices and movement outside my berth!"

Henry said, "Don't mind! You'll sleep better when you reach Rome."

"In that old palace, probably full of insects and mold!" Aunt Isobel said with a tiny shudder.

Della smiled across the table at her. "How can you say that? It may be a fine palace full of elegant rooms."

"That creature, Madame Guioni, said it was badly run down!" Aunt Isobel reminded her.

"She can't be trusted for an opinion," Della said.

"She's likely right about the palace," her aunt said, determined to be pessimistic.

Following breakfast they all three made their way back to their compartment. They passed Madame Guioni at one of the tables along the way but she was so busy calling down her waiter about something, she didn't notice them passing. Which pleased them.

Della was in the lead and when she reached the door of the compartment and opened it she stood still with shock. Father Anthony was bent over one of her suitcases which had been taken down from the rack and was apparently in the act of opening or closing it.

Chapter Six

Della was stunned at finding the friendly priest in such a compromising position. But she entered the compartment followed by the other two, and in a calm voice asked, "May I inquire what you are doing, Father?"

Father Anthony turned and glanced up at her with his oval face showing surprise. "Dear me!" he gasped.

She stared down at the suitcase. "That is mine, is it not?"

"Quite so!" the fat priest said embarrassedly. "It is your suitcase. And I suppose you must wonder what I'm doing with it?"

Aunt Isobel was staring at him bleakly. "The question has crossed my mind!"

"And no wonder!" Father Anthony said, his usual likable self, but seeming to be stalling for time.

"Perhaps you will be good enough to enlighten us," Henry said sharply.

"Of course," Father Anthony said. And he brought out a large white silk handkerchief and mopped his perspiring brow. "This must look strange to you."

Della said, "We simply want to hear from you."

"Yes," the fat priest said, putting the handkerchief away in a back pocket of his robe. "I went to breakfast at the same time as all of you. I bade Madame Guioni good morning and was snubbed for my trouble. Then I ate rather hastily and came back here. I found a man in the compartment!"

"A man?" Della echoed.

"Yes," Father Anthony said. "And the fellow had this suitcase of yours down on the seat. He was fumbling with the locks when I entered."

"And?" Henry said in a tone which indicated he was not too convinced by the explanation.

The priest said, "I at once asked him what he was doing."

"And his reply?" Della asked.

"He said he was a customs official and that it was his belief that our compartment had been somehow overlooked at the border."

"That is not so," Della said. "You were here with the rest of us when the officials made their examination."

"I knew that," Father Anthony said. "And I told the fellow so. He at once apologized and quickly made his way out. Not even bothering to place the bag up where he had found it."

"And he told you nothing else?" Henry inquired.

"No. He seemed in a great hurry to leave," Father Anthony said. "It at once occurred to me that he was no customs official but a thief. And I was bending over the bag trying to see if the locks had been forced when you all returned and found me."

Della listened with growing conviction that the jolly priest was telling the truth. He was truly the picture of innocence. She said, "It would seem we owe you thanks, Father."

"Not at all," he said genially. "I saw the suitcase locks were intact and I was about to return it to the rack when you came in."

"I knew there was nothing wrong," Aunt Isobel said and went to take her usual seat by the window.

"Forgive us for being so brusque," Henry said. And he examined the suitcase and then shoved it up on the rack where it had been.

Della sat next to the priest. "We are somewhat on edge," she explained. "We had some unpleasant things happen in the night. That is why we were so quickly suspicious of you."

Father Anthony showed interest. "Did that unpleasant Madame Guioni insult you also?"

Della smiled grimly. "A little worse than that. And Madame Guioni was in no way involved."

Henry leaned forward earnestly, saying, "I'm sure you can be trusted, Father Anthony."

The fat priest shrugged. "I have often served in the confessional. My discretion has never been questioned."

"I think we should tell him," Della said. She turned to Aunt Isobel. "We also want you to know!"

The old woman frowned. "Know what? Have you been keeping things from me again?"

"I'm afraid so," Della said. "But only for your own good."

"I will not have you treating me like a child," her aunt protested crossly. "What is it now?"

Henry spoke for both the benefit of Aunt Isobel and the priest, saying, "There were attacks made on both myself and Della last night."

"Here on this train?" Aunt Isobel said, amazed.

"Where else?" Della asked.

Father Anthony looked puzzled. "You say attacks, my son. I'm not sure I understand. Why were you attacked and in what manner?"

Henry said, "That is rather a long story. But last night someone tried to shove me off the open platform to almost certain death."

Della nodded. "And only a little later I was choked by an unseen attacker in my berth. I fainted and this may have saved my life. I don't know."

"But why?" the priest asked.

"We are not sure," Della said, taking over the explanation from the young lawyer. "One possibility has to do with my journey to Rome. I'm on my way to greet a girl who may be my long-lost twin."

"A missing twin!" Father Anthony exclaimed. "That sounds like an ancient Roman or Greek play."

"This is no play," she said grimly. And she went on to explain to him the details of Irma's kidnapping and of the Prince adopting her and finally learning she was a child stolen from England.

"A most amazing story," the priest said. "I'm sure the girl has had good treatment if she has been raised by Prince Sanzio. He is of a fine family."

"So we have been told," Della said. "The other possibility is that I've somehow been used as a decoy in a remarkable theft."

"What sort of theft?" Father Anthony asked.

"You will recall I spoke to you about a jeweled Madonna," she said.

"Yes," he said.

"And you told me that there were several of them in the Vatican museums."

"That is true."

"I asked you about the Madonna because I was kidnapped in London by a criminal, an Italian, who insisted that I had the Madonna or knowledge of where it was hidden."

Father Anthony showed bewilderment. "I'm not sure I can follow all this. What has this stolen Madonna to do with your missing sister?"

Henry Clarkson smiled ruefully. "We can understand your being puzzled, Father. We are, also. We can only guess that someone close to Prince Sanzio heard Della being discussed as sister to his adopted daughter. For some reason they hit on her to be used in this incredible theft. Deciding to send the valuable stolen loot to her, in this case the jeweled Madonna. But in transit there must have been a double cross and the Madonna never did reach London or my fiancée. But the ones who sent it refuse to believe this. So they are hounding Della for the valuable piece."

Father Anthony considered this for a moment. Then he shook his head. "I find this account of a stolen jeweled Madonna unlikely. If such a precious item had been stolen from one of the Vatican museums a report would surely have gone out to the world. Police would be searching for it. It would be front-page news!"

Della sighed. "You're probably right."

"Unless," the fat priest mused, "the theft took place without anyone yet being aware of it."

"Could that happen?" Henry asked.

"It is possible," Father Anthony said with a frown. "Though not likely. But some of the very valuable items are often stored away and put on display only at intervals. If this jeweled Madonna were in storage, it might be stolen and its loss not known for a period of time."

"Perhaps that is it," Della said. "These men seem very certain there is such a Madonna and that it was sent to me by messenger."

The priest continued to look troubled. "We must face this. If the Madonna was stolen from a storage place it had to be an inside job. That could only mean that some member of the Vatican staff was the thief or a collaborator with the thieves."

Della said, "Again, I ask, could that happen?"

"We have had instances over the centuries," the priest said. "Not many. But it has been known to happen."

She said, "So there may be a stolen Madonna after all?"

"Maybe," Father Anthony said. "When we reach Rome I shall make some discreet inquiries. I can let you know what I'm able to find out."

"Do you think I should complain to the Roman police?" she worried.

"I'm not sure they could help you," Father Anthony said. "Leave it with me and I shall get in touch with you as soon as I've had an opportunity to make some contacts."

Della gave Henry a troubled glance. "What do you think?"

"I think we should try and find out who these criminals are and make sure they understand that the Madonna never reached you."

"All this must have stemmed from the palace of Prince Sanzio," she worried. "And I don't want to involve him if he has played only an innocent role."

Father Anthony said, "That is quite likely the case."

"Can we not wait until we talk to Prince Sanzio before approaching the police?" Della appealed to Henry.

"If that is your wish," he said. "Though I'm sure Sir Roger would prefer that we contact the police."

"I don't want to start off on a bad note with the Prince," Della said. "Attempt to get some information from him before we do anything. And I shall count on your help, Father Anthony."

The jolly priest smiled. "Be assured that I will keep this in mind and attempt to find out whether such a theft has been committed."

"And while we're being so discreet we may all be murdered," Aunt Isobel spoke up acidly.

Father Anthony showed concern. "I promise I shall pray that nothing of the sort happens."

The trainman came by with word that they would soon reach the railway station in Rome. They were passing through a colorful countryside dotted by white houses and occasionally they caught a glimpse of farm animals in the fields. The sky was a startling, deep blue with hardly any clouds and the vegetation was vivid in its coloring: dark green trees, lighter green fields and dark-colored bushes and vines all mingled in lovely contrast.

Madame Guioni arrived importantly with a porter and her stout maid trailing behind her. She came into the compartment with the usual arrogant expression on her ugly face and informed them all, "I'm having my hand baggage removed early. It is a mistake to wait until the last moment. Then you are invariably caught in a long line!"

She pointed out her things and the porter took them down and left with them. She turned to Della and said, "You will hear from me, Miss Standish. As soon as I have settled in I shall have a small party for you!"

"There's no need!" Della protested.

"No," the big woman said imperiously, "it will be my great pleasure. I shall contact you at the palace of Prince Sanzio." Snubbing the others, she made a grand exit with the stout maid forlornly following her.

When she was safely out of the way Father Anthony gave a deep sigh. "I shall not miss her," he said. "I trust you will enjoy the party she is planning for you, Miss Standish."

"I doubt very much if I'll ever hear from her again," Della said with a wry smile.

"Which might be a blessed thing," Father Anthony told her.

"Amen!" Aunt Isobel said sharply. At which they all laughed.

The train was now moving slowly through the outskirts of the city. They were passing through congested areas of buildings on either side of the tracks. The rear of the buildings faced the tracks and so everything looked rather run down.

Everyone in the compartment prepared to leave. The train reached the station yard and it was dark, noisy and full of belching steam and smoke like the Paris station from which they had set out. Only now the shouting was in Italian rather than French.

Father Anthony bade them a friendly good-bye and rushed off on his own to vanish on the crowded platform. Their group was held back by the slow progress of the porter with their hand baggage.

Della had linked an arm in Aunt Isobel's, so that they would not be shoved apart in the bustle on the long wooden platform. Henry led the way with the porter at his side with their bags.

Aunt Isobel was anxious. "Where can the Prince be? I understood he was to meet us."

"He'll likely be in the station," Della told her.

They reached the station, which was an ornate building with fine scenic murals on the walls. Its vast main area was filled with people, some standing in groups, others making their way in every direction. Trains were constantly arriving and leaving and the hurly-burly of incoming and outgoing passengers never ended.

She stood with Henry and her aunt waiting for some sign of the Prince or her twin sister. She asked Henry, "Did Sir Roger send Prince Sanzio the day and hour we would be arriving?"

"Yes. It was all sent long ago," he said.

Aunt Isobel looked around her with wary eyes. "How can we expect anyone to find us in this huge place?"

"I'm sure he'll come or send someone," Henry said.

Della was all at once aware of a child watching her from a distance. She could not help feeling it odd that the youngster should have singled her out. And it was puzzling that he should be wearing long trousers and a tiny bowler hat. The boy was dressed like a miniature man. And as she took all this in she was further astonished to see him come slowly toward them.

She tugged Henry's arm, saying, "That boy seems to be coming toward us."

Henry said, "He may be merely coming this way."

"I'm sure he's been staring at me," she said.

Aunt Isobel gave her a troubled glance. "I think you are imagining things, Della. And no wonder, with us in this busy, awful place."

Della was in for another shock. As the boy drew nearer there came a strange transformation: he was no longer a boy! Coming gravely toward her in the black suit and black bowler hat was a man less than four feet in height with a sallow, wrinkled face and deepset eyes.

He came up to her and, removing his hat to show gray hair, bowed and in a thin voice said, "I am Guido, factotum for Prince Sanzio. I presume you are Miss Standish and these are your fellow travelers?"

Recovering from her surprise, Della told the staid, little man, "You are correct, Guido. I am Della Standish and this is my Aunt

Isobel Moore and Mr. Henry Clarkson, my good friend and lawyer."

Guido acknowledged the introductions and bowed in his stiff fashion. "I have a carriage waiting to take you to the palace. I shall get porters and see about your luggage."

Della asked, "Are you sure we will not be imposing on the Prince? We could go to a hotel."

The midget lifted a small hand in protest. "He would not hear of it. And may I say you look very much like the Princess Irma. No one could dispute that you are sisters!"

"I'm very excited about meeting her," Della said.

"All in good time," the little man said. "You will excuse me while I see about your baggage." And he hurried away.

"What sort of a household can it be?" Aunt Isobel exclaimed. "Why would the Prince hire a midget to manage it?"

Henry gave the older woman an amused look. "No doubt because he is competent. Good servants are hard to find."

"He seems to know what he is doing," Della agreed.

This was borne out by his return with two sturdy porters who whisked away their hand baggage and then looked after their trunks, mounting all onto the back of a large open carriage. When the things were securely tied on the luggage rack, they took their places in the carriage, and Guido seated himself in front with the driver. They were on their way to the palace at last.

The sun was warm and the skies friendly after the gray mists of London which they had left behind. Della was impressed by the ornate beauty of the ancient buildings they passed as well as the patches of green, even in the middle of the great city, and the dark green and brownish trees which rose high in some streets.

There were just as many people and vehicles in the streets as back in London. This seemed to be a busy time. The Roman squares and fountains were charming and gave the hot city a feeling of coolness.

The carriage rolled on and they came to a more elegant area with four beautiful fountains ornamented with giant figures.

Guido turned to call down to them in his piping voice, "We are at the Piazza Quirinale. Here you will see the statues of the horse tamers, executed in the first century!"

They were all impressed by the magnificent square and the statues. They continued on to the Piazza di Spagna which was one glorious bed of flowers. Artists had easels set up there and models dressed in shimmering, regional costumes posed for them. Next they came to the Via Condotti with its art shops and the nearby Café Greco with its many tables and chairs for outside dining.

The carriage made a sharp right turn into what seemed like an alley but was actually a small side street lined with brick houses with shuttered windows. At the very end of this dead-end street a single building faced them. Its stone was of a light brown shade and the green marble columns at its entrance and the ornamental carved dragons which faced each other above the door made Della at once decide this was the palace of Prince Sanzio.

She was almost at once proven right when the carriage came to a halt before the door. The midget Guido gave the driver some curt instructions then scrambled down to see them to the sidewalk and escort them into the house.

The little man explained, "The Prince is a semi-invalid so he will greet you later in the living room rather than meet you at the door. You may get settled in your rooms first. Your baggage will be sent up to you."

He led them into the palace and Della's first impression was of dark and dampness. Yet she saw that it had a shabby sort of elegance. There were fine tapestries and paintings on the walls, though the carpets which they traversed were worn and thin. They mounted a curving marble stairway to the second floor where their rooms were located.

Her room was far down the corridor at the rear of the palace. It had once had a rich crimson and gold decor but now the crimson was faded and the gold had lost its luster. The golden fringe of the canopied bed was forlorn-looking, as were the crimson drapes at the tall windows. The floor was of ceramic with rugs at suitable places. The furniture was carved, heavy mahogany.

The views from her windows were lovely. Nearby there was a canal with a stone bridge across it and beyond that a section of small houses. In the background houses on hills extended into the distance. The sun touched the dome of some cathedral, giving it the shining glory of pure gold.

She moved about the room and studied the small portrait of a long-ago beauty hanging in an oval frame on the wall near her bed. Inside the palace it seemed as if the present had ceased to exist. And she wondered what it had been like for her sister to have grown up in this place.

She had not heard anything from Guido about her sister, aside from his comment that there was a strong family resemblance between them. She found herself growing progressively more excited about their first meeting. She had even allowed the unpleasantness of the stolen Madonna to slip from her mind for a while. This was the moment for which she had made the long, strenuous journey. She hoped that the girl would be truly her sister and that they might become friends.

A burly manservant in livery had brought up her luggage. She was gradually unpacking without the assistance of a maid when there was a knock on her door. She went to it and found the diminutive Guido standing there.

"The Prince will greet you and your friends now," the little man said importantly.

"Very well," she said. "Have you notified the others?"

"I will knock at their doors," he promised.

"What about my sister?" she asked. "Will she be down below with the Prince to greet us?"

"No," the small majordomo replied. "Princess Irma has not returned."

She was disappointed. "But she will be here later, won't she?"

"I would hope so, miss," Guido said. "She was supposed to be here for this gathering."

He left her and she hurried to prepare herself for her reception with the old Prince. She had no idea what he might be like but she badly wanted to make a good impression on him. She had chosen a smart yellow gown which she felt showed her to advantage.

In the corridor she met Henry and Aunt Isobel. From their comments their rooms were much the same as hers. The house had once been outstanding, but years of neglect had taken their toll. The house had taken on an old and melancholy air.

They made their way down the curving marble stairway to the living room. Seated there in a wheelchair was a frail, white-haired man wearing a black velvet coat and velvet string tie. His face was lined and sallow and showed a look of resigned sadness.

Della went straight to him and curtsied. "I am Della Standish, and you are Prince Sanzio!"

The old man smiled and took her hand in his. "I would have known you even if you hadn't told me. You bear a striking likeness to my Irma."

"I should," she said with a smile. "She is my twin."

"Without question," the old man said in his cultured, even tone. "I first doubted the woman's letter when it came to me. But I gradually began to believe it was true. Seeing you has satisfied my last doubts."

Della turned to the others, saying, "You must meet my Aunt Isobel and my lawyer, Henry Clarkson."

"Delighted," Prince Sanzio said, greeting them with his gracious smile. "Sir Roger Drexel wrote me about both of you."

"I have come to take care of the legal details, Prince Sanzio," the young man said.

"That is good." The old man spoke excellent English though he occasionally hesitated to dredge the right word from his mind. "My lawyers will be at your service."

"Where is my sister?" Della said.

The thin face of the old man saddened. "You must forgive her. It seems that she has been detained."

"I have so waited for this moment," Della told him.

"I understand," he said. "And she is most desirous of meeting you. I cannot guess why she is not here!"

"At any rate she will be returning home soon," Della said.

"For dinner, surely," the old man said. "We take a siesta from noon to four in this city, and dinner does not usually begin until eight or nine in the evening. In that way we rest during the warmest part of the day."

Aunt Isobel spoke up, "It sounds very practical, Prince Sanzio."

He smiled again in his sad fashion. "Rome is a most practical city as well as being a saintly one." And to the small Guido, he said, "Would you take Mr. Clarkson and Miss Moore on a tour of the house. Let them see my art collection in the other rooms. I have something of a personal nature to say to Miss Standish."

"Yes, your Highness," the little man replied at once as he bowed to the old man in the wheelchair. And to Henry and Aunt Isobel, he said curtly, "You will follow me."

Della was amused at the expressions on the faces of the other two as they were so peremptorily dismissed by the Prince. When they were alone he gave her a troubled look.

"Did this cause them any unpleasantness?" he asked.

"Sending them away?"

"Yes."

"I think they were surprised but I'm sure they will understand," she said.

"I hope so," Prince Sanzio said. "I'm a frail old man and I sometimes behave without grace."

"Do not concern yourself," she said. "I'm sure they will enjoy seeing your paintings and sculpture."

"There are enough of them," the Prince said wearily, his pale hands clutching the chair arms. "I can barely walk with the aid of crutches, so severe is my rheumatism. So I prefer to use this chair to get about. And for convenience I now live on this lower floor."

"That seems wise."

He studied her with his ancient gray eyes. "You are even lovelier than my Irma," he said. "I have words only for your ears."

"Do tell me," she said, drawing up a plain chair to sit near him in the shadowed old room.

"I was once a wealthy man and this house was a show-place," the old man said sadly. "But imprudence at the gambling tables and other financial reverses have brought me to near poverty. I have only my title and barely enough money to run this house left."

"That is too bad," she said. "But at least you still have the palace."

"I have clung to it. We are without the proper number of servants, that is why I have no maid for you," he explained.

"I can manage without one."

"When the Englishwoman died and I received the letter from her lawyer it seemed like a blessing from Heaven. I have long been worried bout Princess Irma."

"Please tell me," she asked him.

He sighed. "She grew up an ideal girl and blossomed into a lovely young woman. In spite of our poverty the noble name of Sanzio brought her many suitors. And in due time she became engaged to one, Prince Raphael. They were to have been married last month."

"But the marriage was postponed? Because you knew I was coming?"

"Irma used that as an excuse," the old man said. "But I do not think it was the whole reason. For a long while she has been behaving strangely."

"Strangely?"

Prince Sanzio nodded. "Do you believe in evil spirits?"

"In what way?"

"This house is said to be inhabited by evil spirits of some of my ancestors," he explained. "I sometimes wonder if they have put a curse on me and my adopted daughter."

"What is this Prince Raphael like?" she asked.

"A fine young man without much money," the old man in the wheelchair said. It was clear that money occupied his thoughts a good deal. "But he was excellent family alliances and with some luck can look forward to a career in the service of our government. First as a minor official, later as a full-fledged diplomatic emissary."

"That sounds exciting!"

"So I have told Irma! But she is impatient for wealth and I think that is why she has changed her mind about him."

"Has her manner toward her husband-to-be changed suddenly?"

"In the last year," the old Prince said. "Since she has come under the influence of that foul Barsini!" He spoke with rising anger.

"Barsini? Who is he?"

"A wastrel! Inherited a fortune from his father and gives his time to spending it in wanton fashion. He is twice Irma's age with the reputation of being a roué, and yet she has all at once fallen under his spell!"

"An older man of bad reputation."

"The worst. He is the sort no man would wish his daughter to know. And Prince Raphael stupidly introduced Irma to him.

From the moment they met, this Barsini has sought to undermine Raphael with my daughter."

"That is too bad."

"She is with Barsini at this moment! That is why she is not here to greet you. He sent for her earlier today and she always goes to him as if she were under his spell. Which she may well be!"

Della raised her eyebrows. "Why do you say that?"

The Prince gave her a worried look. "I should not speak of this perhaps."

"Please tell me all."

He stared at her in silence for a moment. Then he said in a low voice, "Barsini is a Satanist! He leads a band of mad Devil-worshippers. I fear that Irma has become one of them and we Sanzios have always given our allegiance to the Church!"

Della was shocked. "Satanists here in Rome!"

"It is considered fashionable by many here in Rome to revile the Church," the old man said with sadness.

"And you think my sister has become one of the group?"

"There is much to indicate it."

"I'm glad I'm here," Della said earnestly. "Perhaps I shall be able to help her. If she returns to England with me it would get her away from this dreadful man, Barsini!"

"I pray you'll be able to reason with her since I have surely failed," the invalid said.

"I shall certainly try. Does my sister speak English well?"

"English has always been a second language here," Prince Sanzio said. "And most of the educated group in Rome are fluent in both French and English."

"That will make things easier," Della said.

The white-haired man studied her with his sunken eyes. "There is also the financial aspect of it. As an heiress to part of the Standish fortune, Irma will no longer have to cope with genteel poverty."

"True," Della said.

"This may make a change in her," the old man said. "It can open other avenues of living for the unhappy girl, such as travel, fine clothes and possessions."

Della said, "Mr. Clarkson is here to represent the law firm taking care of my estate. If he is convinced that she is truly my sister the estate will accept her."

"I have not a single doubt," the old man said. "You two look enough alike to be identical twins. Having you by me makes me feel that it is Irma here."

"I find that exciting," she said. "The dearest wish of my parents was that she should be found and restored to her proper place in the family."

Prince Sanzio said, "I shall not stand in her way. I want her to have the security the Standish name can give her."

Della said, "There is no question that she will always be grateful to you for bringing her up."

The invalid shrugged. "That is difficult to predict with Irma in her present state of mind. She is very confused. The main thing is to get her away from Count Barsini and his evil crowd."

"Cannot her fiancé, Prince Raphael, take a leading part in that?"

The old man shook his head sadly. "No. I'm afraid not. He is a good man but rather weak. He hesitates to take a stand against Barsini."

"That is too bad."

"Most unfortunate! But then, despite his charm he is a person of vacillating character. His family have had their headaches with him."

"I'm glad you've filled me in on all this," Della said. "I'll know better how to approach her."

"That is why I insisted on seeing you alone," the old man said.

She stared at his lined, sickly face. "Now may I ask you something, Prince?"

"By all means," he said. "I am at your service."

"A series of strange happenings has tagged me since your letter about Irma arrived in London."

He frowned. "I do not understand."

"For one thing I have been hounded by a tall, dark man who seems to think I know something about a valuable, jeweled Madonna which evidently was stolen here in Rome."

"Jeweled Madonna?" the old man echoed. "I know nothing of such a thing. Nor would I suppose any of the others here have knowledge of it."

"Yet it all followed my hearing from you," she pointed out.

"Could that not be coincidence?"

"I doubt it," she said grimly. "I was actually kidnapped and threatened with death if I would not give information about the Madonna. And I know nothing about it."

"Sounds like the work of a madman!"

"Perhaps it is," she said unhappily. "But it has made life complicated for me. I'm in almost constant fear. And both I and Henry Clarkson were attacked during the train journey here from Paris. I might not have arrived here alive."

Prince Sanzio eyed her with shocked amazement. "This is distressing information. I do not know what to say."

"Please understand we are in no way blaming you," she said.

The old man looked pained. "Yet all this began only after you received my letters concerning your lost sister."

"Yes. We think it may be that someone knowing about my coming here decided to use me in a bizarre theft scheme."

"Continue," the old man begged her.

"Suppose," she said, "that someone close to you, a friend or maybe a mere acquaintance, heard about the discovery that Irma was my sister. And that I was coming here to check on the authenticity of her claim. Let us assume this person or persons has stolen a valuable object which they must get out of the country.

And in an impulsive moment hit on the idea of sending it to me for safekeeping. Perhaps as a belonging of my sister."

"And?"

"Let us further imagine that a messenger was sent to London with the stolen Madonna. But some other criminal knew about the scheme and intercepted the messenger, killed him and took the stolen treasure. This man brings it back here. But in the meanwhile the original thieves assume I have it, come after it, and when they get nothing but denials from me, decide that I'm unwilling to return it to them. So they harass and threaten me!"

The old man heard her story with astonishment. "It all seems to fit," he said. "Except that I cannot conceive of any of my household being capable of such a crime!"

"Could not Irma have told this evil Count Barsini about me?"

The Prince's mouth gaped. "Of course! No doubt she has told him all about you!"

Della said, "Then the first thing I must do is try and find out from her what she has told him."

The Prince nodded. "I warn you it will not be easy. Your sister is a difficult girl where that evil man is concerned."

Chapter Seven

"It is a scandal that you should come all this way and she not be here," Prince Sanzio said. "I must be truthful. I cannot truly say when she will come back."

"I see," Della replied.

He sighed. "We shall have dinner at nine. Prince Raphael is invited. Perhaps she will come with him. Or it could be she is with that villainous Barsini. In that event there is no telling about her!"

"Then we'll all gather for dinner at nine," she said. "And if Irma returns before then please send her to me."

"The moment she comes home," the frail Prince Sanzio said. "I am now going to rest for a while. I advise that you and your friends do the same."

"Thank you," she said. "And especially for being so frank with me."

"It is well that you should know what you are facing here," the old man said. "And it is also best for my adopted daughter."

She left him sitting forlornly in his wheelchair. When she reached the second floor she met Aunt Isobel and Henry on the landing.

Della asked them, "Did you enjoy your tour?"

Aunt Isobel gave her a knowing look. "Not too many left but a few prints and some tapestries dirty and in need of repairs. According to Guido, the Prince has sold most of his valuable possessions."

"That's apt to be the sad truth," Della said.

Henry asked her, "How did you make out with the Prince?"

"I learned a few things which may be of value to us," she said. "My sister is not here and she's been behaving in an irrational fashion lately. The Prince doesn't truly know when she'll return."

"A fine state of affairs," Aunt Isobel said with some anger. "After all we've gone through to get here."

"You look weary," Della said. "Dinner is not until nine. You should go to your room and have a rest."

"I'm not unpacked yet," her aunt said. "But when I finish that is exactly what I shall do. You'd expect the Prince to at least have a maid to take care of us." And with that she went down the corridor to her own room.

The good-looking young lawyer smiled wryly. "I'm afraid this is bringing out the worst in Aunt Isobel."

"I know," she said, frowning. "And I dare not tell her all since it will only upset her."

He gave her an inquiring look. "It sounds as if you had a pretty important talk with the old man."

"I did," she said. "Come along to my room where it is more private and I'll tell you."

In her room she repeated all she and the Prince had discussed. The young lawyer listened with a serious look on his pleasant face. He did not speak until she had ended her account.

Then he said, "I pinpoint Barsini as the criminal who must have sent the Madonna to you in London."

"I'm inclined to agree," Della said. "But we're only guessing."

"It sounds like an educated guess," Henry said. "In any case we know Barsini is a bad influence on the girl."

"Without doubt."

"The first thing to decide is whether she is truly your sister," Henry told her. "If it seems unlikely that she is I suggest we leave Rome at once."

"We've only arrived!"

"We came here for a single purpose," Henry said. "Once that is settled we have no business here."

"What if she is my sister?"

"The situation becomes complicated."

"And whether she is my sister or not, we have to find out whether Barsini or some of her other underworld friends were involved in a theft and whether the stolen treasure was sent to me."

Henry sighed. "All of which is gobbledygook until we establish the identity of the girl and how much she has told others about you."

"Prince Sanzio seems badly upset about her actions."

"Why not?" Henry asked. "He has given her his love and his name. He will not enjoy it being gossiped about Rome that Princess Sanzio is an ardent Satanist!"

"How could she do this to him?" Della wondered.

Henry gave her an amused look. "If she's a Standish she has a mind of her own. You should realize that!"

She smiled at him shyly. "Then by all I've heard she is likely my sister."

"At the moment I'm more concerned about you," Henry Clarkson said. "As long as they have this mad idea that you know where the Madonna is, you're a target."

"I have one trump card."

"What is that?"

"They dare not kill me if they think I've the sole knowledge of where it may be hidden."

Henry nodded. "That's true. But it's a small benefit. They could work you over badly short of death."

"That's been done already," she said. "Remember Limehouse! I know I will!"

"I'd prefer to forget it."

She shook her head in wonderment. "Here we are talking about the Madonna as if we knew it really existed and that it had been stolen!"

"It's a kind of madness that is catching," he agreed.

"As long as they, whoever they are, think it, I suppose we have to go along," she said.

Henry glanced at his pocket watch. Did you say dinner was to be at nine?"

"Yes."

He returned the watch to the vest pocket of his brown suit. "I'll go and let you get some rest. You want to be at your best tonight. And if dinner is not until nine we are apt to have a long session."

"I would say so," she agreed, rising. "Especially when we don't know what time my supposed sister will show up."

"That complicates everything."

"Her fiancé, Prince Raphael, is to be here," Della went on. "And the old Prince appeared to think she might come with him."

"We shall see," Henry said. Then he took her in his arms and kissed her. "I'm glad our rooms are all on the same floor," he observed as he let her go. "At least we are close together in case of an attack."

"Let us hope there won't be any," she said. "It's a very old house. Did Guido show you any secret passages or dungeons?"

Henry smiled. "As a matter of fact, he did tell us about there having been dungeons underneath the original building on this site. He claimed they were part of the cellars now. He didn't say anything about secret passages."

"I'd be willing to say there are some."

"Don't," he protested. "We have problems enough without anything like that. Do try and rest!"

"I shall," she said as she saw him out.

She finished unpacking and it was true that it was awkward without a maid to help. She supposed she had been spoiled at home by having plenty of servants. Perhaps it was a good thing for her to learn to be more self-reliant. She imagined that there had to be a cook and at least a housekeeper. She could not see the small Guido doing all the household work.

She pulled the velvet drapes at the two wondows and then stretched out on the canopied bed. Within a few minutes she had fallen asleep, for despite the heat of the day the palace's thick stone walls kept its interior cool. If anything, it was a little too cool and damp.

She dreamt not at all and woke with a start to find that it was nearly eight o'clock. Startled by the swift passage of time, she quickly went about washing and dressing. She had chosen a light muslin in pale blue for this first evening and she went to some trouble to get her hair as right as possible. A few added touches of makeup to hide the pallor she suffered from the long, tiring trip and a discreet touch of perfume completed her toilet. Now she was ready to go down and join the others at dinner.

No one was in sight when she went to the landing. She started down the curving marble stairway wondering what was keeping Henry and her Aunt Isobel. As she reached a halfway point on the stairway she saw a dark-haired young man with a waxed mustache standing at the foot of the stairway gazing up at her.

He was formally dressed and so handsome she had not the slightest doubt that this must be Prince Raphael. She smiled at him as she continued on down and he returned her smile. But she was not prepared for what happened when she came face to face with him at the bottom of the stairway. He abruptly swept her into his arms and kissed her ardently.

She was stunned by this unexpected behavior on his part and, when she was able, pushed him away from her. In a taut voice, she exclaimed, "Really!"

The moment she spoke the young man's happy expression changed and he looked badly upset. He said, "What have I done? I took you for Irma!"

She could not help smiling a little. "Well, I'm not Irma, whatever you thought!"

He put a hand to his temple in lamentation. "But, of course, I recognize that now. As soon as you spoke I knew my mistake. You have to be the sister, Della!"

"I am," she said.

He stared at her. "But the likeness is striking. I find it hard to believe!"

"We are twins."

"I'm most terribly sorry!"

"You needn't be," she said mildly. "You are, I'm sure, Prince Raphael."

"Please," he begged her. "My name is Frederico. I would prefer that since I am to be your brother-in-law."

She said, "I fear I haven't yet met the bride-to-be."

He frowned. "I was positive she would be here. I thought you were she."

"Yes," she said, realizing that as an aftermath of his warm greeting she was still blushing.

"Wait until I tell her what happened," he said. "It is incredible. You even wear your hair the same way!"

She laughed shyly. "That, I fear, is purely a consequence of following the current style. It wasn't intended."

The Prince had a warm smile which he used often to reveal perfect white teeth against his olive skin. He said, "Irma is always in fashion! And she has hair just a shade darker than yours. Your relationship is obvious."

"I was disappointed not to meet her when I arrived."

He frowned. "She was to be here. The old Prince made her promise."

"She broke her promise."

"So it would seem," the young man in the white tie and tails said. "You did not make the journey alone?"

"No. My aunt came with me and so did my lawyer." She hesitated slightly and then added, "He also happens to be the man I plan to marry."

Prince Raphael arched an eyebrow. "How fortunate for him to be able to join you on the trip."

"I consider it lucky for me," she said.

"But, of course," the handsome young man said with another of his smiles. "And who better to take care of you in this baffling matter."

She said, "You think it baffling?"

"It has to be," he said, spreading his hands. "The finding of a sister after so long a time. The testing and the checking of credentials. Surely you would not have wished to approach such a task alone?"

"You are right," she said. "I could not have come on my own."

"But there will be no problem," Prince Raphael assured her. "The old man is a person of great honesty and he has brought up Irma as his own beloved daughter. She has even enjoyed the title of Princess."

"I know," she said. "I have no fears about him."

Prince Raphael's alert black eyes met hers as he asked, "So, what are your concerns?"

"What about Irma?"

A shadow of embarrassment crossed his aristocratic face. "You cannot expect me to criticize my betrothed!"

She still met his eyes with a firm glance of her own. "Prince Sanzio tells me that her absence today is only too typical. That she has caused him many worries."

He looked down. "It is probably true," he said in a low voice.

"He places most of the blame on a man named Count Barsini," Della went on. "I'm sure you know him."

"Too well!" the Prince said bitterly.

"He thinks she is with him this evening."

"I know," he said worriedly. "I'm aware of what is going on. And to a degree, I blame myself since she first met Barsini through me."

"Why did you introduce them?"

He shrugged. "It was a courtesy that could not be avoided. We were fellow guests at a party. I had no choice."

"And you had no idea what would develop?"

"I gave Irma credit for better sense than to become involved with one of his reputation," the young man said with anger.

"Have you postponed your marriage because of it?"

He shook his head. "Irma put the date off. She cannot seem to make up her mind about anything lately."

"Except seeing this Count Barsini," Della said with meaning.

"That is about the sum of it."

She eyed him sharply. "I think you should show better authority over her. She is your fiancée. So her actions must reflect on you."

"I have tried," he said. "Believe me I have talked to her."

"Apparently without much result."

"That is right," he said.

"Is Barsini truly a Satanist as Prince Sanzio fears?"

Prince Raphael looked uneasy. "Did the old man tell you that?"

"Yes. He said it is the gossip of Rome that Count Barsini holds court to a group of Satanists."

"It may be true," the young man said with a grim look. "I cannot prove it. But he has dealt in every sort of debauchery."

"Has he ever indulged in criminal activity? Theft, for instance?"

Prince Raphael looked shocked. "Why do you ask that?"

"I'm trying to find out what depths of evil he is capable of," she said.

"Barsini is a rich man!" the young man protested. "Why should he steal?"

She smiled grimly. "Men steal for more reasons than gain. It would appear he is a thrill-seeker. What greater thrill than to steal a fabulous treasure?"

The dark handsome man gazed with new interest. "You are a remarkable young woman!"

"You have not answered my question?"

"How can I?" he said. "I do not know the answer. Try Irma. She is much closer to him than I have ever been."

"I shall," she said.

Their conversation was interrupted by the arrival of Henry and her aunt. She introduced them to the friendly young Prince. They were all in a group talking when Prince Sanzio appeared in his wheelchair from the other end of the room. She saw at once that he had changed to evening dress. And she was thankful that Henry had decided to bring his along. It seemed that dinner was a formal occasion in the palace.

Prince Sanzio wheeled himself up to join them and gave Prince Raphael a special greeting. "I am happy you are here," he told the young man. "But where is my daughter?"

Prince Raphael shrugged. "I regret I do not know."

"May I add that I also regret it, most sincerely," the old man said with irony. "Well, we shall have to make do without her. I shall lead the way to the dining room."

He went at the head of their group with Della at his side chatting with him. The dining room was on the other side of the huge reception hall and by candlelight looked less shabby than the rest of the house. The candelabra on the table gave the room a rich warmth which was enhanced by the gleaming white cloth, the rows of fine china, silver and cut glass.

Prince Sanzio wheeled his chair to the head of the table and placed Della on his right and Aunt Isobel on his left. Prince Raphael sat next to Della and Henry sat across the table with her aunt. It was an arrangement for good conversation and she assumed that had her sister been there she would have been seated on the other side of Henry.

Aunt Isobel showed a thin smile as little Guido entered in waiter's uniform to serve them solemnly. The little man was barely the height of the table but he managed well with the various courses from soup, to fish, to grouse and then the flaming desert which he wheeled in on a tray.

Prince Sanzio proved a brilliant table partner. He gave a great deal of attention to Della, saying "You must get to know this old city."

"I want to," she told him. "Rome has always been a magic word for me."

"People call it the Eternal City, you know," the old man said with a wry smile. "Yet in no other city does a visitor see more tangible and tragic evidence of the fragility of human creation."

"You are thinking of the many ruins, I suppose?" Aunt Isobel ventured.

"In a sense," the old man said. "In the heart of this city you can lose your way among ruined temples. Grass grows on the Via Sacra along which princes rode in celebration of great victories. All that remains of that glory are traces on the ground, truncated columns, inscriptions on stone worn away by the centuries."

Henry spoke up: "It is because this was such an early seat of civilization."

Prince Sanzio smiled bitterly. "Civilization! A much-abused word! Has man ever been truly civilized?"

"We Romans pride ourselves on our culture," the young Prince Raphael contributed.

The old man gave him a withering look. "Is that why some of our titled young people are turning to Satanism?"

Prince Raphael's face crimsoned and he stared down at his plate. Della entered the discussion to ease the tension, saying, "Perhaps when people refer to the eternity of Rome they are thinking of its perpetual rebirth. The city is made up of ruins as life is made up of its dead, it rises from death to new life. After ancient Rome came the Rome of Christianity, and then the Renaissance, and now the new Rome of today."

Prince Sanzio's wrinkled face showed approval. "You speak wisely. Only in Rome have the centuries not been erased. Here poverty and pomp exist side by side. Nothing lasts but nothing dies! History is not abstract, it is present!"

"You love your city," Della said with a warm smile. "And that is good. I'm sure every English person has a special affection for London."

"And the Queen!" Aunt Isobel said emotionally.

Prince Raphael raised his glass and stood, "A toast to the Queen! And to our English guests!"

The toast was drunk and the mood at the table became most amiable as the long dinner continued. At the end the men remained at the table to enjoy their brandy while Della and Aunt Isobel went to repair their makeup before joining the gentlemen later in the living room.

As soon as they were away from the dining room Aunt Isobel touched Della on the arm and complained, "I don't like the way this is shaping up! Not at all! Where is the girl?"

"I hope she will soon arrive," Della replied, wishing to placate the older woman. Though the situation was also distressing to her.

Aunt Isobel said, "Something is wrong!"

"According to the Prince she has fallen in with bad company and has been misbehaving," she said.

"She should have been here to greet you!"

"I know."

"I think she's a fake and afraid to meet us," Aunt Isobel decided.

"We can't jump to conclusions until we know more," Della warned the older woman.

Aunt Isobel sat down dejectedly on the end of a divan. "They are pretending! They don't really like us! I can tell!"

"I'm sure I don't know how," Della argued. "I think we're being treated well. Prince Sanzio couldn't be more hospitable and Prince Raphael is charming."

"All false front!" was her aunt's emphatic reaction.

When the men rejoined them a little later the talk turned to the Vatican. Prince Sanzio said, "You must all spend some time exploring the Papal State. You will be well rewarded."

"It is one of the memorable sights of Rome," Prince Raphael agreed.

"Even though our sons and daughters no longer have love or respect for the Church," the old man said severely.

"I'm excited about St. Peter's and the square!" Henry said.

"It has majesty and beauty," Prince Sanzio said. "The four rows of columns from the basilica opening are all-embracing. In the center is the red granite obelisk which Caligua imported from Heliopolis and Nero later placed in the Circus Maximus. On each side stand two fountains, their spouting water the mobile and fluid element in what is a symphony of stone!"

Prince Raphael took Della slightly aside as they stood together with their wineglasses in their hands. In a low voice, he said, "I'm weary of this endless talk. May I show you the gardens by moonlight."

There was a twinkle in her green eyes. "I think I could do with some air."

They left the living room quietly and went outdoors by a side entrance. Descending several broad marble steps they entered a garden whose perfumed aroma filled the night. On either side of the flower beds and walks there were rows of straight, sentinel-like dark green trees. A full moon shone down to light the area.

"Magnificent!" she said.

The man at her side shrugged. "It is nothing to what it once was. Would you believe it is maintained by a single gardener?"

"He must work from dawn to dusk!"

"Probably he does. Some simple fellow who has great affection for the old Prince."

She looked up at him sharply. "You sound as if you think that wrong?"

"It is outdated."

"I can't wish to believe that loyalty, respect and affection will ever be dated," she said.

Prince Raphael laughed lightly. "You are a creature of sentimentality. I thought only we Italians ran to such sentiment, that the English are cold and prudish."

"Prudish perhaps," she said teasingly, "but never cold!"

They strolled along the walk and he said, "You must be sick of my friend Prince Sanzio raving on about the glory of Rome."

"I enjoyed it."

"He was a poor imitation of a tour guide!"

"Don't say such things," she pleaded. "Or I shall think less of you."

They had come to the end of the walk and now he halted to ask her, "That brings me to the point of asking you what your opinion you hold of me."

She smiled and considered. "I think you have a great deal of charm but I fear that it is in danger of being spoiled by your cynicism."

"To think is to be a cynic!"

"It depends on one's viewpoint," Della told him. "Henry is much duller than you. But he shows enthusiasm at times and that livens him. You heard him going on about St. Peter's and the square."

"I grew up playing in the square. Why should it mean anything to me?" he asked.

"I'm sorry you have become blind to beauty and history," she said.

"And I may think you naïve about Rome."

"Do so, I don't mind," she said, starting to stroll back and beginning to think the garden interlude might turn out to be a mistake.

Prince Raphael said, "It is too bad about Irma. Her absence naturally has upset you."

"I'm sure it has upset us all," she said.

"Do not worry, she will show herself in her own good time. I think she is with Barsini."

"That should bother you," she told him.

"It will not last," he said, gazing up at the moon so that its full light shone on his handsome face. "She will come back to me. Barsini soon tires of his playthings. She will have no choice!"

"You shock me!" Della said.

"Why?"

"An Englishman would have a showdown with your evil Count and take his girl back from him by strength! You are content to wait and let it happen by default."

"So I am an Italian."

"I'm not sure I approve of you," she said.

He halted again and, turning to her, said, "I have been thinking of something you said earlier tonight."

"Oh?"

"Yes," he said. "You spoke of Barsini and suggested he might be a thief."

"I don't think I actually said those words."

"It amounted to that."

"You think so?"

"Yes," the young Prince said. "And that leads me to believe that something prompted you to make such a statement about Barsini. What?"

"You are jumping to a number of conclusions," she told him.

"Will you not tell me?"

"I have nothing to tell you. I was making a comment on his character. Offering a guess as to the sort of person he is."

"It didn't sound like that!"

"I'm so sorry," she mocked him.

He stared at her long and hard. "I don't think you are anything like Irma."

"No?"

"No," he said. "And I like what I find in you much more!" Without warning he took her in his arms and kissed her again, perhaps more ardently than he had when first they met.

When he released her, she said, "You didn't mistake me for Irma this time!"

"I did not," he said gravely. "That embrace was for you. I have lost my head to you, my English Della."

"Better be more cautious," she said. "I don't like being pawed over whenever someone takes it in their head. I reserve my kisses for good friends and the man I love."

"Can I not be a good friend?"

"It is much too early to say."

"Or even the man you love?"

"You are too late for that!"

"I will not believe it!"

"You had better," she said. "And now I'm sure we ought to go in. We've probably caused talk as it is."

He laughed. "Do you care?"

"Yes, I think so," she said. "It is my first night under Prince Sanzio's roof. I do not wish to have him think badly of me."

"He won't," the man at her side assured her. "But perhaps I will."

With these somewhat enigmatic words the young Prince saw her back inside the palace. They rejoined the others, who were in deep conversation about the condition of the Church in the late-nineteenth century. Della was grateful that no one seemed to have missed them. Prince Raphael smirked at her when she glanced up at him, as if to underline the fact their absence had caused no comment.

Della spoke up to say, "We met several people on the train. One of them a jolly old priest named Father Anthony."

Prince Sanzio said, "The only Father Anthony I can think of died two years ago. But Rome is crammed with priests and many of them must surely be named Anthony. It is an Italian name."

Prince Raphael added, "To find him would be like seeking out a John Smith in London!"

"What about that wretched woman?" Aunt Isobel said. "I think her name was Gonia or something like that!"

Henry said, "Madame Guioni. A widow who claimed to be the owner of the Guioni Brothers winery."

"I have never heard of her," Prince Sanzio said. "But that does not mean she is not an important figure here. I'm very out of touch. I know few people of the new generation."

"She's an Englishwoman who married into the Guioni family," Della explained.

"I do not know the lady but I'm familiar with the wine," Prince Raphael said. "It is very poor stuff!"

"So Father Anthony said," Henry put in.

The intimate conversation went on and the tension within Della grew. It was growing late and the sister she had traveled so far to meet had not shown herself. She was badly worried about it all. She felt relief when Prince Raphael announced his intention to leave and the party broke up.

The Prince kissed her hand in leaving and bade a courtly goodnight to Henry and her aunt. He spoke a few words with the older Prince and then went on his way. Prince Sanzio looked deathly pale, as if on the point of collapse.

He addressed himself to Della: "How can I apologize for my daughter's snubbing you in this fashion?"

She said, "I'm sure she must have had a good reason."

"I would hope so," the old man said. "Yet I seriously doubt it."

Della said, "She will return. Then I'll talk to her and so will Mr. Clarkson. We will then decide if the woman's letter was valid."

The old Prince looked shattered. "I would not blame you for repudiating her even if she should be your sister."

"If the facts are proven I will not let anything else stand in her way," Della said quietly.

"That is charitable of you," the old man said with sincerity. "Sleep well this first night in the Palazzo Sanzio."

"I'm sure I shall," she said.

The old man wheeled himself off into the shadows and she mounted the stairway, following Aunt Isobel and Henry, who had already gone upstairs. The landing was deserted with only a single candle burning there for light. The Prince appeared to rely entirely on candles for lighting the palace. Perhaps because he found it less expensive.

The evening had left her depressed and tense. She felt things were not going well and she was not at all sure about Prince Raphael. She had a suspicion he might not be the carefree man-about-town he pretended, but something much more sinister.

He had reacted strangely to her mention of a theft of a treasure and whether Barsini might be related to it. She was filled with these troubling thoughts as she opened the door to her room and went in. A single candle on the dresser offered light.

She was closing the door when hands reached out and grasped her by the arms. She cried out in terror and twisted around to find herself facing Henry!

"You!" she exclaimed. "Why did you do that? You gave me a dreadful fright!"

"Not my intention," he said.

"You should have spoken, given me some warning."

"I thought of that in the garden," he said, his tone meaningful.

She stared at him. "The garden? Were you spying on Prince Raphael and me?"

"I would hardly call it that," he said. "I went out to join you for a breath of air expecting nothing. And I found you two most romantically in each other's arms!"

"Henry!" she said in reproach.

"I was a gentleman," he promised. "I turned straight about and went into the house."

"You gave no hint of it when we returned!"

"I have some discretion," he assured her.

She touched his arm. "I promise you it was nothing. He is an Italian and a Prince!"

"I know that."

"He simply caught me by surprise! Swept me into his arms before I could resist! I was shocked and I gave him a good lecture!"

Henry smiled knowingly. "I shall believe you. I shall not let my mind be filled with nasty, suspicious thoughts as I have known you to do in the past!"

"Will you never forgive me?"

"Forgiven, my dear," the young lawyer said warmly. "I guessed the situation was as you described it."

"Mind you," she said, "he most brazenly went on making love to me as if he weren't engaged to that Irma at all! I'm sure I may have trouble with him."

"He will require handling," Henry said. "And as for Irma? Do you think she exists?"

"Of course," she said. "The old Prince was in despair at her behavior."

"There is something very odd about it," Henry ventured.

"I'm sure Prince Raphael knows more than he lets on," she continued. "I mentioned Barsini and conjectured whether he might be a thief."

"That was bait," Henry said, at once interested. "How did he react?"

"At first he said Barsini would not steal as he is too rich."

"Then?"

"Then I made him admit there might be other motives for theft. The thrill of taking a great treasure!"

"He reacted to that?"

"Yes and brought it up some time later in the evening. So I think we have hit a vein. It may mean a low follow-up, but I say Barsini is our man!"

Henry offered, "He seems to be at the bottom of a good deal of the trouble here. So why should he not be mixed up in the theft of the jeweled Madonna?"

"If there ever was one," she said. "Now I must get some sleep. I'm dead on my feet!"

Henry smiled at her. "Would a kiss from me be an anticlimax after all your earlier romancing?"

Pertly, she thrust up her mouth, "Why not try it and find out?"

"Very practical!" the young lawyer marveled as he took her in his arms.

It worked very well. And when he smiled down at her she said wistfully, "It was really very good!"

Henry looked pleased. "Thank you and good night." And he left her.

She smiled dreamily after him and then began to prepare for bed. She had not exaggerated in saying she was completely exhausted. It had been a long evening at the end of a long day. Within a few minutes she was in bed with the candle extinguished. And almost at once she fell asleep.

She awoke to the darkness of the big room and a confused sense of how long she might have slept. As she tried to collect her thoughts she became aware of the menacing sound which must surely have awakened her, the loud creaking of the door to the corridor. As she sat up in bed, staring in that direction, she felt her blood freeze! For the door was being slowly opened!

Chapter Eight

The door edged open a little farther. Della leaned back against the head of the bed, shocked into muteness and immobility, her horrified eyes fixed on the slowly opening portal. Then in the doorway she saw the figure of a young woman holding a candle. A young woman in a crimson silk low-cut gown, with a head of dark auburn hair flowing about her bare shoulders. A young woman with her face!

"Irma!" she gasped as she found her voice.

Her look-alike glided into the room a look of scorn on her lovely face. When she was within a few feet of the bed she halted to stare at Della. In a low voice, she said, "So it is true! You are my sister!"

"Yes, I think it must be," Della said, leaving her bed to go to the young woman.

"You should not have come!" the other girl said and now it became noticeable that she spoke with a slight slurring of her words.

"Why?" Della asked, aware that her sister was drunk or drugged.

The girl stared at her with green eyes that matched her own. She said, "You should have stayed in England."

"I came to find you," she said.

"I'd prefer to remain Princess Sanzio," the girl said. "I don't want to be your sister."

"But if you are my sister, isn't it important that we both know it?"

The lovely girl who so resembled her, swayed slightly. "Go home and let us be!" she said, her words thickening once again.

And then she turned and glided out of the room in the same phantom way in which she had entered. Della gazed after her wondering what it all meant. Her supposed-sister surely had not welcomed her warmly. In fact she had made it clear that she wished their meeting had not occurred.

Still shaken by the experience, Della returned to her bed. She did not sleep for a long while. Her mind was in a whirl over all that had happened. And it became clear to her that she must seek out this Barsini as soon as possible to try and find out the truth about the stolen Madonna. And his method of keeping this girl who might be her sister under his influence.

She slept until sun began to pour in around the drapes. Then she got up to find that the diminutive Guido had already left her hot water for her morning bath. Later she donned a plain cotton print with the motif of grapes clusters and oranges.

The dining room was empty, but after she'd taken a chair at the set table, the little Guido came hurrying out to serve her.

She greeted him with a smile. "Am I the first or the last?"

The small man stood at attention, betraying no hint of expression on his lined, sallow face. "You are the last, *Signorina.*"

"I fear I overslept," she apologized.

"It does not matter," the little man said. "The Prince has his breakfast in his suite."

"Better for him," she said.

"He is now enjoying a siesta in the morning sun on the patio outside his room."

Della ordered a light breakfast and he went off to get it. She wondered about Aunt Isobel and Henry. Perhaps they had decided on a stroll in the gardens while they were waiting for her.

Guido returned with the first course of her breakfast, some sliced fruit. She was enjoying this when her look-alike came into the dining room wearing a plain white dress with many ruffles at the sleeves and in the skirt. The girl looked pale and apologetic.

Taking a stand across the table from her, the girl said, "I have come to ask your pardon for last night."

Della smiled. "There is nothing to apologize for!"

"I think there is," the girl insisted. "I was not at all myself."

"Won't you join me for breakfast?" she asked.

"I'll have some coffee," the girl said and pulled out a chair at a place near her and sat down.

Guido came in with the eggs which Della had ordered and bowed to the other girl. He asked, "What may I bring to you, Princess?"

The girl asked him to fetch her coffee and he hurried away to get it. Della kept staring at her look-alike with a fascination she could not conceal. The other girl's hair was just a hint darker auburn than her own and her nose was perhaps more aquiline. But aside from that she might have been gazing into a mirror.

"I cannot get over it!" Della said, staring.

The other girl shrugged. "We are much alike."

"Almost exactly alike!"

"So be it!" The other girl seemed embarrassed, casting her eyes down on her plate. "It is strange to have a look-alike."

"Not so strange! Even though we've grown up apart we are twins," Della said.

"Doesn't that have to be proven?"

Della said, "Now that I have seen you I have no doubt it will be."

The other girl looked up at her uneasily. "And then where will we be?"

"You can take your place in English society and assume your proper name of Irma Standish."

"I do not want any of that," the other girl objected. "I could not desert the Prince in his old age nor do I wish to leave Rome."

Della said, "But it is the Prince who had me come here and who is pressing your claim to the Standish name and fortune."

The girl's lovely green eyes flashed angrily. "I opposed his doing so!"

"But he has gone ahead with it. I am here with my lawyer to find out the truth about you. It has gone too far not to be settled."

"It is a mistake!"

Della raised her eyebrows. "Do you not wish to be my sister? To be restored to me. Have you any idea the anguish your kidnapping caused my parents?"

"I did not know them!" the other girl protested. "My father, the only father I will ever think of as mine, is Prince Sanzio."

"Your devotion is touching," she said. "But if you are proven my sister you will have money to help the Prince. And even he is willing to admit his need of such funds."

Their frank discussion was interrupted by the return of Guido with a silver coffee service. He poured them each steaming cups and retired.

The girl sipped her coffee and said, "I'm sorry I frightened you last night. It did not occur to me that my entrance that way would seem unusual."

"I was scared for a moment."

The girl shrugged. "I had too much to drink. But I wanted to see you. To see if you did truly look like me."

"I understand."

"Please do not complain to my father," the girl said in a pleading manner. "Let him think we met at breakfast."

"If you wish," Della said. "He was upset by your not being here for our arrival."

The other girl's pale face showed crimson spots at the cheekbones. She said, "I had to be somewhere else. I made a promise to a friend."

She gazed at her knowingly over her coffee cup. "Was the friend Count Barsini?"

"How do you know about him?" the girl gasped.

"I know much which might surprise you," Della said. "I have been told he is an evil man and that his power over you is unfortunate."

The girl had not expected such a reaction from her lovely look-alike. Trembling with anger, she demanded, "How dare you repeat such things?"

"I'm sorry. It is only what I've been told."

"Then someone told you wrong," the girl went on, still in a rage. "Count Barsini is one of the most charming and cultured men in all Rome. I'm lucky he has chosen me as a friend." She halted and then exclaimed, "Of course, it was Raphael who told you this nonsense. He is stupidly jealous of my friendship with Barsini!"

"That may be," she said. "I do not know. I would like to meet this Barsini."

The other girl stared at her. "Why?"

"Because he sounds like an interesting person," Della said.

A veiled look came over the girl's face. "You will no doubt meet him sometime."

"I would like to," Della said.

"How long do you plan to remain here?" the other girl asked her.

"Until my lawyer is satisfied of your identity."

"I resent being judged like some sort of animal," the girl said tensely. "I want none of this."

"I'm afraid it has been started and we'll have to go through with it now," Della said in placating fashion. "My lawyer is a fine young man named Henry Clarkson. We plan to marry."

"He is your fiancé?"

"Yes. And you are to marry Prince Raphael. He seems an attractive man."

"He takes too much for granted."

"Is that why you delayed your marriage to him?"

The girl looked down. "That and other things," she said.

At that moment Prince Sanzio wheeled himself into the room. In a tone of relief, he observed, "So you two girls have met."

"Yes," Della said with a smile. "We are almost old friends now."

The other girl spoke up: "I have told her she should go back to England, Father. That I'm content with things as they are here."

The frail old man smiled sadly. "I had no choice but to notify Miss Standish. The letter that woman left behind was clear. You were the victim of a kidnapping."

"Am I not still the victim?" the girl asked bitterly. "My life is being upset by this discovery. I would be happier to go on as I am."

"I disagree with you," Prince Sanzio said. "None of this will make you any less my daughter. I did adopt you. But it will bring you your rightful inheritance."

Della said, "I can understand it is still a shock. I'm sure Irma will feel differently later."

Irma said, "I grew up thinking I was the child of a servant fortunate enough to be adopted. Now it seems I was cheated from the start."

"The pain you may feel is small beside that which our parents felt," Della told her. "And I have often known grief at wondering what happened to you. So we should try to make this a joyful reunion."

"Perhaps," the other girl said, rising. "But do not blame me if I hope that your lawyer decides I'm not your sister!" And with this she turned and left the dining room.

Prince Sanzio stared after her sadly. "I'm afraid she is in a badly mixed-up state."

"I hope she feels better about it later," Della said.

"I'm sure she will," the old man agreed. "Meanwhile, I'm having my lawyers meet with Mr. Clarkson, beginning today. There are the various documents to be authenticated as well as certain articles which the dead woman left to verify her statement. Some children's clothing, several written notes from your parents, items of that nature to substantiate her story."

"I will leave all that to Henry except when he wishes me to identify any personal objects or letters in my parents handwriting," she said. "My aunt may also be helpful in this regard."

"So you will enjoy Rome while you wait to learn the answer," the man in the wheelchair said.

She smiled grimly. "I do not need to wait to know. Having seen Irma and talked with her, I'm positive she is my sister. There is a feeling which tells me so. I think she has experienced it as well. That is why she protested so much. She knew we are on the right path."

"That could well be," the old Prince said with a sigh. "As I explained to you, she is not an easy person to deal with."

"It is a Standish quality, I fear," Della said wryly.

When she and the old man went out to the patio they met Henry and Aunt Isobel, who were returning from a stroll in the gardens.

Prince Sanzio told the young lawyer, "You may go to my lawyer's office as soon as you like."

"I will leave at once," he said.

"My carriage will take you," the Prince said. "And afterward it will take the ladies anywhere they might enjoy visiting."

"I should just like to be driven about the city and enjoy its atmosphere without stopping anywhere special." Aunt Isobel said. "It wearies me to trudge through museums and ruins."

"I think I shall let you go alone," Della said. "I wish to rest a little and later I amy seek out some special place by myself."

Prince Sanzio told her aunt, "I shall deem it a pleasure to accompany you if I may. With help I can get into the carriage and I can point out places of interest to you if I do not have to leave the vehicle."

"I don't wish to impose," Aunt Isobel said, looking pleased at the prospect.

"It will be a rare and excellent outing for me," the old Prince said with gallantry. "I shall enjoy seeing the city through your eyes."

So it was all arranged. Della took Henry aside for a moment to speak privately. She said, "Try and get this settled as soon as you can."

"You may be sure of that," he said. "What was your impression of Irma?"

"A strange, troubled girl."

"I agree," he said. "I'm sure whatever sinister thing has taken place, she knows a good deal about it."

"I agree," Della said. "That is why I want to know as soon as possible if she is my sister."

"Then we can get away from here," Henry said.

"Perhaps," she said. "I'd like to see some of the city and find out why we've been trailed and attacked."

"I'd just as soon not find out as long as the attacks end," Henry said bleakly.

Then he left for the city and she went upstairs. She did not see Irma again until after luncheon. Then the girl came to her and said, "It is siesta time. Everyone rests until about four in the afternoon. Then we resume our activities again. I'm going to do some shopping. If you came along it would give us a chance to know each other better."

"I'd like that," Della agreed.

"Very well," Irma said. "Be ready at four. I shall hire a carriage to take us to the street where I wish to see my cobbler. I have left favorite shoes with him and wish to pick them up."

A strange calm came over the old palace during the quiet two hours of the siesta. Prince Sanzio and Aunt Isobel were also leaving around four in the Prince's single carriage."

Della was dressed with straw hat to shield her from the afternoon sun and also a dainty parasol to use when riding in the carriage. Irma met her in the reception hall and they went out and almost immediately were able to get a carriage.

As they drove along they passed a small, informal piazza. Street vendors had their little carts set up and were crying out their wares. There was a fountain and an area for children to play. Small boys, brown as eels, splashed in the generous basin of the fountain while their little sisters looked on wistfully. Irma told her this fountain was the sole supply of water for the tangle of small streets around it.

They reached a short street called the Via Leonina. Irma paid the driver and they left the carriage and strolled along its narrow width, passing cycle shops, a printer's and a weaver of baskets, eventually reaching a dark little cubicle whose smell of leather mixed nicely with the aroma of the cobbler's pipe.

The old man bowed when he saw Irma. "I have your pumps ready, Princess," he said. And he went off into the back darkness of the shop to get them.

Irma said, "There is a fine little café a few doors down. We'll stop by for espresso."

"I'd like to," Della agreed.

The old man returned with a pair of elegant pumps and gave them to Irma to examine. "I think they will be satisfactory," he said. And then he let his ancient eyes wander to Della and a startled expression crossed his withered face. He croaked, "There are two of you!"

Della smiled, "I am her twin."

The old man continued to look astonished. "I did not know," he said. "Welcome to my poor shop, Princess."

Della said, "I'm afraid I'm not a princess. I grew up in England."

Irma broke in, "The shoes are fine. Don't try to understand the mystery of us. Just wrap the shoes up and I will pay you."

The old cobbler bowed again. "Certainly, Princess."

They left the shop with Irma carrying her parcel. She gave her a wry look and said, "You see the confusion our being together causes. Even the cobbler was upset!"

"I'm sorry to embarrass you," Della told her.

"The café is just ahead," Irma told her.

It was a small place and they sat at a sidewalk table. Irma ordered the espresso and while they were waiting for it, said, "Please excuse me for a few minutes. I wish to drop by the shop of the man who makes my handbags. And I don't wish to do a lot of explaining about who you are."

Della smiled. "Very well. I'll wait for you here."

"Watch my parcel," the other girl said. "I won't be long."

The other girl went off down the street and vanished in the host of shoppers who continually filled the area. She sat back to wait for the espresso and enjoy the sights. She saw that the parcel with the shoes was carefully placed under the table where it would be out of the way.

All at once she heard a voice exclaim, "Miss Standish!" It was the fat, jolly Father Anthony. He doffed his hat and came over to her, looking warm in his black priestly robes. "What a delightful coincidence!"

"I'm glad to see you again," she said. "I'm here waiting for my sister."

"May I sit a moment?" he asked, indicating the empty chair across the table from her.

"Of course," she said.

The priest mopped his bald pate. "It is always warm in Rome at this season."

"I find it pleasant after the cool fog at home," Della said.

"True," he agreed. "And so you have found your sister?"

She nodded. "I'm almost positive about it."

"No fear of her being an impostor?"

"I think there is small chance."

"I'm glad for you," the old priest said. "It is a good thing that you be restored to each other."

"She is not as happy about it as I am," Della said. "She claims she would prefer to remain here as Prince Sanzio's daughter."

"Indeed," Father Anthony said. "Well, that is something which must be settled among yourselves."

"Yes."

"About the other matter?" he said warily.

She stared at him. "You mean the stolen Madonna?"

"Yes," Father Anthony said, and leaned close to her over the table, "I do not wish what I'm about to say to be overheard."

"Oh?"

"I have made some inquiries at the Vatican museums since my return," the old priest said. "And I have found out what may be interesting news."

"Please go on," she begged him

In the same low voice, he continued, "A most despicable theft has taken place."

"Tell me," she urged him.

Fear showed on his oval face and he glanced around again to be certain there was no one among the passers-by listening to their talk. He said, "I talked with the director of the museums and I learned that the jeweled Madonna of St. Cecilia was removed from its vault for a check and cleaning. And while it was out for this purpose it suddenly vanished."

"Was it not carefully guarded?"

"Most carefully," Father Anthony said. "The good brother who was engaged in going over the treasure died at his desk, apparently of a heart attack. Only when it was noticed the Madonna was gone did they hold an autopsy to learn he had been poisoned."

"So someone killed him to get their hands on the Madonna?"

Father Anthony nodded. "And the scandal of it is that it had to be someone within the Church establishment who committed the crime. Outsiders are not engaged in the area from which the theft took place. One of our own did this terrible deed."

"So there is a stolen Madonna!"

"Yes. What happened to it, and why the thieves should link it with you, is a mystery."

She frowned. "Perhaps not as much as we think. Have you heard of a Count Barsini?"

The little priest looked scandalized. "Who has not? A sinful man!"

She said, "My sister seems to have become infatuated with him!"

"Most unfortunate," Father Anthony said.

"I agree. And I think he may know more about this stolen Madonna than most people guess. And it may be through him that I have been linked with the theft."

"Ah!" the priest said. "I begin to see."

"It is only a shot in the dark," she was quick to explain. "I may be wrong."

The espresso came and since Irma had still not returned she invited Father Anthony to join her. The priest seemed grateful.

"Very stimulating," he said, smacking his lips over the thick, black brew.

She said, "So we know there was a theft. Why did the Vatican not turn it over to the police?"

"They fear bad publicity," Father Anthony said. "For either a priest or a brother must be involved. And a murder has been committed. They believe that the conscience of the thief will force him finally to confess and return the Madonna to them."

"Do you think this is likely to happen?"

"Not if it has been stolen," Father Anthony said. "The Vatican does not know that. They think the Madonna must still be in the hands of the one who first took it."

"That's not likely," she said. "I'm sure it was sent to London and someone intercepted it on the way. Otherwise why would I be so harried?"

"I agree," Father Anthony said. "Perhaps you will be able to get more information from your sister, as you come to be better friends."

"It's possible," she said. "But not too likely. I think Barsini was mixed up in the theft and that she is his devoted slave. They claim he practices black magic."

"God forbid!" the fat priest said, crossing himself. "If so, she is surely lost."

"I hope to save her."

"You have my blessing, my child," Father Anthony said. "I shall come and visit you soon at the palace of Prince Sanzio."

"Please do, if you learn anything more," she begged him.

"Depend upon it," he said. "And you must keep your eyes and ears open. Who knows what you may discover?"

He thanked her for the espresso and left. She sat there thinking about what he'd told her. So there was no longer any suspicion that the business of the Madonna was mere fantasy. There was a real Madonna of St. Cecilia and it had been stolen from the Vatican. She was still speculating about this when Irma came swiftly up the street toward her.

Irma said, "I'm sorry I was so long. The handbag maker was out and I waited for him to return."

"It didn't matter," she said. "An old friend I met on the train coming here passed by and saw me. He stopped and talked a little. And I'm afraid he drank your espresso."

"It doesn't matter," the other girl said, seeming very tense. "I didn't really want it. Shall we go?"

They found a carriage to take them back to the palace. Prince Sanzio and Aunt Isobel had already returned and were resting before dinner. Henry was also back and waiting for them in the reception hall.

He said, "Where have you two been?"

"Shopping," Della told him. "How did you manage with the lawyers?"

Henry directed himself to Irma as he told her, "You may as well get ready to acknowledge Della as your sister. Everything seems to prove the case."

"I see," the other girl said quietly.

Henry told Della, "I shall need you and your aunt to identify certain items tomorrow. If that works out we must accept Irma's claim to be a Standish."

"I have no wish to be a Standish," Irma said stiffly, her parcel in hand. "But it seems I'm still only a puppet in all this."

"I'm sorry you feel that way," Henry said. "And I'll try to change your mind at dinner."

"I shall not be here for dinner," the other girl said. "I have other plans. I'm sorry." And she left them to go up the curving stairway.

Della and the young lawyer exchanged glances. And then she indicated that they should go outside where they could talk. They left the reception hall for the patio outside the living room which overlooked the gardens.

Della urgently told him, "I met Father Anthony today while Irma was off doing an errand."

"What did he have to say?"

"He confirmed there has been a valuable Madonna stolen. The Vatican is making no publicity about it since one of their own is partner to the crime. They hope he will repent and return the Madonna to them."

"Small chance!"

"I know," she said. "I'm sure it has fallen into other hands since then."

"And they think you know where it is!"

"They seemed to," she said. "All has been quiet since we arrived here."

Henry shook his head. "I don't like the way that girl behaves. She's very strange."

She smiled. "She's likely my sister. Stranger than me?"

"Definitely," he said with a thin smile in return. "I think she and that Count she's always running off to meet must know more than they should about the theft."

"I agree," Della said. "But I can't decide where she fits in."

"I say get out of Rome as soon as we have finished the legal business."

"Perhaps."

"Why stay here?" he worried. "It could be dangerous for you?"

"Sometimes a certain type of danger attracts me," she confessed.

"I might have known," he groaned.

Dinner was very much a repeat of the night before. Prince Sanzio was very apologetic about Irma's decision to go out. They enjoyed an excellent meal served as before by the tiny Guido. Then Prince Raphael came to join the party and was almost overfriendly with Henry.

They were all gathered in the living room when a message came for Prince Sanzio. He read it and exclaimed, "Botheration!"

Della asked, "What is it?"

"One of my lawyers wishes to settle a point with me. He is coming over here tonight." He glanced up at Henry from his wheelchair. "And he requests that you be on hand."

With his best professional cheerfulness, Henry said, "That will be no hardship since I'm already here."

"But no doubt you and Della had something planned?" the invalid said.

"No," she told him. "We'd discussed nothing."

Aunt Isobel said tartly from her armchair, "I know what I shall be doing. I'm weary from the heat. I'm going up to bed."

Prince Raphael turned to Della and said, "We may as well make the best of our time. Let me take you to one of our famous restaurants for a little."

She laughed, "I couldn't eat anything more."

"For drinks," he said. "Merely for drinks and to see the place and the people!"

Most generously Henry said, "Why not go, my dear? It will save you from a lot of dull lawyer's talk."

"Well, if you say so," she said, blushing.

Prince Raphael was at his most charming. "It is time you saw Rome at night," he told her. "And I'm the best guide possible."

Della was ready to believe him by the time he had taken her by carriage through romantic gas-lit streets. There was a fragrance in the air that spoke of unseen blooms and every so often a snatch of distant music caught her ears. They passed strolling couples obviously also caught up in the enchantment of the warm, moonlit night. Occasionally another carriage passed them. Finally they came to a main street and the carriage came to a halt.

Prince Raphael smiled at her as he helped her down to the street. "This is Grass Snake Street, the site of the fine Ristorante Pancrazio. It is located on the site of a long-vanished theater dating back to 55 B.C. No one should visit Rome without seeing it."

She found herself before an ugly archway with only dim gaslight to outline it. "Strange-looking place," she said.

He laughed. "The restaurant windows are lighted but the glass is opaque. Come along!" He took her by the arm.

They entered a dark tunnel to a level which he told her was fifteen feet below the ground. Inside, it was filled with people who seemed to be having a fine time. It gave no hint of being a cave. The decoration was excellent and the waiters moved about rapidly serving steaming, savory-smelling dishes. Raphael pointed out that several of the original columns still existed and were part of the stage.

When they were seated at one of the many tables, he asked her, "How do you like it?"

"I adore it," she said. "Where else but in Rome would you find such a place?"

"Signor Machhione, the proprietor, is a friend of mine," the Prince said. "I do not see him but I shall look for him after we order."

She said, "And this is truly on the site of an ancient ruin?"

"Definitely," Raphael said. "The restaurant is located on what was the proscenium and the stage of the theater. From here ran a famous arcade of one hundred huge columns. It was in one of the adjoining halls that the Senate met on the Ides of March and Caesar was struck down!"

Della was thrilled by this and by the general feeling of the place. A strolling violinist came by to play at their table and Raphael tipped the old musician generously when he finished. It was apparent that he was well known in the place.

Della was about to ask him another question when all at once a familiar figure came toward their table. Wearing an evening gown and a tiara, and smoking a cigarette, came the formidable Madame Guioni, looking as large and ugly as ever but showing a smile on her excessively made-up face.

"Dear Miss Standish!" Madame Guioni gushed, coming up to the table. "What a delightful surprise meeting you here."

"And for me!" Della agreed. And she introduced the Prince.

Madame Guioni appraised the Prince with unabashed interest. "What a charming young man!" she exclaimed. "A pity we have never met before."

"My loss," the mustached young Prince said with gallantry.

"Pray do not stand," she told him. But he continued to do so as she told Della, "I mean to look you up, my dear, and have that party I promised."

"There's no need," Della said. "But I would like to see you again."

"You shall," the big woman said. A grimace crossed her ugly, made-up face, and she said, "What a journey we had! That awful little priest and his cigar!"

Della smiled. "Strangely enough, I met him for a few minutes this afternoon."

"You did?" Madame Guioni raised her eyebrows. "Well, that is Rome! Did he have anything to say?"

"Very little," Della said with caution.

The woman turned her interest to Prince Raphael again, saying, "What a delightful young man you are. I regret we do not fraternize in the same social circles. Mine is an older set."

"But that is a mistake," Raphael told her, his eyes twinkling.

"Thank you, dear boy," Madame Guioni said, pleased by this compliment. "I shall ask you to my party for Miss Standish. Everyone wants to attend my parties! Everyone!"

"I'm sure of it," he said.

"We must meet again," Madame Guioni said. And in a confidential aside to Della, she said, "I dare not stay longer. I'm with a most charming man and he worries when we are together because of his jealous wife."

"I understand," Della said, smiling.

"Don't forget to drink your toasts in Guioni Brothers wine," Madame Guioni said gaily, and moved on back to another part of the restaurant where she was lost to their view.

Prince Raphael sat down. "That is a character! So that is your Madame Guioni?"

"Yes," she laughed. "She is usually not so friendly, but your good looks charmed her."

"I hope she does not make good her threat to put me on her party list," he said.

Della was amused. "She would consider she was doing you a favor."

"The sort of favor I must escape," he said with a wry look. "Let us get away from here before she decides to return."

"If you like," Della said.

They left the restaurant and returned to the carriage which the Prince had paid to wait for them. He said, "Now I shall take you to an enchanted place."

"Where?"

"The Forum by moonlight," he said, and leaned forward to give the driver instructions.

Once again they drove through the streets of what seemed to her an enchanted night city. They finally came to a halt and left the carriage waiting once more while the Prince guided her toward the ruins of the Forum.

They stood on a slight rise with the splendor of the famed ruins spread before them, the fragments of buildings and columns cast into silhouette by the moon's silver light. In the distance were the outlines of dark, tree-crested hills.

"Is it not magnificent?" he asked.

"Truly," she said in a taut whisper.

The handsome Prince turned to her and told her softly, "All Rome holds no sight more lovely than you!" And he took her in his arms and kissed her.

Again, caught unexpectedly, she found herself responding to him. And then her feeling of guilty enjoyment was caught short by her becoming aware they were not alone! Fear smote her as she saw a dark figure rise up behind the Prince and hit him on the head with something.

Chapter Nine

She saw the hand raised behind Raphael and felt his body slump as the blow hit him. She neither screamed nor hesitated, but as he fell before her she turned and ran down the. steep hill as fast as she could. She heard a man curse and another cry out but she neither halted nor turned. Instead she ran a zigzag path between patches of brush, attempting to escape the moonlight and disappear in the shadows.

She managed this very well. But they were still after her. Reaching a fragment of ancient wall, she bent down behind it. After a matter of seconds she saw two figures rush past her as they pursued her. She was breathing heavily and her side was hurt from the effort of her race.

As soon as they were past her, she retraced her steps. Her aim was to get back to Raphael and try to help him. And if she could not rouse him then at the least she would get back to the waiting carriage and alert the driver. But when she reached the bottom of the steep bank which led up to where the attack had taken place she heard the curses of the two men as they returned.

This meant a change of plan. She scurried along the bottom of the bank, frantically searching for somewhere to hide. Then she came to what seemed like the mouth of a cave with something draped over it. She made her way past the dirty cloth covering the entrance, to her surprise, found herself in a cave with a fire glowing at the far end. Over the fire was a pot suspended on sticks set in the ground. And in the pot there was boiling some sort of delicious-smelling stew. Presiding over the cooking, seated on his haunches, was a very old man. He glanced at her and she saw that he had one eye missing and his face was a mass of wrinkles.

She went nearer to him and apologized, "Please, I didn't mean to intrude."

The one-eyed man grinned at her to reveal gums without teeth. He seemed not to mind her presence at all.

She spoke in a low voice: "You do not understand, I know. But I mean you no harm and I will leave shortly!"

The ancient paid no attention to her. He was too occupied with stirring the stew. She was regaining her breath and not as panic-stricken as when she had stumbled into the cave.

"You are very kind," she said, and produced some Italian coins from her pocket and placed them on the ground close by him.

He snatched at them with emaciated hands and held them before him. Then he gabbled something she could not understand, grinned at her again, and stuffed them in the side pocket of his ragged jacket.

She said, "If you don't mind, I'll just remain here a little longer."

His back was to her and he seemed to be paying no further attention to her. She went to the opening of the cave and, holding back the cloth a little, peered out. The immediate area seemed to be deserted.

Her concern for Raphael's welfare out-weighed her good judgment. She was frantic to know what had happened to him. The attackers had taken their venom out on him but she was sure that it was because they had been after her. She gave a final glance at the old man crouched by the fire and then risked going out into the night once again.

There was an eerie stillness which bothered her almost as much as if she'd heard the sound of distant voices. She felt there was something unnatural about it. She advanced a few steps at a time, keeping crouched like an animal at bay. That was how she felt. The beauty of the ruins no longer meant anything. Now this was simply a place for her to hide.

The silence was broken by what was surely a footstep on the gravel. Then she heard an anguished low cry of: "Della! Della! Can you hear me!"

Only because she recognized the voice of Raphael did she reply: "Over here!"

A moment later the young Prince came stumbling to her out of the shadows. He took her in his arms. "Della! Della! I thought I had lost you!"

"And I was sure you were badly hurt!"

"Not their fault I wasn't," he said angrily.

"They came after me. I hid in a cave!"

Raphael said, "They've gone now. I heard them leave. I stayed on the ground playing possum. They thought I was still unconscious but the blow didn't hit me full on as they had intended."

"You are all right?"

"Yes," he said grimly. "Except for a good-sized bump at the back of my head."

"I'm sorry," Della said. "I'm sure they were after me."

"Why should they be?"

"Let us get back to the carriage and I'll tell you," she said.

He led her back through the darkness to the waiting carriage. Ironically, while all this had been taking place, the driver had fallen asleep in his seat. Raphael wakened him and told him to drive them back to the palace. Then he climbed into the carriage beside her.

"Now you will tell me all this mystery, why those two, whom I regard as common thieves, came to be after you?"

She said, "Did they take your wallet?"

"No," he said with a hint of surprise. "I hadn't thought of that."

"If they had been thieves, isn't that the first thing they would have done?"

"I'm not sure," he said cautiously. "Maybe they were too concerned about your escaping, perhaps to get help, to remain with me."

"But after they lost me they still didn't return to you," she pointed out.

"No. They didn't. So?"

"I say that proves my point. They were not ordinary thieves but the same men who have attacked me before."

"Attacked you? Why?"

"It's rather a long story," she said. "And it begins with the theft of a jeweled Madonna from the Vatican."

"Go on," he encouraged her.

She told him the entire story beginning with her being kidnapped in England. She finished by saying, "It is my belief that Count Barsini was behind the theft and conceived the idea of sending the Madonna to me to keep until later. But the messenger bringing it to me was murdered and the Madonna stolen. He refuses to believe this happened and assumes I'm lying and keeping the treasure for myself."

Prince Raphael looked stunned. "If this is true it means that Irma is mixed up in it all."

"She probably suggested that it be sent to me with a message asking me to hold it for her. It had just come out that she was supposedly my sister."

"Has she made any mention of it to you?"

"No. But I think she soon will."

"Why do you say that?"

"Because of her manner. I feel she also suspects that I may still have the Madonna."

"It all comes of her associating with that Barsini," the young Prince said despairingly. "He has taken her from me and mixed her up in all this evil business."

"He cannot have been in the theft alone," she said. "I talked with a priest, Father Anthony, whom I met on the train from Paris, and he claims it was done by some of the Vatican staff. That is why the Church officials have not turned the theft over to the police to investigate. They hope whoever committed the theft will repent and bring the Madonna back."

Raphael frowned. "It seems to me this should be reported to the police."

"How can we?" she asked. "If they approached the people at the Vatican museum they would likely deny the theft."

"In that case there is a problem."

She said, "Somehow I must establish that I did not ever receive any parcel from Italy. Perhaps they would not bother me if I convinced them."

"Who?"

"I wish I knew," she haid. "As I said, I suspect Barsini is the ringleader."

"The way to him is through Irma."

"I've thought of that," Della agreed. "I'm going to talk to her about meeting him tomorrow."

The handsome Prince took her hand in his and gave her a warning look. "If you do meet him, be cautious. I warn you he is a dangerous man. Especially where women are concerned."

"You let him meet Irma."

"A mistake for which I've paid heavily," the Prince sighed. "I doubt that Irma will ever marry me now."

"Perhaps you are giving up too easily."

"Perhaps," he said. "Or it may be that I no longer love her in the same way I did."

"Because of her turning to Barsini?"

He glanced at her. "That, and the fact I've met you."

She blushed. "Don't forget I'm engaged to Henry."

"Maybe that could change," Raphael said.

"I'm afraid that's unlikely," Della replied.

"I see," he said quietly and stared ahead of him in silence as the carriage rolled on in the night.

"Are we far from Prince Sanzio's palace?" she asked.

"Not now," he said. "I'm sorry our visit to the ruins turned out so badly."

"I enjoyed everything up until the moment we were attacked," she told him. "And we were fortunate to escape as easily as we did."

"What I took to be a simple case of robbery and assault you see as something else," he said. "I wonder which of us is right."

"I think I am," she said. "But I won't argue the point."

"Do you plan to tell them at the palace?"

She considered. "No. I think we might be wise to say nothing. It would only frighten Aunt Isobel and upset Henry and Prince Sanzio. And I would prefer that Irma didn't hear about it from us."

"You think the thugs will report to Barsini and she will know in that way?"

"It's possible," she said

"I shall be more careful in the future," Raphael promised. "There is so much of Rome I'd like to show you. But we must see that you are protected."

"Perhaps we'd be better off to do our sightseeing in daylight," she said with a rueful smile as the carriage brought them up before the entrance to the palace.

It seemed that everyone was in bed. The handsome Prince saw her safely inside, gave her a goodnight kiss on the back of her hand and left. She went on upstairs to her own room and quickly prepared for bed. She fell asleep almost at once, and though her rest was troubled with nightmares featuring swarthy, cruel-faced men coming after her, she slept until morning without waking.

Henry Clarkson came to join her for breakfast in the dining room. He kissed her on the temple and sat by her saying, "You were late getting home last night."

"I know," she said. "Everyone was in bed."

"I waited until midnight and then it seemed pointless," the young Englishman said.

She gave him a quick glance. "You knew I'd be all right."

"After what has been going on I didn't know anything of the sort," he said. "I think you might have tried to get back sooner."

"We went to the Forum to see the ruins by moonlight and spent some time in a restaurant on the way."

"I see," Henry said quietly.

She gave him a troubled smile. "You surely aren't jealous of my going out with Raphael?"

"He is a Prince and very charming," Henry said.

"He is also engaged to marry Irma."

"I understand there's now some question of that," Henry said meaningfully.

"Please!" she begged him. "It was an innocent night out."

He smiled ruefully. "I'm sure that it was. Sorry." But there was something in his tone that suggested he was merely saying this without fully believing it.

Guido came in and took their breakfast orders. And as they waited to be served Henry explained that she must come to the lawyer's offices along with Prince Sanzio and Irma for the final session of the claim to the estate by her sister.

Henry complained, "Irma has made all this doubly hard for us by insisting she doesn't want to be recognized as a Standish."

"I know," Della agreed.

"We have gone too far with it now to change course," he said. "There is no question in my mind. She is your missing sister and must be declared so."

Della said, "I'll do what I can to make her happy about it."

And she did. When the carriage came to take them all to the lawyer's office, she sat next to Irma and talked as pleasantly as she could. Irma looked pale and seemed distracted. She sat restlessly clasping and unclasping her hands in her lap. She had not arrived home until very late in the morning. Della heard Prince Sanzio reproving her for waking Guido in the small hours to open the door for her.

The offices of the law firm were much the same as one might have found in England. The two senior partners were gray-haired and grave in manner. Together with Henry they went over their findings, including letters, personal items and the final confession of the woman who had kidnapped Irma as a child and taken her to Italy.

Prince Sanzio had used his crutches to get from the carriage to the lawyer's office and seemed to be intrigued as he listened to the evidence in the case. Irma sat between Della and the old Prince, and kept staring at the hardwood floor of the office most of the time.

Henry Clarkson did the final summing up in his most professional manner, saying, "Since all doubts have been removed, I declare Irma Sanzio to be Irma Standish. I shall make a detailed report to my seniors when I return to London. In due time she will be given the full rights of her British citizenship and her share of the Standish estate." He paused and went over to shake Irma's hand. "May I congratulate you, Miss Standish."

Looking frightened, Irma shook hands with him and then burst into tears, her face pressed against her foster-father's chest. The old Prince consoled her, speaking in Italian, which he rarely did when he was in the company of English people. Perhaps, Della felt, he spoke in the tongue with which Irma had grown up in order to reassure her that she would always be his daughter as well.

Henry remained at the law office to complete a listing of documents while the old Prince, Irma and Della went back to the palace. Prince Sanzio, exhausted by the morning's effort, begged to be excused. Helped into his wheelchair, he went to his bedroom to rest. This left Della alone with her newly declared sister, which was exactly what she wanted.

Guido suggested, and the girls agreed, that they dine outdoors on the patio. The little man set up a table under the shade tree out there and served them a pleasant salad lunch.

Over the table Della told her sister, "I'm glad it is settled. Over with."

Still pale, Irma said, "I don't think I shall ever feel it over with. I cannot accustom myself to thinking I am an English girl."

Della smiled. "Being an Italian princess is much more glamorous."

"It is not that," Irma said. "It is that I wanted no change. I prefer to remain here with my father in Italy."

"You can do that if you like," Della said. "But you should at least visit England and see if you like it. You speak the language well enough."

"I look at you and see myself," Irma said. "I cannot believe that two people could be so much alike in appearance."

Della laughed. "It gives me an eerie feeling as well. But we are twins and we must get used to it."

Irma, lovely in a white dress, sat back in her wicker chair and said, "I have not been pleasant to you since your arrival."

"No need to apologize," Della said. "It is a sort of intrusion."

"You mean well," Irma said. "And it seems you truly are my sister. I hope we can also be friends."

"I hope so," Della said. "And you can do me a favor."

"What?"

"I wish to meet Count Barsini," Della said. "I have some questions to ask him. I know you and he are friends. You can take me to him."

Irma eyed her in a strange fashion, saying nothing for a moment. Then she told her, "By a strange coincidence he has spoken to me about you. In fact, expressed a desire to meet you."

Della leaned forward. "Then it should be easy. When will you take me to him?"

"When do you wish to go?"

"As soon as possible."

Irma shrugged. "This afternoon after siesta. I'm sure he will be at his villa. He is having a gathering tonight."

"A gathering?"

The other girl nodded. "Yes. Perhaps he'll decide to invite you."

"Do you mean a Satanist gathering?"

Irma said, "I'd rather you talked with the Count."

• • •

Della wore a lace and silk afternoon dress of pale blue and her straw hat and parasol were of the same delicate shade. She waited in the reception hall until Irma came down to join her. Irma wore a less elaborate dress of pink.

She gave Della a look and said, "I see you wish to catch Barsini's attention."

Embarrassed, Della said, "Not at all. I just wanted to make myself presentable."

"You have," Irma assured her with a small smile.

The carriage had been ordered and was waiting. They sat together talking more like sisters than in the past and Della began to hope she might at last be learning to communicate with her newfound sister.

Irma was clearly making an effort to be more friendly. She chatted about the places they drove past and had the carriage halt for a moment by the *Baracocia Piazza di Spagna*.

"So unusual!" Della said, studying the sunken stone boat, in the thick of traffic, and the flowers on the steps only a few feet away. Water fell from various tongues and spigots in the boat, whose stone was pleasantly corroded.

Irma said, "My tutor once told me it was built to commemorate a flood of the Tiber in 1595 when a barge went ashore on this spot. It is by the father of Bernini, his only conspicuous work in the city. He, my tutor said, happened to have been born in the year of the flood."

The carriage continued on in the warm late-afternoon sunshine until they reached the splendid villa of Count Barsini. It was in no way run down as was the palace of Prince Sanzio. The towering stone house suggested wealth and arrogance both outside and in. They were ushered in by a middle-aged male servant in livery and sent to wait in a living room of massive size with huge portraits lining its walls.

"Barsini lives well," Irma told her.

"That is easy to see," she said.

There was a smile on the other girl's face. "I'm interested in seeing his reaction when he meets you. I mean because your resemblance to me will startle him."

"He knows we are twins, doesn't he?"

"Yes," Irma said. "But I did not warn him how much we look alike."

The servant came for them, informing them coldly, "The Count will now receive you."

They followed the servant up a stairway and along a corridor to the rear of the house. There, in a room with a balcony overlooking the Tiber, was Count Barsini. He was seated at a desk with a glass by his hand when they came into the bright, high-ceilinged room.

He rose and came forward to greet them. Della was first struck by his height. He was at least six feet tall, if not more in a country where most people were short. His head was shaved bald but he had a short black beard. His eyes were strange, too bright and darting, as he glanced about. His face was oval and handsome in a menacing way.

He greeted Irma first. "My dear, I did not expect to see you until this evening. You should perhaps have remained at home to rest."

She said, "Della wished to meet you."

The strange eyes darted her way now and he smiled in a way that made her uneasy. He bowed and took her hand and kissed it. "I call it amazing!" he said. "I could be talking to Irma! You look exactly like her!"

Della said, "We are amused by it."

His eyes were fixed on her, appraising her, studying her physical details so that she felt almost naked before his arrogant scrutiny. "You have her body as well," he said softly.

Irma spoke up: "I want to see something about tonight. If you'll excuse me, I'll leave you two to become better acquainted. I'll be back shortly."

"Just as you like," Count Barsini said courteously. But she had an idea that Irma left because she knew it was what he would wish.

Della said, "You have a magnificent home."

"You have only seen a small part of it," Barsini said. "I also have a fine estate in the country." He pulled up a chair for her by the desk. "Do sit down?"

She moved past him to the French doors opening onto the balcony. At the doors she turned and said, "I'd rather go out here. The sun is going down and the sky and river are so lovely."

"As you say," the bald man said in friendly fashion. "What would you care to drink?"

"A gin and tonic perhaps."

Barsini clapped his hands and a servant appeared from behind a door at the rear of the room. He gave orders for drinks and then came out on the balcony to join her. He wore a white linen suit of finest cut, silk shirt with hard collar and a crimson tie with a pattern of tiny yellow dragons on it.

He said, "I could easily pretend I was standing here with Irma."

"We look alike," she said. "But we are quite different."

"Your British upbringing," he suggested. "The British are a cold lot."

"You think so?" They were standing by the balcony railing above the river. She gave him a challenging smile.

"It has been my experience," he said. "But you have more courage than Italian women."

"I wouldn't want to claim that," she said.

The servant brought their drinks. The Count handed her the gin and tonic and took his own from the tray. Sipping his drink, he studied her and said, "So you wished to know me?"

"Yes."

"Why?"

"Because I think you can help me."

Barsini stroked his short beard. "Why should I?"

"I hadn't thought of that yet."

"Well, we won't worry about it," he said. "Go on."

She looked at him straight in those bright, nervous eyes. "What do you know about the theft of the jeweled Madonna?"

He frowned. "Jeweled Madonna?"

She said, "You needn't pretend surprise for my benefit."

Barsini smiled slowly. "As I said, you Englishwomen are not afraid of anything."

"I'm afraid of being attacked," she said. "And I have been several times bacause some people wrongly think I have that stolen Madonna."

The bald man smiled on. "Suppose I tell you I know nothing of what you are saying?"

"I'll know you're a liar."

He winced. "So unladylike!"

"My English showing again," she said.

"But the English have great ladies," he told her. "No. I think it must be a family thing. Irma also has a great deal of spirit."

"What about the theft?"

Barsini sipped his drink and stared out across the river. He said, "Have you noticed that Rome is built along this ancient Tiber."

"Please let us keep to the subject!" Della insisted.

He gave her an amused look which was close to being contemptuous. He said, "You wish to play a game?"

"If finding out the truth about that theft is a game."

He glanced away again, sipping his drink. He said, "Did you ever hear of a man called Brizzi?"

"No."

"He is a master thief! Notorious, not only in Italy, but in all the world."

"What about him?" she asked.

Still not looking at her, but staring out at the river, he continued, "I have heard, and this is hearsay, that not too long ago Brizzi masterminded the theft of all his long career. With the aid of a renegade priest formerly employed by the Vatican, he managed to steal one of the great treaures of the Church, the Madonna of St. Cecilia."

"The jeweled Madonna?"

"Yes. There was some confusion after the theft and, unhappily for Brizzi, the Madonna fell into other hands. He is on the lookout for it and so are his henchmen. In fact, many people want it."

"Including you?"

He at last turned to her with a cold smile. "Why not?" She said, "Why do these criminals think I have it?"

"Do you?" he asked.

"Certainly not!"

"Then I cannot imagine why you have been bothered. These men are clever. You might call them supercriminals.

They make few mistakes. They must have some reason for thinking you know where the Madonna is."

"I know nothing about it," she said angrily. "And I wish you would let them know."

He shrugged. "I can deliver your message but I cannot promise to make them believe it."

"They must!"

"They are not all that agreeable," Barsini said. "And you are very young to die!"

She put aside any attempt at discretion and, facing him, accused, "I think you masterminded that theft! That there is no Brizzi! And that you gave the stolen Madonna to Irma to send to me in England. But your messenger was intercepted and I never received it. Now no one will believe me!"

"You accuse me of the theft?"

"Yes."

"That is a very serious accusation," the bald man said, touching his beard in his absentminded fashion. "But I will not hold it against you."

"How kind of you!"

He went on, "Have you discussed this remarkable view of the theft with Irma?"

"No. I have said nothing to her."

"Why not?"

"I believe you to be the brains behind the plot. Prince Raphael says my sister has not been herself since she came under your influence."

The tall man laughed lightly. "The Prince is such an innocent."

"Do you say that because he is decent?"

"No. I say it because he is stupid. And I warn you I have a total dislike for stupidity."

"You think me stupid as well?"

Barsini said, "You have to be to come here making such mad accusations!"

"I'm not sure they are so mad," Della told him firmly.

He smiled again. "Still, I like your spirit."

"Thank you."

"I will help you if I can."

"Thank you," she said. "I hoped you might."

"I will make inquiries in certain quarters," Barsini went on. "Perhaps I will find something of value for you."

"I will be grateful."

Barsini's eyes, with their mad brightness, fixed on her again and his gaze was so eerie it sent a chill down her spine. She found herself speculating if he might be a drug addict of some sort.

He said, "I will expect to be paid for helping you."

"I understood you are a very rich man."

"I will not expect payment in money," he said quietly. "But I shall expect your gratitude."

She said, "You will have it as long as the form it takes is not too personal."

"I have a gathering tonight," the bald man said. "Your sister will play an important role in it."

"Oh?"

"Yes," he said, staring at Della. "I would like you to be here. You might discover an entire new meaning to your life."

"I've never been interested in Satanism!"

"My version is rather different from most," he assured her. "I have found great beauty in the worship of Satan. And what better spot to indulge in his worship than here in Rome, the seat of the cult founded by his archenemy."

She turned her back on him. "It does not interest me."

"I have my price," he said. "If I'm to look into the Madonna theft."

"Do something for me," she begged him.

"My condition stands."

"That I must be at you gathering?"

"Yes. It will do you good to see another side of this Holy City."

"I'm sure it is another side."

"Also, you ought to be especially interested. Your sister is playing a big role in tonight's proceedings."

"Oh?"

"Another reason for you to join us," he urged her.

She turned to give him a searching look. "I will in no way have to take part?"

"In no way," he assured her. "You will be merely an onlooker."

"And you will try to get some word about the Madonna?"

"I have said I would," he assured her.

"Very well," she agreed, feeling at the same moment that she was making a major mistake. "I will come."

The bald man looked pleased. "Excellent! It will be the experience of your life! We shall discuss it afterward."

Della was about to make a reply when her twin sister came out onto the balcony to join them. There was a smile on her pale face. She said, "Well, you two look as if you'd managed to get along splendidly."

Barsini chuckled and stroked his beard. "I had to keep telling myself I was not with you."

Irma said, "I wondered what you'd think about us."

"I'm delighted," the bald man said. "To think there are two beauties such as you!"

Della told her sister, "The Count has persuaded me to come to the gathering tonight."

A passing shadow of concern crossed her sister's face. She gave the Count a glance. "Do you think she will enjoy it?"

He towered above them as he said, "I'm sure she will find it educational."

"I see," Irma said, at once more subdued.

She remained in that mood for much of the remaining conversation on the balcony. Then it was time for them to leave and the Count escorted them all the way down to their carriage.

He helped them into the vehicle and for a moment at Della's side. He said, "I did not tell you. The theme of our gathering tonight is a variation on the sacrifice of the Vestal Virgins."

Then with another of his enigmatic smiles he stood back for them to drive away. He waved as they were driven up the hilly, cobblestoned street leading from the villa. Della was startled by this final statement on his part.

She turned to her sister. "What does he mean?"

Irma grimaced. "It is his idea of a joke."

"There was some meaning behind it," she insisted. "Why not tell me?"

Irma said, "He has devised a ritual. You will see it. I will be part of it and you may not approve. It will be like seeing yourself involved."

"I am attending only as an onlooker."

Irma smiled at her grimly. "That was my role at first."

"Tell me about the ceremony."

"I cannot," she said. "We are bound to secrecy. But I will tell you about the original Vestal Virgins. The sect was suppressed in A.D. 394 after having flourished for eleven centuries. The temple virgins were chosen from among the women of the best families, and they were allowed to return to ordinary life after thirty years if they wished. If in the time they were dedicated to the temple they had intercourse with a man, it was termed incest. The punishment for it was being buried alive."

"Not a pretty fable," Della said.

"The woman was taken to the place of execution in a cart. Then she was dragged down stairs leading to a crypt but no further. It was not to be said that a Vestal Virgin died by force or starvation. Food to last for days was placed in the tomb. The condemned woman walked down the stairs, then they were quickly pulled up after her. Then the masons quickly wall up the door."

"Horrible!" Della said. "I hope Barsini treats his Vestal Virgins in a different manner."

"You may be sure of that," Irma said with a bitter smile. "But in the end I wonder if what happens doesn't amount to almost the same thing."

Della said, "And you are going to be part of this?"

"Yes."

"I wish you wouldn't!"

Irma shook her head. "Too late now! I have made my vows. I'm one of the sisterhood! I cannot disobey!"

Della stared at the other girl with concern. "What are you saying?"

Irma's mood seemed to change quickly. She said, "You must not pay attention to my morbidity. I've been trying to frighten you."

"You managed very well."

"Forgive me," her sister said. "I have these spells of depression. You will grow to expect them from me. And if you do not wish to come tonight there is no need for you to be there."

"On the contrary," she said. "I must be there."

"Then you will be responsible for whatever you see that may upset you."

The carriage had reached the door of the Palazzo Sanzio. Della had no time left to question her sister further. But these last solemn words from her, together with the eerie account of the Vestal Virgins left her with an eerie feeling about the night ahead.

Chapter Ten

Shortly before dinner the weather changed. The sky became so dark that the midget Guido went hurriedly about the old palace lighting candles. Thunder rumbled in the distance and there were several great showers of rain. To Della, dressing in her room, it seemed that the abrupt change in the weather might be a premonition of the dark journey she was planning that night.

She was haunted by the vision of the bald Count Barsini with his short, black beard and cruel smile. And she worried that she might have made a mistake in agreeing to go to the Satanist gathering at his villa. But it was too late to back out now. She hoped that by going along with Barsini, he might reveal the truth about the missing Madonna. It was her belief that he was the central figure in the theft despite his reference to a superthief known as Brizzi.

Irma also worried her. Her newly found sister seemed in a tense, troubled state. And tonight, by her own admission, she was taking part in the Black Magic ritual. Della was sickened by this decadence but she felt she must be part of it if she were to rescue Irma from Barsini—and put an end to the situation that made Della herself the target of the thugs seeking the missing Madonna.

She had chosen a black gown for this evening, thinking it might be appropriate. It was low-cut and revealed her shoulders and the fullness of her breasts. She considered it her most daring dress.

There was a knock on her door and she rose from her dressing table to open it. Henry Clarkson, already in white tie and tails for dinner, came in and gave her an admiring look.

He said, "You must really be trying to turn Prince Raphael's head tonight!"

She felt her cheeks crimson. "You are all wrong."

He was smiling. "That is a most enticing gown."

"Thank you," she said. "I've promised to visit Count Barsini's villa tonight with Irma. He is entertaining a few friends and he has invited us. I want to look my most sophisticated."

Henry's pleasant face creased. "You're going to Barsini's?"

"Yes. Shortly after dinner. Prince Sanzio is going to be playing chess With Prince Raphael. You can watch the game."

The young lawyer looked shocked. "You mean Prince Raphael and I are not invited to Barsini's?"

"I'm afraid not."

"Then you musn't go," he said.

Della showed surprise. "Why do you say that?"

"You know Barsini's reputation! He's infamous!"

"I'm going with Irma. I'll be perfectly safe."

Henry began to pace back and forth. "I hardly think so. He already has her under his influence. I don't want you to be next."

"Never fear," she said. "I met Count Barsini this afternoon and I put my cards on the table. I told him I was almost sure he was behind the Madonna theft and I wanted him to call off the thugs who've been hounding me."

"What did he say?"

"He promised to make inquiries. He pretended to know little about it and blamed a thief known as Brizzi, along with some renegade priest."

Henry looked thoughtful. "That sort of fits in with what Father Anthony told you. He said that whoever committed the crime had help from the inside."

"Yes. That is why I'm hopeful. So I agreed to attend Barsini's gathering tonight and he, in turn, said he'd try to have some information for me."

"I don't like any of it!" Henry said.

Della went to him and patted him on the lapel of his evening coat. Smiling up at him, she said, "You mustn't try to interfere with this. It is our best chance to clear up this mystery."

He sighed. "I shall worry about you until you are safely back. And I give you permission to go on the condition you promise to leave Rome as soon as possible."

"Leave Rome?"

"Yes," he said. "Everything is settled as far as Irma is concerned. It is time for us to go back to London. She can come with us if she wishes; if she doesn't want to leave, let her remain here with the old Prince."

"We can talk about it tomorrow," she promised.

Her promise placated him enough to agree to her going to Barsini's. Though had he guessed there was to be a Satanist meeting, she was sure he would have refused to allow it. Irma was quiet and nervous in manner. She was wearing a chic gown in dark green. Prince Raphael had arrived and did most of the talking at the dinner table.

Later the young Prince took her aside and asked, "Is it true you are going to Barsini's tonight with Irma?"

"Yes."

"Why? You know he is notorious."

She said, "I'm starting a campaign to get Irma away from him."

The handsome dark man said, "Barsini is clever. Be sure it doesn't wind up with you joining Irma as his slave."

"No chance."

Raphael said, "Henry is very upset about your plan. And I also am worried."

"Please don't say anything more about it," she said. "Get Prince Sanzio busy with the chess match so he doesn't note our leaving."

"After last night I dislike seeing you leave here after darkness," Raphael said. "And especially on a dark, wet night such as this. A good night for criminals."

"We shall take the carriage straight to Barsini's villa," she promised.

They waited until the chess match began and then quietly went out to the waiting carriage. The old coachman had brought out the closed vehicle because of the rain. Guido was there to open the carriage door and let them in.

As the carriage moved through the rainy blackness of the streets Irma gave her a worried glance. She said, "I feel responsible for your getting into this. You can still return to the palace if you like."

"No!"

"Do you realize what you are getting into?"

"I'm not afraid," Della told her.

"You may feel differently later," was Irma's comment. "If you do, don't be afraid to run. Not even at the last moment."

"I intend to remain," she said. "I want to see your role in the gathering."

Irma looked out the window into the darkness. "I don't want to think about it."

They rode on in silence with Della wondering what was on the other girl's mind. Surely Irma was no stranger to these Satanist meetings. She had become one of them. And Count Barsini had claimed that she would play a leading role in the ritual on this occasion. It must be that an ordeal was scheduled, for Irma was clearly in a state of fear.

Torchlights flanked the entrance to the Barsini villa and other carriages were arriving. Della stared out as some of the passengers in the vehicles ahead descended and made their way into the house. They seemed to be mostly near her own and Irma's age. Evidently Count Barsini wished to be Satan's apostle to a flock much younger than himself.

A servant opened the door of their carriage and helped them to the sidewalk. Then they went on into the softly lit reception hall. Count Barsini was there to greet his visitors; he wore a long, flowing black robe embellished down the front with white crocheted figures of the Black Magic symbols.

He kissed Irma and told her, "You will go to the ritual room at once."

Irma nodded and went on. Now he smiled in his menacing fashion as he bowed over Della's hand and kissed it. He said, "You shall wait down here for a little. Ill have you brought to the ritual room when we are ready for you."

"It is well organized," she said.

"These things must be done correctly," the bland Barsini told her. "Wait over there with Brother Louis."

"Very well," she said, and left the reception line to join a sickly-looking young man in the black cassock of a monk. He was standing in a sort of alcove room which contained only a couple of chairs and a suit of ancient armor.

The balding man showed shock when she joined him. "What are you doing here, Irma? You should be preparing."

She smiled. "I'm not Irma but her twin sister. My name is Della."

Brother Louis looked suspicious. "This is not some trick of Barsini's? I've had my fill of his black jokes!"

"No," she said. "The Count sent me here to wait with you. Irma has already gone upstairs."

"You two look remarkably alike."

"I know," she said.

Brother Louis asked, "Are you converted?"

"No. This is my first time here."

The man in the cassock showed a strange gleam in his watery blue eyes. "The mystery will be revealed to you. It is the only way!"

"I take it you are a convert," Della said.

"I am," he said proudly. "I was once a brother in the Church. But I'm free of all that now. The Devil and God are one and the same. Opposite sides of one coin. What Godly folk think evil is actually good and vice versa."

She said, "So you have left the Church?"

"Yes," Brother Louis said. "I have crosses tattooed on the soles of my feet so I can continually tread on the symbol of Christianity."

Della was disgusted by his words and it struck her the man was slightly mad. At the same time she recalled that a member of the Vatican Museum had been mixed up as inside accomplice in the theft of the Madonna.

Taking a wild chance, she asked him, "Were you ever employed in the Vatican?"

Brother Louis showed pride. "I was a specialist in illuminated manuscripts. I worked in several of the museums within the Vatican."

Her eyes met the watery blue ones of Brother Louis as she asked, "What do you know about the stolen Madonna of St. Cecilia?"

She might just as well have struck him across the face, so strong was his reaction. His thin face went a bit more pale and he asked, "How do you know about that?"

She forced herself to smile calmly and say, "As a friend of Barsini's I know many things."

Brother Louis clenched his fists. "He didn't tell you to bait me? To try and find out if I knew anything?"

"Why do you ask that?"

"I know nothing about where it is!" Brother Louis said angrily. "You can tell him that! I wish I did!"

"I see," she said. Then looking around, she saw that they were alone. The Count and his other guests had vanished. She asked the man in the cassock, "Where have they all gone?"

"To the Black Mass," he said, his face becoming more animated at the thought. "Tonight is a special celebration! Irma is to become a priestess of our group."

"Oh?"

Brother Louis nodded eagerly. "We have a half-dozen leaders. One day I shall become a leader."

"What is your role now?"

"I'm a sort of watchman," he said. "I remain here while the ceremony is going on. And I'm also responsible for guiding in neophytes like you."

She recalled Irma's advice that she might flee at any time if she changed her mind. For a moment she was on the verge of doing exactly that. But if she did she knew she would be deserting her sister and losing perhaps the only hope she had of penetrating the Madonna mystery.

She asked, "Where is the ritual room?"

He smiled bleakly. "I cannot tell you that. When the time comes I will take you there."

Della waited with the strange Brother Louis. There was an uneasy silence between them. She thought about the plight she was in and realized she had always thought of Rome as the great center of Christianity. But she'd forgotten its long dark history. Centuries of paganism were also part of the city's background. It was not so strange that decadent secret societies should still operate within sight of St. Peter's.

A strong odor of incense filled the air now. It seemed to come from somewhere in the cellars of the villa. She found it not unpleasant but it began to make her head a trifle dizzy.

She asked Brother Louis, "What is that smell?"

"Incense," he affirmed. "Part of the ritual." He smiled knowingly. It has a special quality."

"In what way?"

"It releases the emotions," Brother Louis said, his pale face glowing now. "Barsini discovered it and uses it for all our gatherings."

Della made no reply but she began to see how wily this Count Barsini was. He had hit upon some drug which when used as incense had a lifting, aphrodisiac influence on his followers. You could be sure he would use it to help him enslave them.

She began to worry since she could not help breathing in some of it. She still retained all her senses but she was experiencing an odd, light feeling. A feeling of relaxed well-being which she knew was not normal under the circumstances.

As she was thinking all this a woman in a dark brown robe with an attached cowl came in through a doorway of the reception hall. Keeping her cowl pulled over her head so that her face was hidden, the woman corssed over to Brother Louis and whispered something to him. Brother Louis nodded and then the woman gave her a furtive glance before vanishing through the doorway.

Brother Louis eyed her expectantly. "It is time!"

"So?"

He went to a closet and brought out a dark robe much like that of the woman who had just left. He said, "There is a dressing room over there." He pointed to the reception hall. "Strip your clothes and put on this robe."

Alarmed, she said, "Must I?"

"If you wish to join the gathering."

She took the robe. "Why not let me slip it on over my own clothing. No one need know."

"That is impossible!" Brother Louis said stonily. "I have been ordered to take you to the gathering. You must lose no time. Strip!"

Almost ready to run for freedom again, she turned and crossed to the door of what he said was a dressing room. It turned out that it was. Hooks had been installed all along four sides of the room and clothing hung from the hooks. She was not alone in being told to strip naked before donning the robe of the cult. Relaxed by the drug she'd inhaled, she began to strip, a thing she might not have done otherwise. She carefully hung her things on a hook and hastily donned the robe. She returned to Brother Louis in her bare feet, her shoes and stockings left behind with her other clothing.

She said, "I am ready."

He eyed her hungrily, noticing her bare feet. He asked, "You are fully stripped beneath the robe?"

"Even to my shoes."

He nodded. "Now I must blindfold you."

"Why?"

"It is the rule," he said firmly. And he produced a dark band of cloth and tied it about her eyes so that she could not see anything.

"What now?" she asked.

"Come along," he said, taking her arm. "I shall guide you."

He led her across the reception hall and then down a winding stone stairway which seemed to twist about for an interminable time. And as she descended the smell of the incense grew stronger. She found herself coughing from its sweet fumes. Then they reached a level area, and in the distance she heard a monotonous chanting of male and female voices.

The noise grew louder and she felt the chanting worshippers must be all around her. All at once Brother Louis removed the blindfold and she saw that she was truly in the middle of a room filled with the Devil's followers. The walls were painted with views of Satan ascendant and other scenes so erotic she couldn't let her eyes remain on them.

All about her were the cowled heads of the brown-robed men and women of the cult. On a raised stage a few yards before her stood High Priest Barsini in a red robe! Beside him sat a black velvet altar with black candles burning. The walls of the stage bore murals of men and women in every sort of erotic position.

The altar's front was decorated with the image of a goat trampling on a crucifix. Barsini smiled down at the group and she was almost sure he was directing the smile solely at her.

Now two members of the cult brought a naked, young woman from the side of the stage. The nude girl was Irma! Della felt her cheeks burn at the sight of her flesh and blood naked before this assemblage of males and females. It seemed that Irma was more deeply drugged than anyone else, for she moved as if in a trance and her lovely face and eyes were blank of expression.

The two men turned the naked Irma over to the red-robed Count Barsini. He led her gently to the altar and saw her stretched out on it. Then he gave the group a signal and they began to sing a mournful dirge in some weird tongue. A gibberish of a mass was said by Barsini, his face and hands uplifted over the outstretched nude body of Irma on the altar.

Black hosts were passed to be eaten and Barsini placed one between Irma's breasts and spilled wine over her body from a silver chalice. As he finished this he removed his robe to reveal his own naked figure and shocked Della by placing his body over that of the prostrate Irma to indulge in intercourse with her on the altar! The sight of this ignited the worshippers. On all sides the men and women flung off their robes and naked bodies of males and females mingled in a bare-faced sexual exhibition!

Della stood there, her hands pressed to her temples and terror on her lovely face, as the naked couples dropped to the floor on all sides of her to twist and squirm in the mass fornication. Blindly she turned and started toward the doorway at the rear, picking her way amid the moaning pairs, until suddenly she was confronted by a young blond giant!

The face of the young man showed a lascivious grin as he confronted her in his total nudity. His great chest heaved with excitement and he reached out with his large hands and in a single motion tore the robe from her.

"Lovely!" he said, staring at her unashamedly.

She crossed her hands over her breasts and begged him, "Let me go!"

His answer was to laugh wildly and catch her and pick her up in his arms as if she were a child. He carried her sobbing and screaming to another, smaller room which was deserted. She clawed at him and pounded him with her fists, but none of it seemed to bother him. He threw her on the hard floor and as she crouched there panting, he slowly descended upon her.

The giant's lips pressed to hers, his hands pinned her to the floor, and as he painfully penetrated her she passed out. When she opened her eyes again he had vanished and she lay there aching and miserable from her battle with him.

She struggled to a sitting position and looked for something to protect herself but could find nothing. With a moan she got to her feet, feeling soiled and abused. She staggered to the doorway only to be met by Barsini, wearing his red robe again. He carried a black robe which he carefully draped over her.

She gasped, "You—you animal!"

"Easy," he said. "I could give you back to some of those hungry males out there!"

"You tricked me into coming here! Told me it would be safe!"

He smiled. "No harm has come to you."

"I was raped by that giant!" she sobbed.

"Some women would not complain," Barsini told her. "I took you to be more sophisticated!"

Tears streaming down her cheeks, she said, "I'm not used to being defiled! Nor did I enjoy watching you violate my sister before all those people!"

"Irma knew what was going to happen," he said. "It is part of our ritual."

"Your signal for them to break into an orgy!" she exclaimed.

The bald man chuckled. "But orgies always accompany Satanist gatherings. You could not be so much a child as not to expect that."

She wanted to tell him how throughly rotten she believed him, but realized that any protection she might get must come from him. He had threatened to turn her over to the depraved, drug-sodden males in the next room and he had meant it. So she must be discreet for the moment.

Pushing back her hair from her face, she said, "I want to leave here at once and I intend to take Irma with me."

"I'm sorry, that is not possible," he said urbanely.

"Why not?"

"She has left with someone else. A young noble who took a great fancy to her. As a priestess she is free to bestow her favors on any member of our group. I would imagine they are back at his house by now, enjoying each other!"

She eyed him with suspicion. "You could be lying to me."

"I'm not," he promised. "She left with him only a few minutes ago. Before I came to you. It was she who asked that I look after you."

"If any harm comes to her you will pay for it," Della warned him.

"I'm not worried about that at all," the Count said genially. "I expect you'd like to dress."

"I would," she said grimly.

"It would be wise to leave this area of the villa. Come with me to my private apartment. You can wash up there and dress. Then we can talk."

"No!" she said, drawing back from him.

He spread his hands in a plea to be heard. "Why be more difficult than you need to be? You cannot stay down here. These revels will go on until dawn!"

"Sexual orgies!" she said with disgust.

"Whatever you wish to call them," he said, dismissing her scorn. "I'm trying to carry out Irma's wish to protect you."

"A little late," she reminded him.

"Why harp on it? You suffered no serious physical harm," Barsini said. "Now be sensible, come along with me!"

She knew that she truly had no other choice. So she let him escort her back up the winding stairs to the ground floor. Then they picked up her clothing from the dressing room and continued on to his private apartment. It was away from the rest of the house. The sound of the revels could no longer be heard.

She washed and dressed in the privacy of the small antechamber adjoining the Count's bedroom. When she came out fully dressed she found that he had also changed back into his linen suit.

He smiled at her. "I still marvel at your resemblance to Irma. I feel that I have already possessed you!"

She reddened at this reference to his rape of her look-alike and said, "Please see me home safely."

"I will," the Count said. "But first we have some things to discuss over a drink."

"I have nothing to say to you," she told him.

"I think you have," he said calmly. "There was the matter of the Madonna. Remember?"

In the midst of her humiliation she had completely forgotten about the stolen Madonna. Now it all came rushing back to her. She said, "All right, I will remain. But only for a few moments."

"As you will," he said and, as she waited, he brought her a martini along with a large drink for himself. He sat opposite the divan on which she'd seated herself and smiled at her speculatively.

"You interest me greatly," he confided.

"Forget the pleasantries," she rebuked him. "We can never be friends!"

His laugh was knowing. "Irma once said almost the very same words to me."

"I am not Irma, however much I may look like her."

His eyes ravaged her in the smart, low-cut black gown. "Very well," he said. "Let us go on to other things."

"What about the Madonna?" she demanded.

He shrugged. "Give me a moment, I beg you. Since we talked this afternoon I have been in touch with Brizzi."

"I do not believe there is such a person!"

"You think I'm making him up?"

"Yes!"

"You are extremely difficult to convince," he sighed. He got up and went over to his desk and pulled out a drawer. From the drawer he took a folded newspaper and brought it to her. "Read for yourself!"

She took the paper from him and saw the headline: *Brizzi Strikes Again!*

Standing over her, he said, "That story is only a few months old. You see the date on the paper."

Again he was right. She noted the date and putting the newspaper to one side, told him, "All right! So there is a Brizzi! That does not mean he stole the Madonna. I say you engineered that!"

"I wish I had," Barsini said, his smile vanishing. "It would be easier for you to deal with."

She frowned. "Meaning?"

"Meaning that your problem is Brizzi! He is the one convinced that you have the jeweled Madonna!"

"I have never even seen it!"

"Yet you know all about it," he said sharply.

"Because of the attacks on me both here and in England. It began just after I learned that a letter had been found naming Irma as my sister."

Count Barsini nodded. "It is Brizzi's firm belief that the Madonna which was stolen from him fell into Irma's hands and she shipped it to you!"

"Irma will tell a different story! And you know it! You probably have the Madonna!"

The tall, bald man eyed her scornfully. "If I had the treasure do you think I'd be wasting time here talking with you?"

"You cannot believe I have it!" she protested.

"Your protests have the ring of sincerity," he was willing to admit.

"Well, then?"

"Perhaps you have the Madonna without being aware of it."

"How could that be?"

"It may have been delivered to you without your discovering it, hidden in something else."

She frowned. "I received nothing from Rome."

"I'm sorry," he said. "There are those who believe you did."

"That is all you have to tell me?"

"I greatly fear that is true," he said with some disdain. "You will have to battle this for yourself."

She rose, feeling sick and weary. "What a fool I have been!"

"On the contrary," Barsini said. "You may be the most exquisite liar of all. I wish you well if you do have the Madonna. But I warn you, if it is in your possession you would be much wiser to hand it over to me!"

"Let me go!" she cried angrily.

He nodded. "As you say. I will call you a carriage." He summoned a servant and ordered a carriage for her. And a few minutes later he saw her down to it and helped her inside.

She leaned out. "Are you not coming with me?"

"Why should I?" he asked.

"To protect me!"

He smiled coldly. "The driver knows the address!" And he stepped back and signaled the driver to start.

The carriage started with a jolt and she had a final glimpse of the bald, bearded man standing by one of the torches flaring outside his villa. His saturnine features were highlighted in the flare's amber glow. She began to tremble and couldn't stop. She felt nauseated.

How could she have thought herself clever enough to match wits with the evil Count? There was no question that Henry Clarkson had been right in warning her not to go to his party. Now she had been shamed physically and spiritually!

Irma had become so debased under the Count's careful tutelage that after having been raped in public by the evil Barsini, she had gone off for another orgy with some equally decadent man! She suspected that Irma was being kept filled with dangerous, mind-muddling drugs, so that she did Barsini's bidding without question.

Worst of all, her efforts to find out more about the stolen Madonna had been successful in the wrong way. She now knew more about its theft, but she was still under suspicion of having the stolen treasure.

Irma was supposedly responsible for this. But she felt Irma had spread the false story under the Count's instructions and for his benefit. Perhaps to give him time to dispose of the jeweled loot. While the superthief Brizzi and his thugs were after her trying to get the Madonna back, it was likely in the hands of Barsini, who hoped to dispose of it for the best possible price. It would not be an easy item to be rid of, so likely it would be broken up and the jewels sold singly.

It was very late when the carriage let her out at the palace of Prince Sanzio. She was glad in one way, since it meant she would not have to face the others until the morning. That would be soon enough!

She rang the bell at the entrance door and after a long while the door was opened by a sleepy Guido. The midget showed a frown on his small, wrinkled face.

"You are very late, Miss Standish," he observed in a tart voice.

"I'm sorry," she said. "I was delayed." And as he closed the door and stood there in his robe, she asked, "Has the Princess Irma returned?"

"No," the little man said peevishly. "I expect she will be even later. I get little sleep on nights like this!"

"I know," she said. "Do forgive me." And she went on up to her own room.

She hesitated at her door. In the hope that Irma might have come home earlier without the midget being aware of it, she decided to check her sister's room. She made her way quietly down the hall and finally reached Irma's door. She tapped on it lightly and, receiving no answer, tried the door handle.

She opened the door and stepped inside cautiously. A candle burned on the dressing table and she saw that the bed had not been slept in. So Guido had been right. Her sister had not yet come home; perhaps she would remain with the young man all night!

Then something caught her eye. Another candle burning at the opposite end of the room, not far from the bed. It was burning before a carved figure of the Madonna set in a round shelf in the wall. The candle was unusual, set in a giant glass bowl almost two feet wide and three quarters filled with green wax. The candle likely burned day and night without interruption. When the wax was burned down it could easily be refilled.

The sight of this Christian shrine in her sister's room made her eyes fill with tears. It proved that before Irma had been twisted and dragged down by the evil Barsini and his group, she had been a good young woman. Even now, in her degradation, she had not made any attempt to do away with this link to her Christian upbringing.

Della left the room filled with a great sadness. She wished she had somehow managed to get to Irma and saved her from the final disgrace of this evening. Now Irma would know she had witnessed it all. Indeed, without wanting to, she had herself been part of the orgy. Memory of the cruel giant who had raped her made her shudder involuntarily. She was making her way back to her own room when suddenly she knew she was not alone. She heard stealthy footsteps behind her.

Swinging around quickly, she saw the frightened figure of her Aunt Isobel, and gasped, "It is you!"

"Yes!" her aunt snapped. "And may I ask what you are doing roving about the palace at this hour?"

"I went to Irma's room," she said.

"Why?"

"I wanted to talk to her," she said unhappily.

Her aunt frowned. "Didn't you two go off to that dreadful Count Barsini's together?"

"Yes."

"Then where is she now?"

"We were parted during the evening. She went somewhere else. She's not home yet."

"And you have only just come in!" her aunt declared. "I was wakened when Guido let you in."

"Please go back to your room," she begged her aunt.

"What respectable young woman would stay out until this hour?" Aunt Isobel wanted to know.

"I'll explain tomorrow."

"Everyone was upset by you two girls sneaking away as you did," the older woman said. "Prince Sanzio was badly worried. And Prince Raphael spoke of going to find you."

"He didn't," she said bitterly.

"As for Henry," her aunt went on, "he was more upset than all the rest of us together. He kept promising that we would begin packing tomorrow and leave for Paris as soon as he can make bookings on the express."

Avoiding looking directly at Aunt Isobel, she said, "Do go back to bed!"

"You look ill!" her aunt worried. "Is there anything I can do?"

"Just let me alone!" she said with a tiny groan and she ran into her room and shut the door.

She sobbed quietly as she prepared for bed, feeling extremely sorry for herself yet knowing it would do no good. In the morning she would have to face the rage of her fiancé and the questions of the others. No doubt Raphael had guessed they'd gone to some sort of orgy and that was why he had been so uneasy. But he had not dared brave Barsini's wrath to come interrupt the gathering and rescue them!

But Irma probably hadn't wanted to be rescued. Nor had she until she'd come to grief. Now she could only hope it would somehow turn out all right. She would not argue with Henry if he wished them to return to England. But she would surely insist that he bring Irma along. For one thing, she wanted to try and save this sister whom she'd so recently found. In a strange way she had come to love her. Even though they had managed to have little time together, the pull of blood ties was strong. She wanted Irma to be taken from this evil place and recover at home in London.

Also, the business of the stolen Madonna had not been settled. Irma might tell the truth about that once Della had a chance to express her warm feelings for her. Surely her sister would turn on Barsini and tell the truth of the Madonna theft.

Della was still convinced that Barsini had stolen the Madonna from the original thief, Brizzi, and his henchman, the renegade priest. Somehow it had reached Barsini's hands and he'd pretended to pass it on to Irma.

But how had Barsini managed to get the Madonna? All at once it hit her. Brother Louis! The follower of Barsini who had turned from the Church and his position in one of the Vatican museums! Brother Louis must have been the partner of Brizzi in the original theft and then he had gotten the Madonna away from Brizzi and given it to Barsini! Why not? Barsini was his new shepherd! Della fell asleep speculating on all these things.

Chapter Eleven

Irma had been missing for almost two days!

The palace was in a state of turmoil as a result of Della's lovely twin not returning. No one had seen her since the evening she and Della had gone to the Satanist gathering at the evil Count's villa. Della had not dared tell the others of what had transpired at that party. She merely repeated Barsini's explanation to her that her sister had gone off with one of the guests.

Now, in midmorning of the second day, Prince Sanzio had called them all together in the living room of the palace. Even Prince Raphael had been summoned for the occasion.

They stood in a semicircle before the old man's wheelchair. Prince Sanzio looked more frail and ill than ever. He sat huddled in the chair like a lost soul.

He looked up at them and said, "You may well wonder why I have asked all of you here. The past thirty-six hours have been ones I shall never forget. Now, at last, I have word of some kind about Irma."

"What sort of word?" Prince Raphael asked. He also looked as if he'd suffered sleepless nights.

The old Prince said, "A message was delivered to me this morning. Guido took it at the door. I will read the message to you." He produced a crumpled sheet from a pocket of his robe and spread it open. He continued, "It is crudely printed and there is no signature. It says: "We have your daughter. Her ransom price is the Madonna. If you report this to the police we will kill her. If the Madonna is not left for us to pick up within the week we will kill her in any event. The signal for us to pick up the Madonna will be a pot of roses on the sill of one of the lower palace windows. We ask that it be left in a package on the table by the front door.""

Henry Clarkson gasped, "So they've actually taken her hostage!"

The old Prince nodded. "I'm afraid so."

Prince Raphael was standing with a stunned expression on his handsome face. "I didn't think they would do it."

"Outrageous!" Aunt Isobel said with proper British anger.

Della asked the old Prince, "Does Guido have any idea who delivered this?"

Prince Sanzio shook his head. "No. He did not know the contents of the message at the time so he paid no particular attention to the man who delivered it. He says he cannot recall seeing him before."

"The police should be informed," Henry said indignantly. "That is certain!"

The old Prince raised a thin hand in protest. "You have heard the letter. They will kill her if we call the police."

"They threaten to kill her anyway," Henry pointed out.

"But we will have at least a week to deal with them if we handle this privately," the old Prince said. "And I think that is the best plan."

Prince Raphael looked around at the others. "The key to all this is the Madonna. Whoever has taken her captive believes that we know where the stolen Madonna is hidden."

"I have been the target," Della said unhappily. "I didn't think they'd strike at her!"

Prince Raphael said, "It is simple. They hope to wrest the secret from you by threatening her life."

"If I knew anything about the Madonna I would gladly tell them," she said unhappily. "The terrible thing is that they are mistaken. I never received it."

Prince Sanzio asked, "Then why do they appear so sure that you did?"

"I can't think," Della said. "It must have been sent to me. But I never did receive it."

Aunt Isobel wanted to know, "How can you deal with them?"

"I admit that is a grave question," Prince Sanzio said. And glancing at Della, he said, "You were the last to see her."

"Yes," she replied in a small voice.

"Do you have any suggestions about finding her?" the old Prince asked.

"I think she is a prisoner of Barsini," she said. "And I think he masterminded the theft of the Madonna from the Vatican Museum."

"Don't be too sure about that," the slender Prince Raphael said worriedly.

"It seems to rest on their mistaken idea that you are the one possessing the Madonna," the old Prince said.

"And I have not seen it!" Della replied. "Henry and my aunt can vouch for that!"

"That is so," Aunt Isobel said.

"The hounding began back in London," Della told the old Prince.

Henry was frowning. "It is obvious that someone here in Rome believes that Della knows where the Madonna vanished. And no matter what we say, they refuse to believe it isn't in her keeping."

Prince Sanzio addressed himself to Prince Raphael: "What do you think?"

"I think they mean their threat," the young man said worriedly. "I'm inclined to agree with Della that Barsini is behind all this. But I also think it will be impossible to prove it."

"Why didn't they kidnap me instead of my sister?" Della wondered.

"They may think the Madonna is hidden somewhere and you are the only one with access to it," the old Prince suggested.

"And if they threatened to kill you it would make small sense since you are their hope of retrieving the Madonna," Prince Raphael pointed out.

"They needed someone to threaten and so bring pressure on you," Henry said. "And obviously Irma is the one."

Della bit her lip, then said, "We can't let them harm her."

"Nor can we, it seems, produce the Madonna," Prince Raphael said grimly.

Aunt Isobel spoke up: "If the Madonna was sent to my niece and somehow lost along the way, wouldn't the best plan be to trace it from the time of its leaving here?"

"You are right," Prince Raphael said with a bitter note in his voice. "Unhappily we do not know who sent it. So there is no place to begin!"

"Why not begin with the theft?" Della said. "I have been told that a kind of superthief named Brizzi and a renegade member of the Vatican Museum staff are to blame."

"Brizzi!" the old Prince gasped. "Who told you that story?"

"Count Barsini, when I asked him about the threats on me," Della said.

Prince Raphael scowled. "Brizzi may have stolen the treasure, but I cannot imagine him allowing it to get in anyone else's hands. He is a superthief, as you say; I doubt that once he had the Madonna anyone could get it away from him."

"Such things do happen," Henry Clarkson said. "Thieves fall out."

"What do you think?" the old Prince appealed to Raphael.

"Barsini may know. He has close contact with the underworld. But I doubt he can put us in touch with Brizzi," Prince Raphael said.

"Someone must talk to Count Barsini and at once," the old Prince said. "I despise the man and what he has done to my foster daughter, but we have no choice but to turn to him."

Della had been thinking about it all and now she spoke up, "Let me go! I think I might get some information from him."

Henry glanced at her worriedly. "I don't like the idea of your going there again."

"I can protect myself," she said. "Irma is my sister. I want to do what I can."

"Let me go along with you," Prince Raphael suggested.

"Thank you," she told the handsome Prince. "But I feel I can accomplish more alone."

Prince Sanzio nodded. "I agree with Della. I say, let her go at once and see if this man can help us."

So it was settled. She left within a half-hour. As her carriage rolled through the streets she felt her spirits dropping and worried about what she would say to the arrogant Barsini. She was not nearly so certain of his help as she'd pretended.

Reaching the villa, she asked the carriage to wait. Then she went to the heavy oaken door with its giant rapper and knocked on it. After a slight delay the liveried servant opened it with an inquiring look on his aged face.

She said, "I wish to speak to Count Barsini for a little."

"Is he expecting you?"

"Not exactly," she admitted.

"What is your name?" the sober servant asked.

"My name is Della Standish," she said.

"If you will come in and wait a moment," the servant said politely.

She waited nervously in the same reception hall where it had all begun such a short time ago. She noted the dressing room where she had changed her clothes and memory of what had followed brought warmth to her cheeks. She had not dared tell anyone at the palace of her sordid adventures under Barsini's roof or the way Irma had been treated.

After a little the servant returned and said, "The Count will see you."

She found him waiting for her in the same room where they had first met. He was wearing a dressing gown and looked rather weary. He brought a chair forward for her to sit on but remained standing himself.

"What can I do for you?" he asked, studying her.

"I have come about Irma," she said.

"What about her?"

"She is missing."

"Missing?" He showed surprise.

"Yes. She has not returned home since her being here at your Satanist meeting the other night."

"Please," the tall, bald man said. "Do not refer to it as a Satanist gathering; I fear people have an unfortunate resentment of such things."

"Well they may have," she haid grimly. "After what I saw!"

"You would do best," the Count said, stroking his beard, "to forget all you saw. The gathering never took place."

"Is that your story?"

"It has to be to protect my followers and myself," was his reply.

"I see," she said grimly. "All I want is to know what happened to Irma."

He shrugged. "Why ask me?"

"She was here the last time I saw her," Della said. "Playing the role of your high priestess and sexual partner on the altar."

His smile was leering. "Would you like to play the same role some evening soon?"

"I would not!" she said sharply.

"Too bad!"

"Where is Irma?"

He strolled over and stood behind his desk, scrutinizing her closely. "I told you. She went away with another guest."

"With whom and where?" she demanded.

"I would rather not tell you that," he said loftily.

Della said, "You will either talk to me or the police!"

A muscle in his cheek twitched. He said, "If I tell you his name do you promise not to bother me any further?"

"I did not enjoy coming here," she said. "I'll not do it again if I can avoid it."

Barsini said, "The man's name is Gregorio. You will find him about five blocks distant, the Via Angeli, number five."

"You are sure that is where she went?"

"Yes."

"You have not seen her since?"

"She is not here," he said scornfully. "That should be self-evident."

She moved to the door alone, then turned and said, "If this Gregorio is not able or willing to help me find my sister I will be back."

The Count spread his hands. "It will do you no good."

"We shall see," she said.

She left the villa and returned to the carriage and gave the driver the address. Within ten minutes the carriage halted before a white villa only a little less elegant than the one she'd just come from.

She was about to knock on the door when a bronzed face peered at her over the edge of a balcony. She was shocked, for the face belonged to the giant who had raped her at Barsini's Satanist gathering.

Staring up, she gasped, "You!"

"The Signorina Standish," the giant said, leaning over further. She saw that he was wearing nothing from the waist up. A towel was tied about his midriff.

She recovered a little to ask, "Was my sister here?"

"Irma?" the giant said with a smile.

"Yes."

"She was here the night we all were at Barsini's," he said. "She came here with me later. I told her about you and me."

Della found herself blushing furiously. "I don't want to discuss that!"

"That is a pity!" the young giant mocked her as he sat on the balcony railing smiling down at her.

"Where is Irma now?"

"I have no idea," he said.

"But she came here with you!"

"She left before dawn," Gregorio said. "I could not send her home by carriage as my coachman has been ill. Brother Louis came by for a drink and he agreed to escort her home."

Della said, "The same one who was on duty as guard the other night."

He shrugged. "I know no other Brother Louis."

"Did he say where he was going?"

"At dawn he should have been returning home. But he promised to find your sister a carriage and get her home."

"And that was the last you saw of her?"

"It was," Gregorio smiled. "And I'm lonesome for company. Why do you not come up and visit for a while?" He rose as if he were coming down to open the door to her.

"No," she said quickly. "I'm looking for Irma. Where does this Brother Louis live?"

"He is not a romantic," Gregorio warned her. "He will never make you a lover."

"Please be serious," she begged him. "If you have his address give it to me!"

Gregorio smiled down at her, plainly enjoying her misery. He said, "Brother Louis is a renegade."

"I know that."

"He is fearful of his life," Gregorio went on. "So he has buried himself in a room up from the Aventine Hill. It is mostly a poorer-class district. He feels safe there. He has a room on the Via della Reginella, a house on the corner. I think it is number five."

She did not stop to thank him but heard his laughter as she hurried back to the carriage and gave the driver the address Gregorio had just offered her.

The driver showed concern. "You do not wish to go there, Signorina. You must have made a mistake."

"No," she said. "I'm aware it is not a good section of the city but I'm trying to find someone."

"If you have a companion it would be better," the coachman worried.

"You will be with me," she said.

"I cannot accompany you into that maze of narrow streets," he warned her. "Too narrow for a carriage."

"At least you will not be far distant."

"I do not like it," he said.

"Please do as I say," she begged him. "My sister's life could depend on it."

So he argued no more as they drove on. They left the rich section to travel through a commercial area of the great city and then on to the poor district where Brother Louis had his room.

The streets were mean and filled with elderly men and stout women, often in volatile arguments. Little children darted in front of the carriage and ran along beside it begging. Della was fearful that they might be run down but they had an agility born of experience which saved them from harm.

The driver pulled the carriage to the curb of a squalid street and said, "This is as far as I can go."

"The street I'm looking for is ahead," she said. "I will continue on foot."

He helped her down to the cobblestoned street and gazed up at the tall tenements surrounding them. Clothes hung on lines above their heads and neighbors held shouted conversations with each other from their windows.

He said, "There are decent people here and, as in all slums, the other kind. You are taking a chance."

"I know," she said, defiant in her brown dress, and wide-brimmed straw hat. She clung to the tiny white parasol which was the only thing she had which resembled a weapon.

"Don't let the children bully you," he warned. "And don't try to give one of them money or they'll swarm on you and tear you apart."

"I'll remember," she said, glancing grimly ahead. "Ill try not to be long."

She went through an arched passage leading into the narrower streets. The houses almost met above the street, making it so gloomy, even in full daylight, that it was frightening.

She moved on until she came to a corner marked Via della Reginella. A bent old woman shuffled by, dressed all in black, a black shawl over her head. She carried a market basket and was mumbling to herself.

Della halted her and asked, "Where is number five?"

The old woman's wrinkled, toothless face showed no expression. She pointed a gnarled finger to an open door leading to dark stairs. "There!"

"Do you know a Brother Louis?" she asked.

"The drunken one?" the old crone cackled.

"It could be," she said.

"The attic, at the head of the stairway," the old woman mumbled. "He is evil! There is a curse on him!" And at once she moved on.

Della was heartened. She had not hoped to locate the house and the exact location of Brother Louis's room so easily. She went to the open doorway and stepped into the darkness. The stairs were worn and the combined smells of cabbage, garlic and many less pleasant things made the air unfit to breathe. But she braved the stench and started up the stairs.

Reaching the first flight, she was aware of a monstrous quarrel between a man and woman going on behind one of the doors. Screams and angry imprecations were hurled back and forth. She closed her ears to them and climbed the second flight of rickety stairs.

She seriously doubted that the chic and fastidious Irma had come to this place. But she had been in the company of Brother Louis if the story offered by Gregorio were true, and he might know where she'd gone.

At the second landing a door opened and a sluttish-looking young woman breast-feeding a baby came to stare at her. The woman's glance was one of hatred and resentment, making Della feel dreadfully uncomfortable. The woman shut the door as Della moved on toward the attic stairway.

The attic stairs were the most worn and narrow of the lot. When she reached the landing she saw that there was a door facing her. It was painted gray but the paint was peeling and there was a split in one of the wooden panels. Someone had roughly drawn a crude head of Satan on the other panel. The drawing had been done in ink and there was evidence of a faint attempt to scrub it off, but it remained triumphantly there nonetheless. A minor work of art suggesting the character of the room's occupant.

Della knocked on the door. There was no reply. She waited a minute and then decided to try opening it. She turned the handle gently and to her surprise it was not locked. She slowly opened it to be hit by the stench of stale cigar smoke and whiskey. And stretched out on a cot in a corner of the shabby room was Brother Louis.

Guessing that he was drunk, she cautiously made her way the several steps over to him. He was wearing his black cassock and his face was as pale as ever with his watery blue eyes staring into infinity. He made no move as she neared him.

Her heart was pounding rapidly, not from the exertion of climbing the many stairs but from sheer fright. Finding herself in this shabby room atop the drab tenement with its strange denizens was a new experience for her. And she had no idea how she was going to cope with the inebriated Brother Louis.

Then something caught her eye which made her halt and stare at the floor. On the rough board floor by the cot lay a jeweled comb which she recalled having seen in Irma's hair the night of her disappearance! She knelt and picked up the comb and then reached out and touched the shoulder of the man on the cot.

"Brother Louis!" she cried tensely.

As the words escaped her lips Brother Louis' body fell toward her so that it was on its face at the very edge of the cot and she saw the knife protruding from between the shoulder blades!

She felt she must collapse. And then she knew that she must fight her feeling of faintness and nausea. The comb clutched in her hand, she stumbled toward the doorway and then on down the rickety stairs, almost missing a step.

At the foot of the attic stairs she halted, clutching the railing, her head reeling. Then she made herself go down the steps past the landing where the couple were still quarreling and into the comparatively fresh air of the street. She leaned weakly against the door frame.

As she recovered a little she carefully placed the jeweled comb inside her pocketbook. Then, still stunned, she set off along the dark, narrow street, on her way back to the carriage. She reached the archway leading out of the maze of streets almost to bump into the figure of a stout priest.

Before she could apologize the priest doffed his hat and said, "My dear Miss Standish!"

She gazed at him stupidly and then recognized it was jolly Father Anthony. She said, "Father Anthony! What are you doing here!"

"I'm on the track of that renegade Brother Louis," he said. "I hope to find out about the theft of the jeweled Madonna from him. He is supposed to have helped Brizzi in the theft!"

"Too late!" she said weakly.

The priest regarded her with surprise. "What do you mean?"

"He's dead!"

"Dead!" Father Anthony sounded incredulous.

"I was in his room just now. He was murdered! Stabbed!"

Father Anthony took a large white handkerchief from his pocket and mopped his broad brow. "This is shocking news!" he gasped.

"I thought I would faint."

"My poor child." The fat priest was all sympathy. He stuffed the handkerchief back in his cassock, placed his hat on his head and took her by the arm to give her some support. "Is that your carriage waiting back there?"

"Yes," she murmured, leaning close to him for support.

"No point in my going there if he is dead," the fat priest said as they walked on. "It is a grim game with the stakes high! Brother Louis has paid with his life for his greed and turning his back on the Church!"

"My sister is missing! They've taken her!" Della said despairingly.

"The thieves?"

"Yes. That Brizzi or Count Barsini or whoever is at the head of all this. The last person I know her to have been with was Brother Louis."

"They must have killed him and kidnapped her," the fat priest suggested.

"Perhaps. I found her comb on the floor by his bed."

"Then you know she was with him."

"Yes."

"This is a dreadful setback," Father Anthony said. "I hoped to talk to the man and have him repent. Then he might have informed me where the Madonna had been taken. Now I'm at a dead end."

They were nearing the carriage. She asked him, "Should we tell the police?"

"About the murder?"

"Yes. It doesn't seem right to not report it."

Father Anthony frowned. "Better not to get mixed up in it. Especially if your sister is being held by that gang."

"I hadn't thought of that," she admitted. "They have promised to kill her if we notify the police of her kidnapping."

"You see?" the fat priest said. "You must not say or do anything about finding him."

"What will happen?"

"One of the neighbors will discover his body soon enough," Father Anthony said. "These fellows always have some cronies or hangers-on."

At the carriage, she said, "Do you want to share the carriage with me? I'll take you wherever you like."

"No," he said. "I think it might be safer for both of us if we are not seen together in the open."

"Oh?"

"Yes," he explained. "I have another idea. I think I know where Brizzi might be in hiding. I'm going to look for him and if I find him I'll accuse him of murdering Brother Louis."

"That could be dangerous," she said.

"I shall be careful in how I handle it," he said. "But that villain, Brizzi, must be brought to justice."

"And Count Barsini as well if he is mixed up in the scheme," she said.

"Definitely Barsini," the old priest agreed.

"I don't know what to do next," she said. "I must somehow find Irma."

"She's likely in Brizzi's hands," the fat priest said. "If I find him I may learn something of where your sister is."

"Will you try?" she asked eagerly.

"Depend on it, Miss Standish," he said. "This has to be a terrible experience for you. I would like to help."

"When do you think you may know something?"

"Late in the day."

"Can we meet somewhere?" she asked.

"Yes," he said. "But not where we'll be seen. Let us meet at one of the tourist places. There'll be mostly strangers there."

"Very well," she said. "Where?"

"The Mamertine prison," he said. "I'll meet you near its entrance and pretend to be showing you around. In the meanwhile we can talk."

"What time?" she asked.

"Seven o'clock," he said. "I won't keep you long. You will have plenty of time to return to the palace for a nine o'clock dinner."

"Good," she said. "Will I have any trouble finding the place?"

"No. It's close by the Capitoline Hill," the priest said. "Your driver will find it easily."

"Thank you," she said warmly. "We met at exactly the right moment. You have given me some hope."

"And you saved me from stumbling upon the corpse of Brother Louis and perhaps getting in great trouble."

She said, "Perhaps we can go on doing each other good turns."

"I hope so, my child," the fat priest said.

"I would leave Rome but I cannot go as long as they hold my sister hostage. They think I have the Madonna and can turn it over to them."

He said, "Why do they think such a thing?"

"I'm not sure," she said. "I believe Barsini is the one responsible. He heard about me from Irma and used my name. But I can't say definitely."

His eyes searched her lovely face. "And you do not have any knowledge of the Madonna's whereabouts?"

"I wish I did," she said. "I'd gladly give it to them and get Irma back."

The priest nodded appreciatively. "I'm sure you would. There are things beyond the value of jewels!"

He helped her into the carriage, doffed his hat again, and walked off swiftly. She told the driver to take her back to the palace and sat back to think all that had happened.

Prince Sanzio was waiting for her in the living room. As she entered he wheeled his chair forward to greet her. "I have been on edge waiting for your return," he said.

She sat by him. Pensively she said, "I'm afraid I have not managed well."

He let his breath out sharply and clenched the arms of his wheelchair. "Tell me!"

She said, "I believe we may be getting closer to the center of the evil."

"Heaven hope so!" the old Prince said fervently.

"The other night she left Barsini's with a man called Gregorio. An evil young man!"

"Those people around Barsini are all evil," Prince Sanzio said angrily. "I blame Raphael. It was he who introduced her to the scoundrel."

"I do not think he meant any harm by it."

"It was still stupid of him!"

Della sighed. "I must agree. I went to see this Gregorio and he admitted Irma had been with him. But he said she left around dawn."

"She did not return here!" the old Prince said.

"No. She left with a renegade from the Church named Brother Louis."

The Prince frowned. "Are you sure?"

"I found this," she said, taking the comb from her pocketbook.

The old man examined the comb. "Yes, yes, I recognize it. The stones are of second quality but I bought it for her and paid a high price. There are seven diamonds in it."

"It was on the floor of the room where I found Brother Louis," she said.

"And did he tell you how it came to be there?"

"I'm afraid not," she said. "By the time I reached him he was dead. Murdered!"

The old man looked shattered. "Murdered?"

"Yes," she said. "So I found out nothing."

"So your day was wasted?"

"Not quite," she said. "As I was returning to the carriage I met an old friend, Father Anthony. We met on the train from Paris."

"Yes. You told me about him."

"I had asked him to help me in any way he could and told him about the thieves thinking I had the Madonna," she said. "He had traced the theft to a man known as Brizzi and this Brother Louis. He was on his way to question Brother Louis when I encountered him."

"And told him of the murder?"

"Yes," she said. "He was shocked but he claimed to have some knowledge of where Brizzi might be found. He left me determined to try and locate him and find out about Irma. I'm to meet him later."

"Then there is some hope," the old man said.

"Yes," she replied. "I have an appointment with Father Anthony at seven. Where are the others?"

"Henry Clarkson is in the city doing some paperwork with my lawyers," he said. "Your aunt is upstairs resting. And I have no idea where Prince Raphael is. He left here shortly after noon."

"I'd like to talk to him about all that has happened," she said.

"Beware of that young man," the old Prince warned her. "I do not trust his ready charm. He has led Irma to ruin!"

"Surely not by intention," she said.

"I'm not sure," the old Prince said, his sallow face grim. "Count Barsini is a powerful man and very wealthy. I think Raphael would do almost anything to gain favor with him."

"Including betraying his fiancée?"

"Perhaps," the old man said bitterly. "History is filled with many more loathsome betrayals."

"I think we should give him the benefit of the doubt until he is proven guilty," Della said.

Prince Sanzio eyed her with some alarm. "He has cast his spell on you as well."

"No," she said. "But he has never shown himself to be our enemy. With Barsini, it is different! He is the most vile of men!"

She left the old Prince and went upstairs. Something impelled her to go by Irma's room and, as she did, she tried the door and went inside. She was startled to find the room was not empty.

The midget Guido had been standing by the candle before the carved Madonna, touching a taper to the wick in the giant glass bowl. Hearing her, he turned with a look of guilt on his small, wrinkled face.

The little man said apologetically, "Forgive me, you gave me a bad start. For a moment I thought it was Princess Irma returned."

"Do you expect her return?"

"No," he said unhappily. "I came to her room to see that all was in order. I found the candle had somehow gone out. I lit it again. The Princess never wished this candle to be out."

Della said, "I did not think her so devout!"

The midget crossed himself. "Bless her! She was! As a child the Church was all her world! She was educated by the nuns."

Della had memories of the naked Irma on the black velvet of the Satanist altar and contrasted this with what she was hearing about her missing sister now.

"As an adult she has become less religious," Della suggested.

Guido sighed. "It is all too often the case. Yet I think much of her early training remains with her. And here in the privacy of her room the flame always burns before the Madonna's shrine."

"Let us hope Irma will soon be found," she said.

"You are much like her," Guido said, staring up at Della.

"Yes," she said. "I know." And she left him there in the room. He was a strange little man and she did not always understand him. But she was sure he was truly devoted to the old Prince and to Irma.

She rested for a little and was dressing to go meet Father Anthony when a knock came on her door. It was Prince Raphael.

He said, "I hear you are going to meet someone at the Mamertine prison in the hope of finding Irma. You're not going alone. Prince Sanzio says I'm to accompany you."

Chapter Twelve

"I think I should go alone," she protested.

Prince Raphael, handsome in a dark brown suit, stepped into the room. He faced her seriously and said, "No. I cannot allow that. I heard the risk you took earlier today."

"Prince Sanzio told you?"

"Yes."

"I don't want it known I was there or found the dead body."

"I realize that," he said. "There will likely be an account of it in the morning papers. The police are bound to find that renegade by then."

"He had Irma's comb!"

"So the Prince told me," Raphael said. "And you are to meet this Father Anthony at seven?"

"Yes," she said solemnly. "He might not come to me if he sees me with anyone else."

"When we get there I will remain a distance from you," Prince Raphael promised. "But I'll always stay within call."

"I was going to speak to Henry about coming along," she said.

The Prince shook his head. "I will be of much greater use. I know the city and the Mamertine prison. I want to protect you."

"Thank you," she said, looking up into his eyes. "I have always believed in you."

He was studying her and with great gentleness took her in his arms. "You look so like Irma tonight," he said and kissed her.

"Please!" she begged and at the same time pushed him away.

As she did so she saw that Henry Clarkson had come to stand in the doorway of their room and was watching them crimson-faced. He had to have seen their embrace.

Crossing to him, she said, "Henry! I was just going to look for you."

"Were you?" the young lawyer said coolly. "It seemed to me you were pretty busy here."

"Don't misunderstand!" she protested. "Raphael is going with me for a special meeting. I hope to learn more about where Irma is."

"I see," Henry said, unrelenting in his cool polite tone.

Raphael came toward him. "It was my fault, old man! I gave way to an impulse and kissed her. Don't blame her!"

"Why should I?" Henry said. "It is I who should be blamed for intruding on her when she is entertaining a friend in her room. Forgive me!" He bowed stiffly and walked off down the corridor.

"Henry!" she called out the door after him, but he paid no attention. She came back into the room and told Raphael, "We surely didn't manage that well!"

"I apologized and told him the truth!" Raphael said heatedly. "What more could he expect? What is so awful about a kiss between friends? I wished to comfort you."

She said, "Whatever you wished you made him jealous."

"It is his jealousy that is at fault," the Prince said angrily. "Does he not trust you?"

Della smiled ruefully. "You're defending yourself well. But in his place I doubt if you'd have acted better."

"I stepped aside when Irma made it clear that she preferred Count Barsini to me."

She said, "Was that because of your love for her or because you were willing to surrender her to the Count in exchange for his goodwill?"

The handsome young man looked dismayed. "You cannot believe that about me!"

"It was a question."

"The answer is no."

"And when Irma is found will you marry her?"

He shrugged. "That depends on her. Yes, if she will have me. And if you refuse to consider me."

"Why should I come into it?"

"I told you almost on our first meeting," the Prince said "I have fallen in love with you."

"Please!" she raised a hand in protest. "I don't want to hear that again. And especially when Irma is in danger because these thieves think I'm unwilling to part with their precious Madonna."

The Prince smiled. "You should take an advertisement in the newspaper. A whole page! Tell them you know nothing about it!"

She said, "I think I would if I felt it would do any good."

The Prince reached into his vest pocket and produced his elegant gold watch. "If we are to reach the prison on time we'd better leave."

She said, "I wish I could explain to Henry before we go."

"Do not worry," Raphael said. "Prince Sanzio will make it clear to him that he requested me to accompany you."

"Are you certain?"

"Yes."

She took his word for it and they left. They saw no one on the way out. The carriage was waiting and Raphael told the driver where they wished to go and the route they would take to get there.

When they were on their way he turned to her on the seat beside him and asked, "Why did this Father Anthony choose this spot to meet?"

"He said it was a tourist place. That it would be busy and we would not be noticed."

"In a way that is true," the Prince agreed reluctantly. "But I could have thought of other places."

They drove on and passed the Palatine Hill. Raphael told her that in 753 B.C.. Romulus ordered the building of a great wall around it. The wall that was supposed to protect the citizens was constructed along the lines of those put up by the Etruscans, the first builders of Italy. And in time the wall grew to become a circle around the Capitol. Escaped slaves and criminals came to seek the safety of the asylum established on the adjoining Capitoline Hill.

"You can see that even today part of this area remains bare," Prince Raphael pointed out.

"And it is of great elevation," she said.

"It rises at least sixty feet," he agreed.

This conversation did little to distract Della from thoughts about Irma. Her captors had promised they would let her live for a week. But she could not fully believe that And if anything happened she would never forgive herself. She would feel that Irma had died in her place.

Raphael glanced at her and said," You're in a dark mood."

"I know. I'm truly fearful for Irma."

"I hate to think about it," he admitted.

"Why don't you go see Barsini?" she urged him. "He might tell you more than he did me."

"I much doubt it," Raphael said. "Barsini hates me."

"Why?"

"There are many reasons. That is why he gloried in taking Irma from me."

She said, "I only hope nothing happened to Father Anthony. He is such a good old man."

"He is involving himself in a bad business when he tries to track down Brizzi."

"Only to help me," she said. "What is this Brizzi like?"

"Few people have ever seen him," he said. "He is a Sicilian. Crime is his profession. And he is a master of disguise. So those few who have seen him generally are not able to recognize him when they meet again."

They arrived at a series of gardens and she said, "What a lovely setting!"

"Only in these modern times," the Prince told her. "In early days this was the execution spot of Rome. Here stood the gallows with their rotting corpses for all to see. Here were the machines for stretching, decapitation, ripping, cracking, disemboweling—all the most sophisticated torture devices of the time. Any unfortunate punished here died in dreadful agony. Eventually the executioners moved to the riverside, by the bridge of Sant'Angelo, but they left behind them, deep inside this Capitoline Hill, a last grim reminder of evil Rome, the Mamertine prison."

"I don't look forward to it," she said with a shudder.

He checked his watch again. "You are just in time."

They descended from the carriage and mixed with the sizable number of tourists. Raphael pointed out that the prison was now a chapel consecrated to St. Peter, who was said to have once been imprisoned there by Nero. They went to read the notice boards commending the faithful for visiting the shrine.

She looked around. "I do not see him."

"Probably he will be somewhere inside," the Prince said.

They entered the little church and Raphael knelt and crossed himself and she bowed her head. Then they moved on with the tourists and began a descent into the cells below. It was at this moment that fear began to crowd in on Della. She could almost sense the grim horror of history as they descended farther into the earth. Raphael, true to his promise, followed her at a short distance, so that he would not seem to be with her.

An old man with a straggly, gray beard appeared at her side so mysteriously that it seemed he might have come fully formed out of the shadows. He was bowing and shaking his head in awe, making Della even more nervous. She glanced back but could not see Raphael; others had come between them. For the moment her only company was to be this weird old man.

He sniffled and said, "I'm very devout. My sister is a nun."

"How nice," she said as distantly as possible.

They were descending another flight of worn stone steps and she wished she had not asked Raphael to keep a distance from her. She was so frightened and feeling worse every minute.

Seeming anxious to be helpful, the old man wheezed, "The dungeons lie one above the other and now are connected by these stairs."

"I see," she said tensely.

Still at her side, he rambled on, "We will finally reach the Apostle's cell."

She found herself in a long corridor of stone so silently menacing she felt she was in a tomb. There were openings to the dungeons on either side of the corridor. The bearded old man came close to her and she was alarmed to see that they had moved ahead of the others and were alone in this section of the dark, underground place.

"Used to take the bodies up from here and toss them in the sewers," the old man wheezed.

It was not the sort of talk she wished to hear. She turned away from him as they passed another dungeon opening. Suddenly a terrifying and unexpected thing took place. She was given a vicious shove by the old man which sent her stumbling into the dungeon.

She cried out as he came in after and slammed the rusty iron door shut on the corridor. From the rear of the musty dungeon there rose a huge figure which she belatedly recognized as Gregorio.

"You!" she cried.

The giant smiled cruelly at her, his face visible in the narrow streams of light which seeped in from the torchlit corridor.

Behind her the old man hissed, "Make her talk!" Then he opened the rusty door a fraction and eased himself out, apparently to stand guard outside.

Gregorio came slowly toward her, saying, "Why don't you be intelligent and tell us where it is?"

"I don't know!" she protested.

"You have it," he said grimly. "Either here or in England!"

"No!"

"Don't lie!" he snarled, then seized her by the arms, pressing so tightly that she cried out in pain. "We know it was sent to you."

"I didn't get it! Believe me! I didn't!"

"Keep that up and you'll never see your sister alive again," Gregorio warned her. And he tightened his grip on her arms so she screamed with pain again.

Her scream had not entirely died when the rusty door was burst open by an angry Raphael. The Prince's eyes were blazing with fury as he leapt for the giant. Gregorio let her go and moved back to receive the attack. She fell onto the dungeon floor and crawled to the side to be away from their struggling.

In a moment they were on the floor. The battle now attracted some of the other tourists, who gathered by the dungeon door frantically to ask the two assailants to halt their battle. It seemed destined to be a struggle to the death.

Then Gregorio managed to get astride Raphael and deliver a punishing blow to the Prince's face. He lay still. Gregorio gave her an evil look and jumped up and rushed out of the dungeon and past the spectators as he raced to make his escape before the police came.

Della went over to Raphael just as he was stirring and raising himself up. She said, "He's gone! Made a run for it! Are you all right?"

"Hardly!" the Prince said with irony, standing up and ruefully surveying his dirtied and torn clothing. He pushed back his hair and she saw the bruise on his jaw and a cut above his left eye that was bleeding a little.

"What now?" she asked.

"Let us get out of here," he said curtly. "I don't want to have to answer police questions either." And he took her by the arm and led her out into the corridor where a group of the other visitors to the prison were gathered.

An old woman asked, "Was it a quarrel over the girl?"

"Animals!" a thin young man said with disgust.

"More like criminals," a big Englishwoman voiced her contempt.

"And in a sacred place," another woman said. "You would expect them to know better!" There were other annoyed murmurings as Della and Raphael made their way back up to the chapel and then outside.

In the sunshine she halted and took a deep breath of fresh air. "I feel as if I had returned from the tomb!"

"You have," Raphael said grimly. "That Gregorio is a giant and quite mad!"

"I know," she said wearily. "He questioned me and threatened Irma would die if I didn't talk."

"I heard your scream," Raphael said. "I rushed down the corridor and found an old man with a thin beard standing staring at the dungeon entrance. I threw him aside and went on in."

"He was with Gregorio. One of them!"

"I didn't know!"

She looked around grimly. "They're both gone now. How are you?"

"I'll manage," Raphael said bleakly as he tightened his cravat and rearranged his clothing a little.

"There he comes!" Della said suddenly, seeing the little priest hurrying up toward them.

"A bit late!" her companion said with disgust.

"I'll go talk to him," she said. "You wait here." And she was already on her way to meet Father Anthony.

When she reached him, his oval face was purplish and he was struggling for breath from his exertions. He said, "I've run most of the way."

"It's all right," she said. "Catch your breath."

He placed a hand on his heart. "I should not do this sort of rushing."

"I intended to wait for you."

"But I was late."

She said, "Just as well. I think there was trap set for us."

"A trap?"

"Yes," she said. "Down below in the old prison section. Gregorio and another, older man abducted me and tried to torture me into talking."

"All this happened before I reached here?" he asked in an incredulous tone.

"I think someone found out about our rendezvous and planned to attack us."

"How did you escape them?"

She smiled. "I brought along a bodyguard, Prince Raphael."

"That was very wise," the old priest said, still having trouble with his breathing. "I'm sure he was a good deal more help than I would have been. You were lucky it happened before I arrived."

"What now?" she asked.

"There is a small café back down the hill," Father Anthony said. "Let us have coffee there."

So it was that ten minutes later all three were seated at a sidewalk table of the small café. Prince Raphael had washed his face in cold water and it looked considerably less battered. He was in an interested mood as the little priest told Della of his progress.

Father Anthony said, "Would you believe it? I actually have been in the presence of Brizzi."

Della asked, "What sort of person is he?"

"Very ordinary except for one thing," Father Anthony said. "He has an obsession with his reputation as a master thief. He is enraged by the loss of the Madonna after having cleverly stolen it."

Prince Raphael said, "The man must be reasonable. Even if the Madonna was sent to Miss Standish, she never received it."

"Were there not so much at stake I think Brizzi would drop the whole thing," Father Anthony said. "But he thinks his reputation is resting on how this turns out as well as a fortune in precious gems which he is loath to lose."

Della said, "Perhaps if I could talk to him in person he would listen to me."

"I doubt it," Father Anthony said.

"Did you get anywhere with him?"

The priest said, "I made him promise not to harm your sister in any way. And I found out she is hidden here in Rome somewhere."

Raphael asked, "Any approximate idea of the location? Was it here in the center of the city or on the outskirts?"

"Brizzi is a wily one," the fat priest said. "He did not give me a hint of where she might be."

"I'm amazed you were able to reach him at all," Della said.

"Only because I am a priest," he replied. "Brizzi likes to keep in good with men of the cloth."

Raphael said wryly, "He apparently wasn't all that worried about his accomplice, Brother Louis. He either killed him or had him killed."

Father Anthony said, "I dispute that. I say that the unfortunate man was killed by someone else."

"Did Brizzi know about it?" she asked.

"He was shocked to learn it," Father Anthony said. "And I do not think his concern was mere playacting."

"Who else would want to murder Brother Louis?" Raphael wanted to know.

"Many are involved in this game of trying to locate the jeweled Madonna," the priest said. "I think he was killed by someone who received certain information from him which he didn't want passed on to anyone else."

"What is Brizzi's next move?" Della asked.

"He is trying to search out the thief of thieves who stole the Madonna from him and who supposedly passed it on to you. He is still dubious of your insistence that you do not have it."

She asked, "How can I convince him?"

"Give me a day or two more," the priest said. "I will arrange a meeting with you."

"Where?" she asked.

"I will think of a place," he said. "Certainly not the Mamertine prison!"

Raphael frowned. "Which brings up the question of how did Gregorio and that old-man accomplice know Della was to be at the prison."

"A good question," Father Anthony said. "In my opinion you were followed here. They have been waiting for the right chance to get at you."

"It's possible," she said.

"I don't know," Raphael complained. "It seems more likely someone told them we'd be there. Or at least Della would be."

"Brizzi suspects her of having the Madonna," the old priest said. "It may be that I made the mistake of saying where I was meeting Miss Standish. In that case he could have sent those evil people to harass you!"

"That sounds more like it," the Prince said.

"I shall be more careful in future," Father Anthony said. "I believe I have a clue as to where the Madonna went."

"Oh?" she said.

He nodded. "Yes. I'm sure Count Barsini was mixed up in its theft. And since Brother Louis and Gregorio both have been henchmen of Barsini it is possible they were part of the double cross which took the Madonna from Brizzi."

Della said, "You think Brother Louis may have been playing a double role, working for Brizzi and Barsini at the same time. That is likely why he was murdered."

"I suspect so," Father Anthony said. "He likely passed the Madonna on to Barsini, expecting a big share of it. Once Barsini had the treasure he coldly ordered Brother Louis killed."

"Or Brizzi may have done it in revenge," Raphael said.

"He denies it," the priest said.

"Do you believe him?" Della asked.

"No," Father Anthony said. "He lies when it suits him. It is possible he is lying in this instance."

Raphael said, "So for all our trying we are back where we started. With this girl in as much danger as ever."

"It is not through lack of effort on my part," Father Anthony apologized.

"I'm sure it isn't," Della said generously. "Do continue your work on my behalf."

"You may count on me, my girl," the priest said.

They broke up their little discussion with Father Anthony again promising to be in touch with her. He went off somewhere on his own and they took the carriage back to the palace.

Prince Sanzio was completely frustrated. "I say we must risk them harming Irma and bring the police into this."

"And if she is killed? What then?" Della asked.

The old man sank back into his wheelchair. "It is likely they will kill her in any case."

Raphael said, "We mustn't give up. I'm as disheartened as any of you. Yet I can see that something may happen to help us."

Della said, "You might try to talk to Barsini?"

"I will," the young Prince said. "I do not expect any good to come of it. But I shall try."

She left Raphael to talk with the old man and went upstairs to see Aunt Isobel. She found the old woman in her room, standing by the window and looking weary and upset.

Aunt Isobel came to her, "Where have you been? I've been worrying about you!"

"I went to meet Father Anthony," she said, not going into any of the unpleasantness which had taken place.

"You don't tell me any of your plans," her aunt said unhappily. "For all the good I'm doing I might just as well be back in London."

"Please," she said. "It will be all right. Soon I hope we'll be going home."

"Not as long as that girl is missing," Aunt Isobel said. "You have taken it on yourself to rescue her."

"She is my sister! I can't do less!"

Aunt Isobel gave her a troubled look. "What happened between you and Henry?"

She hesitated. "There was a little misunderstanding."

"What sort of misunderstanding?"

Della sighed and turned away from her aunt. Then she said, "It was one of those ridiculous situations. Raphael was in my room talking with me. Something was said and he impulsively kissed me. At just that moment Henry happened to arrive in the doorway to see us."

"So that is what happened!" her aunt exclaimed.

She gave her a guilty look. "I promise you the kiss was innocent enough. I'm so like Irma that I sometimes think Raphael becomes confused."

"I wouldn't accept that as an excuse, and neither would Henry," her aunt said acidly.

"It was a fuss about nothing," Della protested.

"I see!"

"As soon as I can find Henry I'm going to tell him how sorry I am and ask him to forgive me."

"You'll not have that opportunity for a few days at least," her aunt said.

"Why do you say that?"

"Because Henry received word from London of an urgent matter involving his firm. It has to do with a client in Naples and he left for there while you were out."

Della was stunned. "I don't believe it!"

"It is true," her aunt said. "He told me to explain to you and said he'd be back in three or four days!"

"How could he leave me knowing the predicament I'm in?" she lamented.

Aunt Isobel said, "I expect he thinks Prince Raphael will look after you."

"He's done it to punish me!"

"Perhaps."

"But it isn't fair. He knows I'm in real danger! How could he just go off and let me take my chances."

Aunt Isobel sighed. "I'm sure he was badly hurt."

"He didn't give me a chance to explain."

"Too late now," her aunt said. "You'll have to wait until he returns to Rome."

Della sank into a nearby chair. Dolefully she said, "Everything is going wrong."

"This grim old house depresses me," Aunt Isobel said. "I cannot sleep at night."

"If only Irma hadn't been abducted we'd have been on our way back to England," Della said.

"Let me ask you something," Aunt Isobel said.

She looked up at her. "What?"

"Have you been wandering about the house in the middle of the night?"

Della was startled by the question. She said, "No. Of course not. Why do you ask?"

"I have wandered out of my room in the night," Aunt Isobel said. "Twice I have seen a figure in the hall which I took to be you. Each time it went along the corridor and suddenly vanished, as if it had dissolved in the air."

She stared at her aunt's wrinkled, worried face. "That is utter nonsense!"

"It isn't," her aunt insisted. "And if you want my opinion of what it means, it means that Irma is already dead and I've been seeing her unhappy ghost."

Della jumped up. "Don't say such things!"

"I believe it," her aunt went on. "I only had a glance at her face and I was sure it was you. Now I realize my error. I was watching a ghost. Irma's ghost!"

"That's nonsense talk!"

"You think so? Well I saw some phantom figure with your face. If it wasn't you it had to be her phantom!"

She stared at the older woman and wondered. This was an amazing utterance from one who scarcely ever strayed from fact.

Della told the older woman, "You must have been dreaming."

Aunt Isobel said, "I was afraid you might say that."

"I was not in the corridor and Irma, as you well know, is a captive somewhere. How else can it be explained?"

"As I've told you. I think they've killed her!"

Della shuddered. "Don't say that!"

"It is what I think," the older woman said. "This old palace has a curse on it. Prince Sanzio said so. I'll not rest until we're safely away from here!"

Della saw it was not a time to argue. To discuss this further might put Aunt Isobel into a highly nervous state and she had no wish to do that. She was sure her aunt had been suffering from nightmares and because of her insomnia was now mixing up fact and her dreams. The whole business had been a strain on them all and must be especially hard on the older woman.

There was nothing to do but listen to the story and make no definite comment. Once again Della regretted the stupid scene which had put Henry in a frame of mind to go off on an errand for his firm without first warning her. Only now that he was gone did she realize how much she counted on him.

She kissed Aunt Isobel on the cheek and begged her, "Please don't make yourself ill with worry!"

Then she went on to her own room. But she could not rest. She changed into another dress and went downstairs to find Prince Sanzio in his wheelchair by the fireplace of the great living room.

The old Prince said, "Raphael has gone. I believe he plans to stop by and see Barsini."

"I'm glad of that," she said. "I'm sure Barsini is much more involved in this than he revealed to me."

"Irma was a happy girl before she met that wicked man," the old Prince sighed.

"Let us hope that she soon will be back with us arid ready for a fresh start."

The old man frowned. "I do not know. Sometimes I fear they have lied. That she may already be dead."

"Don't think that!" she protested. But at the same time she was recalling what her aunt had said. Was it possible that the phantom figure she'd seen had been the ghost of the murdered Irma?

"You have been most kind to an old man," Prince Sanzio told her. "I fear I brought a great deal of trouble upon you when I brought you here."

"You could not have done anything else," she said. "I wanted to find my missing sister. It is grimly ironic that I should find her and then lose her almost at once."

She had barely finished dinner when a messenger came with a letter from Prince Raphael. She opened it and read it quickly. In it he asked her to come at once and join him at the main entrance of the Sistine Chapel.

She went at once to Prince Sanzio and showed him the letter. "It is evident he must have discovered something!"

The old man examined the note. "It looks genuine enough," he said. "It is on Raphael's notepaper."

"I must go at once," she said. "Will you explain to my aunt?"

"Of course," the old man said. "I will have Guido summon the carriage for you."

She left the palace filled with the hope that Raphael had finally solved the mystery. The fact that he wished to meet her within the area of the Vatican suggested that perhaps the stolen treasure had been restored to the Church officials.

It was still daylight and she enjoyed the street sights as the carriage took her toward the Vatican conclave. She left the carriage near the Bronze Gate and after passing the Swiss Guard on duty there she made her way to the entrance of the Sistine Chapel. But there was no sign of Raphael!

She stood there glancing around at the hordes of tourists coming and going. But nowhere did she see the Prince's tall figure and handsome face. She began to worry that she had been the victim of some hoax. The letter could have been forged. It might not be too hard for someone to get some of Raphael's personal notepaper and use it for their own purposes.

Troubled by these thoughts and fearful that she might have walked into a trap, she was about to hurry back out to her waiting carriage when a scholarly-looking young man wearing thick spectacles and the broad-brimmed black hat and black robes of a priest came to her.

"Miss Standish," he said with a smile. His English was perfect.

She stared at him in surprise. "Yes. How do you happen to know me?"

The priest smiled. "From the excellent description given of you by Prince Raphael. Also I have several times had the pleasure of meeting your twin sister, Irma. The likeness is startling!"

"Did Prince Raphael send you to meet me?"

"Yes," the priest said. "May I introduce myself. I am Father Joseph Walker. I am from London and I'm here taking advanced studies in theology."

"How nice to meet someone from home!" she said.

"Prince Raphael felt you might enjoy my showing you around a little. He will not be here for a while. He is having a meeting with one of our Church officials."

Her hopes rose. "Has it to do with the Madonna?"

The eyes behind the spectacles fixed on her. "The stolen Madonna of St. Cecilia?"

"Yes."

"I cannot be sure," he said. "I am only a humble priest. But I can tell you the Prince must have important business since he is at this moment talking with a cardinal."

She smiled. "I'd enjoy seeing the Sistine Chapel while we're waiting."

"You have never seen it?" Father Walker said.

"No."

"Then let us delay the experience no longer," he said.

Della was astonished by the distance of the chapel from the main entrance. Father Walker led her along at least a half-mile of marble corridor with inexplicable twists and turns. The chapel was down a winding staircase with occasional windows on the wall looking out on grim stonework. She had the sense of descending into a deep fortress of stone.

Father Walker bade her follow him through a low door and she found they were in the chapel at one side of the altar. She had the impression that the many other tourists there were gazing at her in awe. Then she suddenly realized that she had entered underneath Michelangelo's fresco of the Last Judgment. This to the right of the frightening figure of Charon forcing the damned from his boat.

The priest said in a low voice, "It may seem gloomy at first. But it is a place of unbelievable beauty."

"I know," she said in an awed whisper.

The windows of the chapel were set high and the towering walls were painted a third of the way to imitate drapery. The priest knelt on the marble steps of the altar and she with him.

She then followed him back a little and he pointed upward. She gasped at the splendor of the ceiling painted by Michelangelo.

"The task took him many years of his life," Father Walker whispered in her ear. "He was thirty-three when he began the ceiling and started the Last Judgment."

"I have never seen anything so powerful," Della said. "Nothing like it in England."

Father Walker smiled sadly. "I'm afraid not."

She went back to study the Last Judgment. At first it had seemed rather dull in color. But as she moved in on the painting and studied it at close range the majestic figures stood out. It struck her that Christ was more occupied with cursing the doomed than welcoming the saved. She stared at the macabre faces of the resurrected corpses.

Under Father Walker's guidance she moved on. She noted the gold, blue and scarlet figures on the side walls.

"We are proud of our Vatican art and treasures," the English priest said.

"Rightly so," she agreed.

"When there is a theft such as that of the jeweled Madonna, it is greatly lamented," Father Walker said as they started back along the marble passage to the entrance.

"I hope it is soon returned," she said.

"That is kind of you," he said. "I most heartily pray this will be case."

"What a long way," she said, as they continued along the marble corridor.

"There is a door ahead which leads to a shortcut," Father Walker told her. "We can take it. It is here on the right."

He went ahead to a side hall and led her down its short length to a heavy, iron door. He opened the door for her, saying, "Please go first, Miss Standish."

"Thank you," she said, impressed by his friendliness and good manners. But the minute she stepped through the door it was slammed closed after her. And there was no sign of Father Walker and no handle to open the heavy door!

Chapter Thirteen

Della turned and, pounding on the door, shouted, "Father Walker! Let me out of here!"

Her words echoed mockingly in the stone tunnel with its arched roof. She began to tremble, shocked that she had come to danger in such a holy place. But she was no longer sure of anything. Was Father Walker truly a priest? Not likely! He was surely an imposter who had baited her into coming to the Sistine Chapel by using a false message from Prince Raphael.

The light in the corridor was murky and she groped her way forward wondering what she was faced with now. In a moment she stood before another door, a wooden one with an iron handle. She opened the door and found herself in a candlelit room.

A thin voice from the far end of the room called, "Enter, my child!"

Mystified and frightened, she went on into the room, which was richly carpeted and hung with crimson tapestries on all its four walls. At the very end there was a square mahogany table with a candelabrum whose white candles burned with tiny, yellow tongues to lend an amber tint to the high-ceilinged room.

As she took this in she saw an old man hunched in a chair by the table. The chair was ornate with a high back and the old man wore the red robe and cap of a cardinal. By his chair there sat a huge brown mastiff with a black-marked face. The great dog's burning, amber eyes fixed on her angrily and it rose with a growl as she slowly approached.

"Down, Bruno," the ancient Cardinal said in a thin but authoritative tone. The great beast glanced at him dubiously and then with a show of sullenness crouched down beside him again. The Cardinal's thin old face showed a smile. "Bruno is my protector and overly fond of me. He is suspicious of all intruders. You must not mind him."

"I'm sorry to be intruding," she apologized. "I didn't know what was on the other side of the door. I was in the Sistine Chapel and as we left my guide suggested we take a shortcut. To my surprise I found myself trapped in the corridor outside your door."

The red-robed Cardinal touched a jeweled finger to the graying fringe of hair under his crimson cap. He studied her through slitted ancient gray eyes. "You are speaking of Father Walker."

"Yes," she said. "I can only think that it was an accident."

The Cardinal's eyes didn't leave her. "It was no accident." His tone had become cold.

She faltered. "I don't understand."

"I will explain in due time," he said. Bruno eyed her, moved to one side and growled again. "It is all right, Bruno," the old man placated him.

"May I ask what this means?" she said, trying not to show her fear. "Are you really a cardinal or is this all some game?"

"Forgive me for having you stand," the old man apologized. "I am truly a cardinal of the Church and Father Walker is a priest. He sent you to me at my bidding."

"Why?"

The Cardinal smiled thinly and with one hand caressed Bruno's huge head. "You must be as intelligent as you are lovely. Surely you don't need to ask me that?"

She stared at him. "Do you mean you are like those thieves? That you actually think I have the jeweled Madonna."

The Cardinal looked grimly amused. "I am the one from whom the Madonna was stolen. I am in charge of the archives here. I have been for seventeen years and this is the first time such a sordid theft has taken place."

"I'm sorry," she said. "I cannot help you."

The Cardinal sighed. "We have no lack of treasures here, I promise you. Some are of precious stones and gold. Others are more rare. Items which I cherish as an archivist. Would you believe that under my lock and key are such items as Henry the Eighth's application for divorce with its mass of seals, a letter from the nephew of Genghis Khan politely declining to become a Christian, the last letter written by Mary, Queen of Scots, and an impatient demand for payment written by Michelangelo."

"Why do you tell me all this?" she asked.

"To give you some idea of the magnitude of the collection for which I'm responsible, my child," the Cardinal said. "The jeweled Madonna of St. Cecilia is worth a fortune. It was stolen from under my nose and I shall never forgive myself for my failure to protect it."

Della said, "It is presumed that the stolen Madonna was sent to me. I never received it."

The Cardinal studied her in silence for a moment and then, addressing the mastiff, said, "She seems like a truthful girl." In reply, Bruno made a growl resembling a long rumbling.

She said, "I am telling you the truth."

"If I believe you, I shall be the only one involved who does," the Cardinal told her.

"I vow that I'm being truthful!"

"Since you declare it so strongly I hope you are," the old man in red robe and cap said. "But the thieves all still think you have the treasure."

"I know. They have kidnapped my sister and threaten to kill her if I do not return the Madonna."

"They will also kill you," the Cardinal said in his casual way. "Have you any idea of the caliber of men you are facing?"

"Not really. I know they are thieves and desperate."

"Let me tell you," the thin old man said. "The Madonna was stolen by an animal named Brizzi with the help of one of my trusted aides, Father Louis."

She said, "You know that he is dead?"

The Cardinal nodded. "Murdered by Brizzi who no longer needed him. I pray for Brother Louis's soul. There was much good in him but he was weak."

"I have never met Brizzi," she said. "I have been told he is a superthief."

"You are not apt to recognize him when you do meet him," the old Cardinal said. "He is a chameleon! A master of disguise! One day he is an old man, another he is a young one. He has a dozen different identities."

"What about Count Barsini?"

"Ah!" the Cardinal said. "Our Satanist! A truly evil person. You have met him."

"To my sorrow," she said.

"It is a rather complicated story," the old Cardinal said as he fondled Bruno's head. The big dog had now closed his eyes and seemed to be sleeping. "It began with the theft by Brizzi and Brother Louis. Then an accomplice of Barsini, whose name I do not know, managed to steal the Madonna from Brizzi while he was with one of Barsini's Satanist courtesans. Barsini met your sister, Irma, through Prince Raphael."

"That is true," she agreed.

"Raphael, who is not a bad fellow but rather foolish, introduced Barsini to your sister just at the time she'd discovered her true identity. For some perverse reason Barsini decided to get the Madonna out of Rome by sending it to you by messenger. The idea being to ask you to keep it until Barsini and your sister came to London."

"But I never received it."

"In that case the messenger must have been murdered and the Madonna fell into other hands."

"Who was the messenger?"

"I have not been able to trace the Madonna past its reaching Barsini's hands," the Cardinal said.

Della said, "Prince Raphael is going to see Count Barsini again and try and get more information from him."

"He has scant hope of that," the Cardinal said drily. "In the meanwhile this pack of mad dogs will close in on you and tear you to bits as they seek this fabulous treasure of the Church. I ask you, if you have it, turn it over to the Church, then you will no longer be the target for them."

"I can't," she said, near tears. "I don't have it!"

"In the days of the Inquisition I would have had you tortured," the man in the red robe said. "That was their way then but this is 1890. I cannot threaten you. I can only pray for your safety."

"I have been truthful," she said. "There is one other man who may know something about where the Madonna is. He has talked with Brizzi. His name is Father Anthony!"

The Cardinal looked grim. "A renegade! Long ago defrocked! He is no priest of the Church any longer. He is an underworld figure who uses his priestly garb as a façade. He has been a henchman to Brizzi and to Barsini. Do not trust him!"

"I have until this moment," she said, shocked.

"I think he is Barsini's man now," the Cardinal said. "But he is one of the greedy animals seeking to find the Madonna and dispose of it for his own profit."

She said, "I will avoid him. He promised to send me a message. I was to meet him. I've been trying desperately to get the Madonna back so that I may save my sister's life."

"I do not know who is holding her," the Cardinal said. "It could be either Brizzi or Barsini."

"I realize that."

The Cardinal stared at her. Then he said. "I doubted from the first that you had the Madonna. I believe your story. You are free to go."

Relieved, she asked, "How do I find my way out?"

He smiled. "The same way you came in. You will find that Father Walker has left the iron door open to the corridor."

"Thank you," she said.

"If the Madonna does come into your hands do not be afraid to bring it to me," the Cardinal said. "I will ask no questions and I will try and protect you."

"I do want to see it restored where it belongs," she said.

The old man nodded and waved a thin hand as a signal she was dismissed. The dog Bruno rose to its feet again and growled after her as she hastily retreated to the door and out. She reached the short hall and found that, just as the Cardinal had promised, the iron door was open. She stepped out into the wide marble corridor, joining the other visitors. She looked for some sign of Father Walker but he was nowhere to be seen.

She could not believe what had happened to her. A few minutes ago she had stood in the presence of a Prince of the Church. He had talked with her amiably enough under the circumstances. And convinced of her innocence in the theft, he had let her go free.

Darkness had fallen. She made her way out to the gate and the street where she expected her carriage would still be waiting. She was anxious to get back to the palace and contact Prince Raphael and tell him about her weird experience. There was no doubt that somebody had forged the letter from him. Perhaps the old Cardinal had arranged it as a means of questionong her.

She reached the spot where she had left the carriage and to her amazement it was gone! Vanished! She stood there unable to believe the evidence of her eyes. With the coming of night the street was not so busy and she found herself standing there alone. What could have happened to the coachman that he decided to leave in this fashion? She had given him explicit instructions to wait.

Standing there bewildered, she was further startled to see a stout figure hurriedly coming up to her. It was Father Anthony!

He beamed at her. "My dear girl, what luck that I should meet you this way!"

"I suspect you've followed me," she accused him.

The fat priest looked hurt. "You are right. I did follow you but only for your good."

"My good?" she echoed. "I've just heard about you. You are no longer a priest. The Church turned you out!"

"Once a priest always a priest," Father Anthony told her. "I don't know what wicked lies you have been fed inside. I assure you I'm the same kindly Father Anthony who has tried to help you!"

Alarmed by the turn of events, she told him, "You can help me best by getting me a carriage. My own seems to have disappeared."

"You will not need a carriage," the fat priest said with a deceptively warm smile.

She stared at him. "Did I hear right?"

"I dismissed your carriage," Father Anthony said. "I took the liberty of advising your driver that you would be visiting me. I sent him back to the palace with the promise I would take care of getting you home."

She stared at him wide-eyed. "How dare you do such a thing?"

"One dares when one must," the fat priest said. "I have a cellar flat nearby and I would like to play host to you!"

"No!" she said, preparing to run in the opposite direction.

But her awareness of danger had come too late. Already the dark, swarthy-faced man familiar to her from London had come up to seize her arm. Father Anthony seized the other one and between them they propelled her across the street where it was more deserted.

"Let me go!" she cried, struggling vainly to escape from them.

The dark man hissed, "I have a knife at your ribs. One loud shout from you and I plunge it in!"

She looked and saw that he was telling the truth. In his free hand was a knife, its sharp tip poised against her.

Father Anthony was breathing heavily from the effort of struggling with her and dragging her along. He gasped, "Just a few yards more and we shall be at my modest abode."

This proved to be right. They descended a stone stairway into an alley that let to the side entrance of an adjacent building. Father Anthony went ahead and unlocked the door, then the darkman shoved her inside roughly and stood guard. In the meanwhile Father Anthony lit some candles.

Turning to her, he said, "Do please sit down and be comfortable!"

She stood defiantly. "I demand that you let me go!"

"All in good time," he said. And he told the dark man, "Best that you take up guard outside." Without saying a word the dark man went out and closed the door after him.

"Are you hungry?" the fat priest asked her as soon as they were alone.

"No. I want to be set free!"

"Not yet," the fat man said.

"What do you want of me?"

He leaned forward. "What did they ask you?"

"What business is it of yours?" she demanded. "You bring me here against my will and expect me to answer questions. Who told you to do this, Brizzi or Barsini?"

Father Anthony looked hurt. "They have turned you against me. And I'm probably the only one who can help you."

"You are a liar and an imposter!" she shot back.

The fat man looked grim. "I have no wish to be unpleasant, Miss Standish. What did you tell the cardinal?"

"What could I tell him?"

"Where the Madonna is!"

"I don't know! I keep telling you that!"

Father Anthony looked sad. "I do not wish to harm you, Miss Standish. Be sensible. Settle it here and now. Tell me where the Madonna is and both you and your sister will be free and safe."

"I cannot tell you," she said. "I have never seen the Madonna."

The fat priest looked sad. "It seems you are determined to be stubborn!"

"And you to be stupid!"

He said, "Well, there are other, more conventional means of getting information. You must forgive the poverty and bareness of my quarters. I'm sure you understand that I have taken the vow of the priesthood."

"You are no longer recognized by the Church," she reminded him. "At least that is one thing the cardinal told me.

A vicious smile came to the fat, oval face. He said, "I happen to be a collector of Church relics. I'll show you one of them." He vanished into the back of the apartment and then appeared again with a metal object mounted on a wood base. "Do you know what this is?"

She stared at the rather complicated contrivance. "No!"

"It is an ancient thumbscrew, Miss Standish. Used by churchmen and others in the old days for reviving the memories of their enemies. It is still most practical. Works very well. The purpose being to crush and twist the thumb completely out of shape."

She watched him display the torture weapon with true relish and began to wonder if he were mad. She turned her head away. "I don't want to see it!"

"Nor I to use it on you,'" the fat man said amiably. "Such delicate hands too! But if you refuse to tell me about the Madonna, you leave me no choice, do you?"

"You're mad!" she declared, backing away from him.

He followed her, holding up the torture device. "I have only to call my friend back in and have him tie you in a chair. Then we can apply this little device to your thumbs."

"I trusted you and you deceived me," she protested, backed into a corner of the basement room. "But from the first I told you I knew nothing about the missing Madonna."

He smiled madly. "Of course you were lying then and you are lying now. Most impractical of you, I fear."

She stared at him in stunned amazement. "You cannot believe I do not have it?"

"That is quite correct," he agreed in a friendly manner.

"So you are really insane!"

He chuckled. "Names will not upset me, dear girl. I happen to be a man of single purpose. You are standing in my way!"

She stared at him. "You're really Brizzi, aren't you?"

She never did get a reply from him for at that moment a shot rang outside. An expression of fear crossed Father Anthony's fat face and he vanished into the shadows at the rear of the cellar. She stayed in the corner of the room, too terrified to move. Then the door was flung open and Father Walker appeared, pistol in hand.

"Miss Standish!" he called out.

"Here!" she cried in reply and ran to him.

"Where is the other one?" he asked.

"He went on out back," she told him.

Father Walker hurried to the rear where the fat priest had vanished. After a moment he came back with a look of disgust on his scholarly face. He said, "Too late! There is a back exit. He managed to get away! Are you safe?"

"Just barely," she said. "How did you know?"

"The Cardinal felt I should shadow you until you were safely home," the young priest said grimly. "It seems his precaution was wise."

"He was going to torture me," she said.

"I have no doubt." Father Walker eyed her gravely. "You are dealing with the most dangerous of criminals." He kept his pistol ready in his hand. "Now let us get out of here before they come back with reinforcements."

"Yes," she agreed. As they climbed up to the street level, she asked, "What about the dark man acting as guard?"

"A shot scared him away," Father Walker said. "I didn't follow him. I was too interested in getting to you."

"Not a moment too soon," she said. "I think the man calling himself Father Anthony is really Brizzi."

"He could be," said the man walking beside her. "He may have murdered the real Father Anthony as he did Brother Louis. It would be easy for him to pose as our renegade friend. He is clever at disguising himself."

Della shuddered. "He behaved insanely. He refused to accept that I knew nothing about the Madonna."

"The general belief is that you do."

"The Cardinal accepted my word."

"The Cardinal is a man of faith. These others are rogues with no other thought but getting their hands on that stolen Madonna!"

They had reached a busier street and the young priest stood out with his hand raised until he managed to hail a passing carriage. He gave the driver some instructions in Italian and then helped her into the vehicle.

He told her, "You will be safe now. He will take you directly to the Palazzo Sanzio."

"How can I thank you?" she asked.

Father Walker smiled grimly. "By trying to restore the Madonna to us."

"I promise that I will," she said. "And thank the Cardinal for me again."

He nodded and then stepped back. The driver urged his horse on and the carriage started along the wide street. She sat back exhausted in the dark interior of the carriage.

Prince Raphael was at the palace to greet her. The young man was in a state of grim concern. He at once embraced her and said, "We have been on the point of calling in the police! I sent you no message!"

"I found that out," she said with a rueful smile.

Aunt Isobel came to her along with Prince Sanzio in his wheelchair. Her aunt said, "I was imagining all sorts of dreadful things happening to you!"

Prince Sanzio told her, "The moment Raphael arrived and told me he knew nothing of the message, I realized you'd fallen into a trap."

She said, "At least I've survived."

"Tell us what happened," Raphael said.

"I will," she promised. "But first some strong coffee and give me just a few minutes to wash and change."

A half-hour later she sat with the others in the living room and told them of her strange experience. She said, "I had no idea I was being followed as well."

The old Prince studied her with his faded eyes and said, "Then it was actually someone within the Church who sent you the false message?"

"Yes," she said. "I'm sure the Cardinal arranged it. He struck me as a remarkably clever man."

"But he had no intention of harming you," Aunt Isobel said. She was seated on the divan with Della.

"I'm sure that is true," she said. "But he had hoped I knew about the Madonna and would return it to the Church."

Raphael frowned. "I'd like to know how they managed to get my notepaper."

Della said, "Perhaps a servant."

"It could be," the handsome young Prince said.

Prince Sanzio said, "If the carriage had been there when the Cardinal let you go you would have had no problems."

"That was when the so-called Father Anthony took over," she observed with a sigh.

Aunt Isobel frowned. "I always wondered about him. I thought he was rather strange for a priest."

"He has been defrocked," Della said. "And I'm not sure the man we know as Father Anthony really is who he claims to be. It may be someone posing as him."

"Why do you say that?" Raphael asked, puzzled.

"Father Walker suggested it. He pointed out that the real Father Anthony worked with Brizzi. And Brizzi is a master of disguise and impersonation. It is possible the man we accepted as Father Anthony is really the key figure in the theft, Brizzi!"

"That does complicate things," Raphael said. "I'm surprised. I felt the fellow was genuine enough."

"He showed himself in his true colors tonight," Della said. "He was ready to torture me when I was fortunately rescued by the arrival of Father Walker."

"And he managed to escape?" Aunt Isobel worried.

"Yes," Della said. "He had been careful to have an escape avenue ready. He is clever enough."

Prince Sanzio said, "At least he will not be able to deceive you as he did in the past."

She said, "I know him for what he is now, just another criminal after the Madonna."

"I wish we had never heard of it!" Aunt Isobel said in a vexed tone.

After a little both her aunt and Prince Sanzio retired for the evening. She and Raphael decided to take a stroll in the gardens, for it was a pleasant night.

As they walked slowly along the gravel path, he said, "I died a thousand deaths tonight waiting for you to return. I would have blamed myself if you hadn't."

"How could you do that?"

"Because my name and notepaper were used to entice you to the Sistine Chapel."

"That was not your doing."

"But you went because you had faith in me."

"That is true," she said, smiling up at him as they halted by a tall marble figure of a gladiator on a pedestal near the vine-covered garden wall.

"Dearest Della!" the handsome dark man said, taking her in his arms.

She gave him a reproving look. "Thanks to your kissing me in my room I've lost Henry!"

"He'll come back."

"You never can tell," she said. "He's very proud and I know he must have been badly hurt."

Raphael gazed down at her lovely face with an adoring expression. He said, "Why must you worry about him? You know that I'm in love with you."

Still in his arms, she told him, "It happens I love Henry. And even if that were not so, aren't you betrothed to my sister?"

"Irma and I were about to break up before you arrived," he said.

"You don't plan to marry her?"

"No," he said. "Not now. If I can't have you I will marry no one."

Della said, "I find that hard to believe. And I think we are two cold, heartless people. Talking about Irma in this fashion when she is still a hostage and may lose her life."

"I pray that doesn't happen," Raphael said, releasing her.

They began the stroll back to the palace and she told him, "Has it ever occurred to you she may already be dead?"

He looked startled. "Why do you say that?"

She gave a tiny shudder. "It's an eerie feeling I have that she will never return here alive."

"Don't say such things!"

"It's true," she told him. "And my Aunt Isobel has the same opionion. In fact she thinks she has seen Irma's ghost moving down one of the hallways."

He halted. "What?"

"She asked me if I had been in the hall and I said no. And it was then she decided that the figure she had seen must have been my twin sister's ghost."

"We Italians are said to be superstitious, but I'm beginning to think you English outdo us!"

They returned to the palace and said their goodnights. The Prince left promising to return the following afternoon. Della was left to go up to bed and review all the events of a thrilling day. She also thought of Henry Clarkson and worried that the estrangement between her and the nice young lawyer might develop into a permanent thing.

They had gone through several quarrels in the past. The worst one had been patched up just prior to their coming to Italy. Now they were back again where they had started. She could only hope that, after consideration, Henry would come to understand that the embrace he'd seen between her and Raphael had been a casual thing.

Of course Raphael was proving a problem in his own right. He had brought about this embarrassing situation and he was continuing to insist on his love for her. She liked him but she did not love him. And she was distressed that he seemed to have so little feeling for the kidnapped Irma. Raphael was a difficult young man to understand and to cope with.

She could not sleep for a long while. And when she slept it was only to dream of being tortured by Father Anthony. In her nightmare she was tied in a chair, her hands and feet bound. Then the cruel old priest released one of her hands and placed it in the heavy metal apparatus which he had called a thumbscrew. He turned a lever on the outside and she was at once tormented with a searing pain as her thumb was twisted almost from her hand. She screamed for aid, then woke out of the dream feeling stupid.

She was in her bedroom writing a letter the following morning when the midget Guido came with an envelope for her. He said, "This came just a few minutes ago."

She thanked him and, full of excitement that the note might be from Henry, she glanced at the address on the envelope. It was not in Henry's handwriting. So that was that! Disappointed, she tore open the envelope and withdrew the scented notepaper.

She read it quickly. It was a message from Madame Guioni, filled with apologies for having neglected her, and suggesting that they take a ride in her open carriage if the afternoon should be fine. The strong-minded woman ended the note by saying she would call for her around four and so have an hour or two to drive before it was time to dress for dinner.

She took the letter downstairs to consult with Prince Sanzio. He read the brief note and handed it back to her, saying, "I don't know the woman but her offer seems friendly enough."

Della sighed. "I don't know what to do. I dislike leaving the palace for any other wild goose chase. I'm only interested in seeing Irma back here, alive and safe."

"I know how you feel," the old man sympathized. "I feel the same way. But life goes on. It is possible that a late-afternoon drive with the woman might restore your spirits."

She continued to ponder over the message, telling the old Prince, "If I wished to answer this I could not. She gave me no return address."

"Not likely she expected a reply," Prince Sanzio said.

Della smiled and said, "I shall also be breaking my word. I promised I wouldn't accept invitations or go anywhere until Irma was rescued."

"I know," said the old man in the wheelchair. "But this invitation is somewhat different. You are not being asked to a rendezvous anywhere. The carriage will pick you up here, you and this lady will be driven about, and then you'll be returned."

She smiled sadly. "As simple as that! I only hope you are right." And so she planned on the drive.

• • •

Promptly at four Madame Guioni arrived in a large brown carriage that was most impressive. Della was helped up into the carriage by an attractive, young liveried coachman and Madame Guioni showed a smile on her ugly face and kissed her on the forehead. She smelled too strongly of heavy perfume and, as always, her facial makeup was so overdone as to be a caricature of what cosmetics should be. The older woman made room for Della and fussed over her.

"I have so neglected you," Madame Guioni said with regret on her rather monstrous face. The hat she was wearing matched her ugly features and she had on a high-necked brown dress with white gloves. Della felt that beige or brown gloves would have been more desirable.

"No at all," Della said. "Time has passed very quickly since I arrived in Rome."

"I'm sure it has!" Madame Guioni gushed. "But this is a busy social season and I'm so much in demand that I have not had time to plan any parties of my own! Every night I'm invited somewhere!"

"You mustn't worry about it!" Della said as the carriage rolled slowly through the streets. She was sure the ugly old woman beside her was attracting the amused glances of many of those whom they passed. It was not only her loud dress, but she also spoke in an exaggerated way and made a lot of outlandish gestures.

"Notice my carriage!" the vulgar woman said. "Rubber-tired wheels, my dear child! See how easy we ride along! Have you ever been in a more luxurious carriage since you've been in this city?"

Della was forced to say, "No. I surely have not."

"Of course you haven't," the old woman at her side insisted. "This is a magnificent carriage! People plead with me to take them riding in my carriage! But I say no, it is only for me and my firends! Am I not right?"

"You are surely right," Della said wearily. "It is a superior carriage."

Madame Guioni was not listening to her, her attention having been drawn by two young men in the street who had hooted at her and made some obscene remarks. She was gasping with indignation and she waved her umbrella at them angrily.

Turning to Della, she exclaimed, "Did you hear them?"

"Not too well."

"I'm happy that you didn't," the old woman said. "They were saying the most disgusting things! The young! What are they coming to!"

"I'm sure I don't know," Della said, meekly wondering why she'd exposed herself to this experience and how soon it would end.

Madame Guioni was in a mood to reminise. "When my beloved late husband was alive no one dared say a nasty word to me! No one! He was always on the alert to defend me! Poor dear! Now he is gone and his brother also! There is only the label left, Guioni Brothers, and what comfort is a wine label to a sorrowing widow."

Della felt prompted to comfort her. "You have built yourself a good new life, madam."

The ugly, overdressed woman touched a hanky to her eyes. "You are right. Now I must not talk about myself continually but let you enjoy some of the beauty of the things we're driving by."

They came to the Via delle Quattro which Della enjoyed because of its four fountains. And she told Madame Guioni, "Rome has so many fine squares and fountains!"

"True," Madame Guioni growled. She seemed to be tiring as the drive wore on. She pointed to one of a reclining woman which they were passing. "That is said to be nearly four hundred years old. The figure is called 'Fidelity.' "

"Four hundred years is not really ancient in Rome," Della said.

"It is rather new," Madame Guioni agreed. "We have fountains here nearly two thousand years old. So many of them! The Italians love to see water flowing, spraying or just filling a fountain. At the Villa Borghese there is a rabbit's nose which spouts water, at another place water pours out of the muzzle of a bronze wolf. And let us not forget outside the Pantheon, where water flows from a number of grotesque masks!"

"You are right," she said. "I had not noticed it before."

"An obsession," Madame Guioni said. "If only they all spouted Guioni wine I should be richer than I am. But then one must not complain!"

"Certainly not," she said.

Madame Guioni stared at her. "You look pale, my dear. Are you not well?"

Apologetically, she said, "I usually sleep in the afternoon. I fear I'm tired."

"So am I," the ugly woman said at once. She called to the driver and said, "The Palazzo Sanzio at once." Then she slumped back in her seat.

Della was grateful when the carriage pulled up before the palace. She thanked the older woman extravagantly. "It was such a nice treat," she said.

Madame Guioni smiled modestly. "I felt you might like it. I forgot to enquire about your peculiar aunt, and that darling young British lawyer, and that nice Prince I saw you with the other evening, and of course dear Prince Sanzio. Is the poor old man managing to pay his bills?"

Della replied that all were well and that the Prince was managing nicely. Then she quickly left the carriage. But the ordeal was not yet over: Madame Guioni waved to her girlishly and blew kisses until the carriage was far up the street.

As a result Della entered the palace in a totally unstrung state only to be faced by Prince Sanzio in his wheelchair. The old man had a despairing look on his withered face which told her of new trouble.

Chapter Fourteen

Della asked the old man, "What is wrong?"

"Another message from those villains," he said in an agitated voice and held up a sheet of notepaper.

She took it and read: "Time is short! Do you wish to see your daughter alive again?"

The white-haired Prince Sanzio was in a more distressed state than ever before. He moaned, "If I were not a cripple I would somehow settle with those people and rescue Irma."

"I know how you feel," she sympathized.

"As soon as Raphael returns we must settle on some new plan," the old man said.

"Every attempt seems to wind up in a dead end."

"We must persevere," Prince Sanzio said. "How did you manage with Madame Guioni?"

Della shook her head in mock despair. "I hope she forgets all about me. Being with her was an ordeal. She is a loud, vulgar woman and talks incessantly."

"And the Guioni Brothers wine is very bad!"

"I have no doubt," she said. "When do you expect Prince Raphael?"

"In a half-hour," the old man said. "This latest note came after he left. It has shattered me."

"I'm sure we'll manage something." Della tried to bolster his courage although she knew the chances of recovering Irma were getting slimmer as the days passed. They had not been able to discover anything about the Madonna. And it was the key to the predicament.

She went upstairs and met Aunt Isobel on the landing. The old woman brightened on seeing her. "I've been worried all the time you were out."

"I was perfectly safe," she said. "Madame Guioni took me for a carriage ride."

"Is she as obnoxious as ever?"

"Even more so," Della said. "And she thinks only of herself and her problems."

"A very strange person," Aunt Isobel said with a grimace. "You know that the Prince received another message while you were gone."

"Yes. He told me just now. He's very upset."

"Poor old man," Aunt Isobel sighed. "And the worst of it is I think that poor girl is already dead."

Della gave her a troubled look. "Please don't keep on saying that!"

"I think it to be true," her aunt confided. "Again last night I saw a ghostly figure resembling her. This time in the garden."

"Are you sure?" Della asked tensely.

"Yes. It was very late. As usual, I was unable to sleep. I was pacing in my room and I happened to look out the window. And I saw her! I know it was Irma!"

Della felt it was useless to argue with the older woman. It appeared that every shadow had turned into a ghost as far as she was concerned. But she did warn her, "Don't tell the old Prince about seeing the ghostly figure. It would only increase his despair."

Aunt Isobel said, "I will be descreet. I have no wish to see him suffer."

Della went on to her room and changed into a lovely pale-green gown which was one of her favorites. She kept thinking about what her aunt had said, and wondering if Irma might be dead. It seemed too tragic that this should happen so soon after she'd found her. When she had her auburn hair properly done in an upswept style she went back downstairs.

Prince Raphael was there in white tie and tails. He gave her an admiring look as he approached him. "I have never seen you look lovelier," he said. "Your afternoon ride must have been good for you."

She gave him a wry look. "I can promise you I won't repeat that mistake. The next time Madame Guioni suggests I meet her I'm going to be busy."

He smiled, "I take it she was as difficult as ever."

"More so," she said. "Where is Prince Sanzio?"

"He is feeling so unwell he has gone to his room," the Prince said. "It seems we'll have to excuse him from the dinner table. The note he received has been a bad blow."

"He is terribly depressed."

"Not much wonder."

"Is there anything we can do?" she asked.

"I can think of one thing," he said.

"What?"

"Go out somewhere to dinner," the handsome man said. "In a different atmosphere perhaps we'll pick up some fresh ideas."

"It seems heartless to go out and leave him," Della worried.

"He won't mind," the young Prince said. "Here we are beautifully dressed with no place to show ourselves off."

"I'm not concerned with showing myself off at a time like this," she said. "There is also Aunt Isobel."

"Guido can serve her in her room, since he is going to give the Prince his dinner the same way," Raphael said. "Perhaps we may meet someone who'll be able to help us."

She gave him a meaningful look. "I know who can best help us."

"Whom?"

"The police!"

He looked startled. "But we have agreed not to call in the police. Otherwise they've promised to kill Irma right away."

"There are not many days left," she said. "If we don't make some progress I'd say we have to risk it."

"Prince Sanzio would have to be convinced there was no other course."

"I think even he may agree that we are facing a crisis which we cannot seem to cope with. If we let the time go by without calling in the police it could be too late."

"Wait another day or two," the young Prince urged.

"We could then find ourselves with only twenty-four hours left. The police will not thank us for leaving it that late!"

Raphael looked grim. "I doubt if the police can do more than us."

She gave him a sharp look. "What exactly have we done thus far?"

"We've tried to track down leads."

"And wound up exposing ourselves to danger without gaining anything. We are as far from the truth about the Madonna as we were at the start."

He said, "You at least know Father Anthony is in with the gang of thieves."

"If he is truly Father Anthony," she said bitterly. "And whether he is or not I don't expect to see him again."

Raphael said, "I still maintain that getting out of here and having a good dinner in a roomful of people is the best medicine for us."

He finally convinced her and they took a carriage to an elegant restaurant named Mario's. It was in the heart of the city and was filled with a fashionable crowd. The headwaiter knew Raphael and greeted him cordially before showing them to an excellent table in a raised section of the establishment. They were seated near a four-piece string ensemble that played pleasant background music for the diners.

Smiling at the young Prince across the table, she said, "I must admit I feel better."

"You needed this and so did I," he said.

When they had finished their meal they remained in the high-ceilinged, walnut-panneled room to talk in low tones. The lights had been dimmed and the music continued.

Della confessed, "I feel guilty here enjoying myself when I know my sister is a captive somewhere, threatened with murder. And surely badly treated."

Raphael said, "She ought to have stayed away from Barsini. Even though I introduced them it did not necessarily follow that she would become his disciple."

"Perhaps if the police raided his villa they would find her."

The darkly handsome man shook his head. "Never. The place is a maze of secret passages and escape routes. Barsini would spirit her away under the nose of the police."

"I still say Barsini is the one," she maintained. "And what I have learned bears it out."

"He was out when I went by today, but I shall try him again," Raphael said. They continued talking until they were interrupted by the arrival of a voluptuous young woman of twenty or so wearing a revealingly low-cut gown. The girl was blond and beautiful and she knew Raphael.

"My darling!" she said, standing by him.

His face crimson, Raphael at once stood up. "Sophia!" he said.

"I have not seen you for weeks," the girl said with a teasing smile. "Where have you buried yourself?"

"I have been busy," he said uneasily. And then he introduced her: "This is Miss Della Standish from England."

The blond Sophia regarded her with amusement. "Of courre! I remember you! You were at Barsini's last gathering."

She said, "I have been told he does not admit to holding such affairs."

The blonde laughed. "Admit it or not, I know you were there and so was I."

"I think I remember you," she said.

"Your twin was our Vestal Virgin that night," Sophia went on. "How much alike you two are!"

Della quickly asked the girl, "Have you seen her since?"

"Once."

"Where?"

"At Gregorio's after the gathering," Sophia said. "She was making love with him when I left."

Della said, "And you haven't seen her since?"

"No," the girl said. "Why should I? It was her night, wasn't it. Having sex on the altar with the Count and winding up with Gregorio! I wouldn't mind a night like that!"

Prince Raphael raised his eyebrows. "You would enjoy making a spectacle of yourself? Showing your naked body on the stage and going through the sexual act to titillate the group."

"I will be the altar virgin at the next gathering," she said seductively. "You must come and see what a performance I shall give."

"When is it to be?" Della asked her.

"Night after next," Sophia said. "Didn't you get a message?"

"No," she said.

"You will," the blonde said, her eyes studying Della with a mocking light in them. "No doubt we'll meet there."

"Perhaps," Rahpael said cautiously.

Sophia said, "Gregorio was boasting about taking both you and your twin in the same night!"

She blushed. "I'm sure he is capable of discussing it."

"A giant of a man," Sophia said, relishing the picture of him in her mind. "And wealthy as well. But what do you think he does in his spare time?"

"I can't imagine."

"He's fascinated by the opera," the blonde confided in a conspiratorial tone. "Can you imagine? He goes there every night he's free and gives his services as an extra for the crowd scenes."

"Are you sure?" Della asked.

"I've seen him there many times," the girl said. "I find it hilarious! Think of Gregorio as a spear carrier!" And then she moved on.

Della stared at an unhappy Raphael and asked, "Well, what do you say to that?"

"She is one of Barsini's girls."

"Very much so if she's going to do the altar orgy!"

Raphael looked embarrassed. "I'm sorry she spoke so frankly."

"I'm not," she said. "Now we know Barsini is having another of his revels night after tomorrow."

"So?"

"We must somehow get in there with the other guests and try and find Irma."

His eyebrows lifted. "You think that will be easy?"

"No. But I'm sure it can be done."

"You expect me to help you in this mad stunt?"

"I do," she said. "And I expect you to go with me to the opera tomorrow night and see if we can locate Gregorio there."

"Suppose he's not there?"

"At least we will have tried," she said. "You claimed it might do us good to go out. It has. Now we have two new chances to learn something about where Irma is."

"Even if we catch up with Gregorio I doubt that he will talk," Raphael said.

"Are you afraid of him?"

The Prince looked irritated. "No. He may be a giant but I have the reputation of being able to look after myself."

"I should hope so," she said. "I only wish Henry Clarkson were here."

"You think he'd be more help?"

"Perhaps."

"We shall see," he said. "So we have our work cut out for us tomorrow night and the one following."

"You must think up a way for us to get to the orgy," she said. "You know the house and some of its secret passages."

"I'll try," he said carefully. "I'll make no giant promises."

He saw her home and she went to bed that night in a happier frame of mind than on the previous several nights. At least she had some plan now. First they would try to close in on Gregorio and get him to talk, and failing that, they would get to the orgy and explore Barsini's villa.

She slept lightly and was wakened by what she thought was the door opening. But when she raised herself up in bed to study it with frightened eyes she saw that it was closed. At the same time she was sure she heard a floorboard creak on the other side of the door.

Unable to restrain her curiosity, she quickly got up and, throwing a robe around her, went to the door and flung it open. She was just in time to see a ghostly female figure enter Irma's room. The sight of the phantom creature made her gasp and remember what Aunt Isobel had told her.

She rushed down the hallway and opened the door to Irma's room just in time to see a hidden door in the opposite wall of the room closing. She noted that the candle in the wide glass container was burning before the plaster Madonna. She went to the spot where she was sure she had seen motion and began feeling the wood paneling which covered the wall halfway to the ceiling.

She had no luck until she pressed both hands on a section of the walnut paneling and suddenly the secret door swung back, revealing a dark corridor.

She felt the chill, damp air of the dark corridor and found herself trembling. She'd been told that the house had its share of secret passages, yet she had never found one before. Her good judgment told her to venture no farther but her curiosity overwhelmed any caution. She went to the dresser and found a taper. She lit it and went back to the secret entrance.

She knew she had seen someone or something in the hall. And whoever it was had certainly vanished by means of this hidden passage. She did not wish to believe she was stalking the supernatural, that it was the ghost of her sister she had seen. But she knew there was some eerie truth behind the facts.

Slowly she moved into the dark secret passage and found it was of the same stone as the old palace's exterior. It was much damper than the interior of the palace and it smelled of being shut off for ages. She came to a turn and a stone stairway which twisted around as she descended it. The walls of the stairway were wet. She held the candle, fiercely not wanting to be left in the dark in this terrifying place.

She came to the bottom of the winding stone steps and was again in a low corridor of stone. This led her to a door. She hesitated and then cautiously opened the door and found herself in still another passage. She closed the door behind her and stood there a moment.

As she hesitated she suddenly heard a click behind her. She was certain that someone had turned a key in the door and made her a prisoner. She turned and tried the iron door handle. It would not turn now. She knew she had been right. She was trapped!

Ahead lay dark shadows and no promise of any exit. If she were in a dead-end tunnel she could picture herself dying of thirst and hunger while whoever had turned that key would wait silently, knowing that time was his aide.

Sick with fear and shivering from the cool of the deep, dark place, she moved along. The tiny candle flame flickered several times and threatened to go out. In spite of her fear she pressed on. And when she least expected it the tunnel turned again and she came to a set of stone steps rising up six or seven feet.

There was no escape; she had to mount the steps. And when she had gone halfway up she saw a trapdoor above her. With the candle still in one hand she used all her strength to lift the door. The first time it would only go so far, then she pushed a bit harder and swung it back all the way.

A musty storage room was revealed to her. She came up the rest of the steps and used the candle to inspect the room. It was filled with ancient furniture and paintings thick with dust lay against the walls. Flung across a broken chair was a brilliant red cloak. She lifted it and smelled it and recognized the perfume Irma had habitually worn still clung to the cloak.

It was a strange find and she did not know what it meant or what to do about it. She decided to close the trapdoor after her, keep the cloak as evidence of her discovery, and attempt to get out of the storage room by some other means.

After she'd lowered the trap door she went to the room's windows and saw that they were shuttered on the inside. The shutters were locked. She went to the single door and she was not too surprised when on opening it she found herself in a hall at the rear of the ground floor of the palace.

She had covered all this area of the house by means of secret stairways and passages. And the ghostly creature who had sent her on this strange trail must have used the same path of escape. But there had been someone else involved! Someone who had locked that door shut after her. Who? Had it been a human hand or had the ghost been responsible. Irma's ghost!

Della preferred to believe this was all part of the dark business of the stolen Madonna. That there were members of the criminal gang at work in the old palace. The house was deathly still as she made her way back up the main stairway to her bedroom. Now she knew that Aunt Isobel had not been all that wrong. She had really seen a mysterious figure.

She waited until Prince Raphael arrived the next morning and then took him up to her room to show him the cloak. She said, "What do you make of that?"

He took it with a scowl on his handsome face. "It is surely one of Irma's," he agreed.

"I found it in a storage room. Her perfume is still noticeable on it. As if she'd just flung it aside."

He stared at her. "You're suggesting Irma was in the house and left this behind?"

"Yes. I was following close after her. She may have wanted to put on something else when she left the palace. So she left this to don a heavier coat."

Raphael said, "That would mean Irma is a part of the conspiracy."

"Unless it was her ghost," she said. "And I don't think that. My aunt has insisted she has seen her about the palace and in the garden."

He said, "Assuming she is alive and she was here, why would she return without allowing us to know?"

"I can only think she is in this with Barsini," Della said. "They are both still frantically searching for the Madonna. She has a confederate in the house. The person who locked that door after me."

"If what you say is true, Irma is in no danger," the young man said. "She is playing this game to try and make you talk. Thinking you still know where the Madonna is."

"And she may think I brought it here with me and have hidden it somewhere. That is why she returns in the secrecy of the night."

"It's a wild theory," Raphael said grimly. "I do not think Prince Sanzio would accept it."

"Because he adores Irma and thinks she can do no wrong," Della said. "But I know how she is under the spell of Barsini.

I have seen her writhing on the altar with him in a sexual orgy witnessed by dozens of others."

"I know," he said with a deep sigh. "The way things stand, anything is possible."

"I'm glad to hear you admit that," she said.

"Show me the entrance to this secret passage," he said.

"Come with me," she told him. And she took him to Irma's room.

He halted before the Madonna and the giant glass bowl filled with wax, its wick offering a constant light.

He said, "I had no idea Irma was so dedicated to her religion."

"Apparently she kept the candle burning continually. Now Guido sees that it doesn't go out."

"Show me that door," her companion said.

She went to the paneling and applied pressure as she had the night before. Nothing happened! She tried several other places with an equal lack of result.

"I don't understand it!" she said, frustrated.

"If there was a secret door here last night it has to be here now," Raphael said, trying the wall.

Studying the wall grimly, she said, "My guess is that whoever followed me into the secret passage last night, came back and somehow locked the entrance from the other side."

"In that case we are wasting our time."

"We might start at the storage room and work back," she suggested.

"All right," he said. "Let us try it."

She accompanied him downstairs and took him to the storage room, feeling all the while that her credibility was being destroyed. While Raphael had made no comment, she had the feeling he was less convinced by her story than at first.

They reached the dark, dusty storage room and she went ahead of him to the trapdoor. She said, "Once we open this we can work our way back along the secret passage. At least as far as the locked door."

He knelt and took the ring of the trapdoor in his hand and tried to lift it. The door refused to budge. He tried again and again, but had no success.

Looking up at her, he said, "It also seems to be locked!"

"It can't be!" she protested. "I opened it myself last night."

Raphael tried again. "It won't move!"

He was still on his knees studying the trapdoor when Prince Sanzio appeared in the open doorway of the storage room in his wheelchair.

"What are you two doing in here?" he demanded sharply and wheeled himself into the room as far as possible.

"Trying to open the trapdoor and find out where it leads," she said.

The old Prince showed annoyance. "You should have spoken to me first."

"I'm sorry," Prince Raphael said. "We meant no harm. Della has heard so much about there being secret passages in the palace that she wanted to see for herself."

Prince Sanzio scowled. "That trapdoor is sealed. It has not worked for years. There is a passage under it leading to the cellars but it is not used these days."

Della was shocked. She said, "But—"

Raphael interrupted her, telling the old man, "I'm glad you came along. You saved us a lot of useless effort."

The old Prince gave Della a reproachful glance. "Your main thoughts now should be of your sister and how to save her. Not worrying about secret passages."

She was going to tell him that the secret passage was part of her concern, but Prince Raphael gave her a warning glance so she said nothing. The old man turned his wheelchair around and left them.

Neither of them said anything until he was out of earshot. Then she said tensely, "He simply doesn't know the trapdoor has been unsealed and the passage placed in use again."

"I gathered that the moment he spoke," Raphael said. "But we'd gain nothing arguing with him."

"Whoever is responsible has cleverly sealed off the passage at both ends," she complained.

They were out in the hallway now and the young man said, "I want to believe you, Della, but the evidence is all against you."

"Because someone knew I'd discovered the passage," she told him. "They closed it at once."

Raphael said, "In other words we'll need a good deal more evidence before anyone will listen to your story."

They were back in the living room when Guido came in bearing a sealed envelope in his hand.

"For Miss Standish," he said.

She thanked him and took the envelope and tore it open. Inside there was a hastily scribbled message in pencil which she read aloud for Raphael's benefit: "Dear Miss Standish, whatever your opinion of me, I beg you to come in summons to this message. My life is in danger and I have valuable information which I wish to sell you. This is a fair deal with no risks for you. Your friend, Father Anthony. P.S. Meet me at the catacombs of St. Calixtus." She looked up from the note. "Do you know where that is?"

"Yes," he said. "But I'm not going there."

"Why not?"

"You've been fooled by him before. This is another trick to get you in his hands," Raphael complained.

She folded the paper. "I say that Father Anthony is ready to break with the thieves, whichever group he's associated with, and do business with us."

"I don't trust him!" Raphael was adamant.

"Very well," she said. "I'll go meet him on my own." And she started out of the room.

Raphael came hurrying after her. "All right! I'll go! You know I can't let you risk it alone!"

She smiled at him coquettishly. "If you hadn't made Henry leave I wouldn't have to depend on you!"

"You do not need your English lawyer," he exclaimed with annoyance. "I am here."

A short while later they were in the carriage on their way to the catacombs of St. Calixtus. She asked the young Prince, "What is the story behind these catacombs?"

Raphael said; "It began when Marcus Aurelius started to persecute the Christians."

"Wasn't he the last of the Good Emperors?" she asked.

"Yes. But he marred his record by turning against the new Christian community. Many of them had to seek hiding places. And where but the long underground caverns where a large number of people could remain in safety. Caves or galleries of this type are common under many cities in the Mediterranean area. When quarrying opened up a suitable cave, many poor people were quick to move into it. By easy tunneling they often extended the caves. In times when they weren't harassed the Christians buried their dead in the catacombs. They also built simple chapels there where they would not be molested. When dangerous times arrived they simply went underground to live."

"And these catacombs extend for miles under the city, don't they?"

He nodded. "Like a series of underground alleys," he said. "People have been known to become lost in them and starve to death before being found."

She shuddered. "Frightening!"

"I don't see the catacombs as the most desirable place for a rendezvous," he observed.

"Father Anthony likes to select unusual spots."

"He has done it this time."

"He may be afraid he's being watched," she said. "There is a tone of desperation about his message."

Raphael said, "We had better be on our guard. I don't want it to be a repeat of those other times. In every instance you walked into a trap."

She made a brave effort to appear nonchalant. "It has to be different, this time."

"I wonder," he said bleakly.

They reached the Appian Way where it pierced the city walls and came to a church. There were visitors in the area and a number of vehicles waiting. Raphael told the driver to wait while he and Della descended from the carriage and made their way toward the church.

He explained, "The entrance to this part of the catacombs is through the church."

"It seems rather familiar," she said.

He looked about grimly. "Do you see any sign of your fat friend?"

"No," she said. "Should we wait out here?"

"It's hard to tell," Raphael said. "Perhaps we'd better go on into the chapel."

They stepped inside out of the sunlight and the entire atmosphere changed. The visitors spoke in hushed voices and the light was murky.

Just as Della came to a halt within the chapel she felt a tug at her left sleeve. Turning, she was confronted by the remarkable sight of the stout Father Anthony visibly trembling.

"I thought you would never get here," he gasped.

"What is wrong?" she asked.

"I have been followed," he said, looking around him guiltily.

"Are you sure?"

"Yes. I dare not stay here talking to you," he went on nervously. "I will let you go down below and then I will follow you. They mustn't see us together."

Della could see he was badly frightened. "Whatever you say."

"Go on," he insisted. "I will be down there very shortly."

Raphael asked her, "What was he whispering about?"

"He thinks he's being followed."

The young Prince turned around. "Where has he gone?"

"I don't know," she said. "He was here beside me a moment ago."

"He's an eccentric!" Raphael said angrily. "I don't think we should bother. Let us get away from here."

"No. We've come this far. I at least want to have a look at the catacombs."

"I doubt if you'll see him again," Raphael warned her.

"We'll give him a chance," she said.

Raphael guided her down the stairs. Below, it was almost deserted. Few of the visitors chose to go far into the catacombs, their bad reputation probably scaring off all but the most adventurous. She studied the many recesses in the walls of the catacomb in which the dead were placed in twos or threes, sealed in by tablets bearing inscriptions or paintings.

She asked, "How far do they extend?"

"The best guess is about three hundred miles. So it is all too easy to lose one's way," he said.

They came to empty recesses and she asked, "Why are some of the recesses empty?"

"Cartloads of bones have been taken from here and buried in cemeteries above," he said. "Many of them in the Pantheon."

They came to a halt in the candlelit main corridor and she looked behind them to see if there was any sign of Father Anthony. The corridor was empty.

She said, "Perhaps we ought to part for a little. He may not dare come talk to me while you're around."

"That's a dangerous idea."

"Surely not all that dangerous," she said. "Let us stroll back. I'll stay ahead and you walk a dozen yards or so behind me."

"I don't think it will make any difference," he said.

"Let us at least try it," she told him. "I don't want our venture to come to nothing."

"The chances are it will," he warned her. But he gave in to her suggestion and dropped a distance behind her.

She walked on, confident that she was not alone, and a cry for help would bring him quickly to her. Because the catacomb wound about they were not always in sight of each other. She kept watching ahead to see if Father Anthony might turn up.

Suddenly she halted and a strange sensation came over her. She was passing recessed burial places and the painting on it was one which she had not seen before. She studied the crude sketch of the three crosses set against the horizon. And she knew that somehow she had lost her way.

For the past several minutes she had been walking in a side corridor. Not only was she lost but she must have lost contact with Raphael.

She called out, "Raphael! Where are you?"

Her words came back as a taunting echo and there was no reply from the young Prince. She began retracing her steps as quickly as she could, not at all sure that she was even heading in the right direction. An occasional candle burned in a wall holder to indicate that at least she was in a portion of the catacombs which were meant to be explored.

But this was small comfort because it might take hours to find her way out of the maze of corridors. She might even find herself lost in the darkness of the unused sections. Fear streaked coldly down her spine.

She felt her throat tighten with fright and again she halted to call out, "Raphael!"

Again there was no reply and so she now began to half-walk, half-run, her breathing coming faster as she fought her terror and tried to escape the eerie place. She rounded a corner hoping to see some familiar sign, but it all seemed strange to her.

She leaned against the rough wall for a moment, trying to decide what to do. Was it possible she was still heading in the wrong direction? Going farther and farther into the dark recesses of the underground place, she tried to think it all out. To be logical!

Once again she called out, "Raphael! Please! Answer me!"

There was a short pause and then the wonder of a reply. From a distance came Raphael's voice, crying, "Where are you?"

"Here!" she said. "I'll wait!"

Distantly again, he shouted in reply, "Keep calling out and don't move! Stay right where you are!"

"I will," she cried. And then every few seconds she called out to him.

Gradually his replies came nearer and then suddenly he came into view. He ran toward her, his face a white mask.

Taking her in his arms, he said, "I was certain I'd lost you!"

She sobbed. "I know!"

He said, "Now let us get out of here!"

"How?" she asked, pressing close to him and staring at the gloomy passage ahead.

"I'm not sure," he said. "But now that we're together we'll find some way out!"

Chapter Fifteen

Now they were moving cautiously along a fairly straight section of catacomb. Della halted and pointed to an inscription in a recess on their right. "I recognize that!" she cried. "We are on the right track!"

Raphael looked a little less grim. "We'd better stay on it this time."

"We will," she said. "I don't think we are too far from the steps leading to the chapel."

"And no sign of your Father Anthony!"

"Something may have happened to him."

"After all the trouble he's caused us I certainly hope so," he said.

They came to a turning and at once she caught Raphael by the arm and pointed. "Look! Father Anthony! He's sitting on that little ledge of rock ahead on the left!"

"So he is," the young Prince said. "Well, I'll let you go speak to him."

"All right," she said and ran ahead.

Father Anthony was sitting with his hands folded in his lap and his head bent forward slightly. She hurried up to him and said, "Father Anthony! We lost our way!"

He made no reply and so she reached out to tap his shoulder. Her touch sent him falling forward and he lay sprawled out on the catacomb floor. She screamed and stepped back.

"What's going on here?" Raphael asked, running up to her.

She gasped, "I just touched him and he fell! I think he's dead."

"Dead!" Raphael echoed, and he knelt by the fallen priest. Then he glanced up and said, "Look!"

She saw that he was holding the ends of a stout cord. "What's that?"

"The murder weapon," Raphael said grimly as he stood up. "He was garotted! Strangled from behind by someone slipping that cord over his head and tightening it until he was dead! The ideal weapon for down here! Silent and swift!"

She groaned. "Poor little man!"

"He was playing a dangerous game," he said in a taut voice. "Come along!"

She let him lead her the rest of the way to the chapel steps and then through the fairly crowded chapel out into the open. There she turned to him and asked, "Shouldn't we tell someone?"

Raphael's dark, slightly curly hair, was blowing in the strong breeze that had come up. His handsome face was a study in weariness. He said, "We can't afford to get mixed up in this!"

"You mean because of Irma."

"Yes."

"But what will happen?" she worried.

"Someone will find him and report it to the police," he said. "Let it be their problem from then on."

"I think I'm going to be ill," she said, leaning against him.

"You'll feel better once you're in the carriage," he said.

"I hope so," she replied faintly.

As it turned out she did. The fresh air was helpful and she sat back with her eyes closed. Raphael sat in silence beside her as the carriage took them back to the palace.

At last Della opened her eyes and told him, "I'm sorry."

"For what?"

"Placing you in danger for nothing!"

"You were in the same danger."

"It was my idea," she said.

He nodded. "Well, now you know one thing. You won't be hearing from Father Anthony again."

"I had come to like him a little in spite of his being so evil," she said.

"You might have liked him less had he used that thumbscrew on you."

She shuddered. "Don't remind me."

"Consider yourself lucky he's dead."

"I still see him stretched out there! That awful look on his face."

"Strangulation is not the most pleasant of deaths," the young Prince said in a return to his cynical good humor.

She glanced at him wryly. "At least that explodes one of my theories."

"Which one?"

"That Father Anthony was a disguised Brizzi."

"It was likely Brizzi who killed him."

"You think so?"

"They were working closely. Then Father Anthony must have worked with Brother Louis to double-cross our superthief."

"And so he settled with them both," she said grimly.

"It would seem so," Raphael agreed. "Brizzi has the reputation of being a coldblooded killer as well as a thief of great ability."

"Now what?" she asked.

"New contest for the Madonna, I suppose. Between Brizzi and Barsini."

"Don't forget Gregorio," she cautioned him.

He gave her a wary look. "Gregorio may be a giant in size but he is small in influence. He is merely a hired man for Barsini."

"Rather wealthy to be a hired hand," she said.

"Gregorio, like Barsini, isn't in the game for money. It is the thrill he is seeking. That is typical of the Satanists. Of Irma as well, since she joined them."

"Which brings us back to the question, is she being held by Barsini or is she merely hiding out with him?"

"That I would not venture to guess," Raphael told her.

"I wish we knew," she said thoughtfully.

They reached the palace and avoided direct questioning by either Count Sanzio or Della's aunt. Raphael decided to go home but before he did, she reminded him they had a date for late that evening.

The young Prince looked at her aghast. "You're not still planning to go to the opera?"

"Of course," she said. "I want to see Gregorio and ask him some questions."

"Can you honestly think he'll answer?"

She said, "I'll have you there to encourage him. You might bring some sort of pistol if you have one."

He stared at her incredulously. "You're inciting me to violence."

"Would you call it that? I'd say it was an attempt at self-protection."

"Haven't you seen enough effects of violence for one day?"

"What happened this morning makes me all the more determined to bring that murderous crew to justice," she said.

Raphael hesitated. "Perhaps we should turn things over to the police. This is beginning to get beyond us."

"I will if you like."

"You know Gregorio is violent. And he raped you that night at the villa!"

"Don't think I've forgotten," she said grimly. "I mean to settle that debt."

"And I suppose you'll threaten to go after him on your own if I don't agree to help you?"

"Yes, I think I may."

"I'll return for dinner," he said with a resigned sigh. "And then on to the opera and maybe death!"

A day which had begun in a strange, melodramatic way was destined to continue in that mold. Della was still suffering from her experience in the catacombs. The murder of Father Anthony gave everything a new twist. She had hoped to learn something about the Madonna from the stout prelate. Now he had been silenced forever. The big problem was what to do next.

It was her belief that Gregorio could tell them whether Irma was a prisoner of Barsini. She had not seen her twin since that night when they'd both attended Barsini's Satanist orgy. So she had every reason to think that Irma was still being held there. Not that she could ever expect Barsini to admit it.

The whole business seemed to revolve around the belief that the Madonna which had passed through so many hands must have reached her in London. Thus far the only person she felt she'd really convinced otherwise was the old cardinal and his underling, the serious Father Walker. But this did her little good with all the various villains greedy for the Madonna continuing to think she either had it or knew where it was hidden.

She finally went downstairs and discovered the elderly Prince Sanzio in his wheelchair in the drawing room. He was gazing into the remnants of the last log fire. As he stared at the ashes his wrinkled face betrayed his grim state of mind.

"You look ill!" Della told him.

He glanced at her and his thin hands clenched the arms of the chair. He said, "I do not think we should wait any longer. It is time to bring in the police."

"They have threatened Irma's life if we do," was her reminder.

"That is all that has held me back," he complained. "This is madness! None of us knows anything about this stolen Madonna!"

"I wish we could make them believe that," she said.

The old man decided, "I cannot go on like this too much longer."

"I know," she sympathized, placing a hand on his shoulder to placate him.

He gave a deep sigh. "I had expected that reuniting you with your lost sister would give me the great happiness that has somehow always eluded me throughout my life."

"I'm sorry."

"I felt something was wrong even before you reached here," he went on. "Irma changed after meeting that evil Barsini. I felt that he had somehow hypnotized her."

"She was behaving in a tense manner when I first met her," Della recalled.

"Raphael should have protected her from Barsini instead of putting her in that villain's hands," Prince Sanzio went on angrily.

"I'm sure he meant no harm. It just happened that way."

The old man in the wheelchair gazed up at her with some concern. "So Raphael has won you over?"

She blushed. "I think he is my friend. A friend to all of us."

The old Prince eyed her bitterly and advised, "Do not ever be sure of anything. And do not desert your fine, young English lawyer for Raphael. It would be a bad move!"

She was startled that the old invalid would express himself so frankly. She said, "I have no intention of deserting anyone. But Henry is not in Rome at the moment and I need a companion in my search for Irma."

"Do you feel Raphael is being completely honest with you?"

Astonished by the cynical note in the old man's question, she faltered for a moment before replying, "Yes. I'm sure I do."

"Well, I'm not," was the old man's grim reply. "I think he knows where Irma is and whether she is a prisoner or not. And it could be he has more knowledge of that stolen Madonna than he has revealed to us."

She stared at him. "Are you saying that Raphael may also be playing Barsini's game?"

"I think he could be one of Barsini's Satanist slaves," Prince Sanzio said.

She shook her head. "Never!"

"I'd like to see him prove his innocence."

"I'm sure he will when we attend the Satanist gathering that is scheduled at Barsini's tomorrow night. I think I will find Irma there."

The old man frowned. "My advice to you would be not to go near his place."

"I must," she said. "And Raphael has promised to come with me."

"I don't like any of it!" Prince Sanzio said emphatically.

"What is it you don't like?" Aunt Isobel had come into the drawing room.

Prince Sanzio said, "Irma being missing and this business about the Madonna of St. Cecilia!"

"If I had my way Della and I would be starting our journey back to England. I feel nothing is to be gained by staying here and keeping ourselves in constant danger."

Della said, "It's not all that bad!"

"I say it is," her aunt defied her. "In fact I'm sure it is actually worse than you guess."

Prince Sanzio's white head nodded in assent. "I do not think your niece is alert to the great evil which we are all battling."

"I agree," Aunt Isobel said. "My own nerves are in a dreadful state."

"You've allowed yourself to imagine all sorts of nonsense," Della lectured the older woman.

Isobel pursed her lips. "I have seen what I have seen," she said tartly. "I have been tormented by the most amazing dreams and I have watched ghostly visitors in the corridors when I've been fully awake!"

"Please, Aunt Isobel," she said, begging her for silence.

"I will have my say," her aunt insisted. "It is time I told the Prince."

"Told me what?" he demanded.

She looked at him sternly. "I have seen what I believe to be Irma's ghost."

Prince Sanzio returned her angry gaze and then said, "I would not be all that surprised. I think it is a distinct possibility that my dear Irma has been murdered. So you may well have seen her unhappy spirit!"

"I saw something moving about in the corridor again last night," Aunt Isobel went on. "And I had the most awful nightmare. I dreamt that Father Anthony was murdered."

Della gasped. "Your dream told you that?"

"Yes," the prim Isobel went on. "I saw him fall and then come staggering toward me. His eyes were wide and frightened and he seemed to be gasping for breath. Then he collapsed at my feet and I woke up."

The knowledge that Father Anthony had been murdered only a few hours earlier made it difficult for Della to try and react casually. "I do not think you should place too much importance on dreams," she managed.

"I disagree," her aunt replied. "All my life I've had a kind of second sight. Call it intuition or what you like, I have often dreamed things which have come true."

"All of us have done that," Della said in an effort to pass the awkward moment. "It's only coincidence that such dreams turn out to be true."

"No!" Prince Sanzio spoke up from his wheelchair. "I must place myself on the side of your aunt. I have many times had the same experience of predicting things in dreams. In my opinion it happens with many people. I often had the strange experience of entering some building and knowing I had been there before. Then I'd realize that I had dreamed every detail of the place before I ever actually encountered it."

She shuddered. "With all this talk of second sight and ghosts you're making me nervous."

"It is time you were nervous," Aunt Isobel said. "I say the moment that Henry Clarkson returns from Naples we must get away from here."

"Only after I have my sister back safely," Della said.

Aunt Isobel gave her a knowing look and in an even tone said, "I do not think you will ever see that poor girl alive again."

She was startled but she merely replied, "I surely hope you are wrong."

She had no thought of confiding the morning's events to either of the older people, knowing well that if she did they would be in even a worse state and refuse to allow her to continue in her investigations. This must not happen. She excused herself after a while and went upstairs to her room to rest for the evening ahead.

As she stretched out on the canopied bed in the shadowed room her mind was reeling with various speculations. At last she managed to sleep briefly. She came awake with the feeling that someone was in the room with her. She had felt this several times before and had been proven wrong, but she had a sense of urgency this time.

Raising up, she stared about the room and at first thought she'd been in error. Then she saw a movement in one of the heavy, velvet drapes by the wide window. She carefully slid from the bed and crossed to the spot.

Pulling the drape aside, she revealed the tiny figure of Guido standing there. The little man looked more afraid than herself. His wizened face was a picture of misery.

In his shrill, childish voice he protested, "You must not think I mean you any harm!"

Calming a little, she told the little man, "You have to admit your behavior is peculiar. What are you doing in my room?"

"I came here to speak with you!"

Guido made a singular figure in his servant's livery, his small hands clasping and unclasping feverishly in his misery.

She said, "Why didn't you knock on the door rather than come in and hide yourself?"

"I did knock on the door and received no reply."

"So?"

"So I decided to see if the door was open. It was. I came in and saw you on the bed. I thought you were waking and I became confused. I felt you would be angry with me for intruding on you, so I hid behind the drape."

It sounded logical enough but she didn't think he had told her the entire truth. She said, "Have you ever come in here before without my knowledge?"

"Certainly not!" Guido said with dignity, his tiny head held high. "I have long been a trusted servant in this house. You may be sure I have in no way abused my privileges."

"And yet I find you hiding here and spying on me?"

"I have explained that," he said.

She stared at his wizened little face and felt some compassion for him. She said, "I don't know what to think of you, Guido."

"Please do not doubt me," he begged. "I'm not myself these days. I was very devoted to Princess Irma. I am in agony because of her kidnapping. I feel that I may never see her again!"

She said, "We all share that same agony, Guido."

"Yes, *signorina*," the little man said, gazing up at her with sad eyes. "You resemble her so much I sometimes think I'm seeing her when it is you."

"Why did you come to speak with me?" she asked.

The little man looked frightened again. He said tensely, "You must not tell the Prince."

"Tell him what?"

"What I'm about to confide in you," the little man said. "I found another message this morning. Slipped under the front door."

She frowned. "What sort of message?"

"I meant to show it to you, *signorina*," the little man said unhappily. He searched in his inner pocket until he found it. "It is written in Italian and it says 'All who are guilty will pay!' It is unsigned of course!" He handed her the note.

She stared at the plainly scrawled note. She said, "What does it mean?"

Guido was very pale. "I say it is a notice that any of us living here in the palace might be the next victim of an attack. Probably they will strike at Price Sanzio first!"

"But why? He knows nothing about the stolen Madonna."

"It is the way they work," Guido fretted. "They will take their toll of all of us until they get what they want."

She said, "Surely you have no need to fear."

The midget shook his head. "You do not know them! I have been devoted to the Princess. That will count against me!"

"Let us trust this will soon be settled and you will have no more reason to fear," she said.

"I cannot believe that," the little man said in a despondent tone.

"You do not want me to tell the Prince about this?" she asked.

"No. I think it would only needlessly upset him. And after all it was not addressed to him," Guido pointed out.

"Nor to anyone in particular."

"Exactly," he said. "Let it be our secret for the moment. I stop by the room of the Princess every day to make sure the candle before the Madonna is kept burning."

"You have been faithful," Della told him. "When my sister returns she will thank you."

"Yes, *signorina*," the little man said sadly. "When she returns." But he said it as if he didn't expect this to happen.

Guido left the room and she still could not decide whether to fully believe his story or not. She was sure much of it was true. But she wondered that his knock on the door had not wakened her? Or had he knocked. The second message was a disturbing complication. Guido had made her promise not to reveal it to Prince Sanzio but he had said nothing about keeping the news from Prince Raphael.

So she decided to discuss this new development with Raphael when he arrived to escort her to the opera. She did not get an opportunity at dinner, indeed she was not able to confide in him until they were in the carriage on their way to the Opera House.

She told him about the message and Guido's fears, concluding with, "He feels all the household are in danger."

Raphael frowned. "It seems that the old Prince ought to be informed."

"Why? I agree with Guido. It would only worry him needlessly."

"He would at least be prepared should they move against him."

She gave him a rueful glance. "How can that helpless old man defend himself? Telling him will only make him feel more frustrated."

The handsome Raphael sighed. "Perhaps you are right."

"I know I am about this," she said. She had been careful to wear a gown of dark gray which would not be too conspicuous. Prince Raphael was in his usual evening dress of white tie and tails. She wished he had worn something more practical.

He said, "I think this plan of tracking down Gregorio is both dangerous and pointless since we plan to lay siege to Barsini's Satanist meeting tomorrow night."

"Any information we can get from Gregorio may better prepare us for tomorrow," she pointed out.

"I do not like it," the man at her side grumbled as they rode through the dark streets.

"I think it an ideal opportunity to corner him," she said. "Did you bring a weapon?"

He nodded. "My pearl-handled pistol. I felt it more suitable for the opera than a revolver."

"A revolver might have been more useful."

"I know this weapon," he said.

"Gregorio will be dangerous," was her warning.

Raphael gave her a reproving look. "It seems I reminded you of that basic fact long ago."

They reached the Opera House and joined the fashionable crowd entering the great theater with its ornate lobby and many-tiered auditorium. Raphael had been able to get tickets for the first balcony through the good offices of a friend who was a sponsor of the opera company. Their seats were a distance back so that the stage seemed almost postage-stamp-sized. Above them loomed two other balconies and there were boxes on either side of the theater rising to the top level. Soon the vast place was crowded, the lights dimmed and the overture began.

The opera of the evening was *Carmen.* She was not familiar with the stars but they seemed in good voice. She had brought along opera glasses and when a crowd appeared on stage, she scanned the faces of the extras for a sign of Gregorio. He was not in the first group scene.

"I do not see him," she told Raphael and gave him the glasses to use for a moment.

"Perhaps that is fortunate," he said in a low voice as he scanned the distant stage.

She took the glasses again and in the first moment of the second act crowd scene she gasped and tugged at Raphael's arm.

"He's there! On stage! I see him!" she exclaimed.

"Let me see," Raphael said grimly and took the glasses. After a moment, he nodded. "You are right. I see his ugly face."

"We must get to the stage door before he leaves," she said in a whisper.

"That shouldn't be too difficult," Raphael said. "He will have to change from his costume to his street clothes."

The opera based on the Prosper Merimée story went on. In spite of her tension Della found herself enjoying the work. Sympathizing with Don José and thrilling to the final moments of great singing and dramatic action when Carmen was murdered. Then the curtain fell and there was much applause and cheering. The principal artists took their curtain calls and at last the audience began leaving the theater.

Because there had been a capacity crowd it took them a long while to get down to the lobby and then outside. They joined a group of fashionably dressed couples who were making their way to the stage door in the alley beside the Opera House. By mingling with these operagoers wishing to pay their respects to the various stars, they were able to get by the stage-door man and inside to the stage itself.

The others moved toward the dressing rooms of the stars which were on the first level above the stage. They waited at the foot of the iron stairway because the extras dressed high up above. It was likely to be at least two or three flights to that level.

As they waited the stage crew began dismantling settings and taking away the props until only a bare stage was left.

Raphael glanced at the empty stage and then above at the stairway. "I don't like this waiting. I'd rather go up and confront him in his dressing room."

"It wouldn't do," she argued. "There would probably be a half-dozen or more in the room. They'd take his side. We must get him alone."

"Suppose he comes down the stairs with some others?"

She said, "In that case I will show myself and call him onto the stage. You can keep in the shadows here until I have him apart from the others."

"Then I move in with my pistol and keep him covered while you question him?"

"That's the exact plan," she said, gratified that he knew his role so well.

Raphael shook his head. "I'm still not sure this is wise!"

"We'll have to go on now," she said, as they both kept discreetly in the dark area behind the iron stairway.

Tension mounted as some of the couples who had come backstage with them now began to return down the stairs with the stars they were visiting. All was genial conversation and laughter as the fashionably dressed groups came down to the stage level and made their way out. They were followed by some of the minor players and extras. But Gregorio had not yet come down the iron steps.

There was a lull and no one came down the steps for a few minutes. It seemed that she and Raphael were alone in the dimly lighted backstage area. Then she heard footsteps on the stairs and almost cried out as she saw Gregorio.

The bull-like man was hurrying down the last of the iron stairs when she stepped out and stood before him. His broad face showed surprise.

"You!" he said.

"Did you think we'd never meet again?" she asked.

He eyed her suspiciously. "What do you want?"

"I'd like to have you answer a few questions," she said.

He shook his head. "I haven't time!"

"You will take time," she said evenly. And she nodded for Raphael to join her.

The handsome young Prince acted on cue and came out with his pistol in hand and aimed at Gregorio. He said, "We felt you might talk better with encouragement!"

The huge Gregorio gave him a contemptuous smile. "You will not hear anything from me!"

Della was fearful that someone else would come down from the dressing rooms and interrupt them. She told Raphael, "Have him move farther over onto the stage and out of the path of traffic."

Raphael menacingly pointed the pistol at the big man. "You heard her?"

Gregorio looked sullen. "I don't know what kind of game you are playing. You're being very foolish!" But he obeyed her suggestion to move away from the stairs to the dark-shadowed section of the stage beyond.

She faced him again in the near darkness and said, "What about Irma? Where is she?"

"Why ask me?" Gregorio demanded mockingly.

"Because you work for Barsini. You have to know," she snapped.

"Better cooperate," Raphael suggested.

Gregorio made no reply. But suddenly he dodged back into the darkness and in a minute had vanished behind some of the stored scenery. Raphael was left standing there looking stunned with the pistol in his hand.

Della turned on him. "How could you? You let him get away! Why didn't you fire at him?"

"I hadn't time," he pleaded.

She felt this might be true but she didn't think it boded good for them. "We'll have to try and find him," she said in a whisper.

"Where?" Raphael whispered back, keeping his pistol at the ready.

They moved cautiously among the painted canvas flats, Raphael in the lead, crouching with his pistol out. She followed, also keeping low so their shadows would not be too prominently projected agaist the back wall. They were about midway across the area when without warning a heavy sandbag fell from the gallery far above, where the additional scenery was hung when not in use. All these scenic drops were balanced with heavy bags of sand so they could be pulled up or down with ease.

She gave a small cry as the heavy bag barely missed her and moved closer to Raphael. "Almost hit me!" she whispered.

"It was meant to," he said in the same low whisper.

She glanced up into the fly gallery and said, "He must have gotten up there somehow!"

Raphael nodded. "Iron ladder on the back wall."

"I see," she whispered. "We'd better get outside!"

"And leave him?"

"Catch him out there," was her whispered suggestion.

Still crouching, Raphael looked grim. "If we can get out!"

They began slowly crossing the dark, open stage area and had almost made it when down came a second sandbag. This time they were not so lucky. The bag came down almost on Raphael and sent him crashing to the floor. His pistol flew from his hand and skidded into the shadows.

Ignoring her own danger, she went to the side of the fallen Raphael. The bag had burst, splattering sand all around where he lay. His face was deathly white and there was blood trickling from his temple.

She tearfully leaned over him, afraid that he might be dead. "Raphael! Speak to me!" she pleaded with him.

There was no response from the unconscious man. She leaned down to hear if his heart was beating and before she could be sure of this she was seized from behind. She heard the roar of triumph from the giant Gregorio and in the next instant he had tied a rope about her arms so that she could not struggle against him.

"You wanted to talk to me!" he said jubilantly.

"You!" she tried to scream, but before she could properly do it he'd thrust a dirty cloth in her mouth and bound it. Then he picked her up as if she were some sort of cloth doll and carried her away.

Instead of taking the stage door to leave the theater he chose another exit, a small door inside a larger one which could be opened to transport scenery in and out of the theater. She tried to struggle and scream, but she could do neither. She had to be content kicking as hard as she could. This seemed not to bother him at all. He laughed in his mocking fashion as he stepped out into the darkness and down some wooden steps to the ground.

Then he took a succession of alleys rather than the street. She tried to free herself but was as helpless as a child in the giant's arms. They came to a house with a red lamp prominent in one of its lower windows. Della remembered Raphael telling her that this was the sign of the slum brothel. It was the way the keepers of the brothels let all know this was a house of ill repute!

The giant marched toward the house with the red lamp in the window and banged on its door. After a moment the door was opened by a massive woman. She took a look at them and fear spread across her face.

"Go away!" she cried. "I do not want any trouble!"

"You better not refuse me or I'll have this place closed within the hour," Gregorio warned her. "I want a room!"

"No, please!" The big woman was terrified. "You come back later by yourself!"

"Listen to me, Mama Luchini," Gregorio said, "I am a regular and I insist on my rights. Give me a room or expect to be shuttered!"

"Who is she?"

"My girl," Gregorio told the woman. "She has chosen to be troublesome so I tied and gagged her!"

"I do not want trouble!" the massive woman chanted and opened the door to let them in. Still muttering to herself, she climbed the narrow stairway with Gregorio following her, Della helpless in his arms.

They reached the upper level and went down a corridor of closed doors. Della heard drunken male laughter and the shrill cry of a girl. The fat woman halted and threw open a door.

"In there!" she said. "I do not want trouble!"

"Don't worry!" Gregorio said gloatingly. "My girl and I will settle all our differences here on this cot!" And he dropped her roughly onto the narrow cot which, along with a chair, made up the furniture of the tiny brothel room.

Chapter Sixteen

By the flickering flame of the small candle in a tin holder on the windowsill she could see the massive Gregorio looming above her. The young, blond giant had a cruel smile on his face.

He said, "You wanted to be with me again and I never refuse a lady's wishes!"

The terror in her eyes and her repulsion could not be mistaken as she squirmed on the narrow cot in an effort to escape him. But this was not to be! Slowly he bent over and, lifting up her skirts, began to tear savagely at her underclothing until she lay there naked from the waist down.

He unloosed his trousers and as she made a last desperate attempt to roll off the cot, he fell upon her. His tactics were all too familiar! Cruelly he penetrated her with the massive organ that had ravaged her earlier. She groaned and with her eyes implored him to be merciful! Her tears streaked down to the gag which still covered her mouth but seeing her cry only seemed to egg him on.

She closed her eyes and prayed that it would soon end.

His body was heavy upon her and his foul breath seemed to fill the room. He was lost in a wild orgy of enjoying her! And then she saw the door from the corridor open and an old sallow-faced, gray-bearded man in a black cloak and wide-brimmed black hat stepped in. He was the same man she had seen earlier in the catacombs. The old man held a dagger in his upraised right hand and very cautiously he advanced upon the cot!

Gregorio was so lost in the rapture of his lust that he was completely unaware of the intruder. Suddenly she saw the gleam of the dagger as it came plunging down into the blond man's back. Gregorio gave a hoarse cry and shuddered, then he fell off her to land on the floor beside the cot.

The old man moved swiftly to her and pulled down her skirt to hide her lovely nude body. Then he untied the rope about her arms and helped her to a sitting position on the cot as he went on to remove the gag from her mouth.

She gasped, "Thank you!" Then she looked down to see the motionless figure of the partially nude Gregorio on the floor. She glanced away quickly and began to tremble.

The old man said, "Don't worry! He's dead! The scum!"

Still trembling, she managed to ask, "How?"

"How did I know you needed rescue?" the old man formed the question for her. "I've been trailing Gregorio some time. I planned to finish him tonight. When I saw him come out of the Opera House with you I followed."

"What now?"

"You get away from here quickly," the old man said. "I will remain here while you make your escape. Then I will leave."

He helped her to her feet and she stood shakily for a moment. Then she asked him, "Who are you?"

"It doesn't matter," he said.

"I would like to know!" she insisted.

"I could be a friend," the old man said. "There is no time to discuss it. I will give you a suggestion though. Find Pasquale Borgo! Don't forget the name! Pasquale Borgo!"

"Pasquale Borgo!" she repeated with a tremor in her voice.

"Now go!" he said sternly.

He went to the door and glanced out to make sure there was no one in the corridor. Then he nodded for her to leave. She hesitated and then realized there was nothing for her to do but obey the man who had just now murdered to save her. She nodded to him in turn and slipped out quickly. With her long skirt to cover her no one would guess that she was completely nude underneath. Nor that she had been ravaged by a man who now lay dead!

Again there were the bursts of female laughter and male voices low and incoherent as she passed the closed doors. She was too dazed by all that had happened to really hear what was going on. Retracing her way down the rickety stairs, she found herself confronted by the massive, black-haired madam.

The big woman scowled at her. "So he's finished with you, has he?"

"Yes," she said meekly, afraid the huge woman was going to try and hold her captive.

The woman said roughly, "Get out of here! Maybe now hell have a turn with one of my girls! Not like you! They know how to please a man properly!"

The big woman laughed at her own comment and stood aside for Della to rush out into the pleasant fresh air and the darkness of the street. Now she prayed that she might make her way through the maze of alleys unmolested. She was so near collapse than any sort of attack on her would finish her.

She tried to remember the route by which he'd brought her and failed the first time, coming to a dead-end alley. Someone threw slops from a window and she drew back in time to save herself, from a dousing, then ran on.

She was sobbing from the shock of being raped and seeing a murder, all within a short space of time. She was also concerned about Raphael, who could be dead for all she knew. The whole world now seemed a mad confusion of alleys until, just as she was about to give up hope, she came out into the street behind the opera house.

She halted for a moment, pushed back some of her wildly disarranged hair and half-walked, half-staggered to the stage door of the opera house. There on the steps with his head in his hands sat Raphael.

She hurried the last few steps and sank down at his side. "Raphael! I thought you were dead!"

He looked up at her, his face pale, blood congealed on his temple. His dazed eyes suddenly focused and he grasped her by the arms. "Della! What happened to you?"

"Later," she said wearily. "What about you?"

"The last I remember was that sandbag coming down and striking me," he told her. "When I came to I was alone. No sign of you or that Gregorio!"

"I know," she said. "He dragged me off!"

"The theater was deserted," he said. "I called out your name and there was no reply. My head has been aching madly. I searched about the floor and found my pistol. Then I came out here for air and to try and think what I could do."

"Gregorio took me to a nearby brothel."

Raphael stared at her. "You let him?"

"I had no choice. He bound my arms and gagged me!"

"When I was unable to help you."

"Yes," she said bitterly. "I was no match for him."

"And then?"

"What you might expect of Gregorio," she said in a dull voice. "He took me to a room in the brothel and savagely raped me!"

"Della!" His voice was filled with concern.

"I knew it would happen," she said. "I'd gone through it before. But he hadn't finished with me when an old man came into the room and plunged a dagger in his back and killed him!"

Raphael showed shock. "An old man?"

"Yes. I saw him before in the catacombs."

Raphael gave her a knowing look. "Before Father Anthony was killed?"

"Yes," she agreed, linking the two facts for the first time.

Raphael gave her a knowing look. "You surely can guess who it was?"

"Who?"

"Brizzi!"

"The superthief who began it all?"

"Who else?" he said. "It seems plain enough to me. First he murdered Father Anthony and then Gregorio. He is going about eliminating everyone who was involved in the double cross which took the Madonna from him."

She listened with awe, knowing he could easily be right. "It could be Brizzi," she said.

"It has to be! Did you get a good look at him?"

"No! Not really!"

"That's how he succeeds," the handsome Prince told her. "People rarely recall what he truly looks like."

"He had a thin beard and a sallow face," she said. "I would know him if I saw him again."

"In that disguise, you would," Raphael explained. "But next time you'll meet him in some different guise. He is a master of makeup."

"He killed Gregorio and he let me escape."

Raphael nodded. "Sure. He still thinks you have the Madonna. He's giving you a chance to lead him to it."

"You think that is it?"

"I haven't a doubt."

She suddenly remembered what the strange old man had said: "Find Pasquale Borgo!" He had said this urgently as if it were of the utmost importance. And for various reasons she decided not to mention his words to Raphael. Time to tell him later. She had sent him on enough wild goose chases for the moment, put his life in danger too many times.

She said, "I'm sorry."

"For what?"

"Bringing you here. Getting you hurt."

"What about yourself?"

She shrugged. "Gregorio is dead! He'll never attack me again."

"I can understand your being comforted by that," he said. "But the fact remains you've suffered as badly as I."

She said, "I was wrong in coming here after him. You told me so."

"That can't be helped now," he said, rising and helping her to her feet. "We can be thankful we're still alive."

"Yes," she said. "You're right." She looked up into his white face. "About tomorrow night, going to Barsini's and trying to get into his orgy. I can't hold you to it. Not after tonight."

He said, "Are you ready to give up the project?"

"That doesn't matter."

"It does to me," he said. "I want to know."

"Irma is my sister. I must try and find her."

"And she is my betrothed, remember?" he said.

"It could be much more dangerous than tonight," she warned him.

"At least we won't have Gregorio to contend with," was his reply.

"You want to go through with it?"

"I do," he said. "Now we must find a carriage and get you back to the palace as quickly as possible."

They trudged several blocks of cobblestoned streets before they were able to hail an empty carriage. Raphael was grimly quiet and when he kissed her goodnight, she told him he should consult a doctor if his head continued to ache.

"It's better now," he told her. "What about you?"

"I'll be all right," she said wearily.

"I hope so," he said, his eyes grave as he stared at her. "I'm glad Brizzi or whoever it was killed that bully."

"I know."

"I'll be here to pick you up tomorrow evening," he promised.

She went inside and saw Prince Sanzio in his wheelchair, his white head slumped in sleep as he waited for her. She felt sorry for the old man. As she watched him he raised his head and opened his eyes to stare at her sleepily.

"You are back," he said.

"Yes, a little late," she told him. She hoped he would not notice her rumpled dress or undone hair.

He seemed not to look at her as he said, "I'm afraid I fell asleep. It's a problem of my old age."

"You ought not to have waited up for me," she told him, then bent and kissed him on the cheek.

"I feel so useless of late," he said with a sigh. "The least I could do was wait up and see you safely inside."

"You have," she said with a wan smile. "Now let us both get to bed at once."

They said their goodnights and she went upstairs and was happy to find a supply of hot water had been left her in a clay jug. She used this along with some cold water to make a bath for herself. After stretching out in the enamel tub for a good while and thoroughly soaping and washing herself she felt less contaminated.

The events of the evening now seemed unreal to her. She found it hard to believe that all this had happened. Suddenly a wave of utter exhaustion came over her. She felt she would sleep in spite of everything.

• • •

With the coming of the sun through her window the next morning she awoke feeling better than she had hoped. Not that she was at all herself. The scars of the grim doings of the previous night could not be erased that easily. She somehow managed to get through breakfast and answer her aunt's questions about the opera.

Aunt Isobel said primly, "You don't seem to have properly enjoyed the opera! I think *Carmen* a most moving experience."

She said, "The opera was only part of our evening."

Aunt Isobel showed disapproval. "I imagine you spent much of the evening at some expensive restaurant after the performance. In my day a young woman was content to be taken home from the opera without expecting fine food and drink! And I must say you look none the better for it!"

Prince Sanzio wheeled himself into the room and told the older woman, "Don't nag at her, dear lady." And to Della he said, "Did you enjoy the opera?"

"Very much," she said.

"Ah, yes," he mused. "I dare say *Carmen* has to be one of the all-time favorites. Di Carlo sang last night. Was he in good voice?"

"I would say so," she said. "Though I'm truly no judge."

Aunt Isobel told the old Prince, "These young people are interested only in themselves and in being seen in their finery. It was different when I was a girl."

"I'm sure it must have been," the old Prince said with a smile for Della.

She was glad to escape and leave them in a discussion of old times and old customs. Upstairs she paced her room and debated what she should do. She wanted to try and discover who Pasquale Borgo might be. But she hadn't told Raphael anything about it and Henry still had not returned to help her. Who could she turn to?

And then she had an idea! Father Walker, the priest attached to the Vatican Museum. He had knowledge of the theft. She decided to journey to the Vatican on her own again.

She went out and found Guido supervising the cleaning of the hallway. The little man came to her and bowed. "Can I help you in any way, *signorina?*"

"Yes," she said. "I want to use the carriage. And I don't wish to attract any attention."

His wizened face was grave. "Yes, *signorina*."

"Would you have the carriage ready and waiting at the side entrance to the palace? In that way I can escape without my aunt or Prince Sanzio being aware of it."

Guido nodded. "I will arrange it, *signorina*."

"I'm going to the Vatican to see someone," she said. "I do not know how long I will be. If they ask where I've gone you can tell them."

"Depend on me," the wizened little man said.

She hesitated. "One more thing. I doubt if you can help me."

"Anything I can do?"

She gave him a searching look. "Have you ever heard of anyone named Pasquale Borgo?"

He showed surprise. "Borgo! The name is a familiar one. I know many Borgos. There are several families of them in my native village. But I do not know any Pasquale Borgo."

"Thank you," she said. "I doubted that you might."

"If there is any urgent reason to find out about this Pasquale Borgo I could make some discreet inquiries?" the midget suggested.

"Let it go for the moment," she said. "I doubt it is all that important."

"Very well, *signorina*," the little man said. "Your carriage will be ready in ten minutes."

She ordered the carriage to drop her off at the entrance to St. Peter's Square. It was a warm day with the blazing sun beginning to reach its peak. She wore a white dress with lace jabot and trim and a straw hat with a wide brim and daisies. As she made her way across the broad square to look for Father Walker she was impressed that there were already a goodly number of pilgrims visiting the area.

Reaching the inquiry desk of the museum where she had been told Father Walker was a staff member, she asked for him. "May I speak with Father Walker?"

The bald-headed old brother in charge of the desk stared at her with weak-eyed interest. "Are you a relative?"

"No, a friend," she said. "My name is Standish. He will know it. I have an urgent need to talk with him."

The elderly brother looked baffled. "I cannot go to him now. He is attending a staff meeting."

"How long will that be?"

The old man in the black robe shrugged. "The better part of an hour."

She said, "Will you give him my message as soon as he comes out?"

"Yes, of course."

"I shall come back in about an hour," she promised.

"Very well," the old brother said with a smile. "Enjoy our museum. It has many treasures."

Della thanked the friendly old man and strolled around the museum for a while. She went from one rich corridor to another, with each succeeding one seeming to hold more opulent treasure. There were Flemish and other tapestries, masterpieces of the goldsmith's and jeweler's art, gifts from various foreign countries and a library begun by Nicholas the Fifth.

This concentration of art treasures dazzled her. She found herself wondering what the stolen Madonna of St. Cecilia had looked like and whether it had ever been on display with these other valuable pieces.

She had an overwhelming desire for air and went out to St. Peter's Square again. She walked to one of the great fountains and enjoyed the cooling spray that came from it.

Suddenly from behind her a familiar voice exclaimed, "Dear Miss Standish!" She turned and saw it was none other than Madame Guioni.

"Madame Guioni!" she said. "I never thought to meet you here."

The big woman was wearing another of her monstrous, garish outfits, something purple with yellow trim and a large, wide-brimmed purple hat which drooped and was decorated with lush-looking grapes! She was truly a study in purple, her parasol included.

"I have been showing a visitor from England around," the woman said in her loud voice. Several people nearby turned to stare at her.

"I see," Della said politely.

"My friend wanted to see the basilica inside and I did not feel up to it, so I told her to go on and I would wait for her here. Now I regret that I did it; she's bound to be gone for an eternity!"

Della smiled. "I'm also waiting for someone. A priest employed in the Vatican Museum."

"How interesting!" the older woman said. "And what about that vulgar little Father Anthony?"

She said, "I have heard that he is dead."

"Dead?" Madame Guioni looked surprised. "Well, I suppose one shouldn't be too startled. The way he ate and no doubt drank. He had a gigantic paunch."

Since Madame Guioni had assumed he'd died a natural death Della decided to let it go at that. She said, "I have found Rome most interesting."

"I told you that you would," the ugly woman said. She indicated St. Peter's and said, "Look at that! A wonder of our civilized world! The magnificent dome and the façade! You will note the various figures perched on the edge of the roof at the front! Each a sculpture of perfection!"

"It is awesome!" she agreed.

"The façade alone is 374 feet long and 136 feet high," Madame Guioni told her. "Eight columns and four pillars support it. Between the columns is the Papal window from which the Pope gives his blessing! Not that any of the religious aspect impresses me, but the beauty of it all cannot be ignored."

"I remember," she said. "You are a free-thinker."

"My late husband was a devout Catholic," Madame Guioni went on. "And so was his brother and the others of his family. Fine for them. But not for me, I say."

"I'm sure you respected each other's views," Della said.

"You can believe that," the big woman said. With a gesture of her parasol, she informed, "Beyond the portico with its statues of Constantine and Charlemagne is the 'Jubilee Door' which is opened only every twenty-five years during Holy Week."

"For a person outside the Church you are very familiar with it," Della said.

"One cannot live in Rome and not know a great deal of Catholic lore," Madame Guioni said. "And how is the Prince Sanzio?"

"He is well considering his age," she said. "Of course he is confined to a wheelchair because of his rheumatism."

"How soon we all grow old," Madame Guioni said with a sigh. "You are fortunate in having your youth."

"It can also be a difficult time."

"But you have so much ahead," the older woman said. "Ah, but I must not bore you with my philosophy. The last time we talked you mentioned having some sort of problem, but it seems to have completely fled my mind. Do not think ill of me."

"Certainly not," she said. "I'm sure you have many problems of your own."

"Being a widow and trying to operate a business is most difficult," the garishly dressed woman said with a sigh.

"I'm sure it must be," she agreed politely.

"That is why I have not had any parties lately," Madame Guioni said. "And my parties were the talk of Rome."

"I'm sorry I won't be attending one."

"And so am I, my dear," the woman sighed. "My parties were wonderful! Everyone wanted to come! Everyone! But now I'm too old and tired to give another."

"Perhaps one day," Della said.

Madame Guioni brightened. "What a lovely child you are! You are quite wise as well. I may yet live to give another grand party. And I shall send you an invitation even if you've returned to England."

"And I shall try to attend," Della promised.

Madame Guioni gave an impatient gasp. "I really must go and find that impossible woman," she declared. "No doubt she has lost herself somewhere."

"The basilica is vast and takes a while to see."

"Surely not this long," Madame Guioni said. "You will excuse me, my dear, while I go look for her."

"Of course," she said, relieved to be left alone. "I hope we meet again before I leave Rome."

Madame Guioni smiled at her. "How nice of you to say that. And I'm sure that we shall!" She waved daintily to her as she walked away toward the entrance to the basilica. Della remained in the square for a short while and then returned to the museum.

When she reached the desk she felt a surge of hope as she saw Father Walker standing talking with the elderly brother to whom she'd entrusted her message. She at once went to them.

"Father Walker," she said with a smile.

The serious-faced young priest turned to her and studied her good-humoredly from behind his glasses. "Good day to you, Miss Standish."

They shook hands. She said, "You received my message?"

"Yes. I hoped you might have brought something back to us."

"Not quite that."

"Too bad."

"I agree," she said. "But I think I may be getting closer to the details of the theft. And from there I may be able to locate the Madonna."

Father Walker said, "That would be fine."

She hesitated, then asked, "I feel weak. Is there anyplace near where we can get good food and drink?"

"Yes," he said. "There's an excellent sidewalk café not far from here with umbrellas at all the tables. Let us go there."

"You shall be my guest," she said.

"My vow of poverty isn't all that encompassing," the young priest smiled. "I insist on being the host for the occasion."

"If you insist," she said with a smile.

The walk proved longer than she had expected. But it was a pleasant one in the company of the friendly young priest. He pointed out places of interest all along the way and when they reached the outdoor café with its many tables, she felt the journey well worthwhile.

Across the table, she said, "I feel I want to help your Cardinal get his Madonna back. He was kind to me and he accepted what I told him as the truth."

Father Walker looked amused. "The Cardinal is a shrewd judge of character. He did believe you."

"It meant a great deal to me," she said with a sigh. "So few other people have. Are you still looking for the Madonna?"

"Yes. We are working in our own way."

She looked down at the table. "My luck has all been bad. My sister is still missing and they still threaten us with worse if the Madonna is not turned over to them."

"So they are of an opinion opposite to the Cardinal's. They continue to think you have the Madonna."

"Unfortunately, yes."

"Well, you must make the best of it. In their very desperation they may foolishly reveal themselves. We have much to discuss. But first let us order."

Both chose light salads and wine. The food and drink proved excellent and set the mood for conversation.

Father Walker smiled at her. "As I recall our last meeting, I rescued you from defrocked Father Anthony and his thumbscrew torture weapon."

"I'm not liable to forget that night," she said. "Did you know he was murdered?"

"Yes," Father Walker said. "A pity! But he was living a sinful life."

"I know."

"So he joined Brother Louis in death," the priest said.

"Do you think he was murdered by the same person who murdered Brother Louis?"

"No question."

"Who?"

"Brizzi," Father Walker said.

"There has been still a third murder," she told him. "One of Barsini's staunch Satanists, named Gregorio, was stabbed to death last night."

The priest nodded. "In a brothel."

She gasped. "How do you know?"

"I told you we are still working on the return of the Madonna. Gregorio was a partner with Barsini in its theft. They took it from Brizzi with the help of Brother Louis and Father Anthony. It seems Father Anthony persuaded Brother Louis to steal the Madonna from Brizzi, this after he'd helped in its theft."

"So Brother Louis turned the Madonna he and Brizzi had stolen over to Father Anthony."

"Exactly. Father Anthony promised him a larger share of the proceeds when it was broken into pieces and sold. It had been their plan to sell the precious stones and the gold separately. The Madonna is of pure gold decorated with a treasure in precious stones. Fabulous enough to attract the most jaded."

"Then Brother Anthony turned the Madonna over to Barsini and his group."

"Which includes Gregorio and your sister," the priest said. "Somehow, after Barsini got hold of it and decided to send it to you in London, the Madonna was stolen by someone else. The question is who."

"And that someone left the impression that I had actually received it."

"To throw the jackals off his trail," Father Walker said. "With Gregorio finished, it could easily be Barsini's turn next. Brizzi is vindictive; whether he gets the Madonna back or not he will murder them all!"

She gave a tiny shudder. "I think I have met him."

"Brizzi?"

"Yes," she said. "He's an old man, sallow with a wispy gray beard."

The priest looked grim. "That's one of his disguises. Actually he is not old but middle-aged. He is a most ordinary-looking person. No one ever notices him when he is not in one of his disguises."

She said, "I want to ask you something. This old man told me I should find someone called Pasquale Borgo. Have you ever heard of him?"

Father Walker showed interest. "I have."

"This man I think is Brizzi told me I should find Pasquale Borgo."

"Excellent advice," the priest said. "The unfortunate thing is that nobody has been able to find him."

"Who is he?"

"The messenger."

"The messenger?" she repeated.

The priest said, "Yes. The one hired to take the Madonna to you in England."

"So he was the one!"

"Yes. Unhappily he seems to have decided to skip and keep the Madonna."

"That must be what happened," she exclaimed.

Father Walker studied her with keen eyes from behind his glasses. "Unless the Cardinal is wrong. That you do have it. That Borgo delivered it to you and then something happened to him."

"You mean that I arranged for something to happen to him?"

"It is possible."

"Possible but not the truth!" she protested. "I never saw or heard from this Borgo. As far as I know he never came to London."

"Barsini still thinks that he did. Which is why he is holding your sister."

"But he is wrong!"

"Do not be upset," the friendly priest said. "I believe you as much as the Cardinal does. I was only testing you just now."

She sat back in her chair. "Please don't do it again. I have so few friends. I can't afford to lose them."

"Prince Raphael is your friend."

"Yes."

"Did you mention Pasquale Borgo to him?"

"I decided not to until I talked it over with you," she said.

"That was very wise," Father Walker said. "Please do not tell him about Borgo."

"Why?"

The young priest shrugged. "Shall we say I have a few reservations about handsome Prince Raphael." There was irony in his voice as he said this.

She wrinkled her brow. "What are you trying to tell me?"

"Barsini and Raphael have known each other for a long period of time. Raphael introduced your sister to Barsini."

"He openly regrets that."

"I wonder if he doesn't protest too much," the priest said quietly.

"Are you telling me not to trust Raphael? He has fought this battle with me! Saved my life on occasion."

"I merely suggest discretion," he said. "Assuming that Raphael is truly opposed to Barsini. He still could find himself a captive of that evil man. And he might be tortured into telling anything he knows. Raphael would break easily under torture."

"You do not have a good opinion of him, I fear."

"I believe I have his measure," Father Walker said. "So I think it in all our interest that he not be told everything."

She pondered on this. Then she said, "How can I work with him if I don't trust him?"

"Trust him. But only to a point."

"We have a plan to try and get inside Barsini's villa tonight," she said. "He is having one of his Satanist gatherings."

"Orgies is the proper term."

"I agree," she said. "You know that everyone dons black, cowled robes. Raphael has access to robes. He thinks we can get in."

"And?"

"Then break away from the crowd and try to find my sister," Della said. "She is bound to be locked up there somewhere."

"It sounds likely," he agreed.

"Then we hope to escape with her and perhaps she will be able to tell us if Barsini has the Madonna and where he has it hidden."

"I do not think he has it," Father Walker told her. "Unless he intercepted the messenger and killed him and then took the treasure. All the while pretending he knows nothing about it."

Della said, "Then there would be no dividing. He would have it alone."

"Exactly," Father Walker said. "Greed for wealth is at the bottom of all this. All have been tainted by it. The only one who cares truly for the Madonna itself is my Cardinal."

"I understand," she said.

"He will be badly upset if it falls into evil hands to be broken and sold in bits."

"Of course."

"I'm not sure I like your plan of attempting to get into Barsini's villa," the priest said. "There could be great danger in it for you."

"And for Raphael if we're caught."

"I think only of you," the priest said. "I cannot prevent you from doing this. But I can warn you against it."

"Our plans are pretty well made."

"Think carefully before you go ahead with them."

"I will," she promised. But she knew that she would make the attempt however foolhardy it might be.

"We come back to Pasquale Borgo," the priest said. "He is the key to it all. Your strange friend was right."

"What sort of man is Borgo?"

"A failed artist," Father Walker said with a hint of disgust. "He has wound up being somewhat notorious in Rome for his pen-and-ink studies of erotic nudes. I understand his pornography sells well at modest prices. That is how he became a member of the Satanist group. He is their official artist."

"I have seen some of his murals on their meetingplace walls," she said. "Not pretty!"

"Pasquale is the sort of man easily bought," the priest went on. "Barsini selected him as messenger to take the Madonna to you in London. What took place after that is anyone's guess?"

She said, "What does this Pasquale Borgo look like?"

Father Walker gave her a glance of grim amusement. "You gave me an excellent description of him earlier. He is an elderly, sallow man with a wispy gray beard."

Chapter Seventeen

Wide-eyed, Della gasped, "Are you saying that I have seen Pasquale Borgo. That he is the man who came to my aid more than once?"

Father Walker shook his head. "No. The man you have seen is Brizzi disguised to resemble the man he murdered."

"I see," she said.

"Part of his clever game to confuse," the priest said. "Now I fear I must return to the museum. I hope I have been of some help."

"You have," she said earnestly as she rose from the table. "I will remember all you told me."

He was on his feet and facing her. "Please remember my warning about your plans for tonight."

"I shall," she said.

"And be cautious about Prince Raphael. Do not place too much dependence on him."

"I will keep that in mind," she promised.

Father Walker sighed. "I wish I could do more to help. But since I represent the Church I must be extremely discreet."

"I understand. It was good of you to talk with me."

The priest smiled. "I have my Cardinal's approval. He has shown great interest in you."

"He seems a fine old man, though his dog did terrify me."

"Bruno?" Father Walker said with amusement. "The Cardinal has to interview many kinds of people. Bruno is his loyal protector."

Della said, "You are enjoying your time in Rome."

"Very much," the earnest priest said. "I had been working in the library. Would you believe that one day I actually touched the manuscript of Dante's *Divine Comedy*. Now I'm being transferred to the Pinacoteca, the gallery of art. It is the newest building and it is filled with priceless paintings."

Della said, "I wish I were under less pressure and had more chance to enjoy all the wonders of this city."

"Perhaps the Madonna will soon be found and this grim business of murders and double-crossing will be at an end," Father Walker said.

He saw her to a carriage and then left her as he made his way on foot to the Vatican. She sat back in the open carriage so besieged by troubling thoughts she paid scarcely any attention to the busy streets and the volatile people. She was lost in consideration of what the priest had told her. The most disturbing thing of all was his seeming lack of faith in Prince Raphael.

She knew Father Walker to be fair and if he were suspicious of Raphael, there must be a sound reason. He did not condemn the handsome young man completely but suggested there was a wide swath of weakness in him. And she realized that she had come to understand this and allow for it. The most severe test of Raphael would come tonight when they attempted to enter Barsini's villa in search of Irma.

When Della reached the palace of Prince Sanzio both the old man and Aunt Isobel were following the Roman custom of taking an afternoon siesta. So there was no one to bother her with questions. She went up the broad stairway to the second floor and then some impulse sent her to investigate Irma's room.

The old house was strangely still as she went along the shadowy corridor and tried the door. It was not locked and she stepped inside. The first thing she noted was that the candle in the great glass bowl before the Madonna was still burning. Guido was showing his devotion to his mistress by seeing the candle flame was kept alive.

Della looked around and saw no change, no indication that anyone but Guido had entered the room. Then she went over to the paneled wall to seek out the hidden door to the maze of secret passages which filled the palace. The last time it had been locked against her. But when she pressed on the panel today it swung back. She cautiously entered the dark, cold passage and then made her way down the stone steps to the level where she had wandered through earlier.

Though the day was warm and sunny it was cold and damp in the hidden passage. She groped her way along and soon found a new corridor and followed it. This led to a short flight of stone steps. She mounted the steps and found herself coming out to a low arched entry to the garden. This was a different part of the garden and there was no walk leading to it directly.

She could see the other section of the well-kept garden from where she stood. In this section the garden had gone mostly to weeds. But she saw evidence of some fresh flower beds being prepared. The new mounds of earth suggested that additional flowers had been planted and were shortly to increase the beauty of the garden.

She stared lazily at the adjoining garden with its row of tall, dark green trees. Then she started back. This time when she came to the place where the passage wound about and broke into two directions, she was unable to find the familiar passage which had led her into the concealed area.

This maze of passages had been installed in more violent days so that no one would be caught in the palace without some means of escape. Raphael had told her that the majority of the majestic palaces of Rome were built with these dark, hidden corridors.

She was now in deep darkness and began to get a feeling of claustrophobia. Suppose she couldn't find her way back, that she was to be trapped down here! The mere thought of it increased her fears and she realized her heart had taken on a quicker beat. She halted and tried to recall where she might have made a wrong turn. It did not seem possible that she had, yet here she was in a tunnel unfamiliar to her.

Then she heard soft footsteps! Footsteps behind her and coming nearer. A chill ran through her as she speculated whose footsteps they might be!

The footsteps came closer and she drew back against the damp wall waiting for she knew not what. She could still see no one in the near darkness but the sound of footsteps was strangely close!

Then a familiar voice asked querulously, "Is there someone down here?"

With a great feeling of relief she recognized the voice as belonging to the midget Guido. And a moment later he came into view with a candle in his tiny hand highlighting his wizened face.

He stared at her with some annoyance. "*Signorina* Standish! What are you doing here?"

She said, "I knew about the secret panel and the passage. I decided to investigate it."

Guido glared at her. "Prince Sanzio does not wish anyone to be in these passages."

"Why not?"

"They are far too dangerous," he said. "Many of them are in poor repair. The brick roofs could cave in and kill you."

She had not thought of this before; it was a chilling possibility. She said, "The arch overhead seems solid enough."

"Appearance means nothing," the little man said. "It is the dampness which plays havoc with the lime. There is no warning before the bricks come down."

"I had no idea of the danger," she apologized. "Also it is good you came along. I have lost my way."

"That is also easy to do," Guido said. "And there are openings in the corridor floors at some points, put there by the first builders to trap enemies who might come after them when they were escaping from the house. I know the locations of these drops. But a stranger like yourself could step in one and suffer a six-or seven-foot fall to a sort of dungeon without any avenue of escape."

"You frighten me more!"

"One man at least fell into one of these holes and it was only years later that his skeleton was found. He was identified by jewelry he'd been wearing."

"So the secret corrdiors are not in use any longer."

"They are supposed to be kept locked," Guido said, his tone still showing a trace of annoyance. "It was through some mistake you were able to enter."

"I shall not do so again," she promised. "You have told me enough to be sure of that."

"Very well," Guido said sharply. "Follow me and I will get you out of this place."

She followed the little man, helped by the light from the candle he was carrying. Within a few minutes they had returned to the main passage and the steps which led up to Irma's room. When they emerged into the missing girl's bedroom, Della noted that Guido snapped a lock on the panel as he closed it.

Later, when she went down for dinner, Prince Sanzio was waiting in his wheelchair at the foot of the stairway. He at once reprimanded her for her audacity in trying to find her way about in the secret passages. "You were most ill-advised," he said in his old man's querulous tones.

"I did not realize the danger," she told him.

"You could lose your life in there," he said.

"Guido explained it to me," she told him.

"Irma used to tease me occasionally by using the secret passages to make a surprise appearance in the gardens. That was long ago when I was able to move about and she was a mere child. I was always upset and gave her many warnings."

"I will not attempt such a thing again," Della said.

He sighed. "I hope not. The entrances are supposed to be kept locked. I cannot imagine how you managed to open the panel in Irma's room."

"Perhaps someone had used it and neglected to lock it," she said.

Prince Sanzio stared at her. "But who? Only a few people know about the existence of that secret doorway."

"Irma does," she said.

The old man frowned. "We know all too well that Irma has been kidnapped and is in the hands of that villainous Count Barsini!"

"I sometimes wonder," she said.

"Wonder about what?" the old man in the wheelchair demanded.

"If my sister was kidnapped."

"She's not here!" the old man exclaimed. "We have the ransom note. They want the Madonna!"

"Could it be some sort of trick?" she asked.

"I'm afraid I don't follow your thinking," Prince Sanzio said testily.

"I wonder if she might have vanished voluntarily."

"Never!"

"I'm not all that sure," Della said. "Perhaps Barsini and his crowd have won her over. They all think I know where the Madonna is. And this is their means of getting it from me."

"By pretending to hold Irma and threaten her life if the Madonna isn't turned over to them?" the old Prince said.

"Yes. That is what I've been thinking."

"However much Irma has fallen under that evil fellow's power I do not think she would be a party to anything like that."

"But none of us can be sure."

The man in the wheelchair reminded her, "There is a time limit. According to their message, she has only about forty-eight hours more to live unless the Madonna is turned over to those Satanist rogues."

"I'm aware of the time limit."

"And yet we have accomplished little in finding her," the old man worried. "Perhaps I should have turned to the police."

"Part of their threat was that Irma would die at once if you dared do that."

Aunt Isobel had apparently overheard them, for she now came down the stairway to stand between Della and the man in the wheelchair. Dressed in somber brown, the old woman was in a mood as gloomy as her dress. She said, "For my part I think Irma is already dead."

"Please! Don't say that!" Prince Sanzio begged her.

"I cannot help it," Aunt Isobel said. "I believe it because on several nights I have seen her ghost."

Della said, "Please, let us not begin that."

"It is a fact," her aunt said stiffly. "I will not change my story to please anyone."

Prince Sanzio eyed her unhappily. "I'm sure it was Miss Standish whom you may have seen. The two girls resemble each other so much even I can hardly tell them apart."

"No," Aunt Isobel said. "Della was not even in the palace at the time I saw the ghost."

Della addressed herself to the old man: "Perhaps my theory is the better one. If Irma is alive and free, she could come back here using the secret passages she knows so well."

"No!" he protested.

Della insisted, "I say she could come back here under cover of night if she were looking for something. The Madonna if she thinks I have it."

"No!" The old man angrily denied such a thing was possible. But more and more she was beginning to wonder about it all.

Della knew about the secret passage and its entrance panel in her sister's bedroom because she had once gone to the room and found the panel door open. Someone obviously had used it. The question was who.

Irma knew the passages and could travel in them safely. If she were truly a free agent and wanted to return to the palace for her own reasons, this would explain the ghostly visitations about which Aunt Isobel was so emphatic.

The old woman said, "I don't think the figure I saw was real. It was a ghost!"

Prince Sanzio shrugged his shoulders. "I cannot help what you may think. It would appear to me I know and understand my foster daughter better than any of you. She would not put me through this torment if she were free to come here."

Della saw that he was sincere in this and badly hurt by her suggestion. Out of sympathy she said, "Perhaps you are right." But she knew that doubts had arisen in her mind and she was not apt to dismiss them until she knew the full story.

Prince Sanzio wheeled himself into the dining room, leaving Della and Aunt Isobel to follow. As soon as he was a distance ahead, the old woman whispered to Della, "I would not talk about this in his presence again. He is very upset and he is old and ill."

"I agree," Della said as they started for the dining room.

Prince Raphael arrived directly after dinner. He was dressed in a dark brown suit and he had a small bandage at his temple.

Old Prince Sanzio at once asked, "What has happened to you?"

"That bandage around your head!" Aunt Isobel chimed in.

Raphael showed embarrassment. "I regret to say my horsemanship is not up to the level I'd hoped. I took a fall this afternoon and this is the result." He touched the bandage.

"I never trust horses," Aunt Isobel declared.

The old Prince frowned. "I do not understand it. You have the reputation of being an excellent horseman."

Raphael spread his hands. "We all fail occasionally."

Della and Raphael left the two older people as soon as they could. They went out to the garden for a stroll before leaving. She was careful to omit any mention of her meeting with Father

Walker or her search for Pasquale Borgo. But she brought him up to date on everything else.

Raphael told her, "The old Prince was right in warning you about those hidden passages. They are dangerous."

"You believe that?"

"I do," he said. "It is true of most of the houses that have them. They were built long ago and no work has been done to keep the majority of them fit to use."

"Irma used them."

"Irma did many things which were unwise," Raphael said grimly. "Including becoming infatuated with Barsini."

Della said, "I do not understand her leaving you for him. I find him repulsive."

He halted and, smiling at her gently, said, "That is because you have better sense than your sister. And why I find myself in love with you rather than with her."

She looked up at him. "Even if you mean that I wish you wouldn't say it."

"Why not?"

"Because you are only making it more difficult for us. You know I hope to reconcile with Henry when he returns from Naples."

"If he returns from Naples," Raphael taunted her. "What if he is already on his way back to London without you?"

"He wouldn't do that!"

"What makes you so sure?"

Blushing, she said, "Because as an Englishman he would not break the trust put in him. He is not only my fiancé, he is my lawyer. Sent here by his superiors to watch over me."

"I'm not sure he has done all that well."

"He did well enough until he caught us in each other's arms and went off in a rage," she said bitterly.

"Good riddance!"

"I can't agree," she said. "But we must not quarrel about that now. Not with our biggest challenge ahead."

He sighed, his mood now bleak. "Perhaps we should give up this plan."

"You can't mean it!" she exclaimed in disappointment.

"After last night I'm not at all enthusiastic," he said. "We both had narrow escapes. We might not be so lucky tonight."

"But there is no time to consider. The threat we received gives us a deadline," she argued. "This is our best chance to locate Irma. And you told me you knew a way to get us into the villa."

"I do," he said. "But the place will be crawling with Satanists. If we are discovered and they turn on us we might be torn to pieces. They're a nasty crowd."

"I know that."

"If Irma is there you may be sure she is well under lock and key. Our chances of getting to her are slim!"

She said, "First let us seek out Barsini and let him turn her over to us."

"You think he is liable to?"

"Not willingly," she said. "But you have your pistol with you, I trust."

"After last night I refuse to leave my house unarmed."

"The prospect of being shot has a beneficial effect on making the most stubborn of men talk," she said.

"So I'm to threaten Barsini with a pistol," he said. "You know what will happen to me if Barsini manages to get the upper hand some way. I'll be murdered."

"And so will I," she said. "But I'm willing to take the risk to find out about Irma. Aren't you?"

"I suppose so," he agreed reluctantly.

"Did you bring the black robes with the cowls similar to those worn by the Satanists?" Della asked him.

He nodded. "Yes. I have them with me."

"All we have to do is put them on and we should be fairly safe," she said. "We can mingle with the others and move about."

"They are only given the privilege of certain parts of the villa," he reminded her.

She gave him a grim smile. "We shall have to do better."

So she set out on the dangerous mission with Raphael an almost unwilling accomplice. She could not help but remember what the young priest had told her. His warning about Raphael seemed to be based on a accurate appraisal of the handsome, young man's character. Raphael's brush with death the previous night had left him uneasy.

They reached the Barsini's villa after darkness and watched it from the vantage point of a dark alley directly across the street. Carriages were arriving and many people were approaching the villa on foot. A single torch flamed at the main doorway and a man in footman's livery was there to check the invitations of each of the guests before allowing them in.

Raphael said glumly. "I've never known him to be so strict about admitting his people."

"He likely is afraid of someone like us getting in there for information."

"Probably," he agreed.

She was watching the movement of people at the door and told Raphael, "I'm sure there are enough in there now so that we won't be noticed."

"Does that mean you want to go in?" he asked.

"Yes."

"All right," he said. "We'll go down to the river bank, get in one of the rowboats that are always tied there and take it to the entrance of the villa at the water's edge. It's there for the convenience of anyone arriving by boat."

"And it isn't likely to be guarded?"

"I have never known it to be," he said.

"When will we put on the robes?"

"After we are in the boat," Raphael said. "It will only take us a moment or two to row to the villa's river entrance."

They moved on down the street and hurried to the river's edge. Raphael took the first rowboat tied there. He helped her into it and then they both donned the black robes and pulled the cowls over their heads and most of their faces so they would not be easily recognized.

Raphael took the oars and guided the boat to the wooden door by the river. He stood up when they reached it and tried the door. It was unlocked. He gave her a signal that all was well and then opened the door and stood to help her out of the boat. She grasped his hands and he drew her up to join him. Then they stepped into the cellar and he closed the door after them.

Della's previous misadventures at the sprawling Barsini villa had given her a fear of the place. And she found the gloomy cellar no different from the rest of the house—indeed it was more frightening. Having Raphael at her side gave her some courage, but she knew that his own fears made it chancy to rely on him.

At least she did not have to face the horror of another encounter with Gregorio. The giant was dead and would do her no more harm. If they were lucky they would locate Irma and get her out of the evil house. But she knew the vicious Count Barsini was no mean adversary.

Raphael led the way looking weird in his black robe and cowl, and she followed him closely. They would be safe as soon as they reached the area where the other Satanists gathered. The others would be an additional cloak to protect them from discovery.

They reached a wide stone stairway and went up to double wooden doors. Raphael listened at the doors and then motioned her to come along. He opened the doors and they found they were in a cooridor of the main house.

The walls were white and a brown carpet covered the broad corridor. At intervals there were examples of sculpture, most of them reflecting the weird character of the house and the man who owned it. On pedestals there were heads of ugly tormented men, snakes coiled in their hair, wanton sirens with daggers in their hands, and various strange figures which seemed to be a combination of human and animal elements. The pieces were all unpleasant to look at.

From above them came murmuring voices. Della supposed that the meeting rooms must be almost directly above them. She followed Raphael along the corridor and they came to an open door. The room looked like a study with a desk and chairs, but the walls were covered with paintings of couples in the act of love.

Even in this moment of danger Della reacted with shame to the shocking scenes depicted on the walls. She turned to make a comment to Raphael and to her utter consternation he was no longer at her side. In just a moment he had silently vanished!

She couldn't believe it. She started for the door to the corridor and found that it was now closed. She ran to the door and tried the knob. It would not open!

"Raphael!" she cried out unhappily, leaning against the door for support.

There was no reply, just as she had feared. She left the door and went to the window. It was high above the Tiber with no balcony on which she might make an escape. Raphael had somehow been whisked away and she was a prisoner in this shocking room!

She went back to the door and tried it without any success. Then she pounded on it and cried out for help. She kept at this until her hands were sore and her throat ached. She was still bewildered by the suddenness of it all. What had happened to Raphael?

She realized the danger had greatly increased. Her presence in the villa was known and Raphael had in some way been removed!

She had spent a long moment staring at the erotic drawings on the walls. In that stunned moment when her attention had been concentrated on the erotica this thing had happened!

Now she was a prisoner and separated from Raphael, who was also in custody of their enemies. If they were still convinced she knew where the Madonna was she could expect a fresh round of torture. That could also mean Raphael would be tortured to make her talk.

She paced back and forth trying to think what she might do. Then, without warning, the door opened and a suave Count Barsini entered in his black robe with the cowl folded back to show his head.

The evil Count bowed to her and smiled. "It seems you are unable to resist us!"

"Where is Raphael?" she asked tensely.

Barsini looked amused. "Not far away."

"What have you done to him?"

"Nothing as yet."

"You dare not hold us here," she said. "I order you to fetch him here and let us both go free."

He said, "You had your freedom until you intruded in my home."

"We came for Irma. You must let her go!"

He continued to mock her. "What makes you think I'm keeping her here?"

"She has to be here!"

He raised his eyebrows. "Merely because you say so?"

"Because you think by threatening her you can make me tell you where the Madonna is!"

"Will you tell me?"

"No. I can't," she said. "I don't know where it is myself. I suspect you or one of your henchmen has it."

He strolled over to stand behind his desk. Giving her a look of appraisal, he said, "I don't know what to do with you exactly. You have made things awkward by coming here."

"You can believe I'm telling the truth when I say I don't know where the Madonna is and end this mad charade!"

Barsini said, "Suppose I tell you that I know the messenger took the Madonna to you in London."

"You mean Pasquale Borgo?"

Barsini stared at her. "So you know his name?"

"I have found out who your messenger was," she said. "That doesn't mean I met him."

"I rather believe that it does!"

"Because you want to," she said. "I can tell you that Pasquale Borgo never arrived in London. He must have been killed somewhere along the way."

"By whom? No one but a trusted few knew his mission."

"Then one of the trusted few must be to blame!" she cried.

Barsini was studying her with a cruel gleam in his eyes. "You have arrived here at a most unfortunate time. Just as we are about to have our Black Mass."

"Then let me go!"

"I cannot do that," he sighed. "But I think I should let you know the facts."

"What facts?"

"That you are in this alone!"

She echoed, "Alone?"

He was smiling nastily now. "You asked me about your good friend Raphael? What happened to him?"

"Yes!"

"Nothing happened to him," Barsini said with silky hatred in his tone. "He deserted you!"

She clasped her hands at her side and told herself not to lose courage. Defiantly she said, "I don't believe you!"

"I will have him come in here shortly and let him tell you."

She faltered a little as she groped for something to say. "I don't understand."

"The handsome Prince Raphael is mine," Count Barsini said. "I own him."

"No!"

"Sad but true," Barsini purred on, his evil face crowned by the halo of his shining bald head.

"It can't be!" she protested, sinking into a nearby chair. "He has been helping me from the start."

"Pretending to help you," Barsini corrected her. "Part of my plan to keep you under surveillance."

She was now thinking of Father Walker and the priest's warning. In a dull voice, she said, "What other facts don't I know?"

"That Raphael and your twin sister have been in on this business of the stolen Madonna from the start!"

She stared up at him. "Irma also!"

He smiled grimly and nodded. "Yes. It was Irma who hit on the idea of making you an agent for us. She gave the Madonna to Pasquale Borgo with passage money and a note asking you to keep the piece in London. I was to go there later and get it from you."

"I never saw Pasquale Borgo," she insisted again.

"I fear that is not possible," Barsini said. "I must leave you now. But I shall have Raphael and Irma sent to talk with you."

"None of what you're saying is true. You're trying to terrify me," she cried.

He spread his hands and said blandly, "Whatever you like to think? Just remember one thing! I'm not finished with you until I get the Madonna!"

With that he marched past her and out the door. She heard a key turn in it and the lock click into place and knew that he intended to keep her in the room, a prisoner. Whether the rest of what he'd told her was true she found it difficult to decide.

She felt weak and ill. Sitting in the chair again, she knew that she should have listened to Father Walker's advice. He must have known more than she did. He had warned her about Raphael, but his warning had not been strong enough. If he suspected that Raphael was one of the thieves, he should have told her that outright.

Her thoughts were interrupted by the key turning in the door again. She jumped up to face the door, tense and waiting. It opened to reveal her sister.

Irma was wearing one of the Satanist's robes and she looked well enough, except for a strange pallor, which might have been accentuated by the grim, black robe. She entered the room and the door was closed and the lock turned again.

Her sister's first words were, "I'm sorry."

She stared at her in disbelief. "You have not been a captive here?"

"No."

"You stayed here to play along with Barsini's rotten scheme to get the Madonna?"

Irma nodded, looking like a sad, lovely reflection of Della. "I know you must hate me," she said. "I was in this before I knew about being your sister. That I would have money. After all the years of poverty I was mad to have wealth!"

Della said, "I'm sure you never suffered as Prince Sanzio's foster daughter. He is a good man. I'm sure he was a fine father to you."

Irma took a few steps away and with a grimace said, "I never starved. But we were genteel poor in a city of wealth!"

"You could look forward to your marriage to Raphael," she reminded her.

Irma gave a bitter laugh. "That meant trading a girlhood of poverty for a womanhood of the same. Raphael is as poor as my unhappy father except for his title. He is a penniless prince."

"So both you and he threw your lot in with Barsini?" she said, at last beginning to believe the nightmare.

"We are bound to Barsini by closer ties than that," her sister said. "We are his disciples. He is leading us into a new existence!"

"Leading you to destroy yourselves," she said with contempt.

Irma said, "I'm not interested in your opinions of our leader. I want to hear all you know about the Madonna."

"Nothing!"

"That is impossible!" Irma said, showing anger. "I sent Pasquale to you. He was a trusted agent."

"Then where is he now?" Della asked, hoping she had found something on which to reason with her enemies.

Irma said, "It was part of the agreement that he was to go underground for a few months. He had some trouble with the police here in Italy. An attack on a young girl. He needed to get out of the country and lose himself. We supplied him with the means to get away in exchange for his handling the Madonna."

Della felt despair at hearing this. So the absence of Pasquale Borgo from the scene could be this easily explained. She made another attempt to talk her way out of her plight, saying, "In my opinion he ran off to Paris with the Madonna."

"You're saying he stole it from us?"

"Yes."

Irma shook her head. "He wouldn't dare! Not with the police after him already. He would be caught between Brizzi, the law and us. He'd never escape!"

Clutching on a last straw, she said, "Brizzi! He must have taken the Madonna back to Brizzi and thrown his lot in with the original thief!"

"Brizzi is still searching for the Madonna," Irma said. "So that rules out your last alibi. You must be reasonable. Dreadful things will happen to you if you don't tell us where the Madonna is."

She backed away from her. "You're mad!"

"You are the mad one! Why do you not tell us? You do not need the money! What can the Madonna mean to you?"

Della stepped back from her angry sister who was following her across the room. She said, "No, you are the mad ones! Mad with greed! You cannot make yourselves accept that you've lost this treasure. That someone has been able to outsmart you!"

"No!" Irma cried, close to her.

"Yes!" Della said. "You've lost! Don't you see? But you prefer to think I can give you the Madonna!"

Rage distorted Irma's lovely face. For a moment it seemed she might strike Della. Then she relaxed a little. And in a grim voice, she said, "I wanted to help you! You are my sister! But you're determined to destroy yourself!" With that she went to the door and asked that it be opened. The door was unlocked and she went out, leaving Della alone once more.

Chapter Eighteen

Della stood there sickened by the discovery that her sister was not only a dedicated Satanist but also part of the group who had stolen the Madonna. She now realized why her aunt had thought she'd seen Irma's ghost moving about the midnight halls of the palace. Irma had probably returned to pursue her own plans and then vanished again before being discovered.

What made the situation so hopeless was the almost insane belief among the thieves that she had possession of the Madonna! They could not accept that their agent Pasquale Borgo had either gone underground with the treasure entrusted to him or had been somehow eliminated by still other thieves and the treasure stolen from him.

She sank down in the chair, again terrified at what might come next. She knew that Barsini was not finished with her. He would torture her until he was finally convinced she could not produce the Madonna for him.

She was lost in these grim thoughts when the lock clicked and the door opened again. This time it was a shamed-faced Raphael who came slowly into the room. As the door was closed after him he came to her side.

"Forgive me, Della," he said.

She looked up at him in disgust. "All along you were playing Barsini's game. You knew that Irma was in no danger."

The handsome Prince pleaded, "I had no choice."

She felt nothing but contempt for him. "Barsini said you were his slave!"

"It's not quite like that," he said. "But we were partners in getting the Madonna from Brizzi. And I can't afford to lose my share of the treasure."

"Your share! You are entitled to nothing! It was stolen from the Vatican by Brizzi. That is where it belongs."

Raphael's handsome face became hard. "Is that what you've been doing? Bargaining with the Vatican for its return? Have you made some deal with your good Father Walker?"

"If I had the Madonna I'd return it to them," she said with spirit.

"We know you have it."

"You are terribly wrong."

"And it seems you are terribly stubborn," Raphael said. "I don't want to see Barsini harm you. I'm in love with you. I told you that earlier."

She offered him a jeering smile. "In love with me or the idea of my money? I am heiress to a good fortune."

"Which Irma will share," he was quick to remind her. "And I'm willing to turn from her to you. That ought to prove it isn't the money."

"After the way you've deceived me I can never trust you again," she said.

He frowned. "I want to be your friend. And I warn you Barsini is becoming impatient!"

"I don't care," she replied.

"You may before all this is ended," was his grim warning. "You look as if you might faint any moment. Have some water!" He went to the desk and poured out a glass of water from a glass decanter there.

She accepted the water and drank most if it down. Her mouth had been parched and she was closer to collapse than she would ever have admitted. She handed him back the glass and said, "Thank you."

He stood watching her carefully. "Irma is upset about your attitude. She was our link with the messenger, so in a way she feels responsible for the failure of the project."

"I cannot help that," she said.

"Be sensible! Tell us what happened to the Madonna and you'll be free. Irma will return to the palace and maybe she and I will marry. I'll be your brother-in-law. The story could have a happy ending."

"Not the way you see it," she said. And then without warning her head began to spin. She prayed that it was only a momentary weakness that would soon pass. But it didn't. She groped for the arms of the chair and clasped them to support herself.

Staring up at Raphael with blurred vision, she asked in a weak voice, "What is happening? What was in that water? You've given me something!" She crumpled back in the chair, unconscious.

When she opened her eyes her vision was blurred for a moment and her head spun. Then the giddiness left her and she became aware of herself and her surroundings. She had drunk some drugged water that Raphael had pressed on her. In her innocence she'd taken a lot of it. Now she was on a stage before a roomful of the Satanists, seated like rows of black birds in their dark robes and cowls!

The stage was in near darkness and she was not alone on it. She was tied, entirely nude with her arms stretched out, to a kind of wooden cross. This last realization shocked her. She glanced to her left and right and saw that on both sides of her other naked girls were tied on other imitation crosses. It was a mock Crucifixion scene to titillate the Satanists!

They were known for staging anti-Christian rituals to mock the Church. Now she was to be publicly humiliated as part of one. She struggled to free herself without any success. Then Barsini appeared at the left of the stage with a black-robed assistant holding a torch to light him.

As the torch highlighted the figure of the Satanist leader he threw off his black robe and stood naked before the assemblage. Smiling he turned and moved toward the girl on the cross nearest him. The crowd cried out in anticipation. And Barsini catered to their lust by pressing himself to the girl and engaging her in sexual movement.

Della averted her eyes from the degrading spectacle, sickened by the knowledge she would be the next to be publicly defiled by the monstrous Barsini. The excitement of the audience grew as the sexual engagement on the stage moved to a climax! She closed her eyes and as she did so a miracle happened!

She felt the cords binding her arms and ankles cut. A voice whispered in her ear, "Step back!"

She did so, moving into the shadows behind the middle cross. The crowd below was so caught up with the sexual orgy on the lighted left side of the stage they paid no attention to her escape.

There in the shadows was a naked Irma. She told her, "Your clothes are out back. I will take your place. You can make your escape before anyone knows it!"

Della had no chance to thank her sister. Irma stepped forward and leaned her nude body against the cross in the same position in which she'd been. The only difference was that Irma had not been tied there at wrists and ankles. But it was unlikely Barsini would notice this as he moved on to her to continue the orgy already underway.

She ran out back and there on a table found her clothing as Irma had promised. She quickly dressed and then put on the black robe and cowl which Irma had apparently left for her. The sounds from the stage and the company of Satanists told her the ugly spectacle was moving to its finish.

She ran out into a wide corridor and down along it in what she hoped was the right direction. As she made her way quickly, there was fear in every fibre of her being that she was to have another shock.

From an ell there sprang a black, robed figure who took her by the arm and hissed in her ear, "Come with me!"

She did not question the newcomer or ask his purpose. It was obvious to her that whoever this was had to be helping in her escape. She and her robed partner stumbled down a flight of stone steps and then out a side door of the villa into the street.

They did not hesitate in their flight until they were several streets away. Then her rescuer halted and took the cowl from his head to reveal himself as Father Walker.

She gasped as she stared at him. "You!"

"Yes!" he said grimly.

"What were you doing in that wicked place?"

"I could ask you the same question," he said. "I knew when I talked with you earlier you were bound to make the mistaken attempt to rescue your sister."

"She didn't want to be rescued."

"I knew that."

"But she made my escape possible, just the same," she said with a shudder. "She took my place in that ritual orgy on the stage."

Father Walker looked grim. "I saw," he said. "Barsini must one day pay a terrible price for destroying the souls of so many people."

"I agree," Della said.

"Get that thing off you," the young priest said, and at the same time he removed his Satanist's robe to reveal a priestly one. He took both robes and threw them in an alley.

"What now?" she asked.

"Get away from here as soon as possible," he told her. "They may send someone after us at any moment!" He took her by the arm and guided her through the dark, deserted streets.

At last they came to a busy thoroughfare and he hailed a carriage. He saw her into it and gave the address of the Sanzio palace. Then he got into the closed carriage at her side.

He explained, "I dare not leave you until I see you safely to your door."

"This is the second or third time you've come to save me," she said. "How can I thank you?"

"No thanks needed," he said. "It is because of the Madonna you are in all this trouble. Both the Cardinal and I feel a responsibility."

"How did you get into that place?"

A grim smile showed on his face. "We are at least as clever as Barsini. I impersonated a member of his group. Once I donned the black robe and cowl I was safe."

"I felt there was no one," she said.

"I understand."

She glanced at him. "You were right in warning me against Raphael."

Father Walker nodded. "The fallen Prince!"

"He has sunk low," she agreed. "I could not believe he was capable of such deceit."

"Barsini's influence and his own greed."

"So he is finished," she said sadly. "Both he and my sister."

"At least she helped save you. If she had not released you I would have had to risk going on stage and doing it myself. And she gave us extra time by taking your place!"

"I know," Della said. "She has much good in her yet. I think she might be saved."

"Barsini will punish her for allowing you to get away, be certain of that."

She shuddered. "I wish she had left with me."

"She wanted to give you plenty of time," he said.

"And it was Raphael who deliberately gave me that drugged water. I took it without even suspecting him. I must have been mad!"

"You had come to trust him and acted without thinking," he said.

"What next?" she worried.

"They won't give up," the priest warned her.

"I know that," she said.

"Like any criminal group, they will work out some other strategy," he said. "At least you won't make it easier for them by walking into their trap."

"Depend on that."

"And Prince Raphael can hardly show himself at the palace now that he has revealed his deceit."

"I'm sure he won't," she agreed. "His only purpose was to watch me and keep me confused."

"In this circumstance that wasn't too difficult a task," the young priest said grimly. "I'd advise you to return to England as soon as possible."

"Yes. I should," she said. Then she gave him a plaintive look. "Do you think there is any hope of rescuing Irma?"

"She wants to be with Barsini."

"She did save me tonight. That proves she isn't entirely lost."

"I wouldn't count on that," he warned her.

"Still, I must consider," she said. "I came to Rome to see her reinstated as a member of the family and take her back to England. Perhaps that may still be possible."

"Dangerous thinking," Father Walker warned.

"Don't you believe in repentance and salvation?"

"Is your question theological or practical? In Irma's case I think there is only a small margin of hope."

"Then how can I return to England and leave her in the clutches of that wicked man?"

He sighed. "I suppose you must make your own decision. But remember, I may not be on hand to rescue you another time!"

"You are too good!" she said warmly.

"I have grown fond of you," Father Walker said with a depth of emotion she had never heard in his voice before. "I do not wish to see harm come to you!" And in the manner of a good friend he kissed her on the temple.

She respected him too much to be misled by his affectionate gesture. "Thank you, Father!" she said in a low voice and squeezed his hand.

The carriage halted before the Sanzio palace and he saw her to the door. When Aunt Isobel opened it to let her in it was to the credit of that prim English lady that she showed no hint of surprise.

Della said, "This is my friend, Father Walker. He has been nice enough to see me home."

Aunt Isobel said, "How kind of you, Father. Won't you come in for some refreshment?"

"Thank you, no," the young priest said with a smile. "It has been a long and wearing evening. And I'm already overdue at the Vatican." With that he bowed to them both and returned to the carriage.

Only as Aunt Isobel saw her inside did she ask with some surprise, "What happened to your Prince Raphael?"

"That is a long and sad story," she replied, taking off her cloak.

"Perhaps it is just as well he is not with you," her aunt said with a rare smile. "Go into the drawing room. There is a surprise for you!"

Della looked at her aunt and her face lit up as she raced toward the living room. When she reached it she saw Henry Clarkson standing there waiting. She ran to him and threw her arms around him.

"Henry!" she said with a sob. "I'm so happy to see you!"

"And I to see you, my dearest," Henry said, embracing her and giving her a long, ardent kiss.

She pressed against him. "I was afraid you might not come back!"

"I was only halfway to Naples when I knew I had acted like an idiot," Henry told her. "It was too late to return then as I had urgent affairs to attend to in Naples. But I arrived back an hour ago."

She looked up at him. "You couldn't have come at a better time. I need you so."

"The business with Raphael is forgotten," he said. "I don't even want to hear why you were in his arms that day. It doesn't matter, that was only for a moment, I want you with me all my life,"

"I shall be at your side, Henry, I promise," she said tenderly.

His arm around her, he led her to the divan and as they sat down, he said, "Now I want you to tell me all that has been happening while I was away."

"So much!" she said.

"Let me hear," he urged her.

So she sat with him until it was very late, filling him in on all that had taken place. She ended with the events of the night and her rescue by Father Walker.

Henry was astounded in the proper British way. "What a scoundrel that Raphael has turned out to be!"

"I know. He had won my trust,"

"And miserably betrayed it," the young lawyer said angrily. "I should like to make him pay for that!"

"Don't think of revenge," she said. "His fate will be bad enough as one of Barsini's slaves."

"Your Father Walker sounds like a proper English gentleman as well as a priest," Henry said. "We surely owe much to him."

"He has been a grand friend."

"Raphael had better not show his sneaking face here."

"I doubt that either he or my sister will return," she said. "The terrible part is that Barsini and all of them, with the exception of Father Walker, think I have the Madonna or know where it is."

"So you will still be a target for those greedy madmen," Henry said indignantly. "My thought is to pack in the morning and take the first available train back to Paris."

"I can't," she said.

He stared at her. "You can't? I'm afraid I do not understand."

She said, "I'd like to make a final attempt at rescuing Irma before I go."

"She's too involved with Barsini."

"Not any longer," she said. "He may even punish her for taking my place in that orgy."

Henry agreed. "She did risk something for that."

"I will think of some safe way to reach her," she said.

"Better that she should come here and we talk it out."

"Perhaps we can get a message to her at the villa without Barsini knowing. She might come in answer to it."

"I still think it would be wiser to go back to England. Let the lawyers here try to help Irma if it is possible."

"There is something else," she said. "I feel I owe the Cardinal and Father Walker something. They have had faith in me and Father Walker's efforts have saved me several times."

"So?"

"I would like to recover the stolen Madonna for the Vatican Museum."

"Who knows where it is now?"

"Pasquale Borgo must know." she said.

"The messenger?"

"Yes."

"But he has to be murdered or hiding out somewhere in Paris," Henry argued.

"I wonder."

He showed surprise. "Meaning?"

"He could be hidden away somewhere here," she said. "I understand the Roman police have a warrant for his arrest."

"If he were here there isn't a chance of locating him in that case."

"There might be," she said. "For a start you could have the Italian lawyers find out everything possible about him. Where he lives and his relatives. We can then check on whether he is around and his habits."

Henry eyed her with perplexity. "I'm afraid you are too mixed up with all this. Why not go and leave it behind you?"

"How can you be sure that would happen? Remember the agents Barsini sent to London for the Madonna? And what they did to me when they couldn't locate it."

"Don't remind me," he said angrily.

"So why could it not happen in England again?" she pointed out. "I say the only way I will ever have peace is for the Madonna to be found. And Brizzi himself told me that this Pasquale Borgo is the key."

"Brizzi is another scoundrel!" Henry exclaimed. "How can you believe anything he has to say?"

"I can believe that," she said. "He wants me to produce the Madonna so he can get it back."

Henry sighed. "What it amounts to is that you're not yet ready to leave Rome!"

"Let's not argue any longer," she said sleepily and pressed herself close to him.

"I'll not argue nor shall I leave you alone for a moment," was his decision.

She was lazily delighted to have him stand up and take her in his arms and carry her up the great winding marble stairway. The eerie old mansion with its hidden passages was silent; all the others had long ago retired. The flickering tongues of candles set out at intervals further enhanced the atmosphere of mystery.

Henry carried her into her room and gently placed her on the bed. Then he bent and whispered to her, "I said I would not leave you and I won't."

It took a moment for her to sift this through her sleepy head and know that he meant to share her bed. Then she looked up at him with a small smile and held her arms outstretched. She saw no reason for denying herself to this man who loved her so much and whom she loved equally well. This moment seemed as good as any.

Soon they were in bed pressed close together, their naked bodies warming and comforting as they kissed. Henry was gentle in his lovemaking and she responded with a rush of ardor she had not realized she possessed. When it was at an end they fell peacefully asleep in each other's arms.

For Della the coming of morning meant a departure from ecstatic happiness to grim reality. The most painful thing of all was telling the old prince about Irma and Raphael. She delayed doing this until after Henry went to call on the Italian lawyers in an effort to learn something more about Pasquale Borgo.

Before Henry left, they took a stroll in the lovely gardens behind the palace. They pledged their love for each other and talked a little of their future back in England. If either Prince Sanzio or her aunt guessed Henry had spent the night in her room they gave no sign of it.

When he was ready to leave, Henry took her hands in his and kissed them. He said soberly, "I'll try to find out what I can. But do not count too much on it."

"I shan't," she said. "But I do think we ought to investigate a little."

He said, "I've just had another thought."

"What?"

"As long as these thieves believe you have the Madonna, the real possessor of it is having a holiday."

"A holiday?"

"From being sought out by that band of killers," Henry said. "You are the innocent decoy protecting him."

"I hadn't thought of that," she admitted.

Warming up to the subject, the young lawyer went on, "So you are giving this unknown person plenty of time to dispose of the treasure in bits and pieces."

She said, "If that is so the most logical suspect from my viewpoint has to be Borgo."

"Perhaps."

"So the first thing we should do is find out all we can about him," she said.

"I'll find out all the Italian lawyers can offer," he promised her. "Don't leave the palace while I'm gone."

"I won't," she promised. They kissed and he left.

Della went to Aunt Isobel's room for a private chat. She told the older woman, "You were right about Prince Raphael. He is mixed up with Barsini and his criminal crowd."

"I never trusted him!" Aunt Isobel exclaimed.

"I doubt if you will see him again. He and Irma are living at the villa with Barsini now."

Her aunt said, "And that Irma is a proper vixen. I can't think of her as a Standish."

"She is one," Della said quietly. "I'm positive of that. I have some hopes she can be saved from her own actions."

"Not if I'm any judge," Aunt Isobel said grimly. "Now that Henry has returned I say let us get on to England."

"In a few days," she said.

"We could all be murdered within a few days," her aunt complained. "I want to see London again."

"You will," Della said. "I promise it."

Then she went downstairs and found the old Prince in his study poring over a richly bound book spread out on his desk. He glanced up as she entered the room and said, "I've been wanting to talk with you."

"And I with you," she said.

He leaned back in his wheelchair and with a wan smile said, "I've been studying your Madonna."

"What do you mean?" she asked in surprise.

He tapped the book. "There's an engraving of it here in the volume of fine art. You will notice how exquisite the workmanship is."

She went to stand beside him and gaze down at the open book. The Madonna of St. Cecilia was shown on a white velvet background in the photo and both its gold background and ornamentation of gems were presented to full advantage. She was awed by the beauty of its design and rows of precious stones.

As she studied it she discovered, "It is not as large as I thought."

"All the more precious for that," the old Prince said.

"Really?"

"Yes. The design is more delicate and the gems of the crown of higher value."

"I see," she said.

He sighed wearily and closed the book. "We ought not to be admiring the piece. It has caused too much trouble."

She said, "More than you realize. May I sit for a moment?"

He indicated an empty chair by the desk. "Please do!"

Sinking into the chair, she hesitated then said, "I find it hard to talk to you about my sister."

"Irma?"

"Yes."

"There would be great happiness in your being brought together again if she had not been kidnapped," he said sadly. "This is the final day. That is why I was looking at the illustration of the Madonna. You recall the threat noted this as the final day."

Her green eyes met his watery blue ones and she wondered what lay in their ancient depths. She said, "It is about the threat and the ransom note which I must speak."

He frowned. "Has something terrible already taken place? Is my daughter dead?"

"No, she is still all right as far as I know," Della said. "But the threat is a hoax. She is not staying with Barsini because she is a prisoner. She is remaining there because she was in on the robbery plot."

The old man's thin, heavy-veined hand was resting on the desk top and now she saw that it was trembling. The Prince gasped, "Are you telling me my daughter has given herself wholly to that Satanist?"

"Yes," she said.

The old man seemed ready to weep. "How could she so deceive me?"

"She deceived us all."

"But I have been her only parent for years. I lavished my love and what little I possessed on her!"

Della felt terribly sorry for the old Prince. She said, "Not all of it was lost. I'm sure that Irma now regrets what she has done. But she is so involved with those evil people it is difficult for her to escape."

Prince Sanzio said, "What of that rogue, Raphael?"

"He is also a traitor. One of them. I learned that last night."

"And he led my poor daughter into the house of the Devil!" the old man said with some anger.

"Again I found his betrayal of us hard to believe. But that is how it stands."

Prince Sanzio said, "If there is any hope of saving my poor Irma I pray that you will do something."

"I'm considering that," she said. "I will not return to England until I know that she refuses to leave Barsini."

"In the meanwhile they still think you have the Madonna?"

"Yes. Even Irma and Raphael appear to think that."

"So you are in grave danger. Nothing has changed to make things better."

"That is about it," she said soberly.

A sudden thought seemed to strike the old man. He gave her a troubled glance and said, "Guido! We must not tell Guido!"

She raised her eyebrows. "Not tell him?"

"About Irma and her behavior," the old man said. "I pray that you let him think she is still a prisoner of Barsini."

"Why?"

"He worshipped her," the old Prince said sadly. "She has been his special delight since she came here. I think he might kill himself if he discovered that she is a Satanist and a criminal."

"Then he need not know."

"You will not tell him?"

"No," she said. "And I'll warn Henry to be careful not to let it drop."

"At least for a short while."

"Aunt Isobel as well," she said. "I'd forgotten about her."

"We must all vow silence for a little," the old Prince said in an unhappy voice. "I'm an old man, sorry I have lived to face this moment."

Touched, she said, "You cannot blame yourself."

"Who else? If Irma turns her back on decency I have failed," he said with a deep sigh.

So the strange agreement of silence on the subject of Irma began. She thought that the tiny Guido sensed there was something wrong of which he had not been informed. He went about his duties tensely and many times when she saw him there was a worried scowl on his wizened face.

It took the Italian lawyers several days to assemble the information she wished on Pasquale Borgo. In the meanwhile she and Henry sought some release from the tension by doing some sightseeing together.

They climbed the broad ramp which led to the Piazza del Campidoglio, designed by Michelangelo. Della was enchanted by the fusion of palaces, fountains, steps, trees and shrubs in a single harmonic whole. They halted at the ramp between the great statues of Castor and Pollux. Before them stretched the Piazza del Campidoglio in its full, magnificent beauty, in its center the bronze, equestrian statue of the Emperor Marcus Aurelius.

Henry told her, "I did some reading about the ancient days while I was on my mission in Naples. This statue has a curious history."

"In what way?"

"It survived the fury of the early Christian bigots because they believed it was a study of the first Christian emperor, Constantine. For centuries it stood near the Church of St. John the Lateran. A pope hanged a rebel by his hair from the horse in 955. And in the fourteenth century some powerful but lunatic tribune celebrated his high office by having the bronze horse converted into a fountain that poured wine from one nostril and water from the other."

She laughed. "You have been doing some serious studying."

"That is not the full story," Henry smiled.

"Do go on," she urged him.

"Well, in the sixteenth century Michelangelo was seeking a focal point for his piazza, and he saw this great statue of the mounted emperor still richly gilded. He discussed it with his patron, Pope Paul the Third, who agreed it would fit in well. But the Canons of St. John the Lateran were loath to part with the statue and had to be both threatened and bribed before they let it go."

"And it was brought here?"

"Yes," he said. "Michelangelo supervised the placement of this most famous of Rome's statues, making it seem right in its new setting. The story goes that when he had placed it on its new pedestal he went up to the horse and commanded it to walk."

"Let us take a closer look at it," she said.

They went down by the great statue and she was even more awed by its perfection. The emperor astride the horse was calm and dignified. His hand was raised in a friendly salute. His clothing was plain and the expression on his serious face made her think of Father Walker.

Henry said, "He had great intelligence, this Marcus Aurelius. He not only put aside the affairs of state to write his 'Meditations' but he also refused to listen to ugly rumors that his wife was unfaithful. His reaction to these stories was to raise a statue to chastity."

Della was staring up at the statue. She said, "There are still traces of the gilding to be seen on it."

"I know," Henry said. "There is a prophecy of doom that says when the last of the gilt disappears Rome will perish."

They had a thoroughly enjoyable morning, the sort she had hoped for when they first departed for Rome. But only now were they beginning to savor some of the charm of the city. In the back of her mind there remained concern for Irma, and hurt at the way Raphael had deceived her. But in her new happiness with Henry she was better able to rise above those troubling thoughts.

After their tour they sought out a small, sidewalk café and were greeted cordially by the stout owner. They sat at a table on the outer fringe where they had a good view of the sidewalk and the street.

Della said, "I forgot about some of the unpleasant things for a little while this morning."

"I'd like to put them behind us forever," Henry said.

She nodded at him across the table. "Let us hope we'll soon be able to do that."

She had barely ordered when a formidable female in a long brown silk dress and broad-brimmed brown hat came swooping down on her. "My dear child," the woman with the atrociously made-up face gushed. "How wonderful to meet you again."

"Madame Guioni," she said in a faint voice.

The old woman turned her ugly smiling face to study an embarrassed Henry. Poking him with her parasol, she exclaimed, "And you are that good-looking English lawyer who accompanied us on the train."

Henry was politely on his feet. "It is good to see you again, madame."

Madame Guioni turned her attention to Della once more and said, "Someone told me you had returned to England. All of your party!"

"They were wrong," she said. "I'm still at the Palazzo Sanzio and so is Henry."

"Ah," the garish old woman said. "Then I expect you have heard the sad news about Prince Raphael!"

Chapter Nineteen

As Della heard the woman's words her throat was gripped with fear. In a taut voice, she asked, "What about Prince Raphael?"

"Dead!" Madame Guioni said. "His body found floating in the Tiber. Apparently a suicide!"

"A suicide?" she gasped.

"The morning newspaper said his wrists were slashed. I expect he did it and then threw himself in the river. Likely from one of those yachts!"

Henry said, "This was all in the morning paper?"

"Oh, of course," Madame Guioni said. "You people, not reading Italian, would not have noticed it. Prince Raphael was one of those penniless princes. Like Prince Sanzio, he had a good family name but nothing else."

"I would not expect him to kill himself," Della said, still shocked.

The woman in the brown hat and dress shrugged. "I'm not surprised. You know how it is with that racy set. They live as if there is no tomorrow! Spending money madly one day and having nothing the next! I must say the Guioni Brothers were not like that. They were hard workers and even after their winery made a fortune they spent money prudently."

Henry said, "Did the paper say if there would be a police investigation of the Prince's death?"

"No," Madame Guioni replied with disdain. "In my opinion it will be hushed up. They do that for royalty, however impoverished."

Della found her voice to ask, "You think he may have been on a yacht?"

"That is what the newspaper story suggested," the ugly widow Guioni said. "Prince Raphael traveled with a racy set. He was often in company with the rich. Some of the newly rich like to have titles around them and pay for it. And the Tiber has a host of pleasure yachts."

"It sounds likely," Henry said, glancing at Della to see how she was taking it.

Della interpreted his gesture and said, "It's all right. I'm over the worst of it now." And to Madame Guioni she went on to explain, "Your news was shattering. I spent a good deal of time in Raphael's company."

"Of course! I'd forgotten," the older woman said. "Do forgive me, my dear."

"I'm over the shock," she said. "And, of course, I'm grateful to you for telling us. It might have been more upsetting to learn of it some other way."

Madame Guioni was sympathetic. "You mustn't worry, my dear. People like Prince Raphael often do things like that. I'm sure no one in his social set will think anything of it."

Henry said, "It will also be a shock to Prince Sanzio."

"Ah, yes," Madame Guioni said. "And he is such an old man now. With nothing but poverty in his background. Creditors constantly hound him, I'm told."

Della wanted to hear no more. She got up and said, "We must get back to the palace."

"So nice to see you again," the gaudy Madame Guioni said. "Do you think you will remain in Rome much longer?"

"At this moment it is difficult to tell," she said.

"If you do stay let me know," Madame Guioni said. "I do want to have a party for you. Let you meet the right people. Everyone wants to attend my parties! Everyone!"

"Thank you," she said, coolly polite and anxious to be rid of the woman. "You are very kind."

Madame Guioni beamed on her. "Not at all, my dear. I simply delight in having parties. And do give my love to Prince Sanzio! The poor old thing!"

"Let us get away from here," Della said between her gritted teeth as she tugged at Henry's arm and started him walking away from the formidable woman.

Henry said, "I've never seen you so angry."

"I detest that horrible old woman," Della said in a rage. "How dare she talk about Raphael and Prince Sanzio in that manner?"

"She is completely without feeling," Henry said. "You must have seen that from our first meeting with her in the train."

"When she tried to bully poor Father Anthony! At least he was a match for her!" Della fumed on.

"He's dead too," Henry said. "We seem to be losing acquaintances at a fast rate."

They slowed their pace when they were a safe distance from the arrogant woman. Della said bleakly, "Most of them have been murdered because of the Madonna."

"Do you think Raphael was murdered?"

"I'm sure of it," she said. "He probably had some sort of quarrel with Barsini."

"And Barsini had his wrists slit and then threw him into the Tiber?"

"Raphael would never slit his own wrists. He had a horror of physical hurt."

"So another of the thieves has been eliminated."

"Yes," she said. "Without Barsini being suspected."

"Who next?" he wondered.

"A good question," she said. "Maybe you or I."

Henry nodded. "We are targets for them."

"Maybe Irma."

"Isn't Barsini in love with her?"

"She has been his mistress," Della said bitterly. "There is a difference. Especially when he's probably had sexual relations with all the women in his group."

"You tried to help her."

"And it ended with her saving me."

"What now? Does this change any of your plans?"

"I'm more anxious than ever to locate Pasquale Borgo if that is possible."

"My latest word from the lawyers was to come by their office tomorrow morning."

"I don't want to wait that long," she complained. "But I suppose I must."

"You know these Italians," Henry said. "They take their own time doing anything."

"Except the Barsinis," she said with a deep sigh. "We better get home and see if Prince Sanzio has heard the news."

All the way back she remained silent, thinking of Raphael and finding it impossible to think of him as dead. She had every reason to hate him, he had betrayed her in the most reprehensible fashion. Because of him she had found herself standing naked on a stage before a group of Satanists. She would have been publicly raped had not Irma come to take her place!

Yet she found herself remembering the good times she'd had with the handsome young Prince. When he wished, Raphael could be charming. Yet he had been caught up in all of Barsini's corrupt activities and he was too weak to get away from the group. It had been almost inevitable that he would come to some sort of violent end.

Her last glimpse of him had been in that room at the villa. He'd wound up looking shamefaced and talking utter nonsense. After that she would have found it impossible to have any respect for him. But she was sad to know he had met such a sordid end. He might have been salvaged.

When they arrived at the palace it was Guido who let them in and hurriedly showed them the newspaper. "A terrible business, *Signorina* Standish."

"It is all of that," she agreed.

"You see the story," the midget said, excitedly pointing a finger to the paper.

All Della could make out were the words "Prince Raphael." The rest of the article was lost on her. She said, "How is Prince Sanzio taking it?"

"Badly," the little man said. "I'm sure he is terribly worried about the Princess Irma. After all, she has not yet returned."

Della said, "She is with Barsini."

"They think Prince Raphael fell in the river from a yacht," the midget said. "Barsini owns a yacht! It is well known!" His wizened face was a study in misery.

She said, "I must go to the Prince." She left Guido in his upset state and Henry followed her. They found the old Prince seated in his wheelchair staring disconsolately out the front window of the great living room. He did not turn or show any other emotion as they approached.

Della knelt before him. "We heard the news and came hurrying back!"

Prince Sanzio had the pallor of a man about to collapse. He stared at her with tormented eyes. "I shall never see my lovely Irma again!"

"You must not give up hope," Della told him.

"That is wrong," Henry agreed, standing behind her.

Prince Sanzio looked dreadfully old and weary. He said, "She is with Barsini. I have no question in my mind he had Raphael murdered."

She said, "The papers term it a suicide."

"Never!" the old Prince said. "You know as well as I do Raphael would never do that."

"I would not expect it of him," she admitted. "But no matter what has happened to him it doesn't follow that Irma will meet a similar fate."

"Anyone close to Barsini is in great danger!"

"I know that," she said. "Henry and I are still trying to discover certain things. If we are successful we may be able to rescue Irma and end this nightmare."

"What sort of things?"

"They have to do with the stolen Madonna," Henry said.

The old Prince looked angry. "I do not care about the Madonna. I only care about the beautiful girl I raised as my own daughter."

"We understand," she said. "And we will try to help."

The old man looked at her and said, "All this began with the discovery of that letter! The letter which told of Irma's family! We would have been better off if we had never received that information! If you had never come to Rome!"

Della was taken back. "I'm sorry you feel that way!"

The old man's manner changed at once. He reached out a thin hand and gently caressed her auburn hair. "Please, it is not I who am saying such things! I'm half mad with fear for my darling. I did not mean it. I take pleasure in just looking at you, so much do you look like her."

"It is all right, Prince," she said quietly. "We know what a strain you are under."

"I'm debating whether to call the police and see if they can bring her back," he said.

Henry frowned. "That might be dangerous. If Barsini thinks she knows too much about his evil doings he'd arrange to have her die in some convenient accident before the police could make her talk."

The old man in the wheelchair looked stunned. "You are right," he said. "Barsini will not stop at anything now. He is a desperate man!"

"He is," Della said. "And a greedy one! We hope to trap him through his greed!"

"Only bring my daughter safely back to me," Prince Sanzio said.

They left him still filled with bleak despair. It was then she decided she wanted to return to the Vatican again and ask Father Walker's opinion of what had happened. She was also anxious to have the priest meet Henry.

But before they went out again she had to placate Aunt Isobel. The old woman was in bed in her room with smelling salts in her hand. When Della came in to see her the old woman said, "We are all doomed!"

"Nonsense!"

Aunt Isobel glared at her. "Tell that to your close friend Prince Raphael!"

Della said, "I know his death has been a blow to you. We are all of us shocked."

"I'm a good deal more than shocked," the old woman said. "I'm terrified. I hate this old house. We have had only bad luck since we've been in it."

Soothingly she promised, "We shall soon be leaving for home."

"I have heard that before," Aunt Isobel said. "You have Henry Clarkson to console you! I have no one!"

"We are both ready to help you!"

Her aunt touched the smelling salts to her nose and then demanded, "Where are you off to now?"

"I want to see Father Walker at the Vatican Museum."

"And so you're both running off to leave me alone with that mad old Prince and that wretched little Guido. He is insane also. All morning he's been puttering about in the back garden. A fine time to plant flowers when all this is happening!"

Della said, "He probably went out to try and keep busy and not think about it."

"As for that Irma, I know she is dead, I have seen her ghost many times," Aunt Isobel said defiantly.

Della kissed the irate old woman good-bye and made no attempt to calm her further. As she was on her way out Aunt Isobel called after her, "I refuse to be murdered! I'm not going to leave this bed until we leave for England."

"Yes, Aunt Isobel," Della said patiently and went on out.

• • •

In the carriage taking them to the Vatican, Henry asked, "What did your aunt have to say?"

"A little of everything," she sighed. "She's terribly afraid."

"I can understand that," he said.

She gave him a knowing look. "And from what she said I guess she's aware that we are sleeping together."

Henry crimsoned. "I don't care! I'm not leaving you in there alone."

She gave him a wan smile. "I wasn't complaining, just letting you know in case she says something to you."

When they reached the Vatican she went straight to the museum where Father Walker was employed. She found the same elderly brother at the reception desk.

She told the old man, "I have come again to speak with Father Walker."

The gray-haired brother smiled at her in friendly fashion. "Ah, yes, the English lady."

"Miss Standish," she said.

The brother nodded. "I forgot the name, forgive me, I'm an old man."

"It is all right," she said.

"I'm sorry," the old man said. "You will not be able to see Father Walker today."

"Oh?" She was disappointed.

"He is not here," the elderly brother explained.

"Is he in Rome?" she asked.

The brother nodded. "Yes. In fact he is confined to his room. I understand he suffered a slight accident and will need a little time to recover."

She felt the familiar fear rising up in her. "What sort of accident?"

"I really have no idea," the elderly brother apologized. "But be sure he will be at his post again as soon as he is well enough."

She stood there frustrated. Then she asked, "There is no chance of visiting him at his room?"

"I fear not," the brother apologized. "That would not be permitted."

"I see," she said. "If you should see him or know anyone who will be visiting him, tell him Miss Standish called and she wishes him a speedy recovery."

The brother bowed politely. "I shall most surely do that," he said.

They went outside again and Henry asked, "What did you make of that?"

"I'm frightened," Della said candidly.

"You think something may have happened to him? I mean some violence."

"I'm afraid so," she worried. "The Church can be most discreet."

"You mean there might be more to it than that old brother was willing to reveal?"

"Yes."

Henry stared off across the square. "You could be right."

"I'm sure of it," she said. "After all, he has been working at finding the Madonna. Taking the same chances as we."

Henry eyed her with concern. "You think he may have gotten himself murdered?"

"I pray not," she said. "Raphael was one thing, losing a man like Father Walker would be another."

"I know what you mean."

Her eyes were filled with tears. "He saved my life more than once."

Henry took her by the arm. "Let us stroll in one of the gardens a little."

"All right," she said. "Gardens seem to be a universal answer to stress. Aunt Isobel said that Guido went out to putter around in the back garden after he read about Raphael in the newspaper. She thought it mad of him."

"On the contrary," Henry said. "I think it a wise thing to do."

They sat on a bench in a deserted garden with a lovely fountain protected by a wall of tall, dark green trees. There were times when neither of them said anything for a long interval. Della felt they had reached a point close to mental and physical exhaustion.

Suddenly she turned to him and said, "Let us have dinner somewhere by ourselves. I can't face going back to the palace."

"If you wish," Henry said.

"Prince Sanzio and Aunt Isobel are both bound to be taking dinner in their rooms. We won't be missed!"

'Then there's no reason why we shouldn't find a good restaurant and enjoy the evening."

She sighed. "Too many memories of dinners with Raphael. And the Prince mourning as if my sister were already dead."

"I agree, it is depressing," Henry said.

"Perhaps after we hear from the lawyers tomorrow we can make some headway," she said, searching for something to be optimistic about.

They left the Vatican gardens and went back to the commercial section of the old city. They had. drinks at a hotel frequented mostly by tourists and then moved on to the magnificent Restaurant Palazzi. It was a huge place much like the older, more sedate London eating places of renown. Many of the patrons were in evening dress so the headwaiter placed them in a suitably remote table where they would not be much noticed.

They were on a balcony above the main restaurant and almost immediately below them a string orchestra played pleasant dinner music on a small stage. They had arrived at eight, early by Roman standards, and by the time they were finishing an excellent meal of roast lamb at ten, the place had become crowded.

The music and the excitement of the place made her feel a little less depressed. Henry, aware of her unhappy frame of mind, worked hard to keep the conversation pleasant. She was grateful for this and felt guilty that she wasn't a better dinner partner.

The orchestra began a favorite waltz and she smiled at Henry across the table and said, "Let us dance! I adore that music!"

They went down below and, feeling slightly self-conscious among the more elegantly clad dancers, thoroughly enjoyed a long waltz. Della found herself wishing that life might always be like this, a pattern of measured beauty in which one could submerge oneself.

The dance ended and they went back up the narrow flight of stairs to the balcony. They were barely seated at their table when Della happened to glance across at the opposite balcony and saw a familiar face which at once made her uneasy.

Turning to Henry, she said, "Across from us in the balcony and standing in the background there is a man!"

He glanced across the room and then said, "You mean the thin fellow with the wispy gray beard?"

"Yes!" she said. "That's the man I believe to be Brizzi!"

"The one who stole the Madonna in the first place?"

"Yes," she nodded. "He rescued me from Barsini's henchman. He thinks I'll lead him to the Madonna."

"Apparently he's been following us today," Henry decided.

"He must have seen us at the Vatican Museum," she said. "And the fact he was there makes me worry all the more about Father Walker."

"What do we do?"

"Get out of here as quickly as we can and try and lose him!"

Henry glanced across at the other balcony again. "He seems to have gone."

Still agitated, Della said, "He likely saw that we were staring at him and has moved somewhere else. But I'd be willing to wager he is still watching us."

"You think he is as great a threat as Barsini?"

"Almost," she said. "He is more clever and just as ruthless. The only reason he saved my life was that he expected me to lead him to the Madonna. He still does."

"I'll settle the bill," Henry said.

It took a little while to locate the waiter and look after the bill. All the while she kept watching, positive that the man with the wispy beard was still spying on them. When they left the restaurant they dodged through several alleys to another street before hailing a carriage.

Only when they were in the carriage did she feel safe. Henry ordered the driver to take them to the Castle Sant'Angelo and they sat back to relax a little.

They reached the Tiber and were back in the area of the Vatican once again. After a little while the young lawyer asked the driver to halt the carriage and they left it to stroll toward the famous castle.

"I have been told this is a romantic spot," Henry said with a smile as they strolled arm in arm.

"It is!" she exclaimed, entranced by the scene which met her eyes as they crossed the bridge to the round, torchlit castle. The yellow glow of the torches gave the tower the appearance of being constructed of bricks of gold. Statues of angels by Bernini guarded the approach to the famous citadel.

They remained on the bridge for almost a half-hour before returning to the carriage and starting back to the palace. The change of scene had somewhat eased her tension. But the vision of the thin, bearded man spying on them in the restaurant continued to bother her.

The next morning she and Henry left for the lawyer's office as soon as they finished breakfast. Della's nerves were on edge as they were shown into the office of the senior partner, a Signor Palumbo. He was stout, wore rimless glasses and had a friendly smile. When they were seated he picked up some papers from his desk and began to talk to them.

"I have found out some facts about this Pasquale Borgo," he said. "He has been a kind of artist. But his work is considered third-rate."

Della volunteered, "I think he was hired by Count Barsini to ornament many of the walls of his villa with erotica."

The lawyer showed surprise. "I was about to tell you that. You know something about Borgo?"

"Only a little," she said. "Please go on."

The stout man studied a paper in his hand and said, "Borgo has lately been in the employ of Count Barsini. He is rumored to be a staunch member of Barsini's Satanist group."

"That is correct," she said.

"He is a middle-aged man, thin with a wisp of beard," the lawyer continued. "I have his address here. It is in a slum area."

Henry said, "We'll need that to try and locate him."

"One thing," the lawyer warned them. "I cannot promise you that this Borgo will be easy to find. The police are looking for him and haven't located him."

Della said, "I heard he was wanted by the police. What is the charge?"

"A grave one," the lawyer said. "He is accused of the rape of a very young girl. Well below the age of consent. It is typical of this Satanist lot; their orgies don't satisfy them, they have to prey on innocents as well."

Henry said, "Not a pleasant-sounding character."

"He is anything but that," Signor Palumbo agreed. "He is degraded and dishonest. But he has no criminal record. This rape seems to have been his first serious offense."

Henry said, "Well take the address and see what we can find out."

They thanked the lawyer and left. A carriage took them to a district of narrow streets, somewhat like the slum area where Della had gone in search of Brother Louis. That seemed so long ago. Yet it had only been a matter of weeks.

At last they reached a grim-looking building of four stories. Pasquale Borgo was supposed to have a flat with a studio on the upper floor. They made their way up the rickety stairs to the top landing and knocked on the battered wooden door. There was no response. As they stood there debating what to do, Della glanced down the stairs and saw the hunched figure of an old man staring up at them from the landing below.

She called down, "Do you know Pasquale Borgo?"

"*Sì, signorina,*" the old man said in a wheezy voice.

"Could you help us find him?" Henry asked.

The old man chuckled. "He is not here!"

"We know that," Della said. "But it is urgent that we locate him."

"You are from the police?" the old man suggested.

"No," Henry said, starting down the stairs to join the oldster. "This is a purely personal matter."

Della followed him down. "Yes," she told the bent old man wearing a shabby black suit and a worn velvet hat.

"I am a sick man, unable to work," the old man whined.

"We will pay you well for any information," Della said at once.

The old man's wrinkled face took on a greedy look. "Let me see the money?"

Henry took several notes from his pocket and held them out to the old fellow. "All yours if you can help us find Borgo."

"He has left Rome," the old man said. "His brother lived with him and he went first. Then about two weeks ago this Pasquale suddenly packed his things and ran off to the country."

"Where?" Della asked.

The old man licked his thin, dry lips and seemed reluctant to say anything further. "It could be dangerous for me. Borgo has friends who are evil."

Henry took out two more bills and held the lot in front of the old fellow. He said, "You've told us this much; you may as well tell us all you know. I can't pay you unless you do."

The old man gazed hungrily at the money. Then he gave them nervous looks. "You'll not say where the information came from?"

"Depend on us," Della said.

The ancient swallowed hard. "He is living with a cousin just outside of Hadrian's Villa. It is about twenty-six miles from here."

Henry said sternly, "You are telling us the truth? No sending us on some futile chase."

"I would not lie to the generous *signor,*" the man said in a wheedling tone.

"What is the name of this cousin he is staying with?" Della asked.

"Carlo Turriti," the old man said and reached out an emaciated hand for the money.

Henry let him have the bills with a warning, "If this information turns out to be wrong we'll be back. And I'll have the police on you for swindling us!"

"No, *signor!*" the old man whined. "I am honest! Ask anyone in the area! I have told you the truth!"

Della said, "Thank you," and then turning to Henry she suggested, "We'd better find out about the train service to Hadrian's Villa."

They left the old man on the landing and went back to the street. They had to get to their waiting carriage and drive to the railway depot before they could learn the timetable of trains leaving for the small town. It turned out there were several and they took one which would get them there by late afternoon.

The train journey was uneventful but Della was impatient in her desire to find this Pasquale Borgo who could well clear up the mystery. He might even have gone into hiding with the Madonna still in his possession.

After a relatively short train journey they descended from the railway car and engaged a kind of donkey cart telling the old driver where they wished to be taken. The driver of the cart recognized the name of Carlo Turriti and promised he could drive them to his house.

They sat in the rear of the cart with their legs trailing in the dust. It was a new experience and Della found herself laughing in spite of the tension. Stray animals and giant geese noisily got out of their way as the cart jogged along.

They reached an area of scattered tiny huts and the driver brought the cart to a halt. With his whip he pointed, "Turriti's house is the second one over there."

Henry told him to wait and they walked along the earth road to the hut. An old woman sat on a flimsy chair by the door of the hut, sleeping in the sun.

Della approached her and said, *"Signora!"* loudly enough to wake the old woman with a start.

"Si?" the wrinkled face looked up at her.

"Pasquale Borgo," she said loudly.

The woman looked at her blankly and shook her head as if to indicate she did not understand.

Henry wondered, "Is there anyone inside?"

She peered in the open doorway. "No one."

"There must be someone else around," he said with a frown.

He'd barely said this when a heavy-set old man came walking slowly with a cow on a rope. He had a fierce, black mustache and a weather-beaten face. He wore the shabby work clothes and corduroy hat of a peasant.

Henry went to meet him. "Are you Carlo Turriti?"

The man scowled at him as he held onto the rope by which he was leading the cow. "Who wishes to know?"

"We are friends," Della said. "We mean no harm."

The man sutdied them dubiously. "Are you from Barsini?"

"No," Henry said.

"What do you want with Carlo Turriti?"

"Just some information," she said. "We will pay you for it."

This produced new interest in the mustached man. He said, "How much?"

Henry repeated his performance of taking out several bills and holding them in his hand. "These and maybe more."

The man said, "I am Carlo Turriti."

"Good!" Della exclaimed excitedly. "We are looking for your cousin Pasquale Borgo who came here from Rome to stay with you."

Henry added, "And we know you have him here since you mentioned Count Barsini. Borgo was employed by Barsini."

"He is here," the man said.

"Where?"

"Give me the money, I will get him," the man told them in his stolid way.

Henry gave him the money. The mustached man took it without expressing any thanks or showing any emotion. He lead the cow to the rear of the hut and tied it. Then he leisurely strolled back again and headed for one of the other huts.

Della exclaimed impatiently, "He is surely taking his time!"

"He does not have our problems," Henry reminded her.

The man vanished into one of the huts and was gone for what seemed a long time to her, but which could only have been a matter of a few minutes. Then he came out again followed by another stout, mustached man about his own age.

Della saw them approaching and said, "That can't be Borgo! He is thin with a small beard."

Henry looked grim. "It may be some kind of game they're trying on us. We'll see what they say."

Carlo Turriti gave them a scornful look and went over to talk in a low voice to the old woman by the door of his hut. The other man, who looked much like him except his face was florid and not weather-beaten, came hesitantly toward them.

He halted before them. "Who are you?"

"Friends," she said. "We're looking for Pasquale Borgo."

The mustached man said, "I am Pasquale Borgo."

"But you can't be!" she protested. "He is thin and has a wispy beard!"

The stout man scowled at her. "You are from the police?"

"No," Henry said sharply. "We mean Pasquale Borgo no harm. We simply want some information from him."

Beady eyes appraised them. "You are from Count Barsini?"

"We know him," Della said.

The stout man said, "You are looking for my brother."

"What?" she said, startled.

"He is one of Barsini's people," the stout man said with disgust. "I have nothing to do with such decadent types."

"But you say you are Pasquale Borgo," Henry reminded him. "And Pasquale Borgo has been employed by Barsini!"

"You are talking about my brother," the stout man said with a touch of anger.

"We do not understand," Della told him.

"It began when we were boys," the stout man complained. "Whenever my brother did a wrong, or stole something, he told people he was me. It began to be that Pasquale Borgo was the one everybody wanted punished! But it was not me, it was my brother, Antonio."

"You're saying he has habitually taken on your name?" Della said.

"To save himself from his villainy," the fat man went on, his anger increasing as he spoke more loudly. "Now the police are looking for Pasquale Borgo but it is not Pasquale they want, but my brother Antonio. All through life he has done this to me! Even to signing his rotten paintings in my name!"

Della listened to the furious man and could not doubt him. She said weakly, "So you are not the man we're looking for!"

The mustached man cried, "No! You are looking for that rogue, Antonio! He has brought shame on our name since the day he was born! He went off on some errand to England for Barsini and left the police searching for me!"

Chapter Twenty

Darkness arrived while Della and Henry were still on the train back to Rome. With the darkness came a heavy rainstorm. The stormy evening well matched their turbulent emotions. Della had been sure they were on their way to discovering something worthwhile only to have all her hopes collapse when they found Pasquale Borgo.

Seated side by side in an otherwise empty compartment, they discussed the weird events of the day. Della said, "The only single thing we were able to confirm is that the pseudo-Pasquale did leave for England on an errand for Barsini."

"We knew that before," the young lawyer protested.

"We had their word for it only, now we have this other information," she pointed out.

"Are we any better off?"

"Very little," she said wryly.

"What next?"

She gave him a weary glance. "Let us sleep on it. There's so little time left. We can't afford to wind up at another dead end."

Henry stared out the train window at the darkness and the rain. "It wasn't bad enough; it had to turn like this!"

"I'm so tired," Della said. "The big question still is: What happened to the messenger?"

"From the time he supposedly accepted the Madonna from your sister," Henry speculated.

The train rocked a little and she braced herself against the motion, a troubled expression on her lovely face. She said, "I think Borgo must have absconded with the money. He had every reason to."

"Barsini seemed to believe Borgo didn't have the nerve to go out on his own," the young lawyer recalled.

"Perhaps he had been a coward in the past," she said. "But this was his big chance. The police were after him in any case. He could not return to Rome. And in his keeping was the Madonna worth a fortune."

Henry admitted, "I doubt if many men could resist the temptation of taking the Madonna for themselves."

"Greed always blinds people," Della said, reviving a little as she tried to reconstruct the crime. "Borgo may have thought he'd be safe enough if he remained out of sight and held on to the Madonna."

"He had planned to hide himself in Paris after taking the Madonna to you in London."

Della nodded. "So perhaps he headed straight for Paris and is still hiding there."

"With the Madonna waiting until it is safe to surface," Henry agreed.

She groaned. "In the meantime we have these wretched madmen harrassing us to give them the treasure. It's strange they do not see this as we do. That the man to find is Borgo!"

Henry said, "You forget that they see Borgo with different eyes than we. They know him better. And they think he would not dare double-cross them."

The rain was literally pouring down when they left the train at the station in Rome. Della thought she had never felt more miserable or depressed. She had come to the ancient city full of hope, happy to have at last located her lost twin sister and expecting that she would enjoy a wonderful new experience in having Irma return with her to London.

None of this had turned out as she'd expected. Her meeting with the long-lost Irma had been shadowed by the theft of the Madonna. And through Irma falling under the spell of the evil Count Barsini, it was inevitable that she be drawn into the maze of evil. Worst of all she had found herself the target of the thieves!

Henry came back to her with a cloak on to protect him from the rain and an open umbrella held in his hand. He said, "I've been lucky enough to find us a closed carriage. Hurry before someone else tries to take it!"

She stepped close to him and with the umbrella giving them both a small amount of protection, they hurried across the wet cobblestones to where the carriage was waiting.

When they reached the palace the mood was still somber there, as might have been expected. Both Aunt Isobel and old Prince Sanzio were keeping to their rooms. Guido was still tense and far from his usual obliging self. However, they did persuade him to prepare them a cold supper. Della had eaten so little during the tense day she now gorged herself.

The heavy rain went on. Because they were both exhausted they went to bed soon after their late meal. Della found sleep difficult and lay awake pressed close to Henry long after the young lawyer's even breathing let her know that he had fallen into a deep slumber. She wracked her brain to think of some clue which she might have missed and which could solve the mystery of the missing Madonna. No matter how far her thoughts wandered they al-days came back to Borgo, the messenger who had vanished.

She was thinking of him somewhere in Paris when she fell asleep at last. She opened her eyes with a start sometime later because she heard footsteps by her bed. She looked up into the shadows and found herself staring into the evil face of Count Barsini!

Henry roused at almost the same instant and said, "What is this?

But he said no more for the dark man who had hounded her in London stepped up and struck her bed partner on the head with the butt of his revolver. Henry gave a gasp and fell back beside her, unconscious.

Barsini whispered, "Make one sound and both you and your gentleman friend die!"

Irma appeared beside the evil Count and in a low voice, told her, "There will be no violence if you come along quietly with us! Please don't refuse!" Her sister appeared in an unhappy frame of mine.

Della knew she had little choice but to obey them. Henry had already suffered a dangerous blow to the head. And they would kill her in a moment, just as they had done away with Raphael. The only thing saving her was their hope she would break down and reveal where the Madonna was. The nightmare had come to a full-scale climax!

"Let him be," Barsini said, glancing at Henry who still lay unconscious, his naked torso and arms revealed over the coverlets. Della had also neglected to put on her night-clothes after a short but ardent session of lovemaking when they'd first gone to bed.

Now she was forced to rise nude and stand before the menacing trio. Irma came back with a robe and helped her into it. Then each of the men took her by an arm and led her out of the bedroom. They went along the hallway to Irma's room, where the candle in the glass container before the plaster Madonna still burned.

Her captors paid no attention to this but under the direction of Irma went through the secret door into the passage beyond. They were led by Irma with a lighted candle in her hand. The silent procession went down the stone steps and through the confusion of dark corridors to emerge into the garden.

At this point Barsini lifted Della and carried her in his arms. She knew it was useless to struggle or try to cry for help but remained a limp burden for him as he hurried through the rain to the street and a waiting carriage.

They were all drenched by the time they reached the carriage but none of them seemed to care. As the carriage rolled through the dark, wet streets she stared across at Barsini and Irma, who sat opposite her. The dark man was at her side, his revolver pointed at her.

She asked Barsini, "Why? Are you going to treat me the same as you did Raphael?"

Barsini's oval, black-bearded face showed a leering smile. "It might be an excellent idea. You've given us far too much trouble!"

Della said, "You don't seem to understand yet. I know nothing about the Madonna! I have never seen it!"

The evil Barsini said, "Why have you been visiting the Vatican so often? And why did you go to Hadrian's Villa today? Is it hidden there?"

"No," she said. "But the real Pasquale Borgo is there. You have been doing business with his brother and you haven't known that Antonio Borgo was using a false name!"

Barsini said, "We know you have the information. This time we get it or you die and we'll find the Madonna anyway."

"I doubt it," she said grimly. "Borgo tricked you just as you tricked Brizzi!"

Barsini became enraged. "Shut up!" he cried. And he gave her a cruel slap across the mouth which left her upper lip bleeding.

Irma tugged at the Count's arm and pleaded, "You told me there would be no more violence after Raphael. You must go easier with her!"

Barsini shoved her roughly away from him. "I shall be the judge of what shall be done!"

His savage anger left Della in no doubt that this was likely to be the end for her. Even the brow-beaten Irma was clearly concerned. That her sister was showing some concern for her welfare was the one hopeful aspect of the terrifying situation.

The carriage halted and the dark man with the revolver jumped out first. Della was then passed down to him. She was at once beset by the wind and rain as she stood a prisoner, on what was surely a wharf. Barsini and Irma joined them and the carriage drove away.

"This way," the dark man said and took her by the arm as he led her across the wharf.

They came to a fairly large yacht and the dark man stood by while she took the long step down to its deck and then joined her. The others followed. The craft was shrouded in darkness except for light which showed at the portholes of the cabin below.

After descending several wooden steps she was in a large lavishly decorated cabin with mahogany moulding and woodwork and crimson wallpaper in an intricate pattern. Two oil lamps swung from the ceiling of the cabin and gave the room a warm amber glow.

The dark man shoved her into a chair and then left to go back on deck while Barsini and her sister took their places between her and the only exit.

Barsini said, "Now we will have our talk!"

"I can tell you nothing," she said.

Irma came close to her, her face pale and tormented. She said, "Don't be a fool, Della! I don't want to see you die!"

Della said, "You let them murder Raphael!"

Her sister gave the evil Barsini a glance. "I know. And I have felt like his murderess ever since!"

Barsini smiled in his cold manner. "Raphael questioned my methods. I do not allow that."

Irma turned to her again. "He is mad with greed for the Madonna. Raphael tried to persuade him that you knew nothing about it. Being with you, he came to believe that!"

"It's true!" Della said.

Barsini said nothing but sneered at her. Irma pleaded with her, "Don't make him kill you as well! The guilt of it will send me into madness! I'm partway there now!"

"You threw in your lot with Barsini knowing what he is like," Della said.

Irma knelt by her frantically. "And I know you have to be lying. You do have that Madonna. Borgo came to the palace and I gave it to him in a wrapped package. The Madonna was concealed within a jewel box. He had his tickets and money for the London journey. And he told me he was then going to hide out in Paris. I saw him to the door and he was waiting for a carriage when I left him and went upstairs."

Barsini spoke harshly: "You're wasting time!"

"Let me explain to her that there's no point in lying," Irma said.

"Be quiet or I'll lock you in the other cabin," the bald man snapped at her. The dispirited Irma gave a deep sigh and went to throw herself on a cushioned sofa in the corner of the cabin behind Della.

Della looked up at the evil Satanist as he loomed over her. "I can tell you nothing!"

"We'll see," he gloated. "And don't think anyone will hear your screams for mercy. We are now well out on the Tiber and while the river is narrow at this point, no sounds from inside the cabin will reach the shore."

She said nothing but realized he had told the truth. The sound of the yacht's engine could be heard and the craft was plainly in motion. No doubt the dark man had taken over the controls.

"Why not kill me and be done with it," she said dully. Her wet dressing gown was clinging to her naked body. She was miserably cold and wet.

"I have better plans for you," the bearded Barsini said smoothly. He crossed to a table and brought back a metal object which was grimly familiar to her. He held it lovingly in his hands and said, "This belonged to someone you knew."

"Father Anthony," she said in a low voice as she stared at the thing in horror.

"The thumbscrew," Barsini said. "He intended to use it on you but was robbed of the opportunity. I promise you we will not be interrupted this time!"

From the sofa Irma pleaded with her, "Tell him anything you can!"

Barsini looked ominously amused. "She will do that, have no fear!"

She stared at the wicked-looking torture weapon and prayed that she might fall into unconsciousness as soon as it was used. She wondered about Henry, who had been stretched out motionless on the bed when she'd last seen him. How badly had he been injured?

Barsini's cold voice penetrated her reverie, as he asked, "What were you doing at the Vatican Museum?"

"It had nothing to do with you," she said.

"Did you return the Madonna to them? Were you fool enough to do that?" His rising anger showed in his tone.

She met his gaze sternly and said, "I would if I had it!"

He nodded in a grim manner. "Would you?" he asked with sarcasm. "Well, perhaps we can make you talk a different tune!"

"It was stolen from the Church," she said. "That is where it belongs."

Barsini carefully placed the thumbscrew on the small table by her and then reached out and gripped her hand and fitted it into the torture instrument. He held the hand in place and gave her a meaningful look.

"Shall we begin?" he asked. "Or do you want to be sensible and tell me what you know?"

"Tell him!" Irma pleaded from where she sat.

"Let us begin," Barsini gloated, and with his free hand tightened the torture weapon.

For a moment she didn't realize what was happening and then a surge of the most excruciating pain she had ever known shot through her hand. It was like biting flame or a host of daggers! She gave a loud moan.

Barsini laughed and said, "Now I think you better understand your position here!" And he relaxed the pressure of the instrument, leaving her hand somewhat relieved yet still paining acutely. He asked, "Will you talk or had we better try it again?"

She had no chance to answer. For at that moment a shot rang out on the deck above them. Irma jumped to her feet and cried out in fear. Barsini let go of the torture device so that she was able to extricate her pain-wracked hand from it. The bald man stepped back behind her and next to Irma and drew a revolver from his coat pocket.

Della realized that he had deliberately taken a stand behind her to use her as a shield. And at the same time she made up her mind to hurl herself quickly to the floor if there was any exchange of gunfire.

She had not long to wait. The door at the other end of the cabin burst open and there in a wide-brimmed black hat and cloak stood the thin man with wispy beard whom she had come to know as Brizzi! Brizzi, the superthief, who had begun it all!

Barsini let out an oath and fired at Brizzi. The man in the black hat and cloak seemed to dodge and Della threw herself down on the floor as she'd planned. Almost in the same second Brizzi fired twice and both Barsini and her sister slumped down onto the floor with blood spurting from what must surely be mortal wounds. They lay silent without a move.

Then Brizzi, his revolver still in hand, came cautiously over to her and said, "Get up!"

She obeyed him and then said, "My sister!"

"She's dead and so is Barsini," he said with scorn. And it was then she saw that he had been hit in the area of the left shoulder and the wound was bleeding badly. Barsini had nearly finished him with that first shot. By missing, the Satanist had lost his chance to live, and had cost Irma her life as well.

"Can I go to her," she pleaded, hoping by some chance Irma might be alive.

"No time!" Brizzi snapped, then seemed to sway a little. "To the steps and be ready to swim!"

She went to the steps and looked back to see him take one of. the lamps and send it crashing to the floor. It exploded and great flames rose hungrily from the spilled oil. He did the same with a second lamp and by this time the cabin was a blazing inferno from which he turned and fled.

He collided with her and forced her up the steps to the deck. She saw they were perhaps a hundred yards from the shore. He was taking off his cloak and hat and kicking off his shoes.

"Jump with me!" he ordered her. "The flames will reach the engine room and the oil tanks will blow her up!"

She hesitated by the rail of the yacht and gazed down at the dark, cold water. "I'm afraid!" she pressed her hands to her cheeks to try and ward off her growing hysteria.

"Can you swim?"

"Yes."

"Then jump! Don't be a fool!"

She glanced back and saw the smoke pouring out of the cabin doors and the flames already cutting through the cabin roof. She knew there would be a dreadful explosion in a moment!"

Brizzi grasped her with his good arm and literally flung her into the river and then jumped in himself. They both began to swim away from the doomed yacht. A few seconds later there was a great roar and flaming debris was scattered all around them. She kept on swimming, praying that she might reach the river bank.

The burning debris that remained on the surface of the water was behind her now. She looked back once and there was only the dark sky; the yacht had vanished as if it had never existed.

Now she called out to Brizzi and received no answer. She felt panic at being alone but there was no sight of him. She forced herself to swim on after deciding that he must have been hit by some of the flying debris and stunned so that he'd drowned! It struck her as ironical! The whole thing became a macabre fantasy in her mind as she struggled on, knowing she was growing weaker every moment. Soon it would be at an end, she would be too weak to fight, and it would be over!

She was only vaguely aware of the sound of an approaching motor vessel. Nor did she know its spotlight had caught her head bobbing in the rough, cold water. The boat came close and hands lifted her into it. Not until then did she finally collapse.

She came to in a modest office stretched out on a cot. And Henry Clarkson was standing beside her. When he saw her open her eyes he bent down and kissed her.

She struggled weakly to an elbow and looked around to see police officers gravely watching. She said, "Brizzi! Did they get him?"

"Brizzi?" Henry asked.

"The superthief," she went on frantically. "He was in the water with me. He blew up the yacht!"

Henry glanced at the senior police officer and asked him, "Did your men save anyone else from the river?"

The police officer shook his head. "Just the *signorina!*"

"You were the only survivor," Henry said.

"Then he drowned when the ship blew up. Something must have hit him!"

"Very likely," Henry agreed. "I saw the explosion, and the flaming debris raining down right afterward. The yacht sank at once!"

"And you?" she said, struggling to a sitting position. "I thought they had killed you!"

"I have a hard head," the young lawyer said with a smile. "Though I admit they did it no good."

"How did you know where to look for me?"

"As soon as I came around I called the police," Henry said. "I remembered that Raphael was supposed to be murdered on a yacht so I thought of you being taken prisoner on one."

"It was a marvelous guess!" she enthused.

"The police drove down to Barsini's villa and the wharf by it. The yacht was not there but we saw a craft out in the river which we decided must be it. But before we got out there it blew up. We barely managed to come along in time to save you!"

"I was ready to give up," she said soberly. Then memory of what happened flooded back and she shuddered. "It was awful!"

Henry apologized, "I'm afraid you'll have to go over it for the police."

She nodded and after a moment began, "They took me on board the ship. There were three: Barsini, the dark man and my sister. Irma was upset over Raphael's murder and tried to plead with Barsini to go easy with me. He wouldn't listen to her!"

Henry said, "The captain is taking it all down. Barsini was his usual villainous self. Please go on."

"He asked me for the Madonna and when I couldn't tell him where it was, he brought out a torture device to crush my hand. He used it once on me and was about to use it again when there was a scuffle on the deck and the sound of a shot. Brizzi must have shot the dark man."

"And?" Henry said.

"Barsini brought out a gun and took a stand behind me with Irma at his side. There was no place for them to retreat. He covered the cabin door with his gun, his only hope to kill the intruder when he came in. Brizzi came bursting through the door, Barsini fired at him, but Brizzi dodged and while he was badly wounded in the shoulder it was not a fatal wound. I dropped to the floor as Brizzi opened fire and hit Barsini first and then Irma."

Henry said, "And he killed them?"

"Both," she said in a taut voice. "He is an excellent shot. Then he helped me up and told me to get out of the cabin and jump into the water. He crashed the lamps and set the yacht ablaze. Then he joined me on the deck and prepared to swim. He forced me into the water. I saw him until the explosion. After that he was missing."

Henry said, "It looks as if they killed each other off. None of them left."

"I'd say so," she agreed. "And the Madonna still missing."

"I think there must be a curse on it," the young lawyer said.

"I'm ready to agree," Della sighed.

The police captain had her statement written down in long hand and he carefully read it back to her. She made a few corrections and additions and he promised to file his report in the morning. Then she and Henry were driven home in one of the official police vehicles.

Alone in the carriage they talked about it all. She said, "I don't know how I'm going to break the news to Prince Sanzio."

"He has to know," Henry said.

"I know," she sighed. "I feel badly enough losing a sister I've known for only a short time and who behaved badly enough in that time. But he has lost a daughter whom he raised over the years and came to love. A girl who was good in character until she was taken over by Barsini."

"It will be hard on him," the man at her side agreed. "Even poor little Guido will feel very badly."

"I'd almost forgotten him," she said. "Of course you are right."

"After we settle with the police tomorrow, as I expect they'll want to ask a few more questions, we must pack and go straight back to London."

"I can't get there quickly enough," Della said sincerely. "Rome has not been a happy place for me."

"Your aunt will not believe her good luck. She's been wanting to leave almost from the moment she arrived," Henry said.

"I know," she said and she lapsed into silence. "I hate to leave with the Madonna still missing," she finally said.

"We shouldn't worry about that."

"We have been involved," she said. "I won't be able to get it out of my mind."

"The next thing you'll probably hear is that Pasquale Borgo has sold a number of fine gems to various wealthy collectors."

"I'm sure that we shall," Della said sadly. "I'm sorry for the Cardinal and for Father Walker."

"You don't even know if Father Walker is alive," her fiancé reminded her.

"I know," she said. "I must find out about him before I leave."

The rain had not let up and they dodged from the police vehicle into the house. The captain had loaned her a heavy police cloak which was both warm and gave her good cover. Guido opened the door to them, his wizened face wearing a look of consternation.

"What has happened?" he wanted to know. "Will the police be back?"

"No," she said. "I do not think there will be a need."

Guido eyed her strangely. "You mean the kidnappers have been caught?"

"They are all dead," she said. "And so, I'm afraid, is Irma."

The little man flinched at hearing the news. Della was certain she saw tears glisten in his eyes. "That is too bad, I was fond of her! The Prince is waiting for you in the drawing room."

He ushered them in and then vanished. Prince Sanzio looked more frail and old than ever. Glancing up at them, he said at once, "I know the news is bad!"

"I'm afraid it is," Della said, kneeling by him and taking one of his thin old hands in hers as she told him.

Della was helped by Henry standing by, and she was thankful that Aunt Isobel had elected not to leave her room. It made her difficult task that little bit easier. Tears came to her eyes and there was a tremor in her voice as she recited the loss of a sister.

When she finished the old Prince stared ahead of him in silence for a long while. Then he said, "So I have lost her. But one way or another I was bound to lose her soon. I'm only sorry that her young life was cut off in its beauty."

Della said, "She would have been a wonderful person had it not been for Barsini!"

"And that Raphael, a weakling and a coward!" The old Prince was angry. "I'm thankful they're both dead!"

"Rome will be a better city without Barsini. The police claim they have been watching him, hoping to get enough evidence to convict him for holding those Satanist orgies. Now that he is gone I doubt that the Satanists will go on," Della said.

The old man smiled at her sadly. "At least in you I have a living memory of my lost daughter."

She said, "I shall always keep in touch with you and perhaps you may decide to come and live with me in London."

The man in the wheelchair shook his head. "Too late for that. I'm an old man who will soon die. I could not leave Rome. And I shall have Guido. He understands me."

"Yes. You are fortunate in that," she said.

The old Prince gave Henry a friendly look. "You are most fortunate, young man, to get a wife with this girl's character and beauty."

"I know that, sir," Henry said warmly.

Prince Sanzio sighed. "You will be going back to England at once. I accept that. And I will not beg you to remain. I understand."

She stood up and, going over to Henry, said, "Both Henry and I feel it a tragedy that so many people should die as a result of their greed for the Madonna. I wish it could be found and restored to the Church."

"I would not worry about it, my dear," the old Prince said. "Perhaps it will never be found. It would seem that way!"

"Not so, Prince," a voice said. And they all turned for a remarkable sight. Madame Guioni garishly dressed in a blue hat with veil and a crimson gown, came into the room with a gun in her hand and an angry-looking Guido marching sullenly before her. The midget glared at them with a look of hatred.

Della recovered first to ask, "Madame Guioni, what does this mean?"

The woman smiled, "You will soon know, my dear. Meanwhile, Mr. Clarkson, will you kindly remove the gun the Prince is hiding under the blanket which covers his legs!" She pointed the revolver to encourage Henry to act.

The old Prince uttered an oath in Italian as Henry lifted the blanket and took an evil-looking revolver from his lap.

In her high-pitched voice Madame Guioni ordered Henry, "Pass the weapon to me, butt first."

Henry obeyed and asked, "What does this mean?"

Della joined in, asking, "Why are you covering us all with that gun?"

Madame Guioni ordered the midget, "I will feel safer if you stand over by the Prince's chair. You make me uneasy."

Guido gave the old Prince a meaningful look and then went over to stand beside him. A strange expression had come over the face of Prince Sanzio—an odd alertness.

Madame Guioni addressed herself to Della while keeping all of them carefully covered with the weapon that looked so incongruous in her well-manicured right hand. She said, "You no doubt wonder why I'm here. Let me introduce myself, my name is Brizzi!" And with obvious pain the left arm raised and in a swift movement stripped off the hat and wig to reveal the face of the wispy-bearded man Della had seen earlier.

"You are Brizzi!" she gasped. "You were nearly killed tonight!"

"I have many disguises and many lives to match," Brizzi said, a smile on the painted face. He made a macabre spectacle, with the man's head and the female clothing. "You want to know about the Madonna, I'm sure. And what happened to Borgo, the messenger.

I have just heard the truth from this tiny gentleman standing before me!"

The old Prince snarled at Guido, "Little fool!"

"He would have killed me!" Guido pleaded with his master.

"He'll kill us anyway!" Prince Sanzio warned the midget.

Brizzi smiled and went on, "The night your sister talked this plot over with Raphael, the servant Guido overheard them. He told his master of the scheme to send the Madonna to England and they concoted a plan."

"Lies!" the old Prince said. "Rubbish!"

"Wait." Brizzi waved the gun at him menacingly. "You were prepared the night Borgo came to get the Madonna from your daughter. It had been delivered to her by Raphael, acting as Barsini's agent. They kept it moving about on purpose. Borgo took the package and Irma saw him to the door and went upstairs."

The old Prince said, "I demand you halt this nonsense!"

"Be patient a little longer," Brizzi said with good humor. "After your daughter retired expecting Borgo to step into the carriage, your man Guido invited Borgo to have a drink with him before he started out. Borgo was an alcoholic and never refused a drink. But he did not expect the drink he took with this little man in the kitchen to be both drugged and poisoned. Borgo collapsed after a few minutes and Guido had the Madonna. He also had to find a way to dispose of the body."

Trembling and white-faced, Guido leaned against the wheelchair. "I am going to be ill!" he said weakly.

"I doubt it," Brizzi told him. "Your little stomach was strong enough to murder. And your little body strong enough to drag your victim out into the back garden. There you already had a trench dug and ready. You placed the body in it and hastily covered it and you've been working at finishing the job ever since."

Della said, "What about the Madonna?"

"What, indeed?" Brizzi said. "I have come for it. At long last it will be restored to me. All this time Prince Sanzio has had it in the jewel case it came in, in the concealed drawer under his chair. He has literally been sitting on it. Now I will ask the little man to reach in there and produce it!"

Guido and the old Prince exchanged a grim look. Then slowly the midget knelt and reached in under the chair and produced a black, velvet-covered box about ten inches square. The sight of it awed everyone in the room including Brizzi. They stared at it in silence, this treasure which had brought death to so many.

And it was not to end. For in the instant of silence the midget produced a pistol that had been hidden in with the box and fired it at Brizzi, catching him directly in the chest. Brizzi staggered and then lifted his revolver and shot the midget through the head; a second shot hit the old Prince in the area of the heart and he fell forward out of his chair. The weapon fell from Brizzi's hand and he also slumped to the floor.

Della stood horrified at the carnage around her in the elegant setting of the drawing room. Aunt Isobel appeared in the doorway and let out a hysterical cry and collapsed. Henry went from the old Prince, to Guido and on to Brizzi.

Kneeling by Brizzi, he told Della, "He is the only one still alive and I doubt if he'll last long."

Della ran to the side of the superthief and as she knelt by him, he opened his eyes and the ugly hawk face took on the shadow of a smile. In a husky whisper, he said, "Now it is yours!"

"Not mine," she said. "I shall return it where it belongs."

The dying man's whisper grew fainter so that he barely formed the words, "The Church!"

Della left him to help revive her Aunt Isobel. Then Henry summoned the police. Only when all this was done and the police were dealing with the three dead bodies, did they open the box to look upon the beauty of the Madonna of St. Cecilia.

Della gazed at the blazing glory of the gold Madonna with its rich decorations of ruby, white, yellow and purple stones. It was a work of genius! Something for the ages! A creation too precious to attempt to appraise and too attractive to man's greed to be anywhere but in a museum.

Father Walker expressed much the same opinion the following day when the police captain, Della and Henry visited him at the Vatican Museum to return the Madonna to him.

"Beauty beyond the ordinary too often brings tragedy," the young priest said. "I think we shall place this Madonna in storage for a time. Until the notoriety associated with it is forgotten."

Della said, "I'm glad we are able to return it."

"The Cardinal will be pleased," he said.

She said, "You were ill last time we came. We were unable to see you."

He smiled ruefully. "A slight stab wound from which I recovered. I was attempting to spy on the Satanists and they almost finished me."

"But you are all right now?" she said with concern.

Father Walker said, "Yes. In spite of my appearance I'm fairly rugged."

She hesitated, awkwardly aware that the police captain was listeneing to all they said with polite interest. Then she said, "I'm afraid this may be our last meeting, Father. We are all returning to London in a day or two."

The young priest offered his hand to Henry. "You are a lucky man, Mr. Clarkson. I'm sure your marriage will be a happy one."

"Thank you," Henry said warmly as he shook hand.

Father Walker then turned to study her through his rather heavy glasses. "It has not been too pleasant a visit for you, Miss Standish. I trust you will not let it spoil Rome for you. Come again when you can enjoy it."

"I will," she said, her throat tight with emotion. "I'll not forget Rome nor will I forget you, Father."

"Nor I you," he said. "We all must know love of one sort or another if we are to survive. Mine is for the Church and for all people. You and this young man know love in each other! You were obviously meant to be lovers. I wish you well."

Della nodded, her eyes blurred with tears. She went to Henry and took his hand in hers. She managed a last smile for the young priest, who remained there watching them. Then they walked toward the museum entrance with the police captain following at a polite distance.